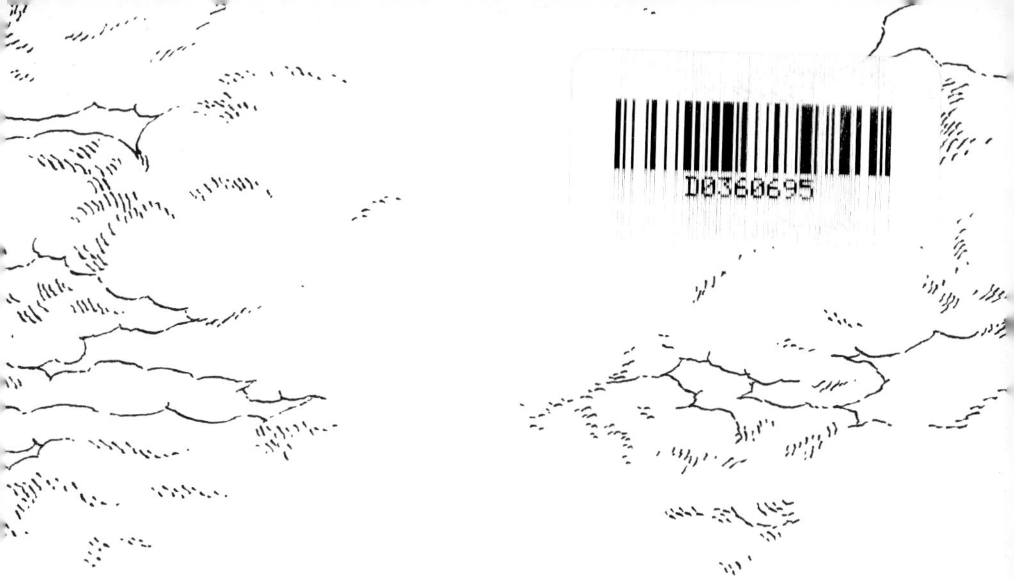

Talli

Daughter of the Moon

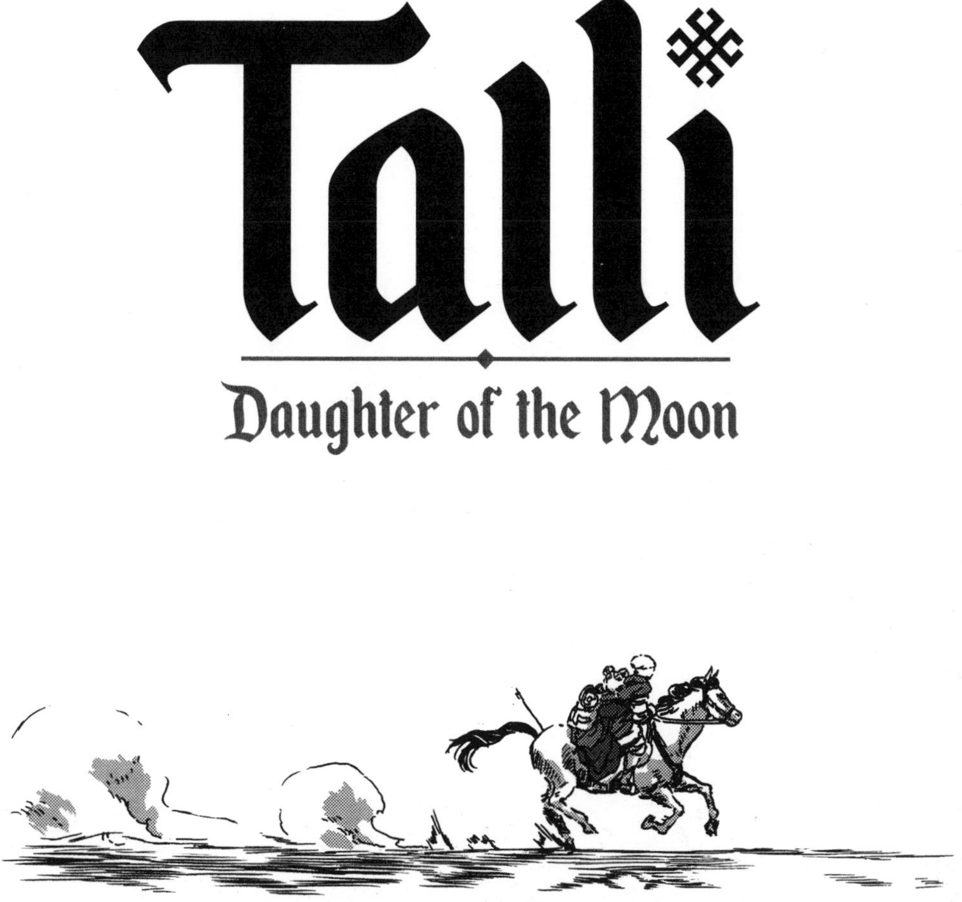

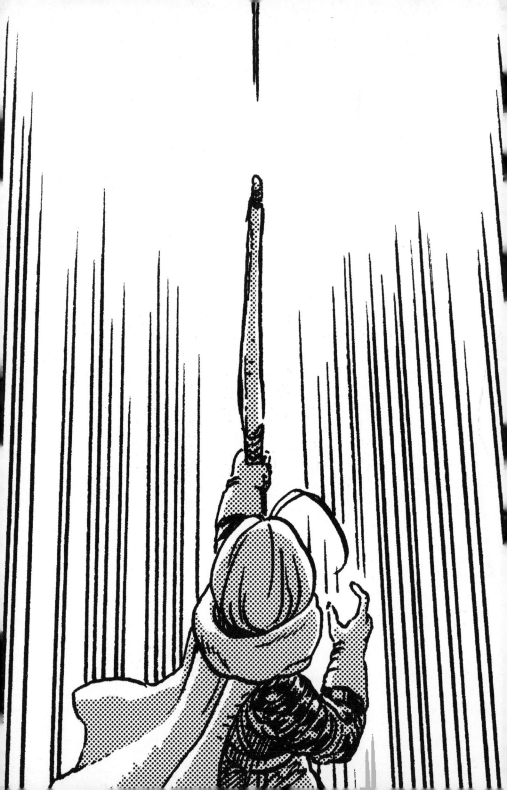

Taïli

Daughter of the Moon

BY SOURYA

Translation and lettering by **FRANÇOIS VIGNEAULT**

Book design by **CAREY HALL** Edited by **ZACK SOTO**

Editor, Ankama Éditions **RUN**

PUBLISHED BY ONI-LION FORGE PUBLISHING, LLC.
1319 SE MARTIN LUTHER KING JR. BLVD. SUITE 240, PORTLAND, OR 97214

JAMES LUCAS JONES, president & publisher
CHARLIE CHU, e.v.p. of creative & business dev.
STEVE ELLIS, s.v.p. of games & operations
ALEX SEGURA, s.v.p. of marketing & sales
MICHELLE NGUYEN, associate publisher
BRAD ROOKS, director of operations
AMBER O'NEILL, special projects manager
KATIE SAINZ, director of marketing
TARA LEHMANN, publicity director
HENRY BARAJAS, sales manager
HOLLY AITCHISON, consumer marketing manager
TROY LOOK, director of design & production
ANGIE KNOWLES, production manager
KATE Z. STONE, senior graphic designer
CAREY HALL, graphic designer

SARAH ROCKWELL, graphic designer
HILARY THOMPSON, graphic designer
VINCENT KUKUA, digital prepress technician
CHRIS CERASI, managing editor
JASMINE AMIRI, senior editor
AMANDA MEADOWS, senior editor
DESIREE RODRIGUEZ, editor
GRACE SCHEIPETER, editor
ZACK SOTO, editor
GABRIEL GRANILLO, editorial assistant
BEN EISNER, game developer
SARA HARDING, entertainment executive assistant
JUNG LEE, logistics coordinator
KUIAN KELLUM, warehouse assistant
JOE NOZEMACK, publisher emeritus

ONIPRESS.COM 🖪 FACEBOOK.COM/ONIPRESS 🗗 TWITTER.COM/ONIPRESS 🖸 INSTAGRAM.COM/ONIPRESS

FIRST EDITION SEPTEMBER 2022 | **ISBN** 978-1-63715-082-5 | **EISBN** 978-1-63715-102-0 | **PRINTED IN** CHINA
LIBRARY OF CONGRESS CONTROL NUMBER 2022932175
1 2 3 4 5 6 7 8 9 10

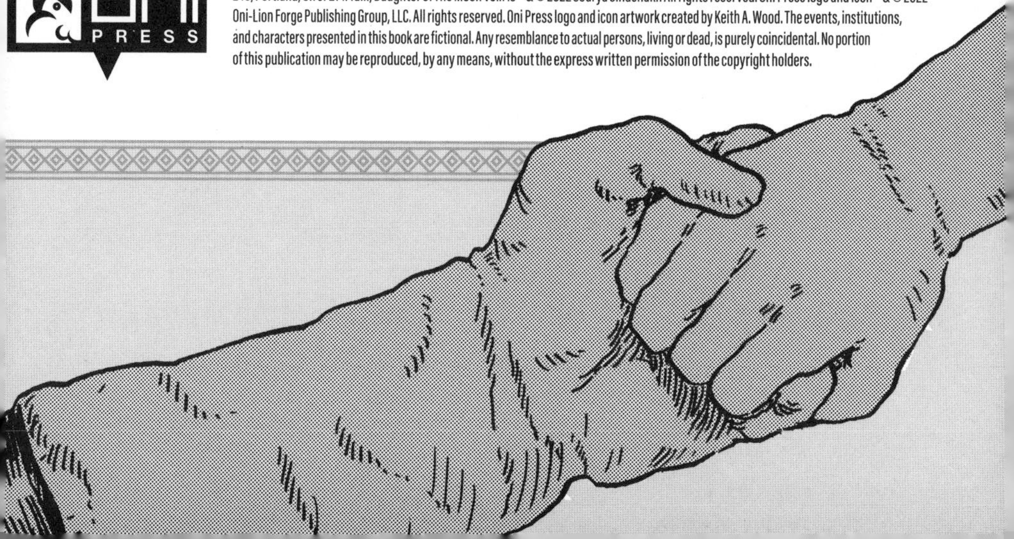

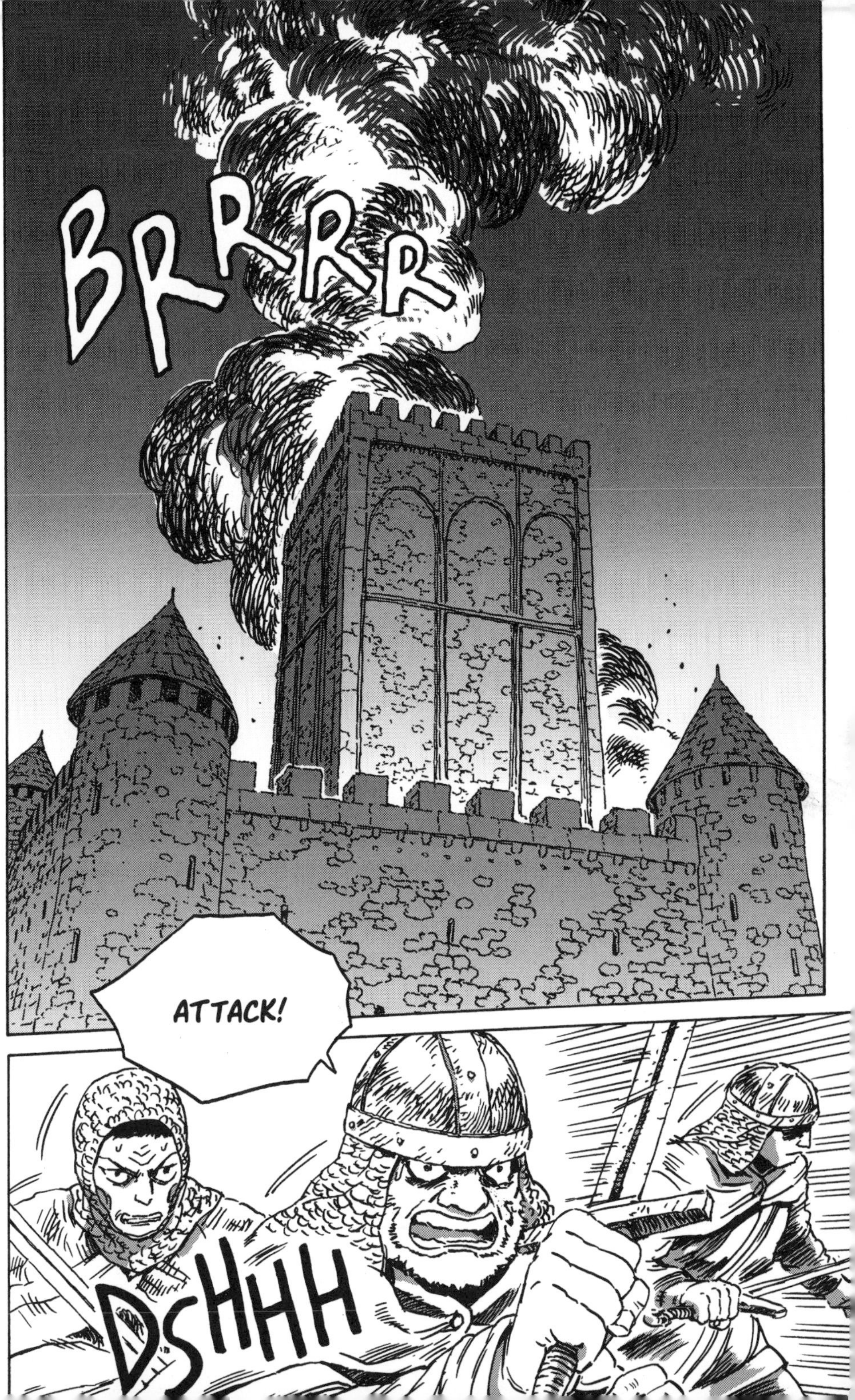
BRRRR
ATTACK!
DSHHH

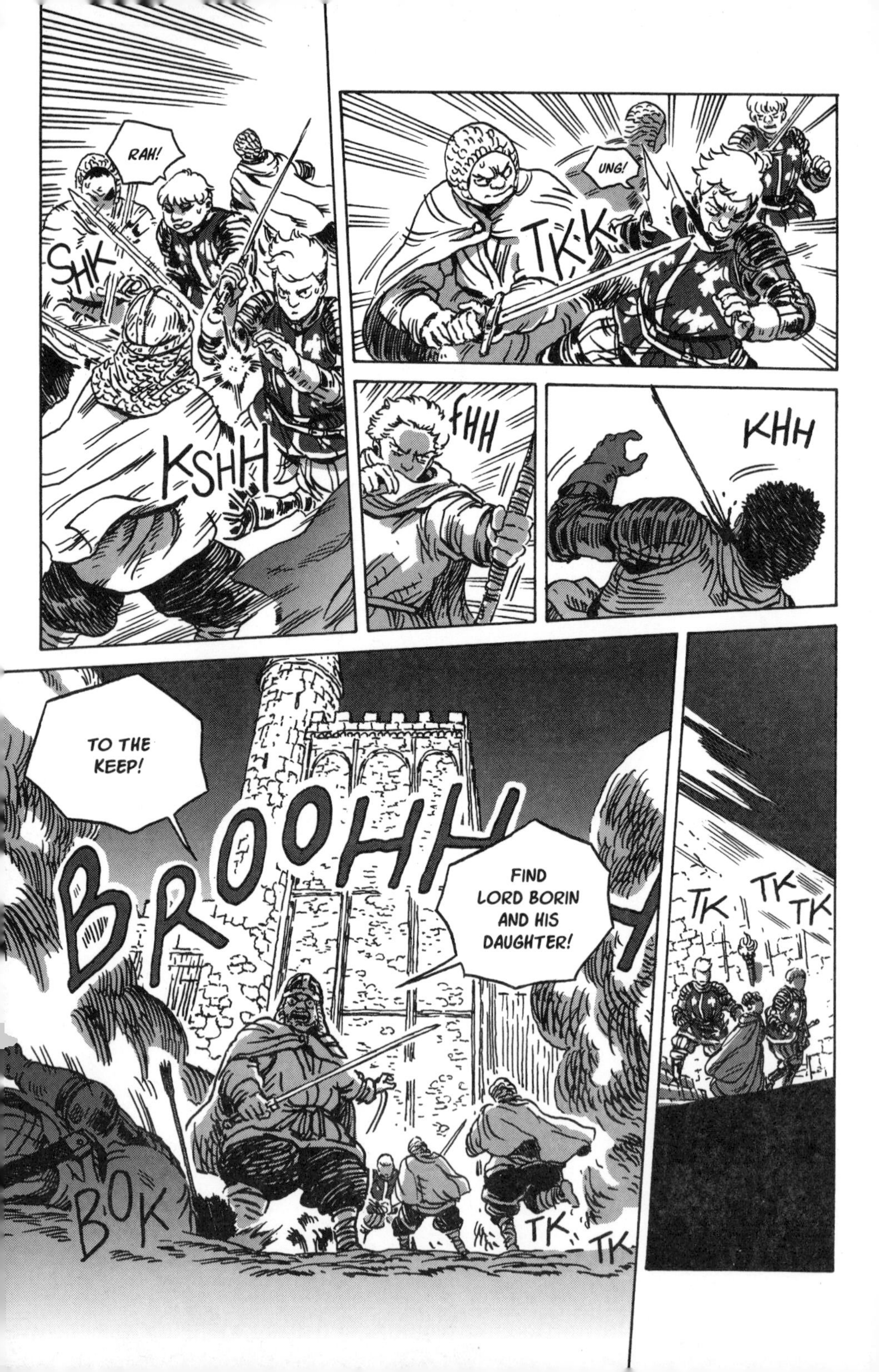
RAH!
SHK
KSHH
UNG!
TK-K
FHH
KHH
TO THE KEEP!
BROOHH
FIND LORD BORIN AND HIS DAUGHTER!
BOK
TK
TK
TK
TK
TK

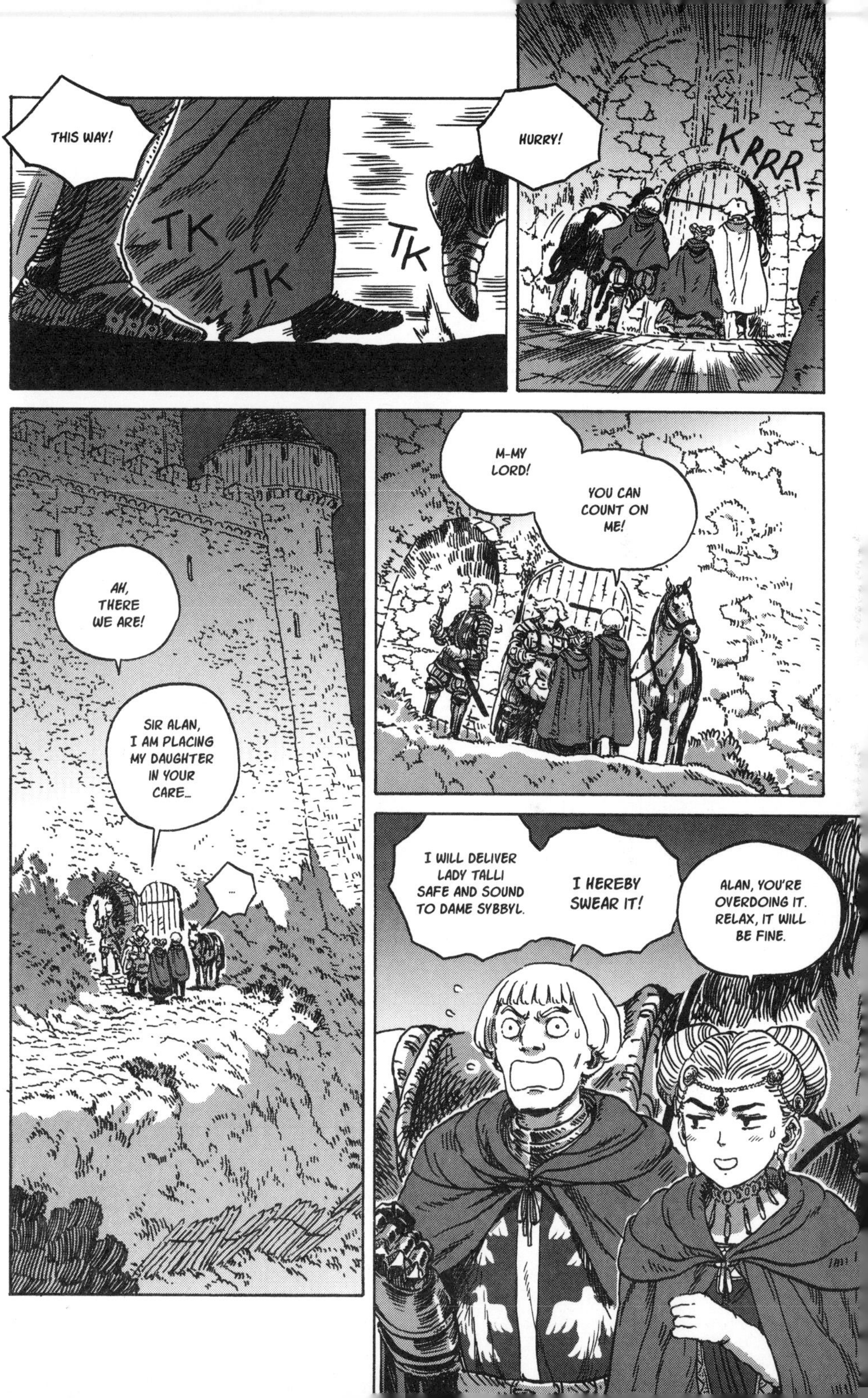
THIS WAY!
TK
TK
TK
HURRY!
KRRR
AH, THERE WE ARE!
SIR ALAN, I AM PLACING MY DAUGHTER IN YOUR CARE...
...
M-MY LORD!
YOU CAN COUNT ON ME!
I WILL DELIVER LADY TALLI SAFE AND SOUND TO DAME SYBBYL.
I HEREBY SWEAR IT!
ALAN, YOU'RE OVERDOING IT. RELAX, IT WILL BE FINE.

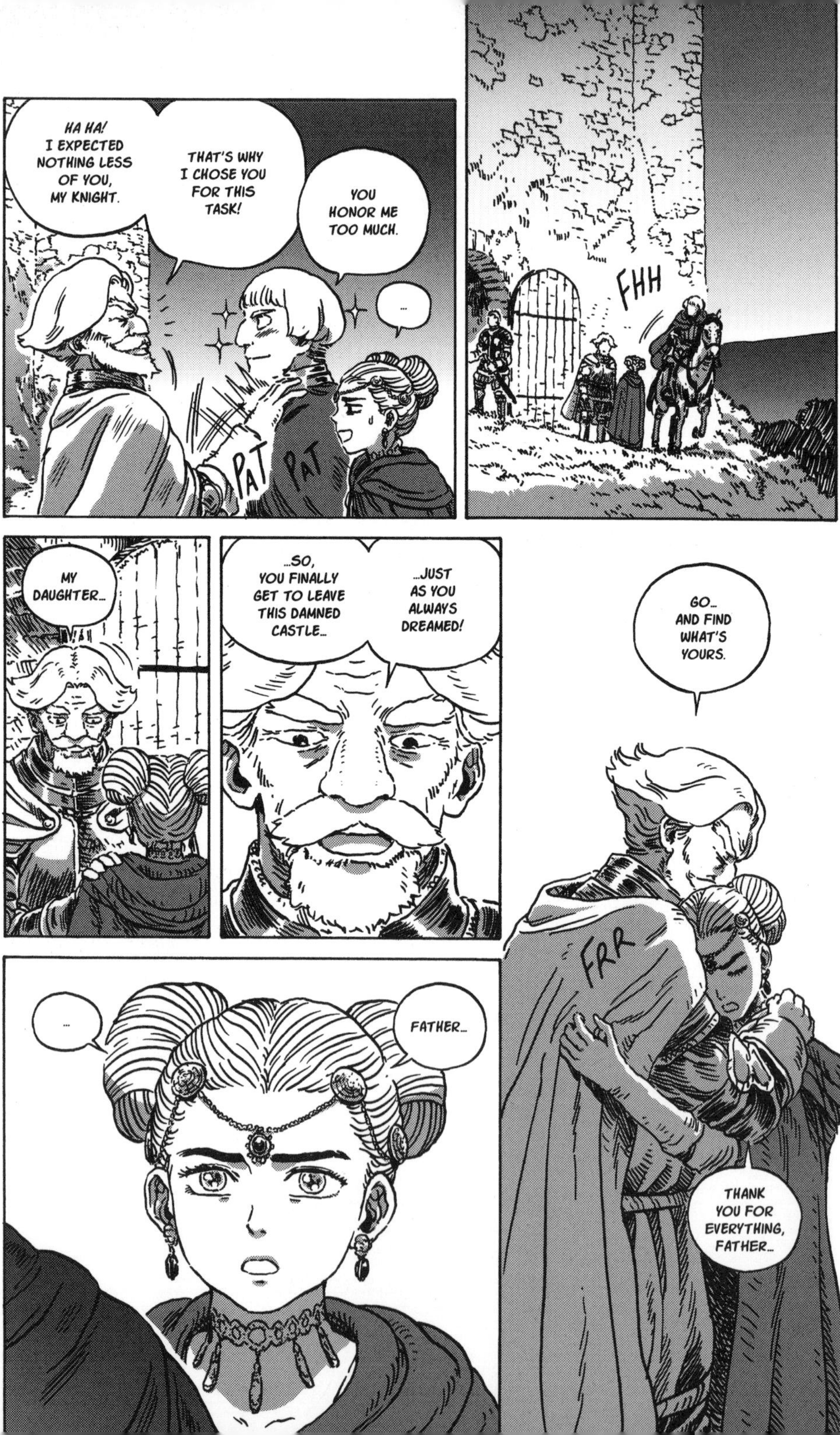
HA HA! I EXPECTED NOTHING LESS OF YOU, MY KNIGHT.
THAT'S WHY I CHOSE YOU FOR THIS TASK!
YOU HONOR ME TOO MUCH.
...
PAT
PAT
FHH
MY DAUGHTER...
...SO, YOU FINALLY GET TO LEAVE THIS DAMNED CASTLE...
...JUST AS YOU ALWAYS DREAMED!
...
FATHER...
GO... AND FIND WHAT'S YOURS.
FRR
THANK YOU FOR EVERYTHING, FATHER...

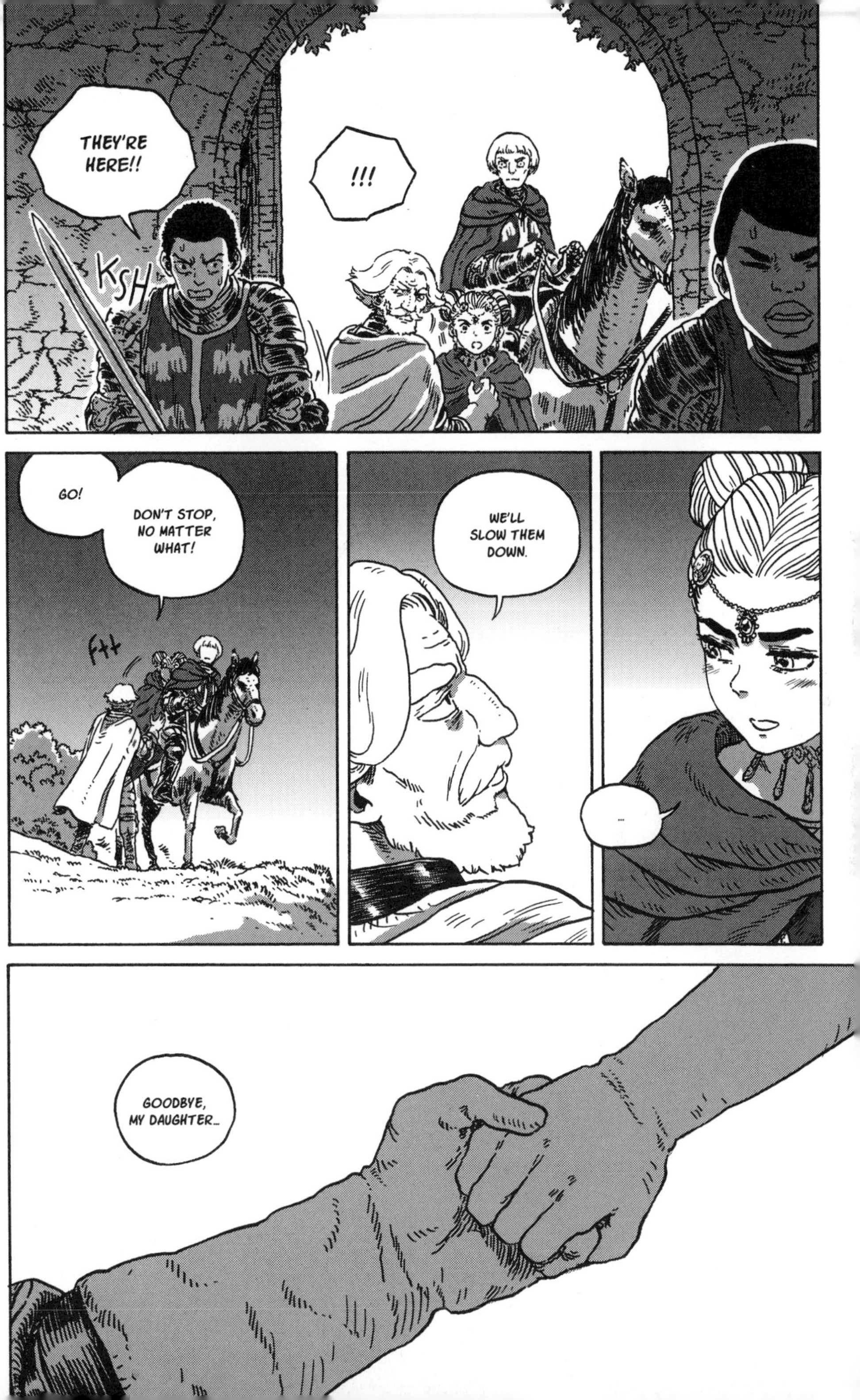
THEY'RE HERE!!
KSH
!!!
GO!
DON'T STOP, NO MATTER WHAT!
FTT
WE'LL SLOW THEM DOWN.
...
GOODBYE, MY DAUGHTER...

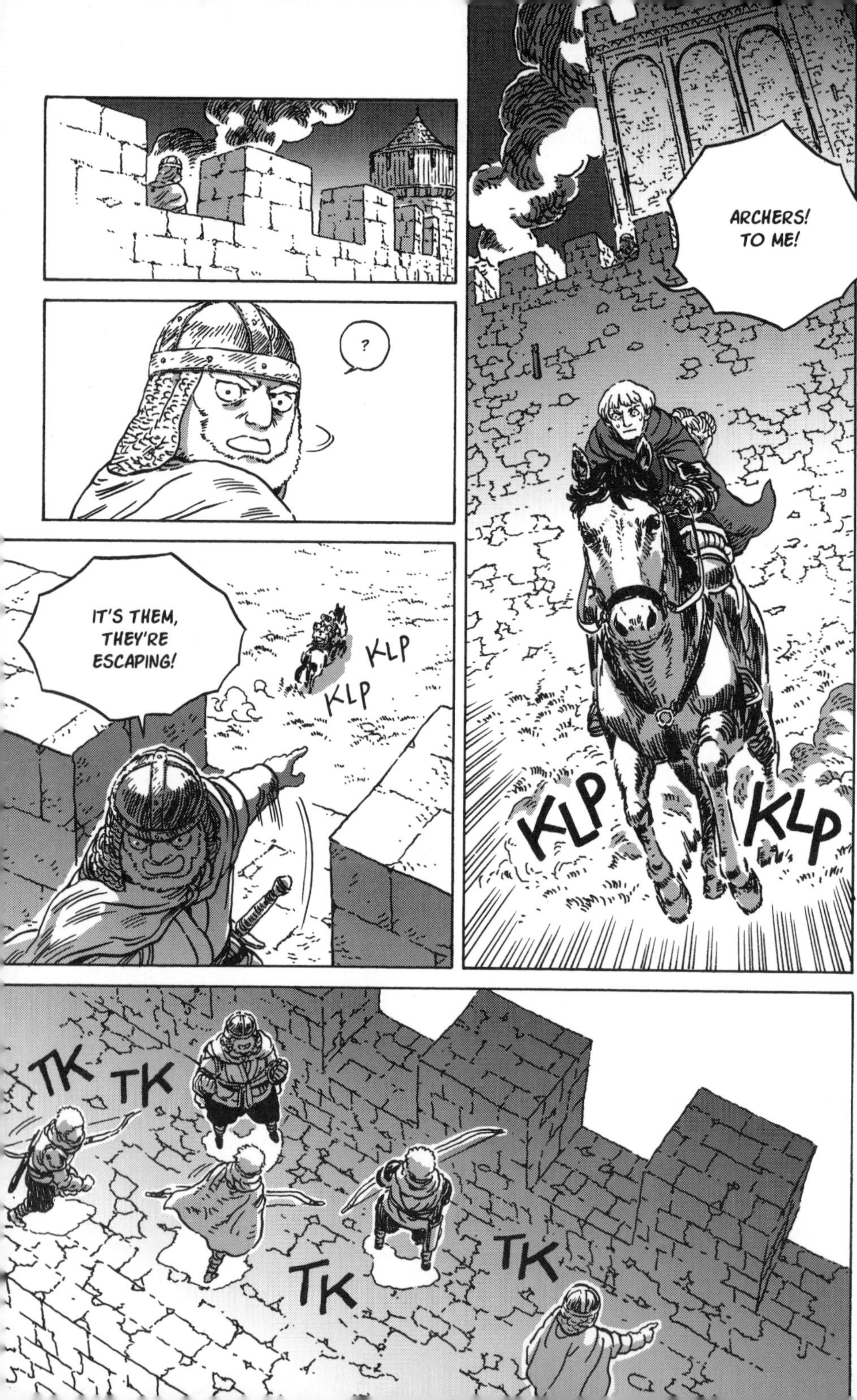
?
IT'S THEM, THEY'RE ESCAPING!
KLP
KLP
ARCHERS! TO ME!
KLP
KLP
TK
TK
TK
TK

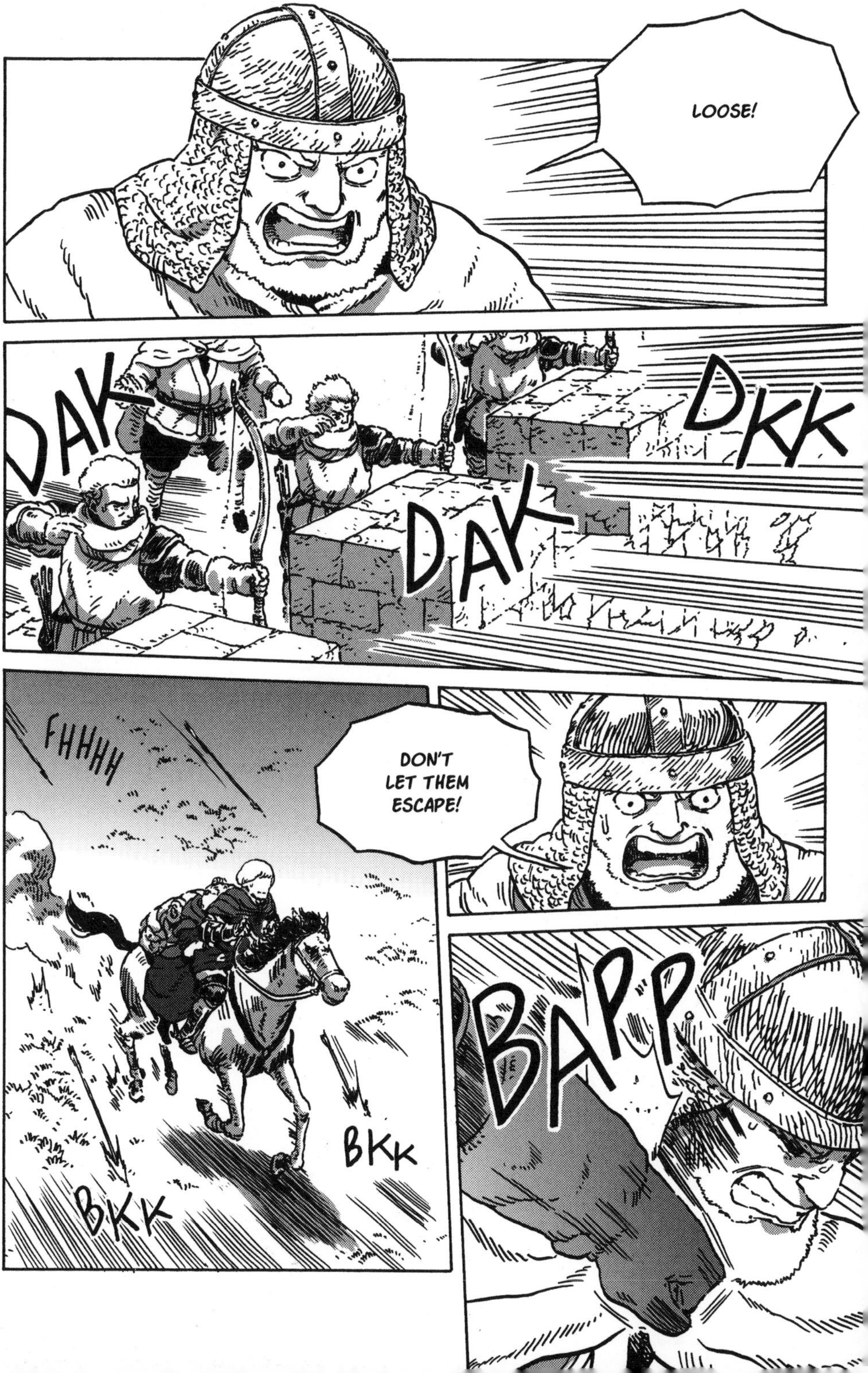

LOOSE!
DAK
DKK
DAK
FHHHH
BKK
BKK
DON'T LET THEM ESCAPE!
BAPP

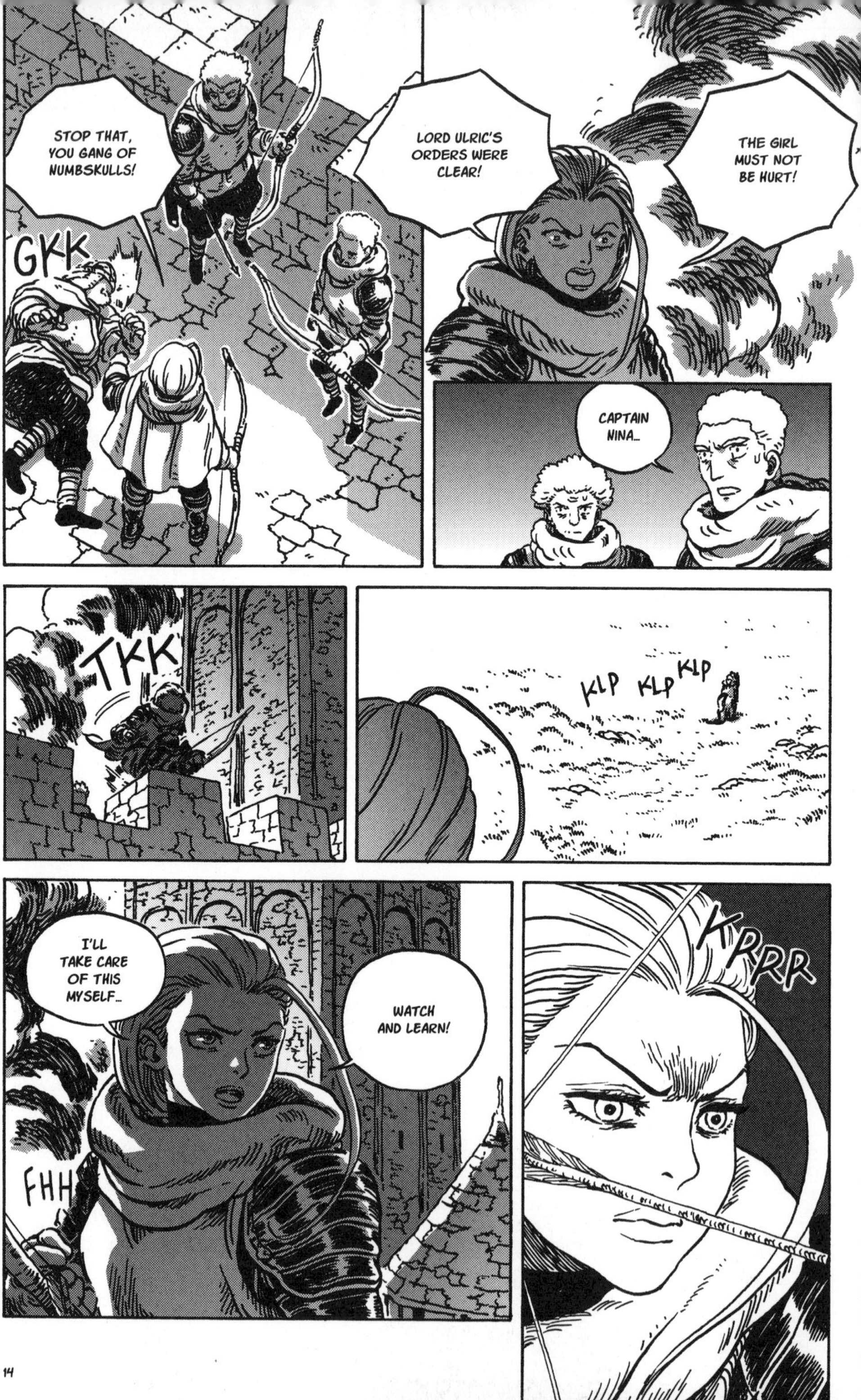
STOP THAT, YOU GANG OF NUMBSKULLS!
GKK
LORD ULRIC'S ORDERS WERE CLEAR!
THE GIRL MUST NOT BE HURT!
CAPTAIN NINA...
TKK
KLP KLP KLP
I'LL TAKE CARE OF THIS MYSELF...
WATCH AND LEARN!
FHH
KRRRR

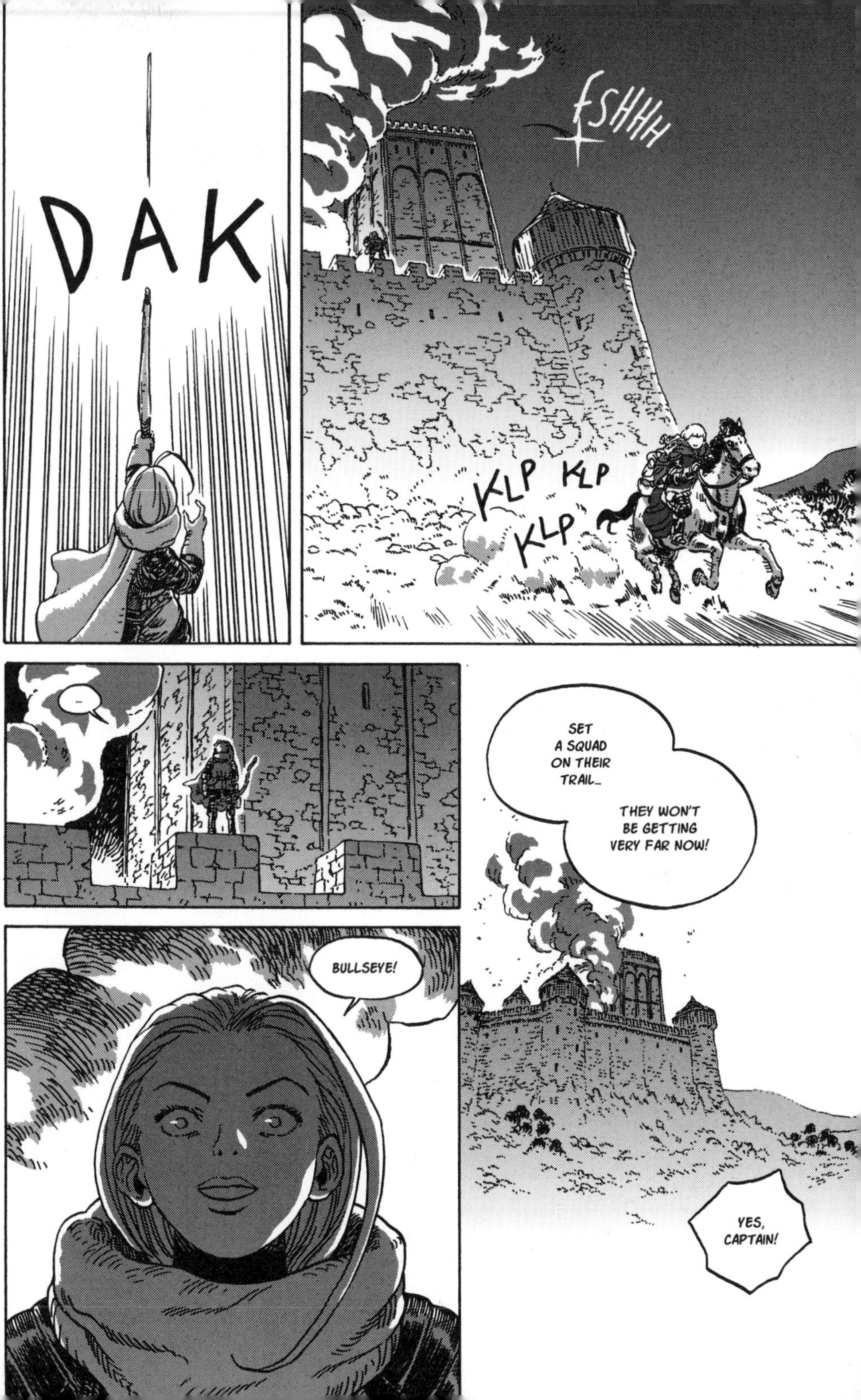
DAK
FSHHH
KLP KLP
KLP
...
BULLSEYE!
SET A SQUAD ON THEIR TRAIL...
THEY WON'T BE GETTING VERY FAR NOW!
YES, CAPTAIN!

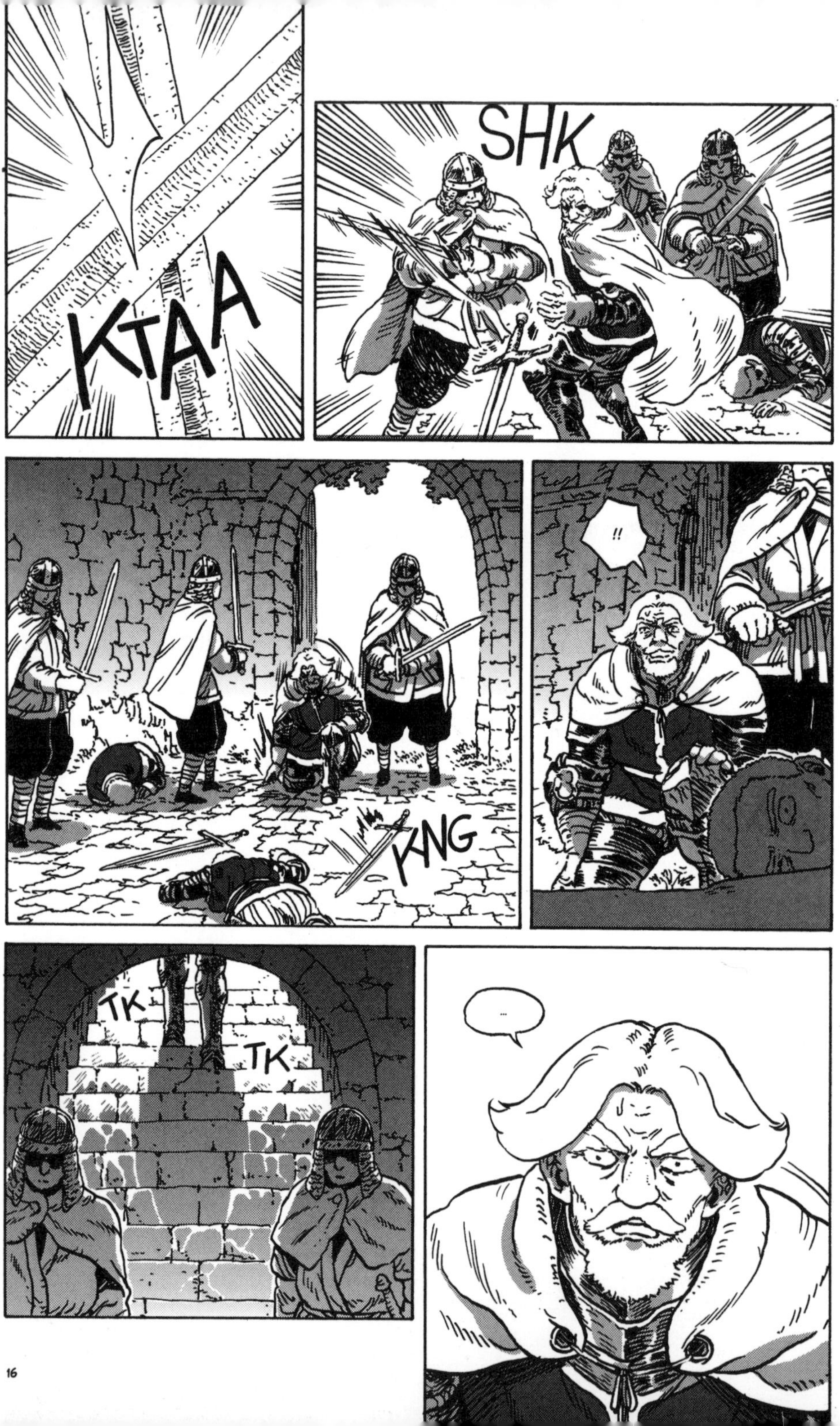
KTAA
SHK
KNG
!!
TK
TK
...

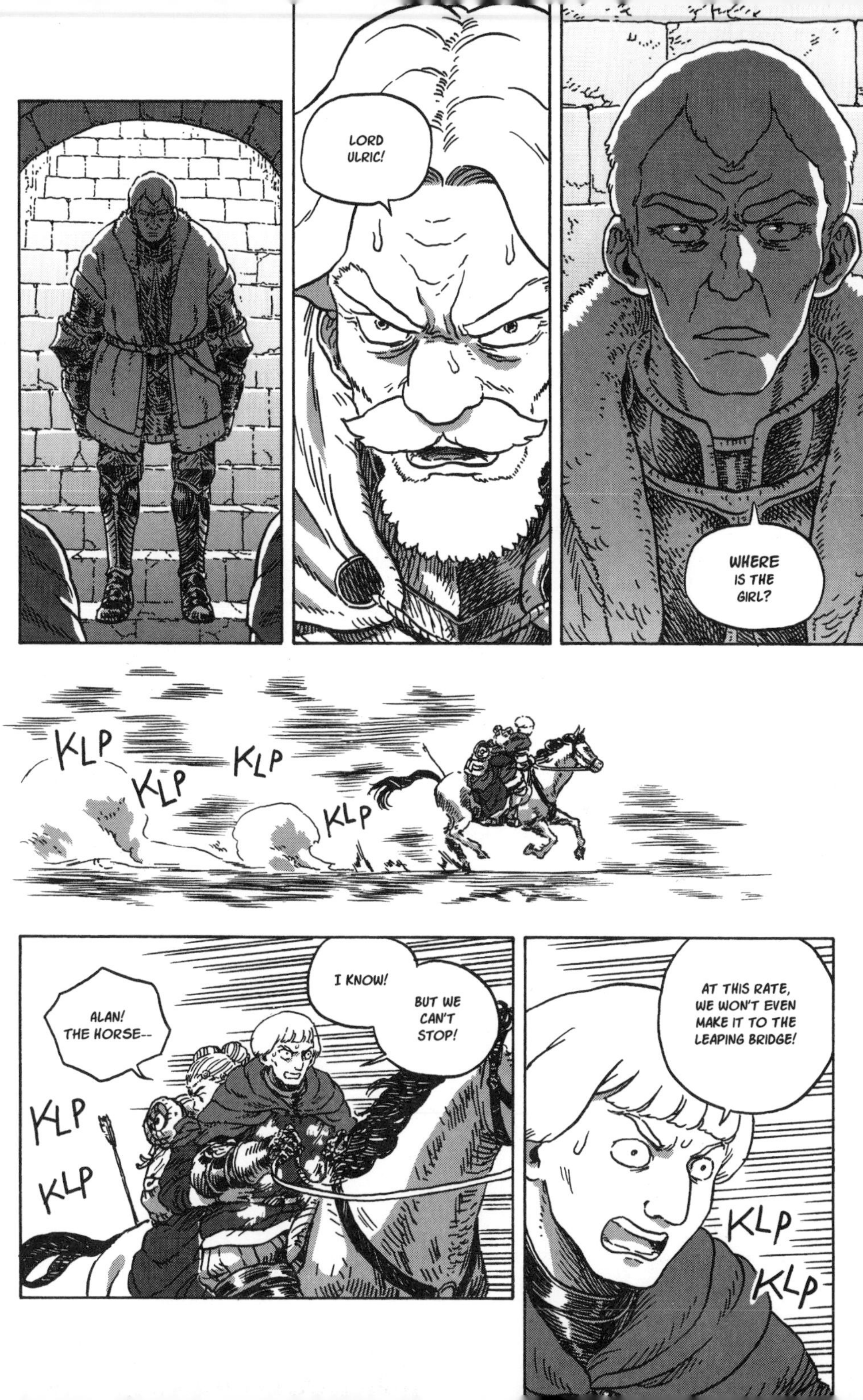
LORD ULRIC!
WHERE IS THE GIRL?
KLP
KLP
KLP
KLP
ALAN! THE HORSE--
I KNOW!
BUT WE CAN'T STOP!
KLP
KLP
AT THIS RATE, WE WON'T EVEN MAKE IT TO THE LEAPING BRIDGE!
KLP
KLP

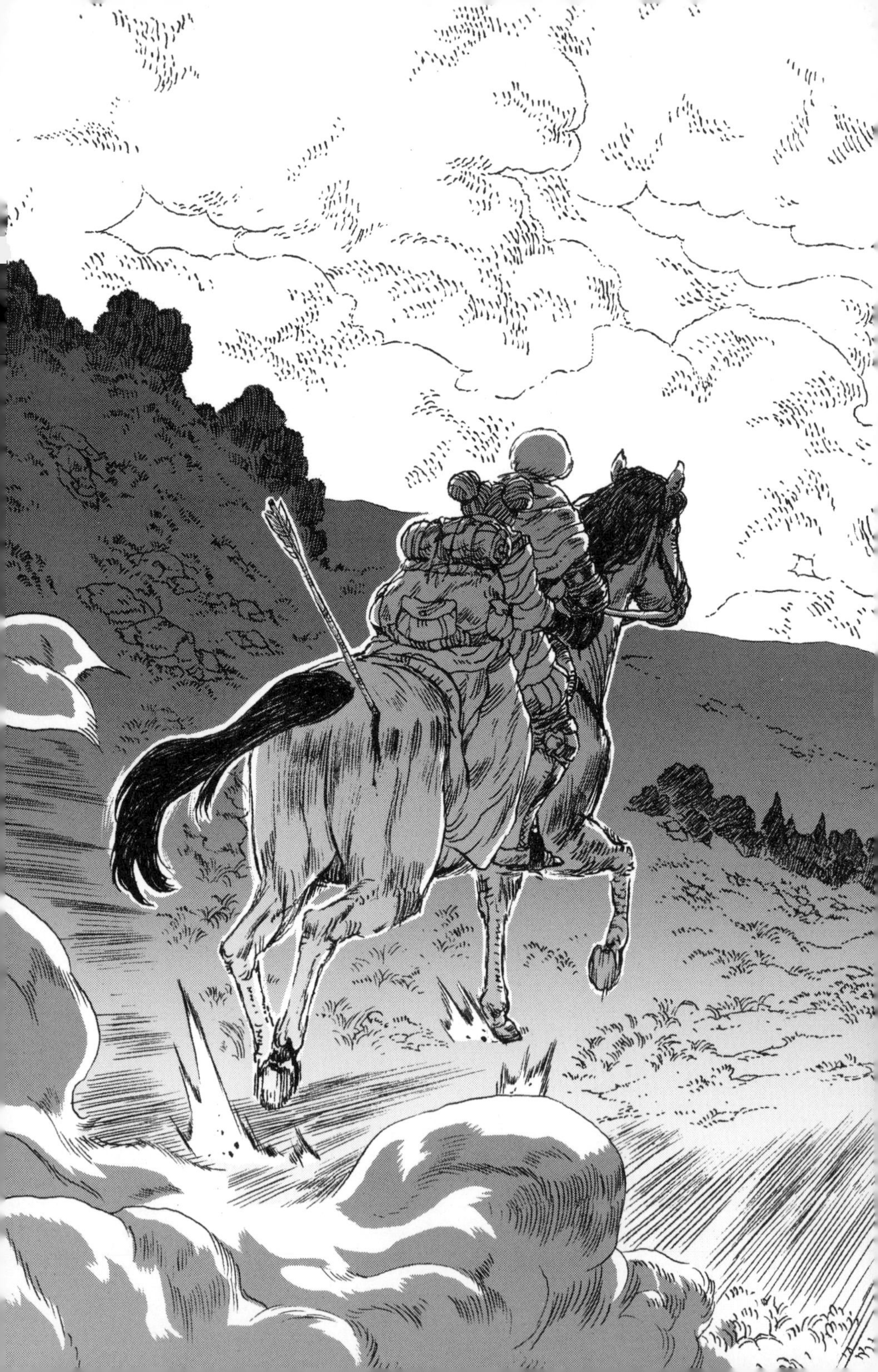

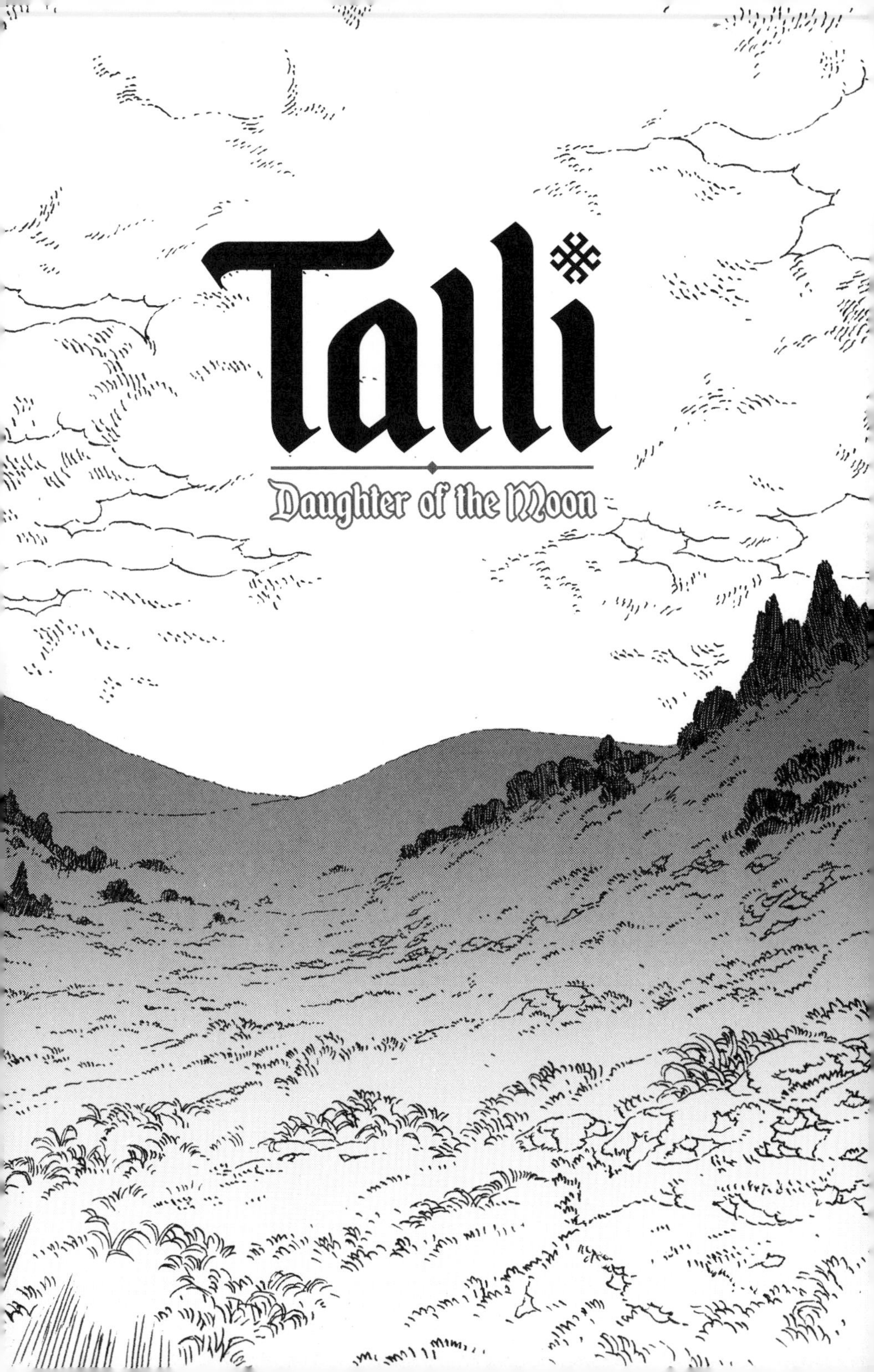
Talli
Daughter of the Moon

Chapter 1

Rare Gems

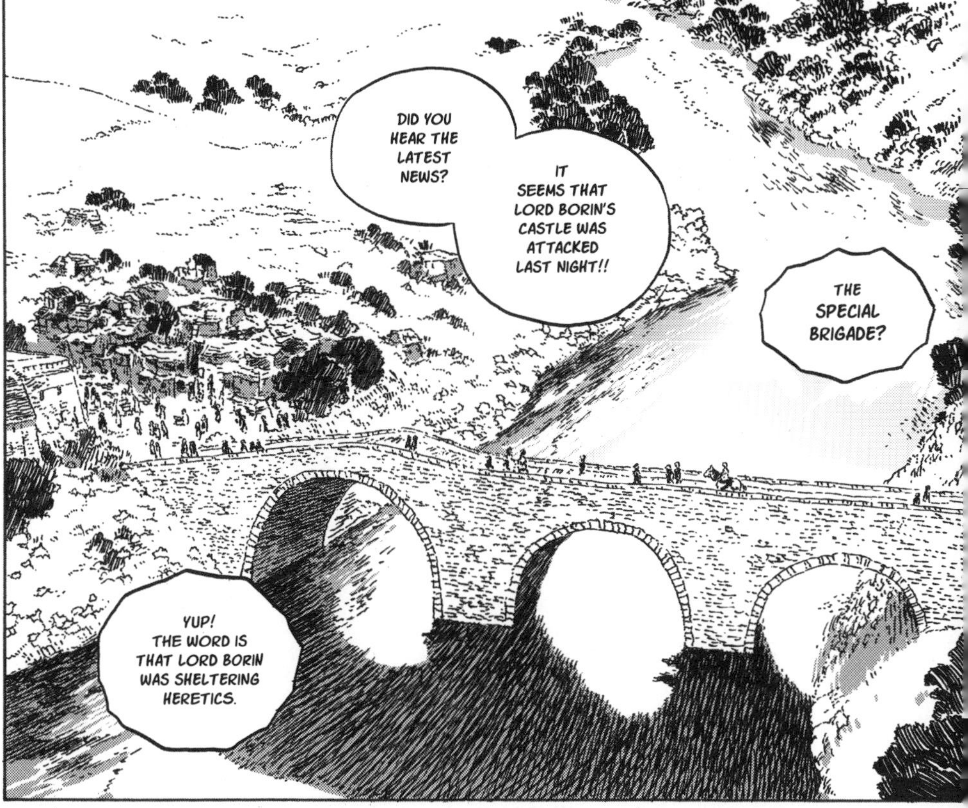
DID YOU HEAR THE LATEST NEWS?
IT SEEMS THAT LORD BORIN'S CASTLE WAS ATTACKED LAST NIGHT!!
THE SPECIAL BRIGADE?
YUP! THE WORD IS THAT LORD BORIN WAS SHELTERING HERETICS.

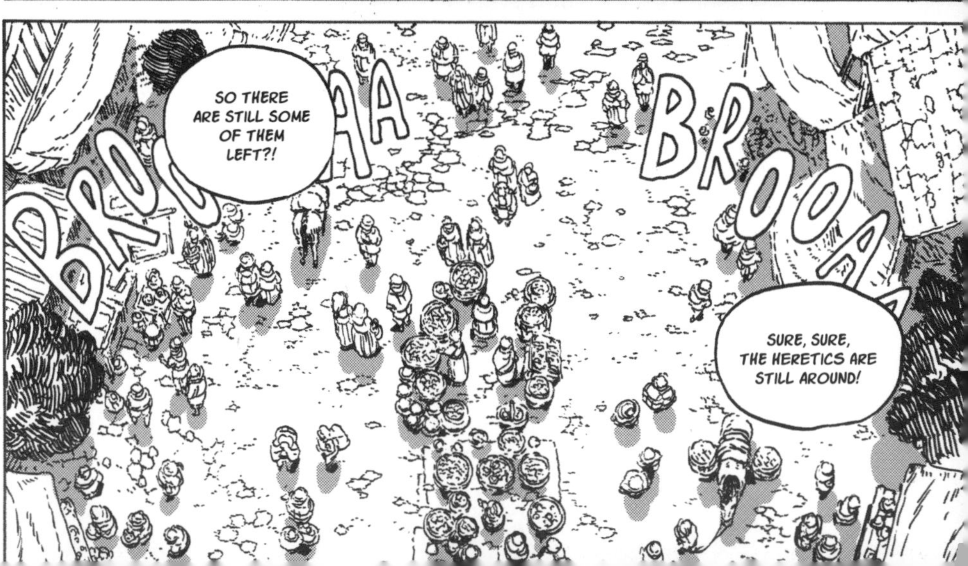
SO THERE ARE STILL SOME OF THEM LEFT?!
BROOA
SURE, SURE, THE HERETICS ARE STILL AROUND!

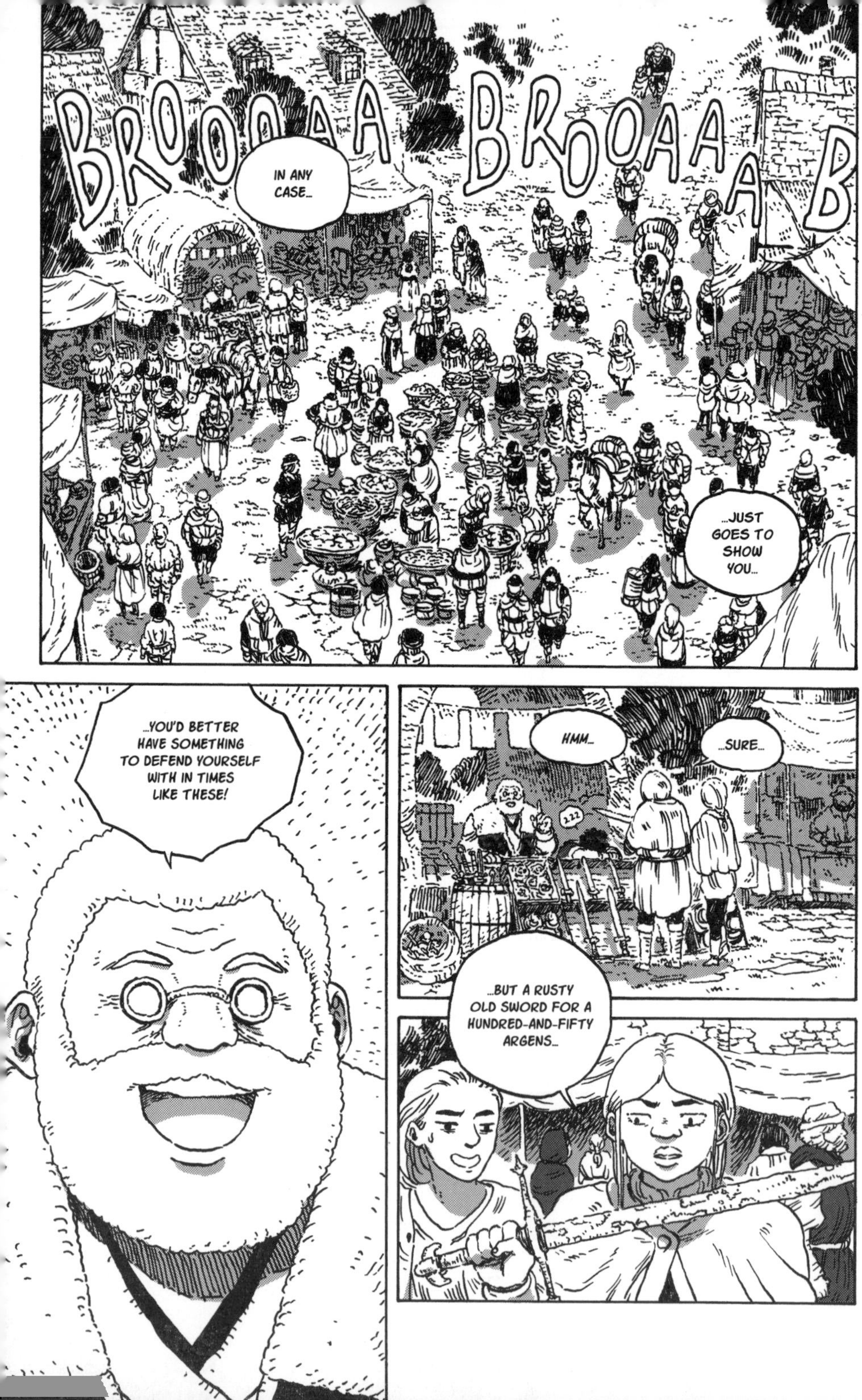
BROOAA
IN ANY CASE...
BROOAAAB
...JUST GOES TO SHOW YOU...
...YOU'D BETTER HAVE SOMETHING TO DEFEND YOURSELF WITH IN TIMES LIKE THESE!
HMM...
...SURE...
...BUT A RUSTY OLD SWORD FOR A HUNDRED-AND-FIFTY ARGENS...

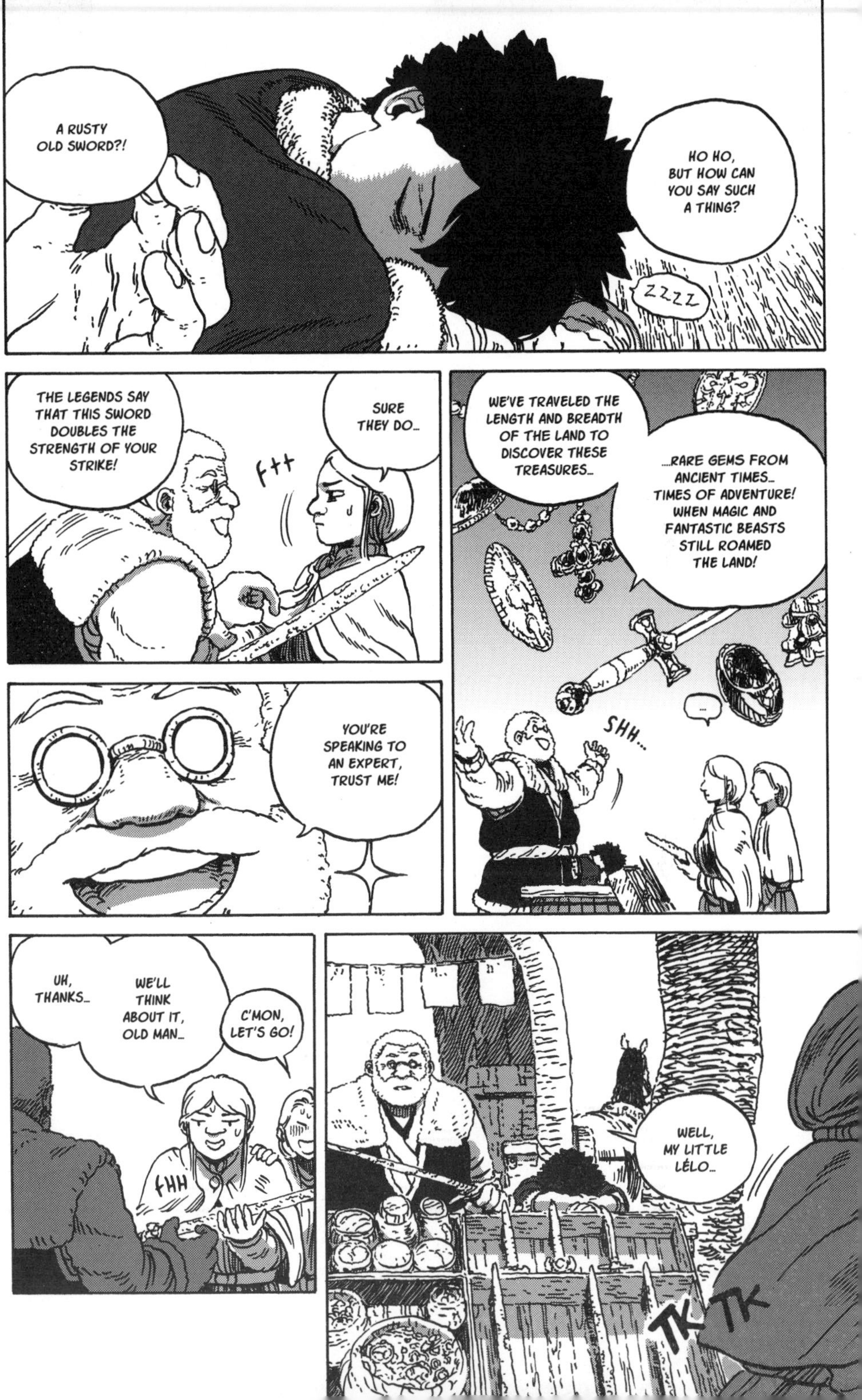
A RUSTY OLD SWORD?!
HO HO, BUT HOW CAN YOU SAY SUCH A THING?
ZZZZ
THE LEGENDS SAY THAT THIS SWORD DOUBLES THE STRENGTH OF YOUR STRIKE!
SURE THEY DO...
FTT
YOU'RE SPEAKING TO AN EXPERT, TRUST ME!
WE'VE TRAVELED THE LENGTH AND BREADTH OF THE LAND TO DISCOVER THESE TREASURES...
...RARE GEMS FROM ANCIENT TIMES... TIMES OF ADVENTURE! WHEN MAGIC AND FANTASTIC BEASTS STILL ROAMED THE LAND!
...
SHH...
UH, THANKS...
WE'LL THINK ABOUT IT, OLD MAN...
C'MON, LET'S GO!
FHH
WELL, MY LITTLE LÉLO...
TK TK

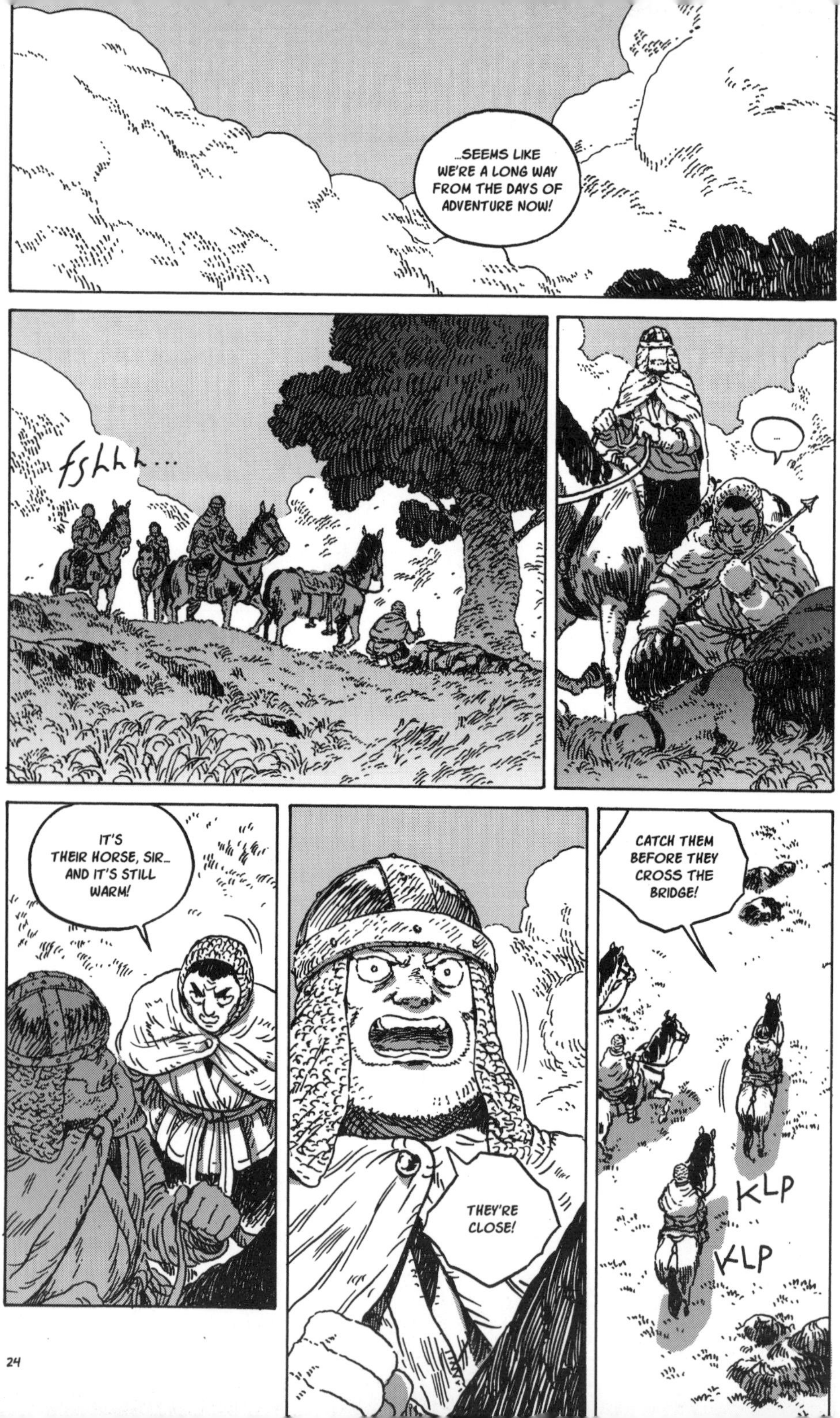
...SEEMS LIKE WE'RE A LONG WAY FROM THE DAYS OF ADVENTURE NOW!
fshhh...
...
IT'S THEIR HORSE, SIR... AND IT'S STILL WARM!
THEY'RE CLOSE!
CATCH THEM BEFORE THEY CROSS THE BRIDGE!
KLP
KLP

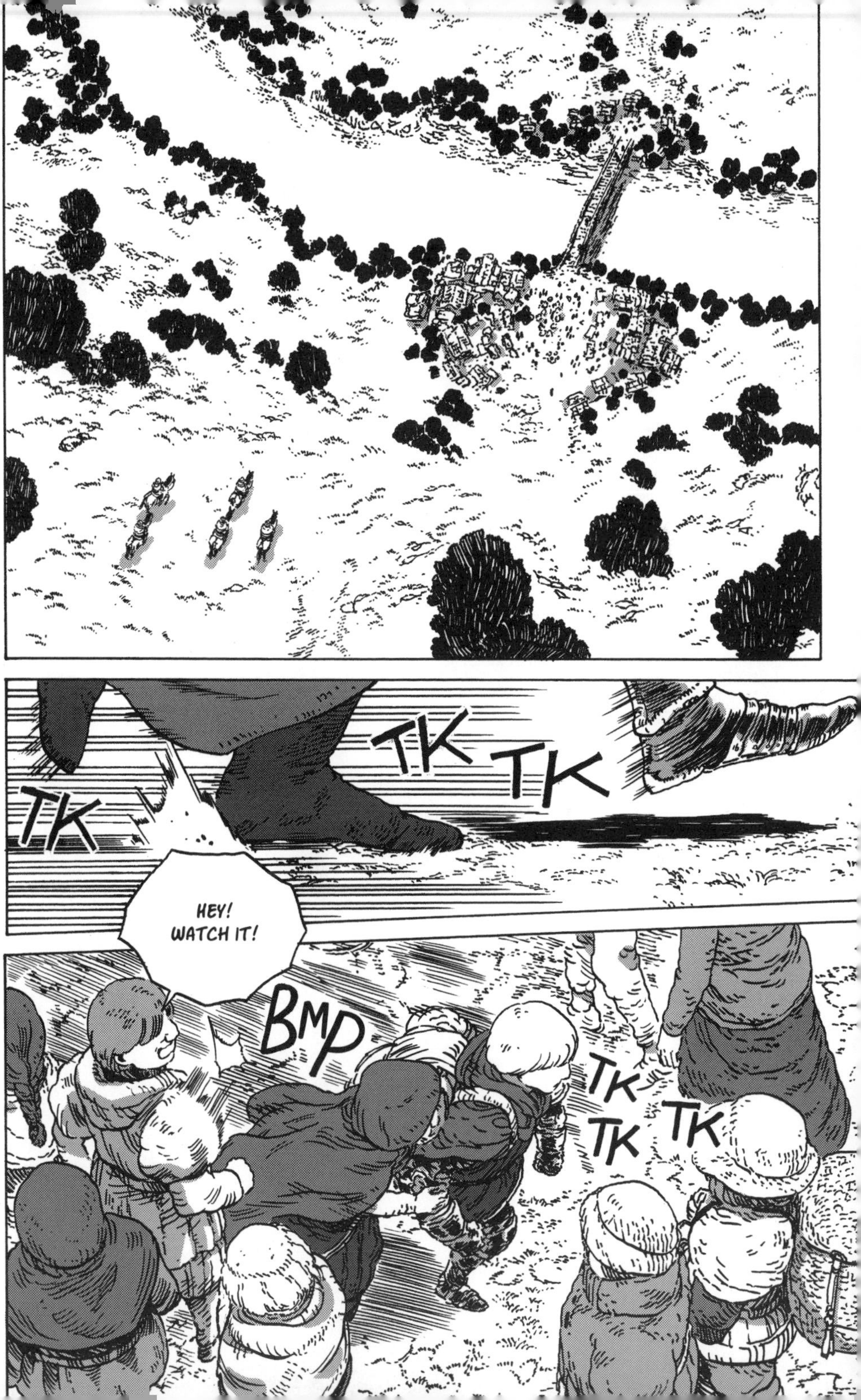
TK
TK
TK
HEY! WATCH IT!
BMP
TK
TK
TK

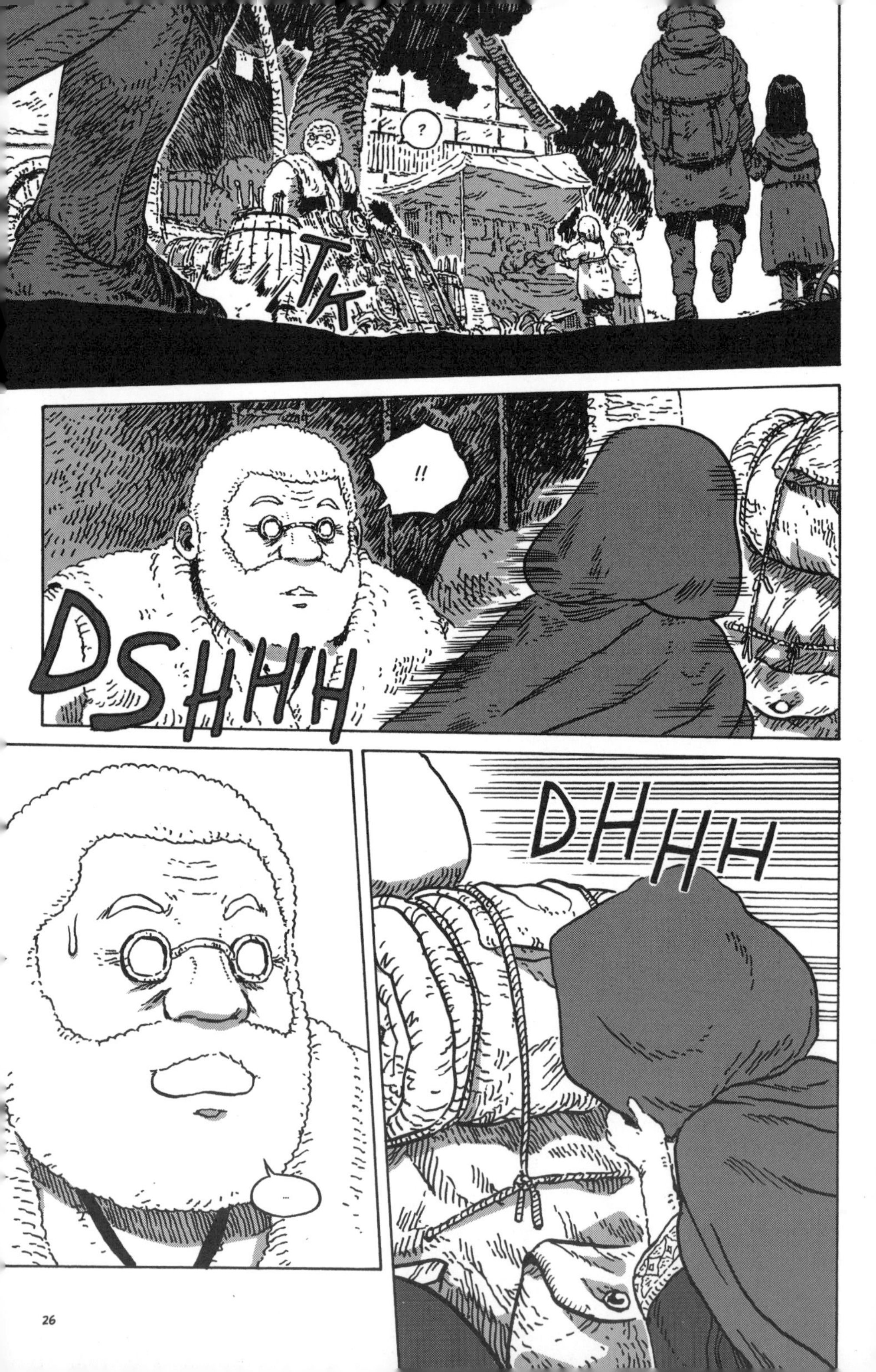
?
TK
!!
DSHHH
...
DHHH

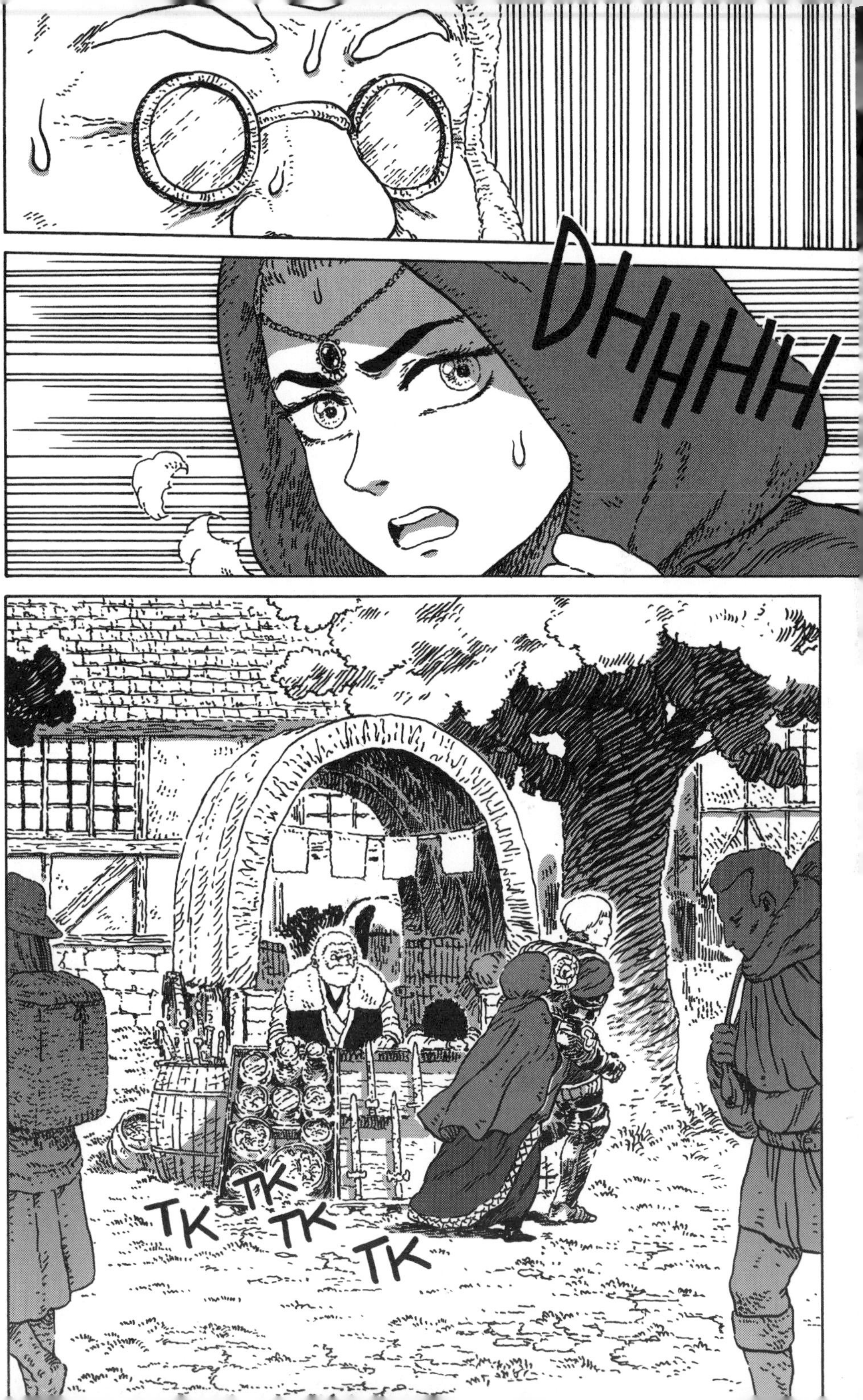
DHHHH
TK TK TK TK

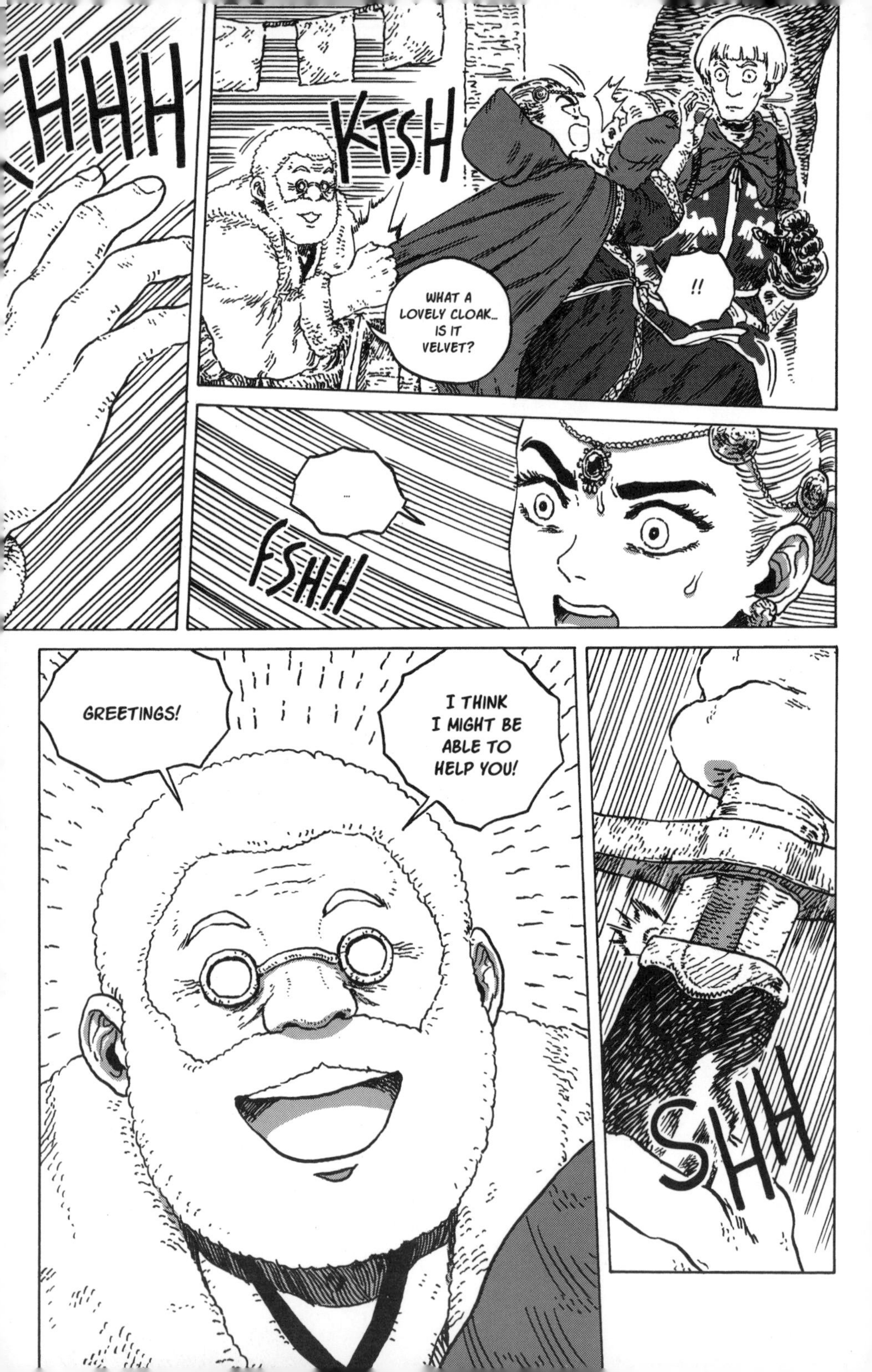
HHH
KTSH
WHAT A LOVELY CLOAK... IS IT VELVET?
!!
...
FSHH
GREETINGS!
I THINK I MIGHT BE ABLE TO HELP YOU!
SHH

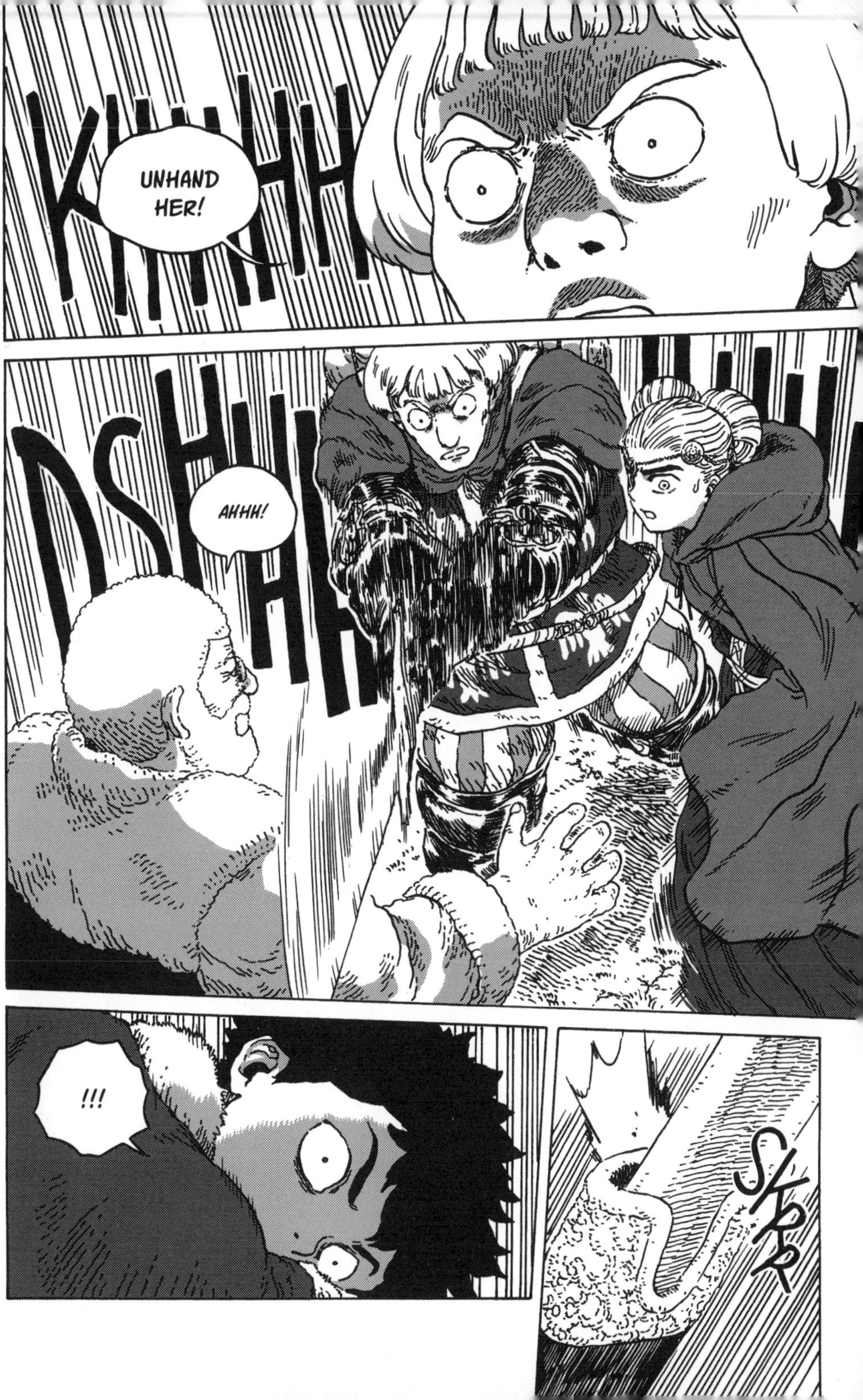
UNHAND HER!
AHHH!
!!!
SKRR

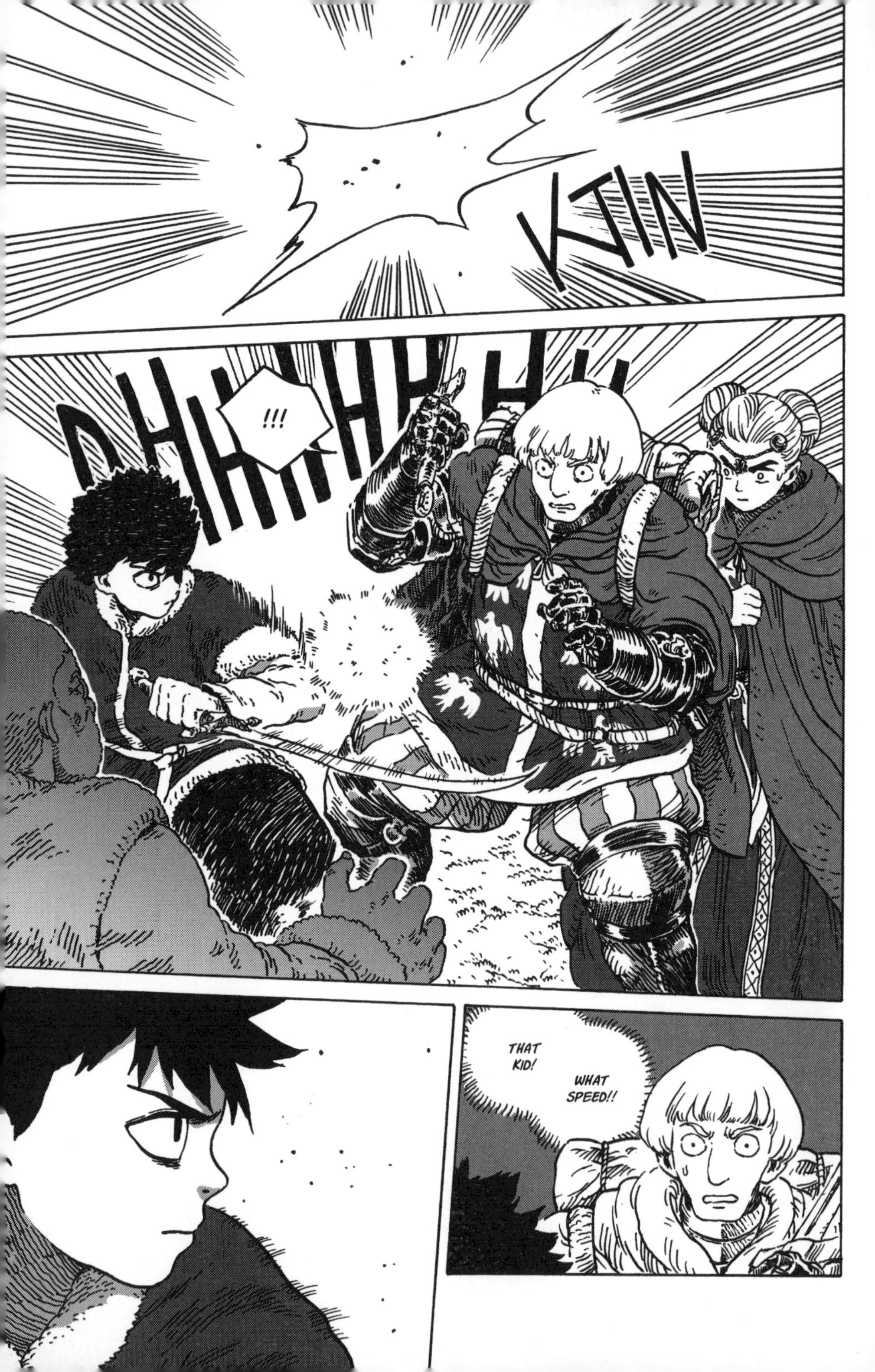
KJIN
!!!
THAT KID!
WHAT SPEED!!

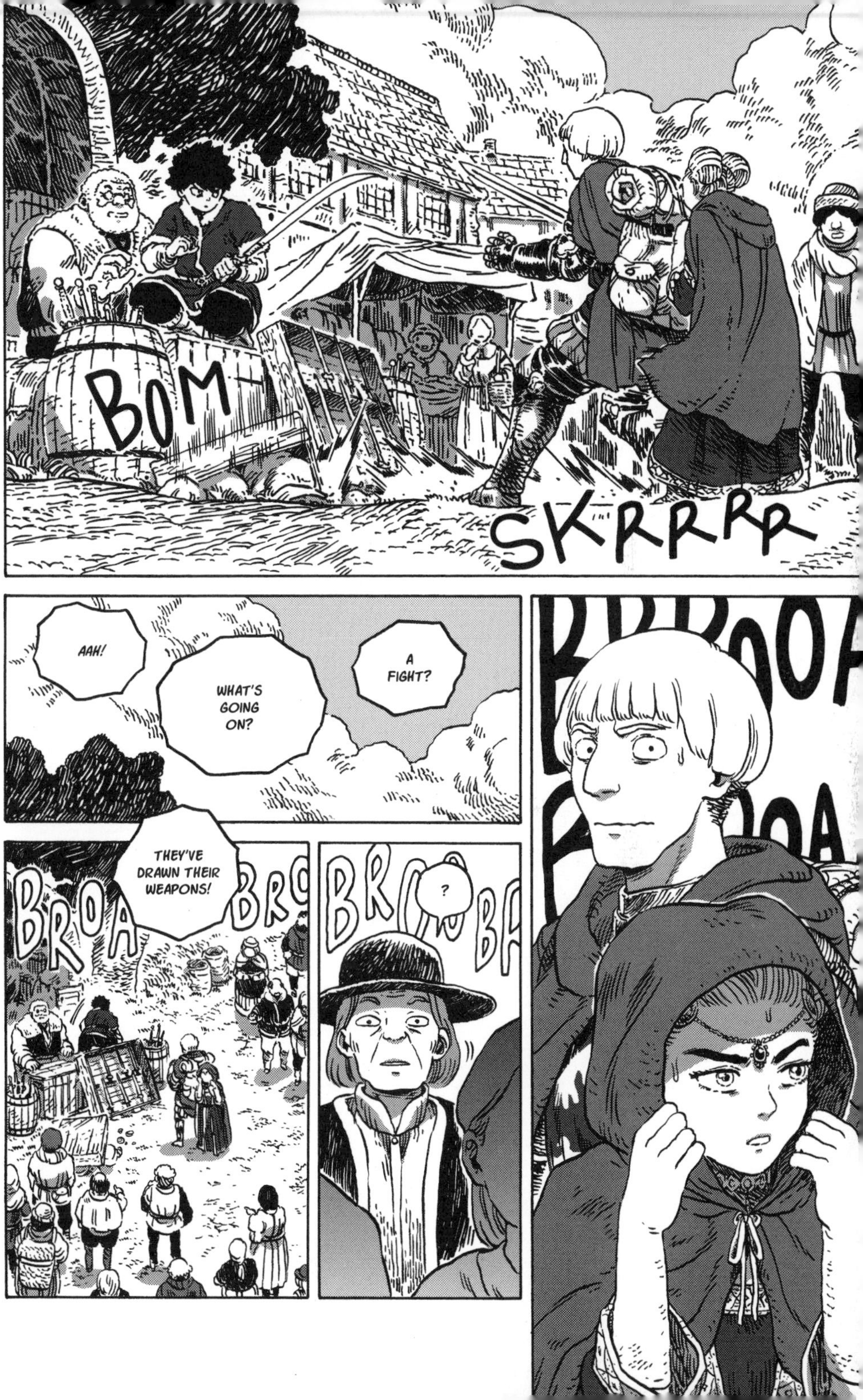
BOM
SKRRRR
AAH!
WHAT'S GOING ON?
A FIGHT?
THEY'VE DRAWN THEIR WEAPONS!
BROA
?

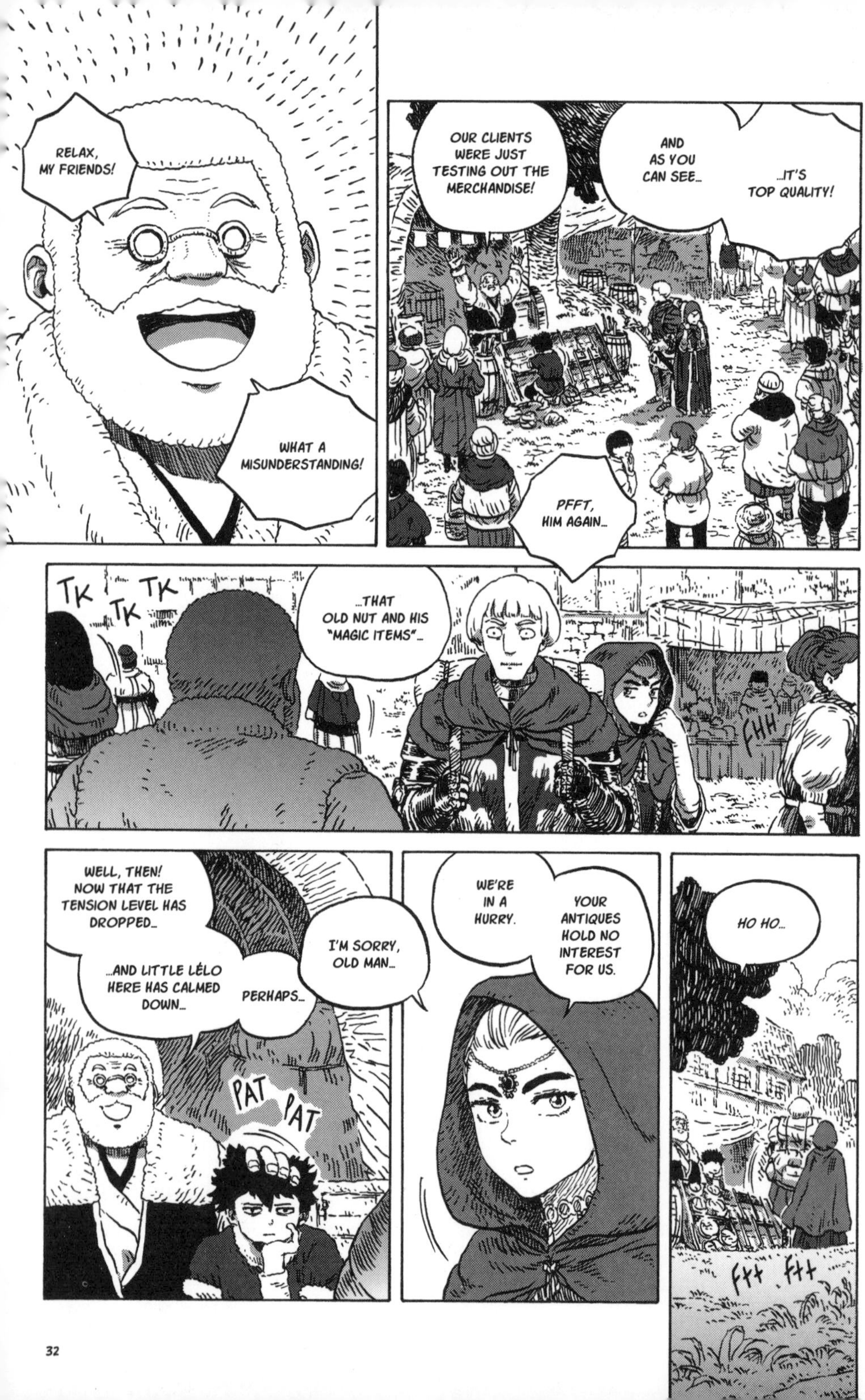

RELAX, MY FRIENDS!
WHAT A MISUNDERSTANDING!
OUR CLIENTS WERE JUST TESTING OUT THE MERCHANDISE!
AND AS YOU CAN SEE...
...IT'S TOP QUALITY!
PFFT, HIM AGAIN...
TK TK TK
...THAT OLD NUT AND HIS "MAGIC ITEMS"...
FHH
WELL, THEN! NOW THAT THE TENSION LEVEL HAS DROPPED...
...AND LITTLE LÉLO HERE HAS CALMED DOWN...
PERHAPS...
PAT PAT
I'M SORRY, OLD MAN...
WE'RE IN A HURRY.
YOUR ANTIQUES HOLD NO INTEREST FOR US.
HO HO...
FTT FTT

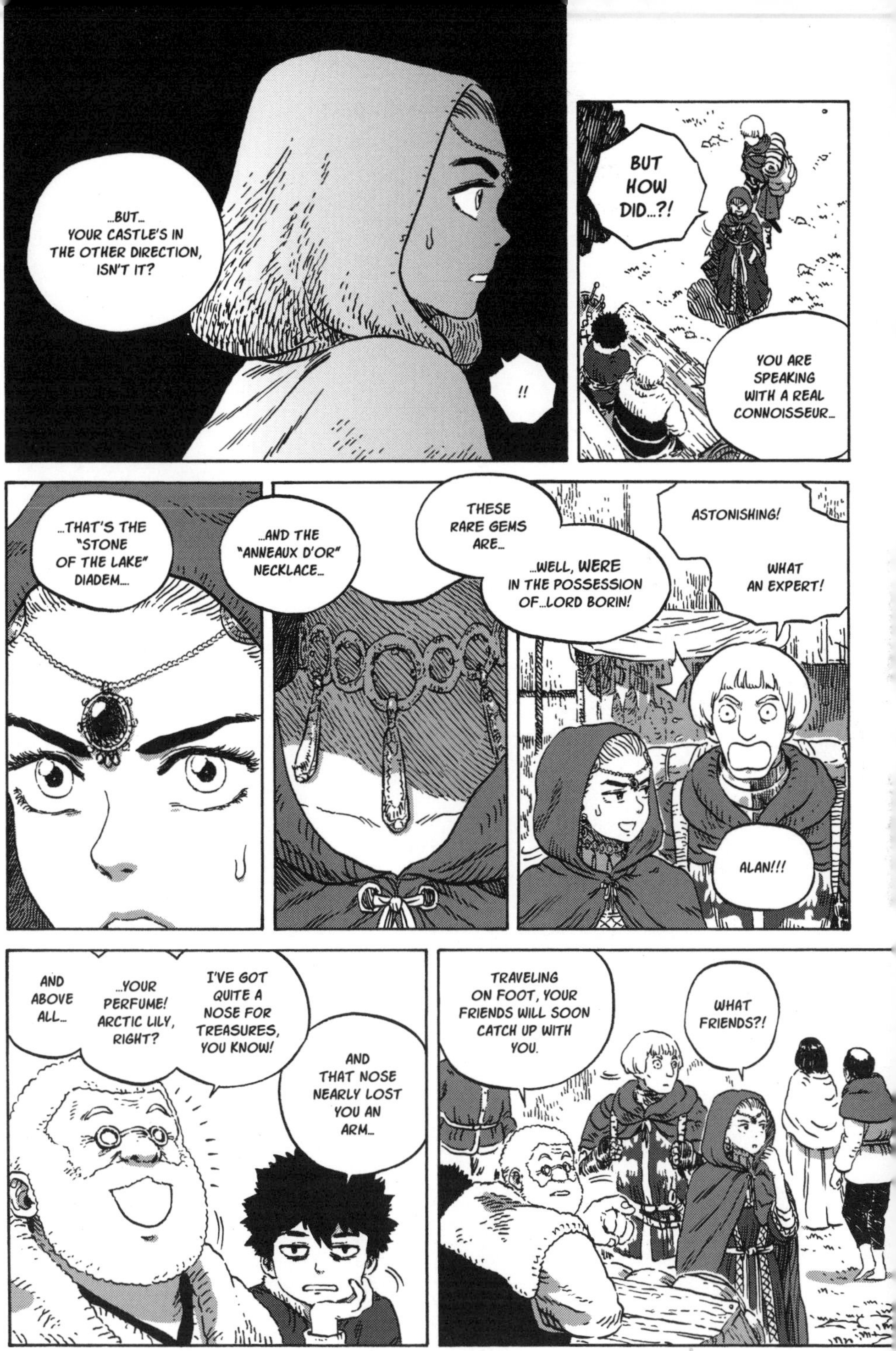
...BUT... YOUR CASTLE'S IN THE OTHER DIRECTION, ISN'T IT?
!!
BUT HOW DID...?!
YOU ARE SPEAKING WITH A REAL CONNOISSEUR...
...THAT'S THE "STONE OF THE LAKE" DIADEM....
...AND THE "ANNEAUX D'OR" NECKLACE...
THESE RARE GEMS ARE...
...WELL, WERE IN THE POSSESSION OF...LORD BORIN!
ASTONISHING!
WHAT AN EXPERT!
ALAN!!!
AND ABOVE ALL...
...YOUR PERFUME! ARCTIC LILY, RIGHT?
I'VE GOT QUITE A NOSE FOR TREASURES, YOU KNOW!
AND THAT NOSE NEARLY LOST YOU AN ARM...
TRAVELING ON FOOT, YOUR FRIENDS WILL SOON CATCH UP WITH YOU.
WHAT FRIENDS?!

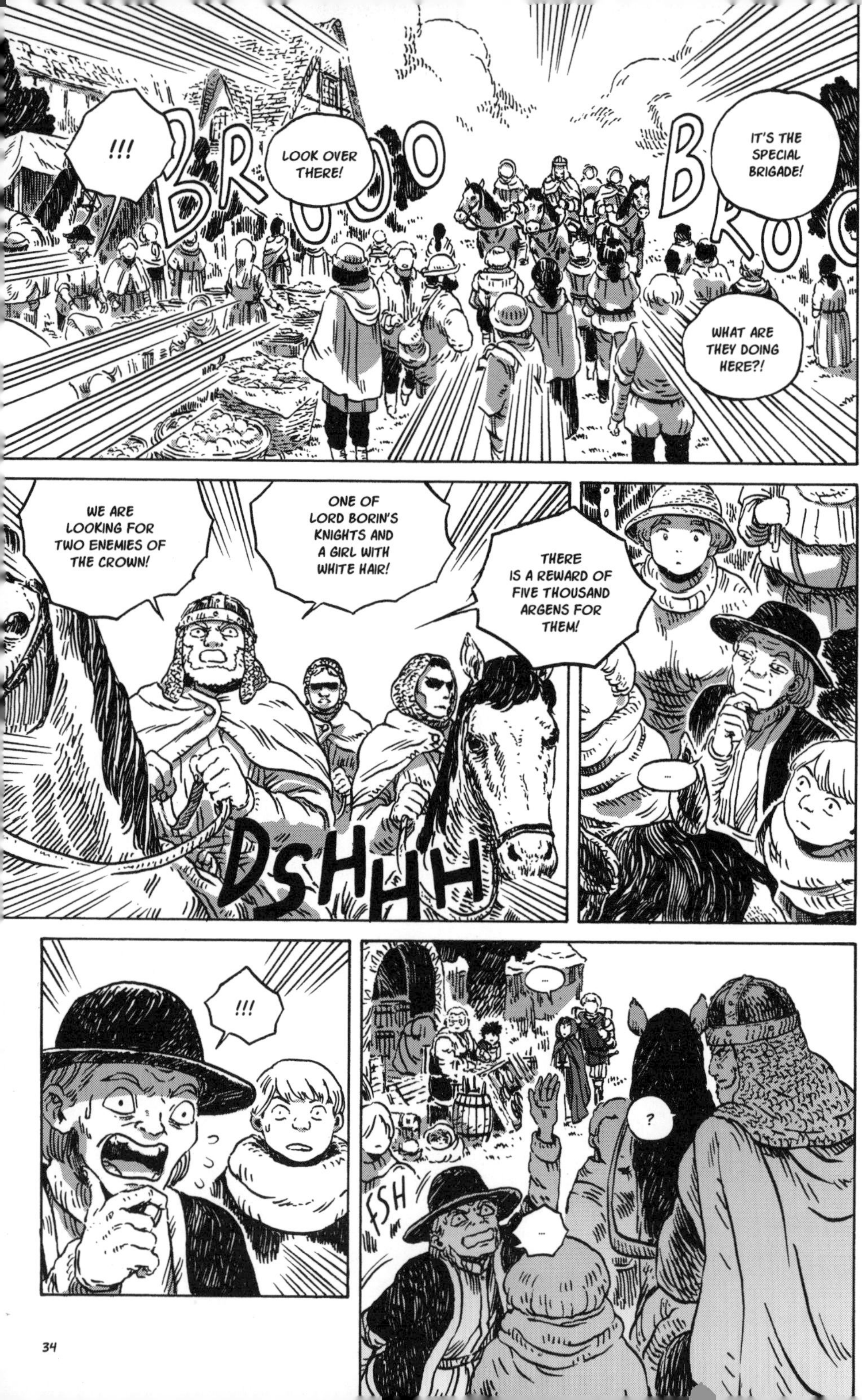
!!!
BROOO
LOOK OVER THERE!
BROO
IT'S THE SPECIAL BRIGADE!
WHAT ARE THEY DOING HERE?!
WE ARE LOOKING FOR TWO ENEMIES OF THE CROWN!
ONE OF LORD BORIN'S KNIGHTS AND A GIRL WITH WHITE HAIR!
DSHHH
THERE IS A REWARD OF FIVE THOUSAND ARGENS FOR THEM!
...
!!!
...
?
FSH
...

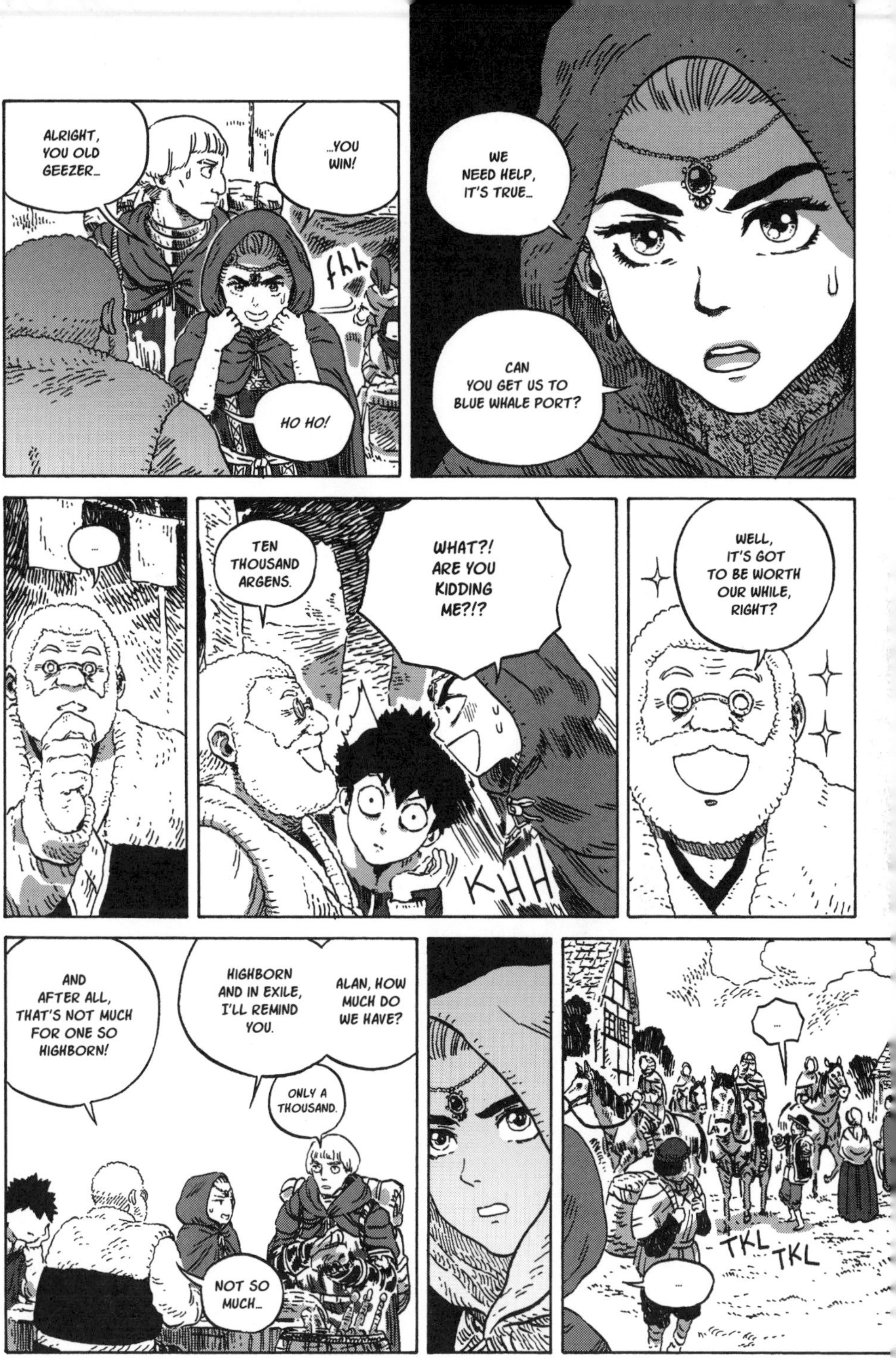

ALRIGHT, YOU OLD GEEZER...
...YOU WIN!
fhh
HO HO!
WE NEED HELP, IT'S TRUE...
CAN YOU GET US TO BLUE WHALE PORT?
...
TEN THOUSAND ARGENS.
WHAT?! ARE YOU KIDDING ME?!?
KHH
WELL, IT'S GOT TO BE WORTH OUR WHILE, RIGHT?
AND AFTER ALL, THAT'S NOT MUCH FOR ONE SO HIGHBORN!
HIGHBORN AND IN EXILE, I'LL REMIND YOU.
ALAN, HOW MUCH DO WE HAVE?
ONLY A THOUSAND.
NOT SO MUCH...
...
TKL TKL
...

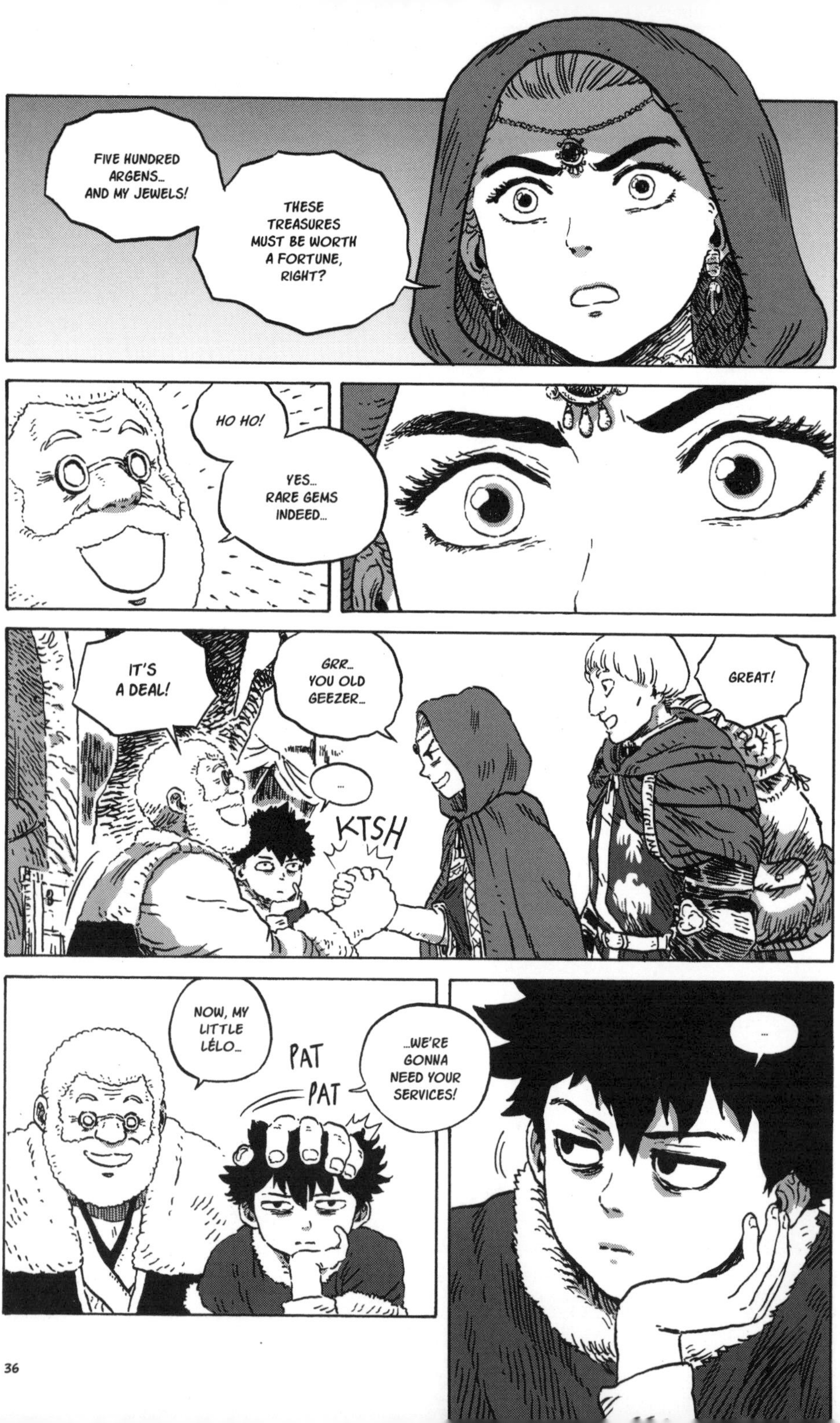
FIVE HUNDRED ARGENS... AND MY JEWELS!
THESE TREASURES MUST BE WORTH A FORTUNE, RIGHT?
HO HO!
YES... RARE GEMS INDEED...
IT'S A DEAL!
GRR... YOU OLD GEEZER...
...
KTSH
GREAT!
NOW, MY LITTLE LÉLO...
PAT PAT
...WE'RE GONNA NEED YOUR SERVICES!
...

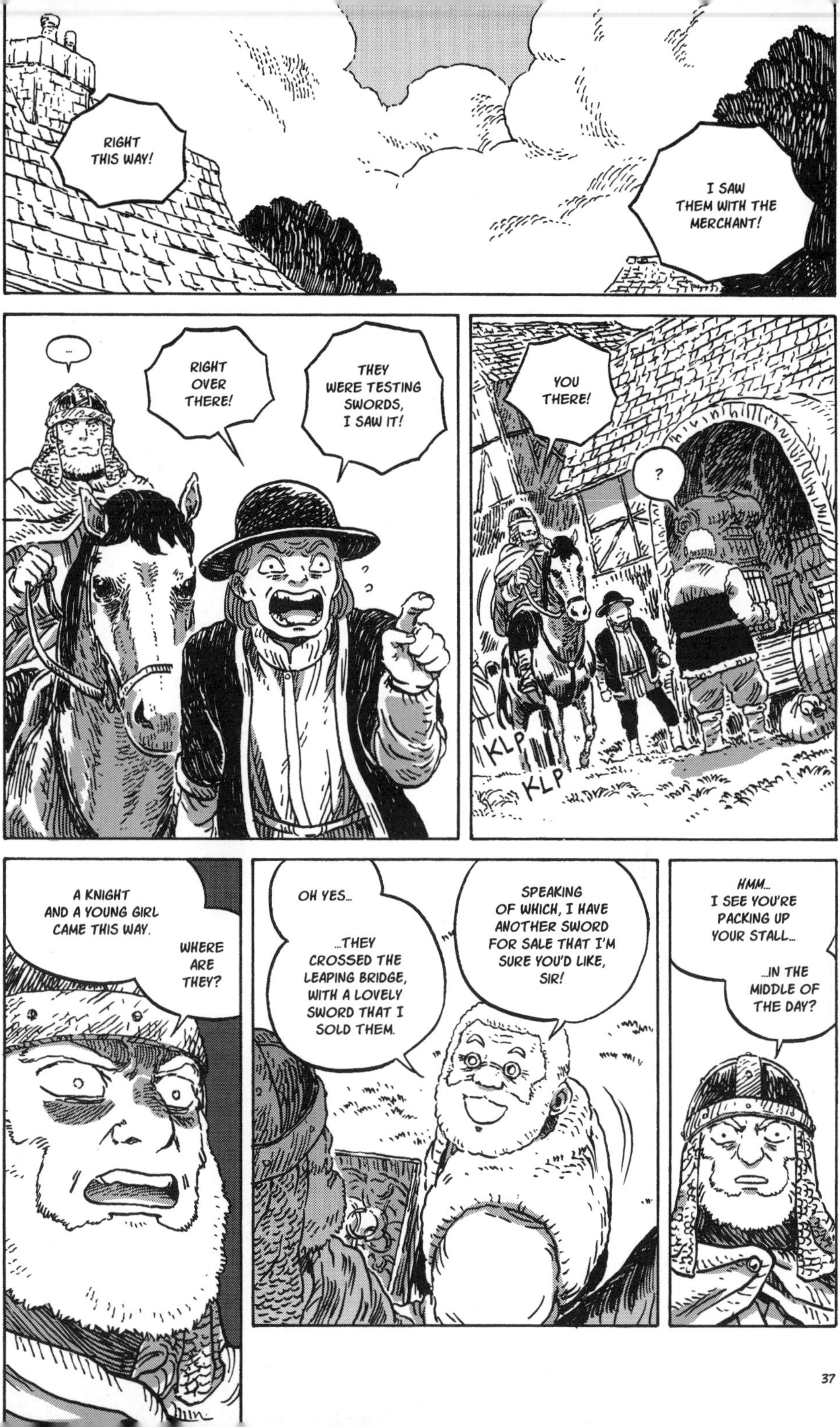
RIGHT THIS WAY!
I SAW THEM WITH THE MERCHANT!
...
RIGHT OVER THERE!
THEY WERE TESTING SWORDS, I SAW IT!
YOU THERE!
?
KLP
KLP
A KNIGHT AND A YOUNG GIRL CAME THIS WAY.
WHERE ARE THEY?
OH YES...
...THEY CROSSED THE LEAPING BRIDGE, WITH A LOVELY SWORD THAT I SOLD THEM.
SPEAKING OF WHICH, I HAVE ANOTHER SWORD FOR SALE THAT I'M SURE YOU'D LIKE, SIR!
HMM... I SEE YOU'RE PACKING UP YOUR STALL...
...IN THE MIDDLE OF THE DAY?

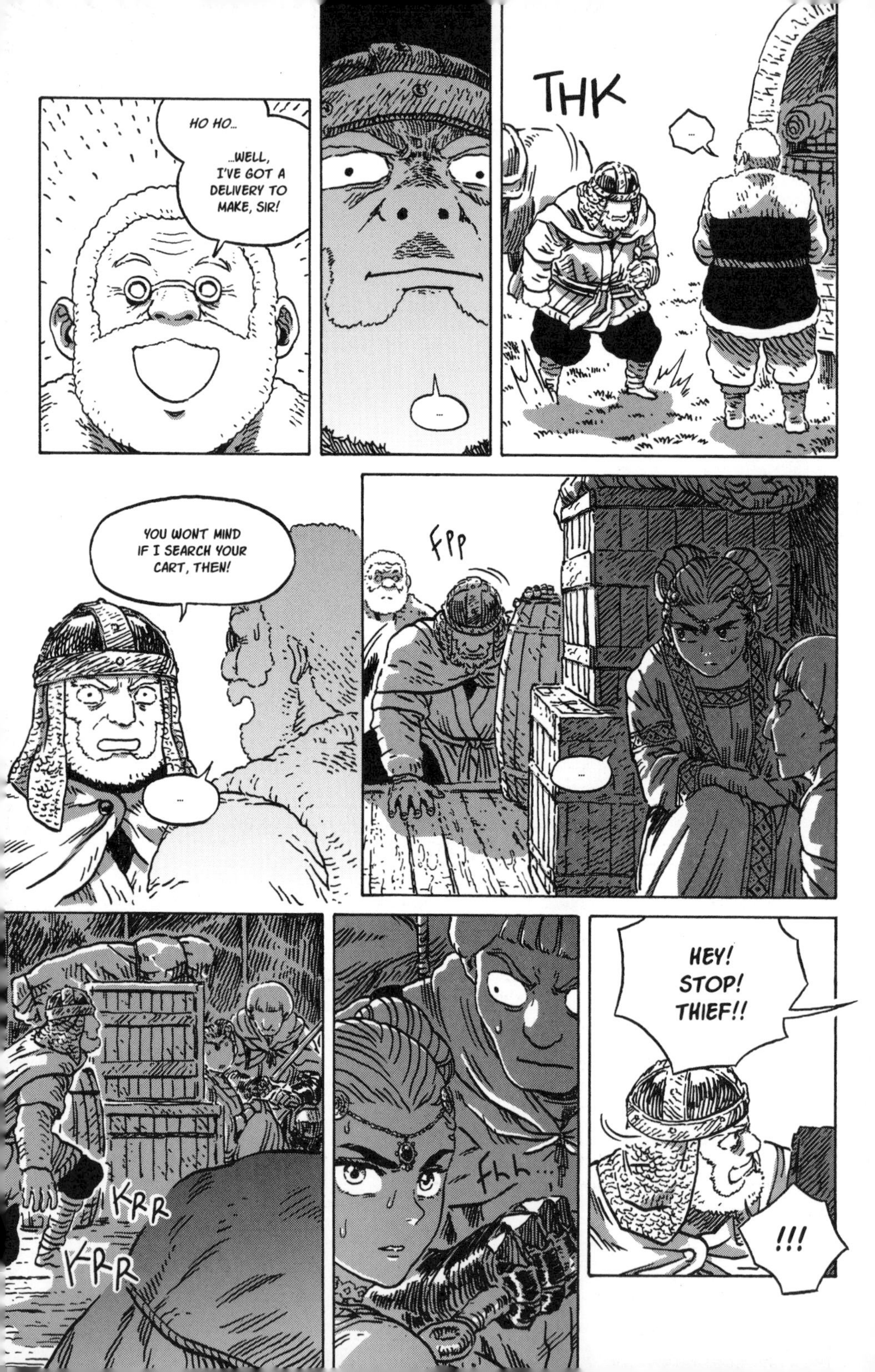
HO HO...
...WELL, I'VE GOT A DELIVERY TO MAKE, SIR!
...
THK
...
YOU WONT MIND IF I SEARCH YOUR CART, THEN!
...
FPP
...
KRR
KRR
fhh...
HEY! STOP! THIEF!!
!!!

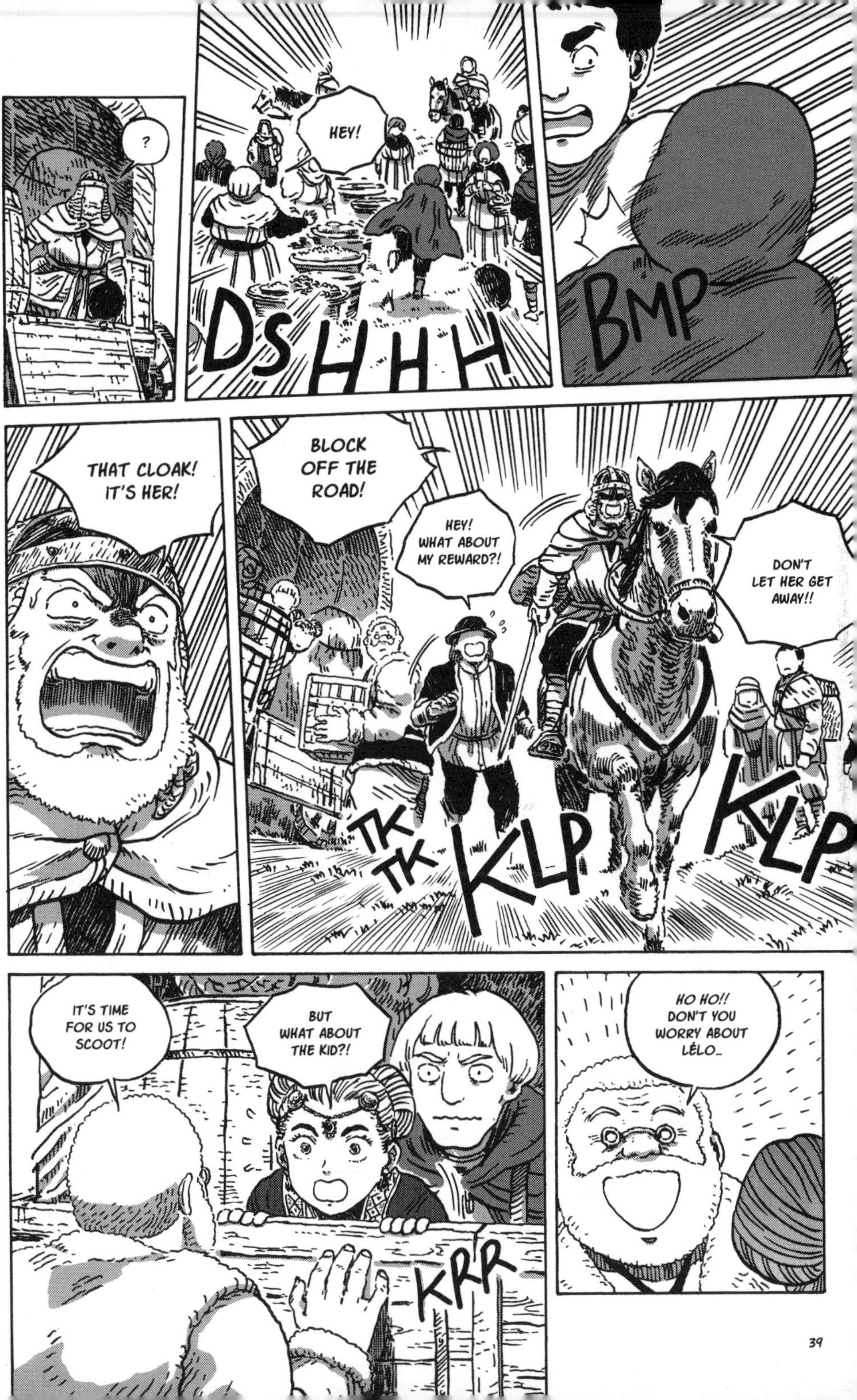
?
HEY!
DSHHH
BMP
THAT CLOAK! IT'S HER!
BLOCK OFF THE ROAD!
HEY! WHAT ABOUT MY REWARD?!
DON'T LET HER GET AWAY!!
TK TK
KLP
KLP
IT'S TIME FOR US TO SCOOT!
BUT WHAT ABOUT THE KID?!
KRR
HO HO!! DON'T YOU WORRY ABOUT LÉLO...

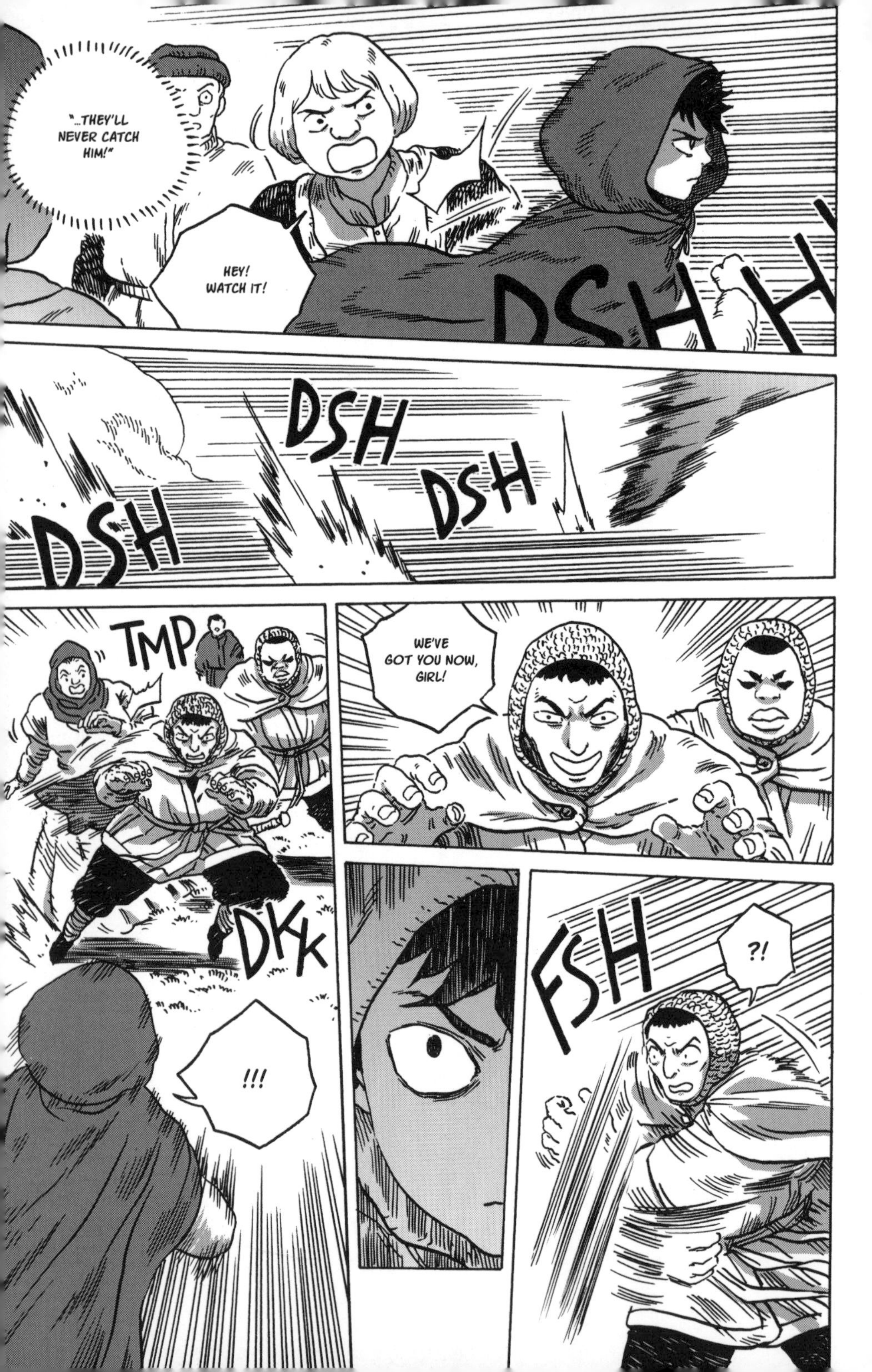
"...THEY'LL NEVER CATCH HIM!"
HEY! WATCH IT!
DSHH
DSH
DSH
DSH
TMP
DKK
!!!
WE'VE GOT YOU NOW, GIRL!
FSH
?!

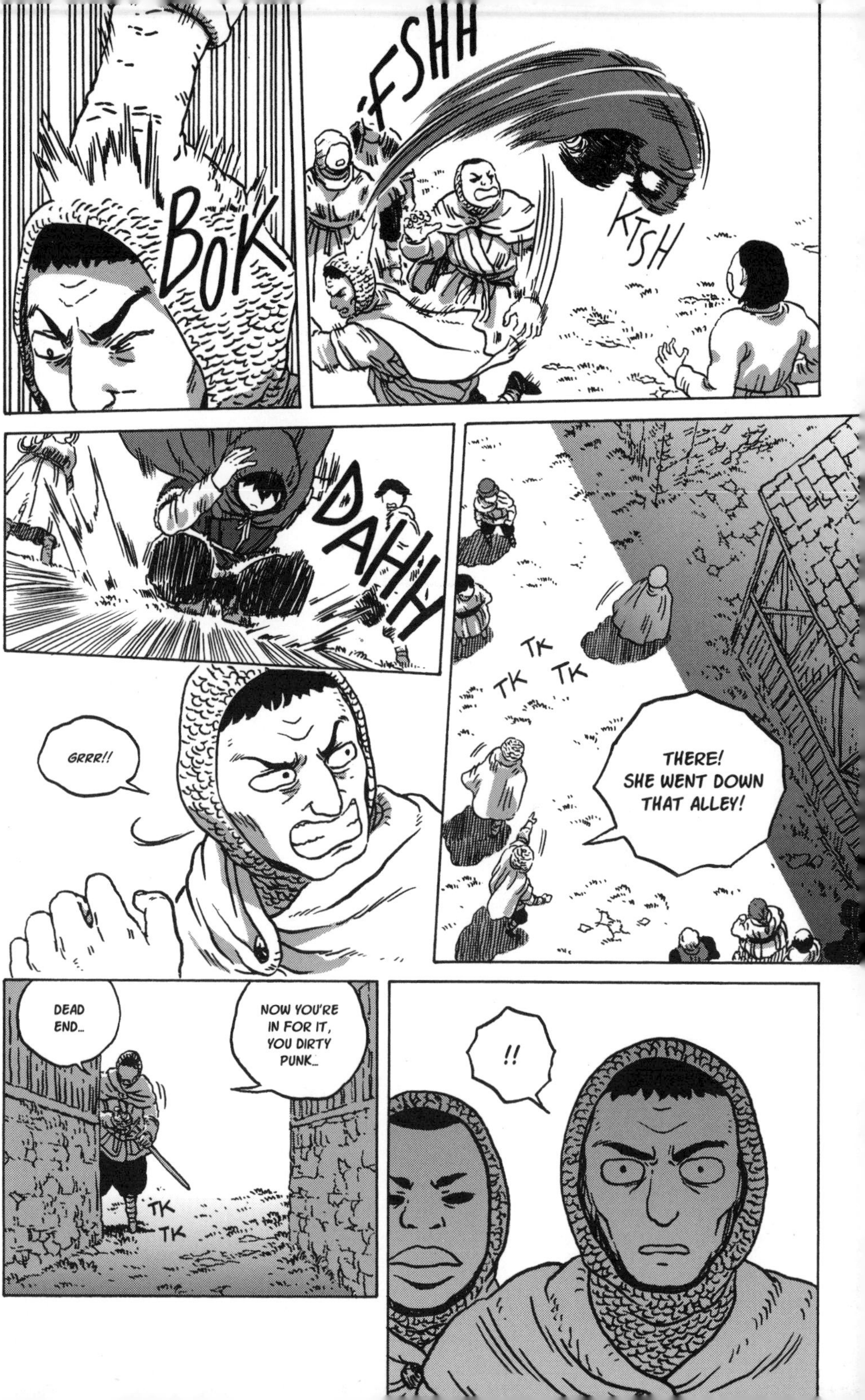
BOK
FSHH
KTSH
DAHH
GRRR!!
TK
TK TK
THERE! SHE WENT DOWN THAT ALLEY!
DEAD END...
NOW YOU'RE IN FOR IT, YOU DIRTY PUNK...
TK
TK
!!

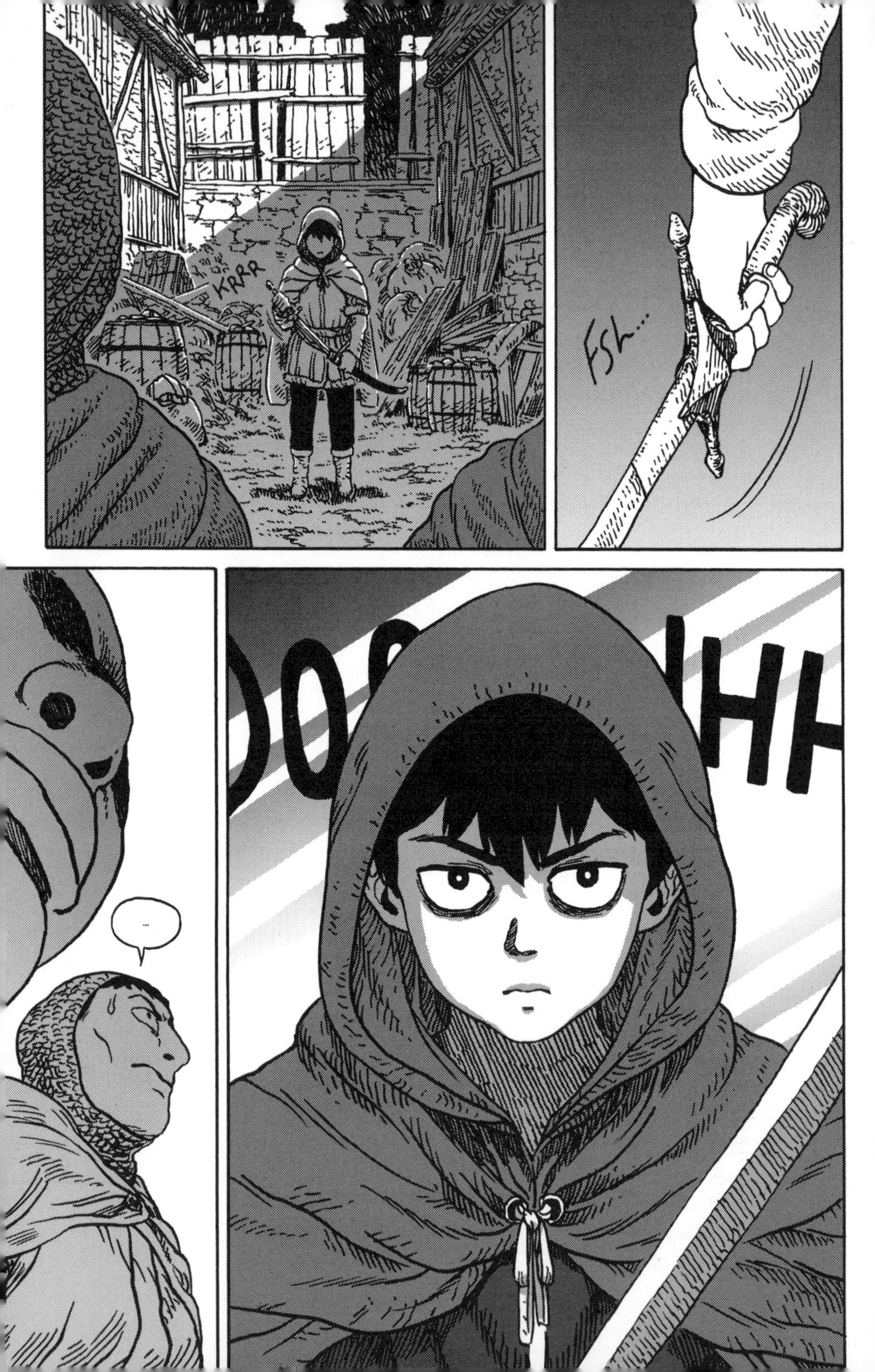
KRRR
FSH...
...
DOO
HHH

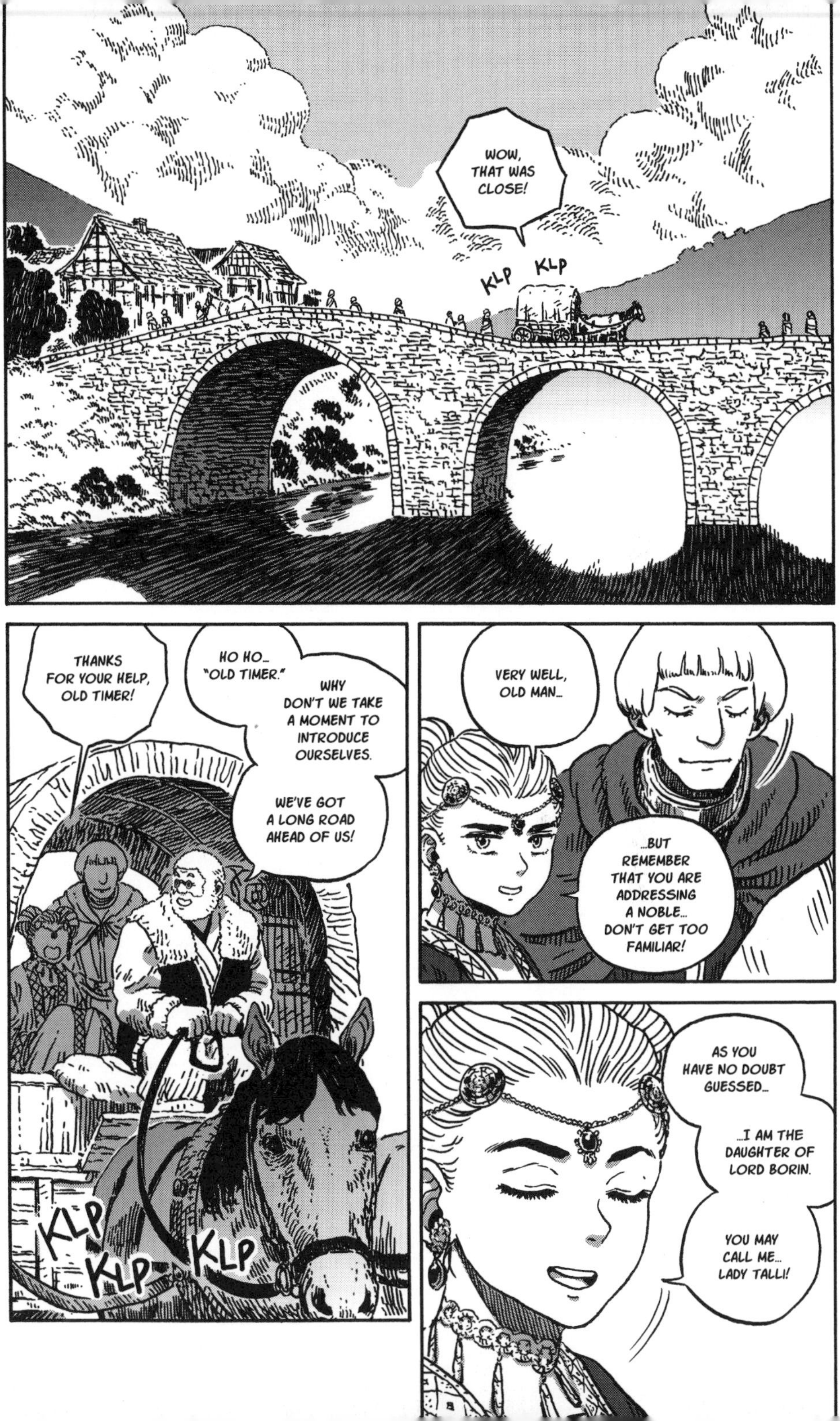
WOW, THAT WAS CLOSE!
KLP KLP
THANKS FOR YOUR HELP, OLD TIMER!
HO HO... "OLD TIMER."
WHY DON'T WE TAKE A MOMENT TO INTRODUCE OURSELVES.
WE'VE GOT A LONG ROAD AHEAD OF US!
KLP KLP KLP
VERY WELL, OLD MAN...
...BUT REMEMBER THAT YOU ARE ADDRESSING A NOBLE... DON'T GET TOO FAMILIAR!
AS YOU HAVE NO DOUBT GUESSED...
...I AM THE DAUGHTER OF LORD BORIN.
YOU MAY CALL ME... LADY TALLI!

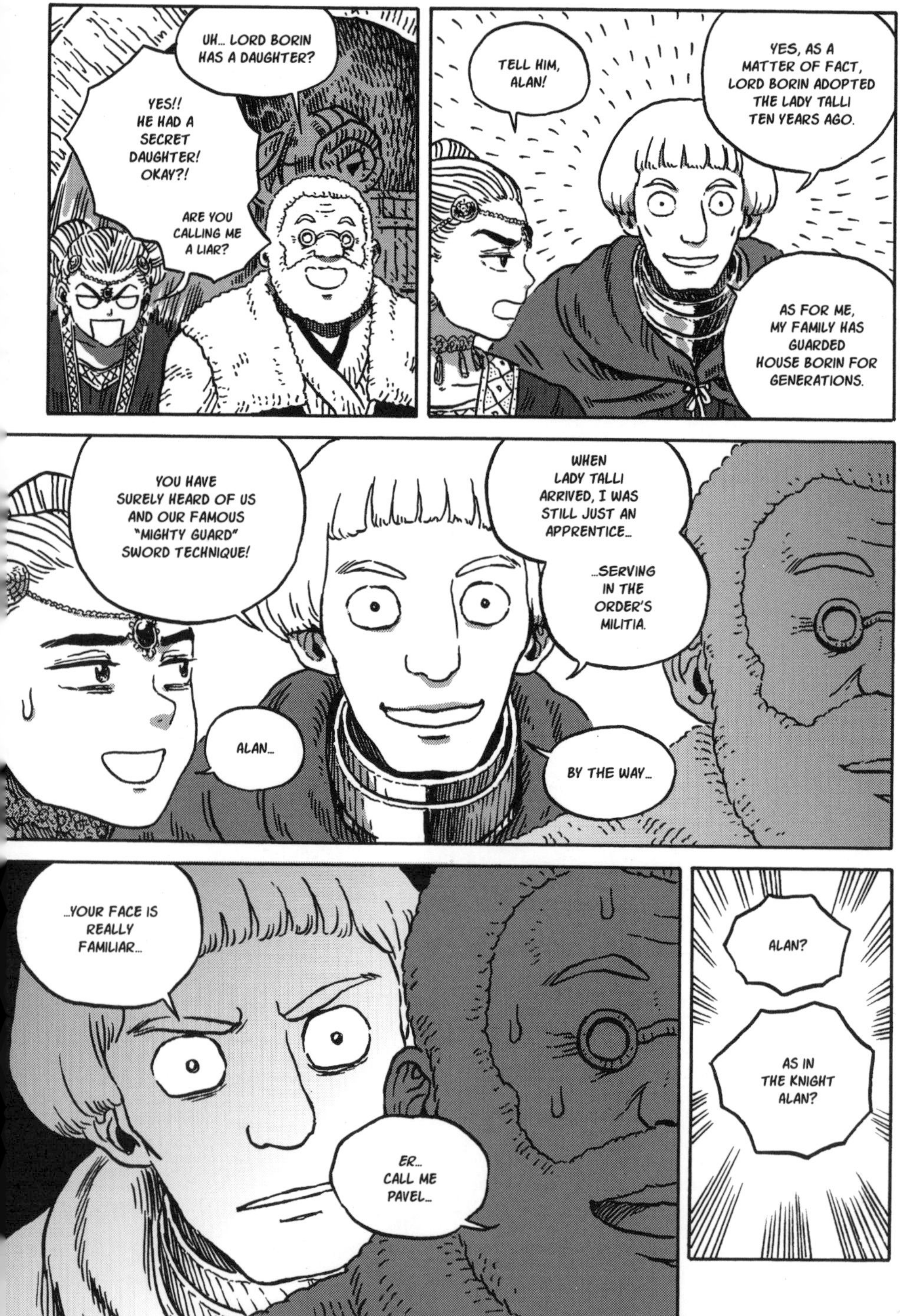
UH... LORD BORIN HAS A DAUGHTER?
YES!! HE HAD A SECRET DAUGHTER! OKAY?!
ARE YOU CALLING ME A LIAR?
TELL HIM, ALAN!
YES, AS A MATTER OF FACT, LORD BORIN ADOPTED THE LADY TALLI TEN YEARS AGO.
AS FOR ME, MY FAMILY HAS GUARDED HOUSE BORIN FOR GENERATIONS.
YOU HAVE SURELY HEARD OF US AND OUR FAMOUS "MIGHTY GUARD" SWORD TECHNIQUE!
WHEN LADY TALLI ARRIVED, I WAS STILL JUST AN APPRENTICE...
...SERVING IN THE ORDER'S MILITIA.
ALAN...
BY THE WAY...
...YOUR FACE IS REALLY FAMILIAR...
ER... CALL ME PAVEL...
ALAN?
AS IN THE KNIGHT ALAN?

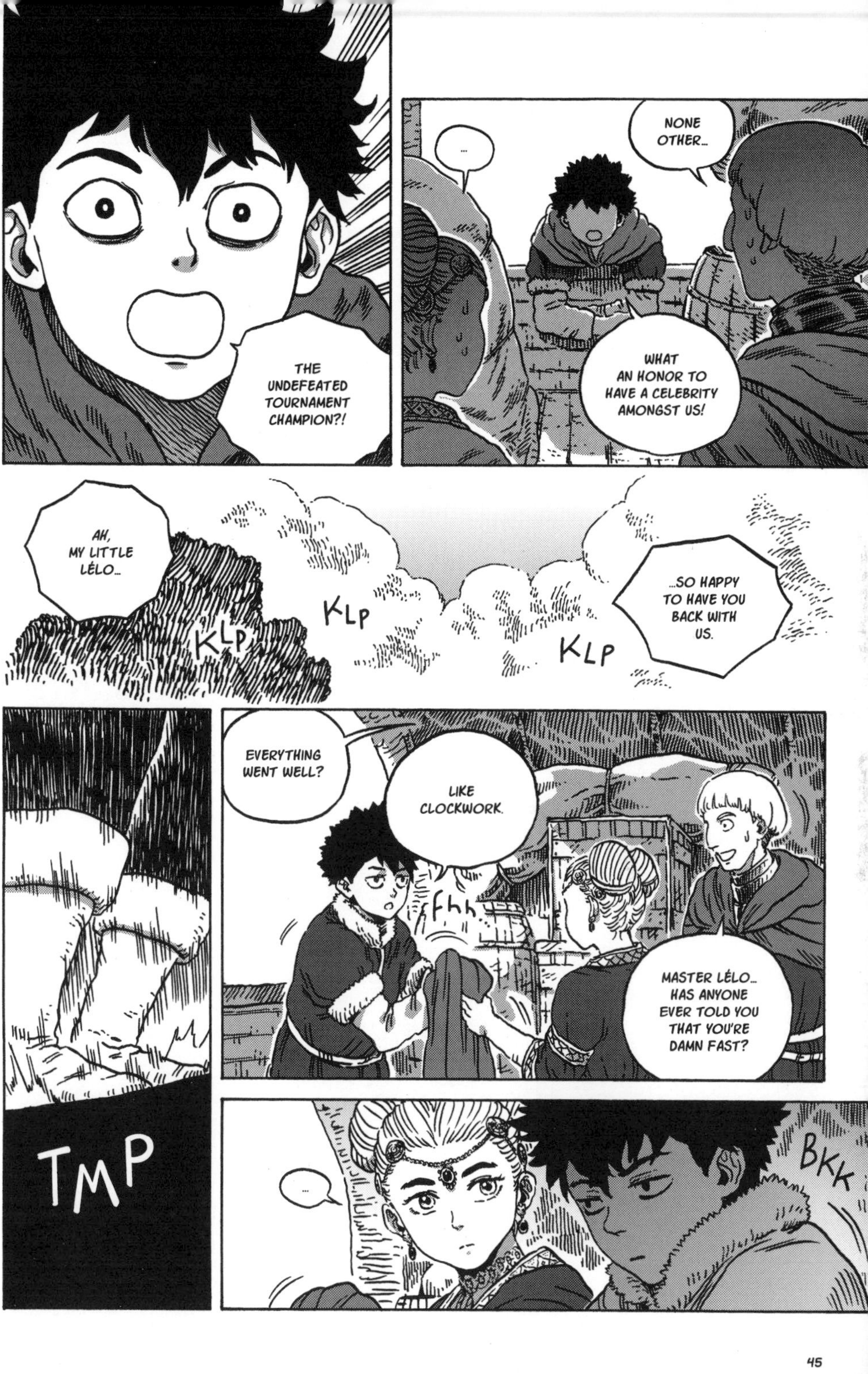
THE UNDEFEATED TOURNAMENT CHAMPION?!
...
NONE OTHER...
WHAT AN HONOR TO HAVE A CELEBRITY AMONGST US!
AH, MY LITTLE LÉLO...
KLP
KLP
KLP
...SO HAPPY TO HAVE YOU BACK WITH US.
TMP
EVERYTHING WENT WELL?
LIKE CLOCKWORK.
FHH
MASTER LÉLO... HAS ANYONE EVER TOLD YOU THAT YOU'RE DAMN FAST?
...
BKK

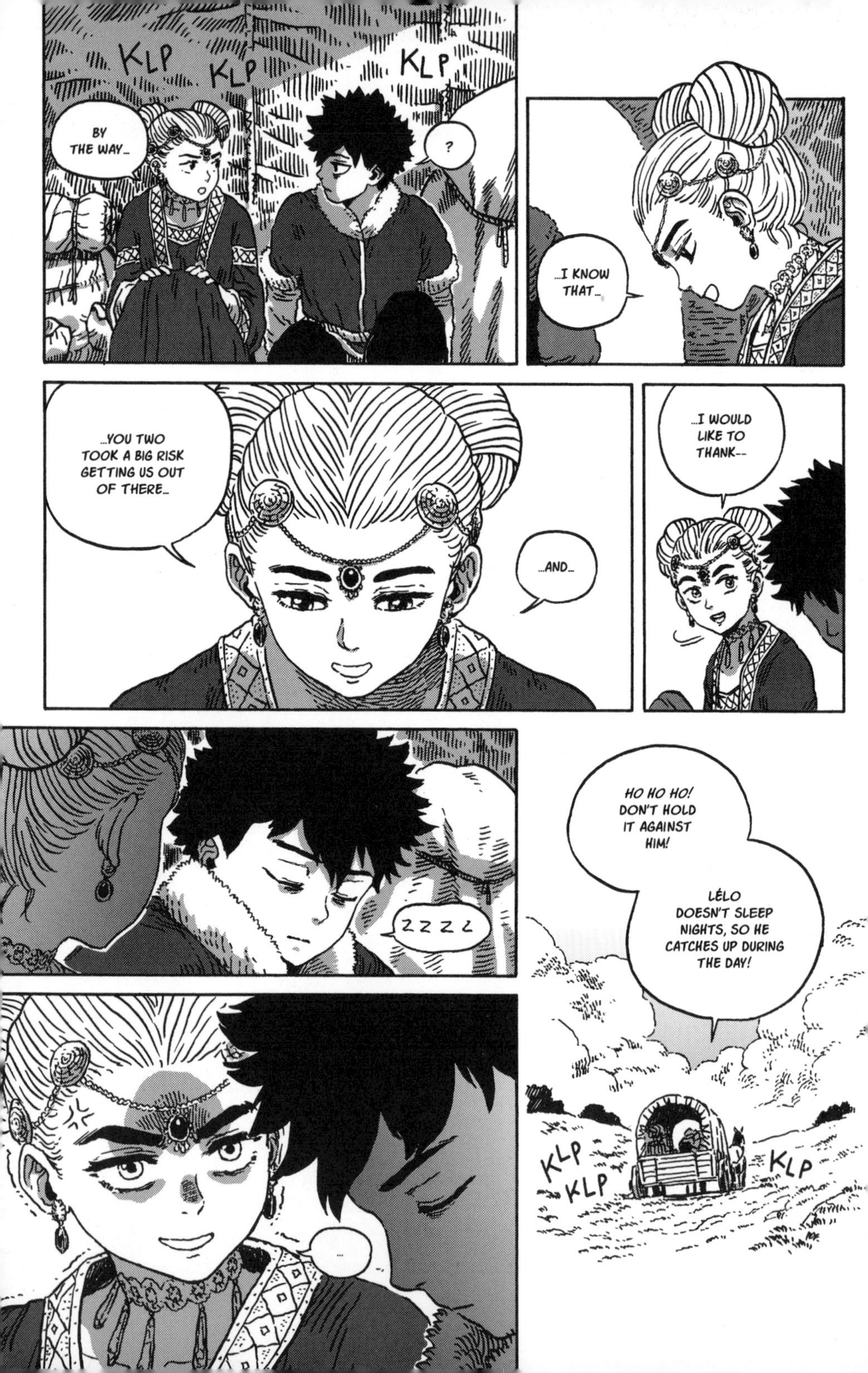
KLP
KLP
KLP
BY THE WAY...
?
...I KNOW THAT...
...YOU TWO TOOK A BIG RISK GETTING US OUT OF THERE...
...AND...
...I WOULD LIKE TO THANK--
ZZZZ
...
HO HO HO! DON'T HOLD IT AGAINST HIM!
LÉLO DOESN'T SLEEP NIGHTS, SO HE CATCHES UP DURING THE DAY!
KLP
KLP
KLP

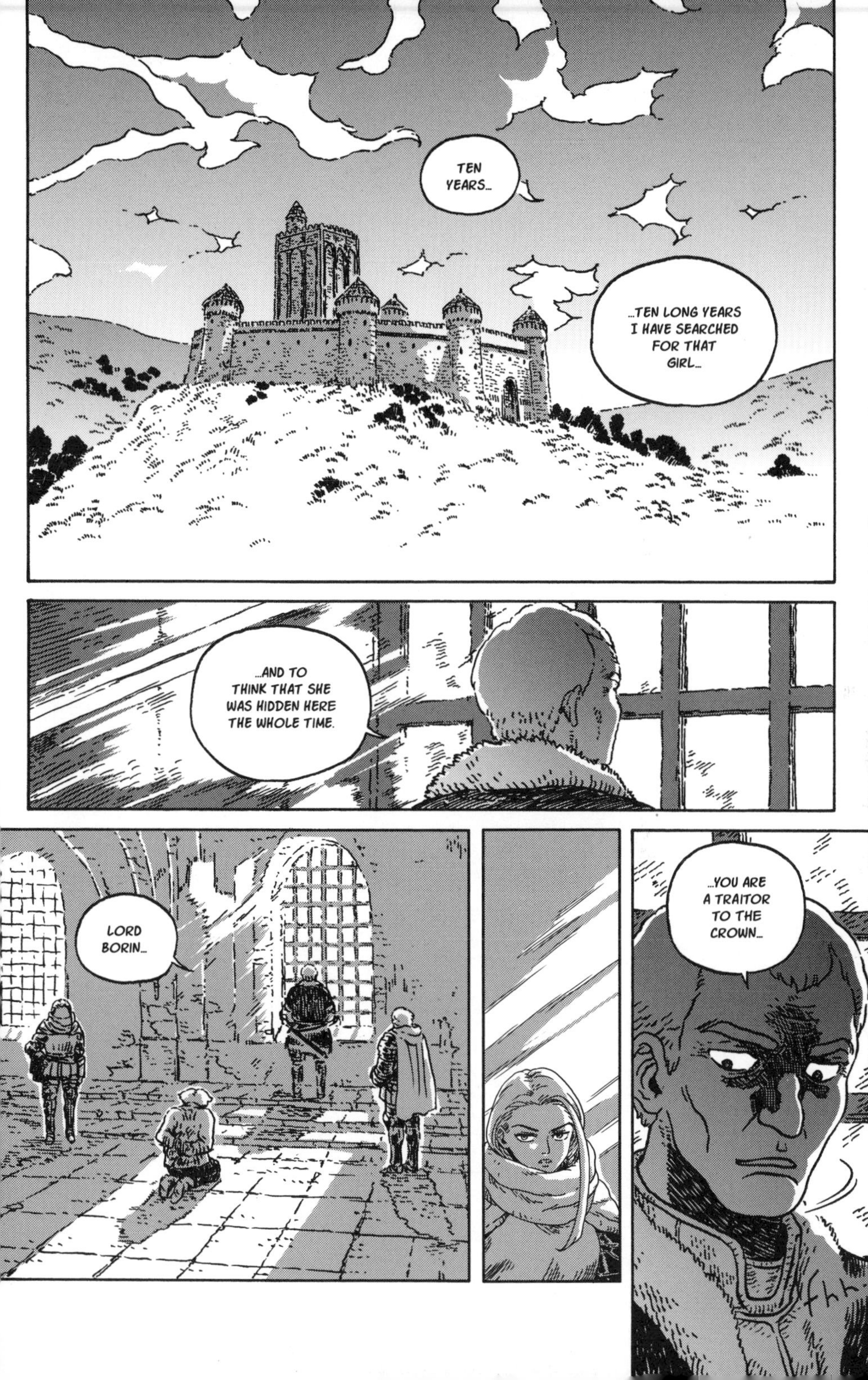
TEN YEARS...
...TEN LONG YEARS I HAVE SEARCHED FOR THAT GIRL...
...AND TO THINK THAT SHE WAS HIDDEN HERE THE WHOLE TIME.
LORD BORIN...
...YOU ARE A TRAITOR TO THE CROWN...

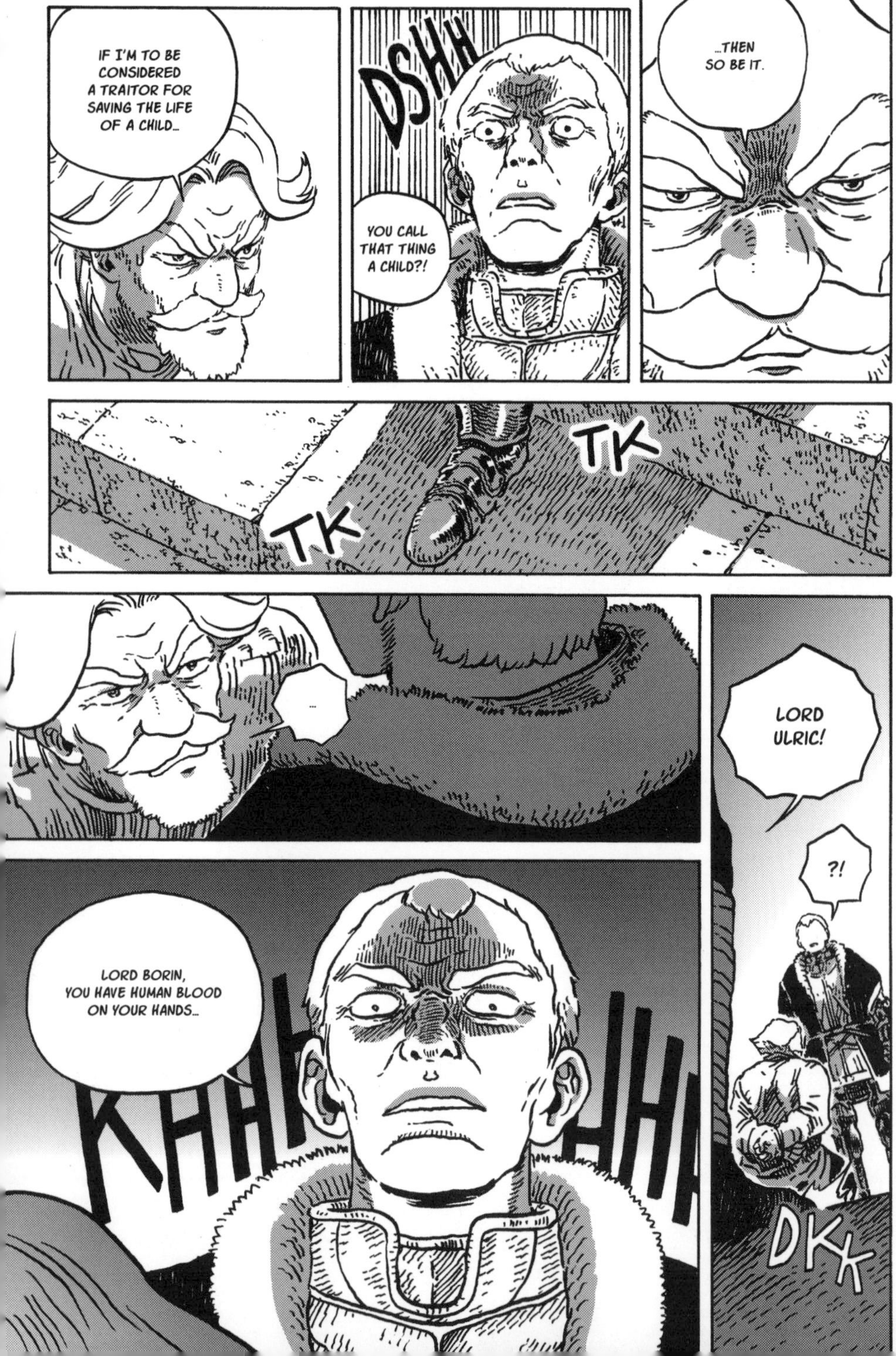
IF I'M TO BE CONSIDERED A TRAITOR FOR SAVING THE LIFE OF A CHILD...
DSHH
YOU CALL THAT THING A CHILD?!
...THEN SO BE IT.
TK
TK
...
LORD ULRIC!
?!
LORD BORIN, YOU HAVE HUMAN BLOOD ON YOUR HANDS...
KHHHHHHA
DKK

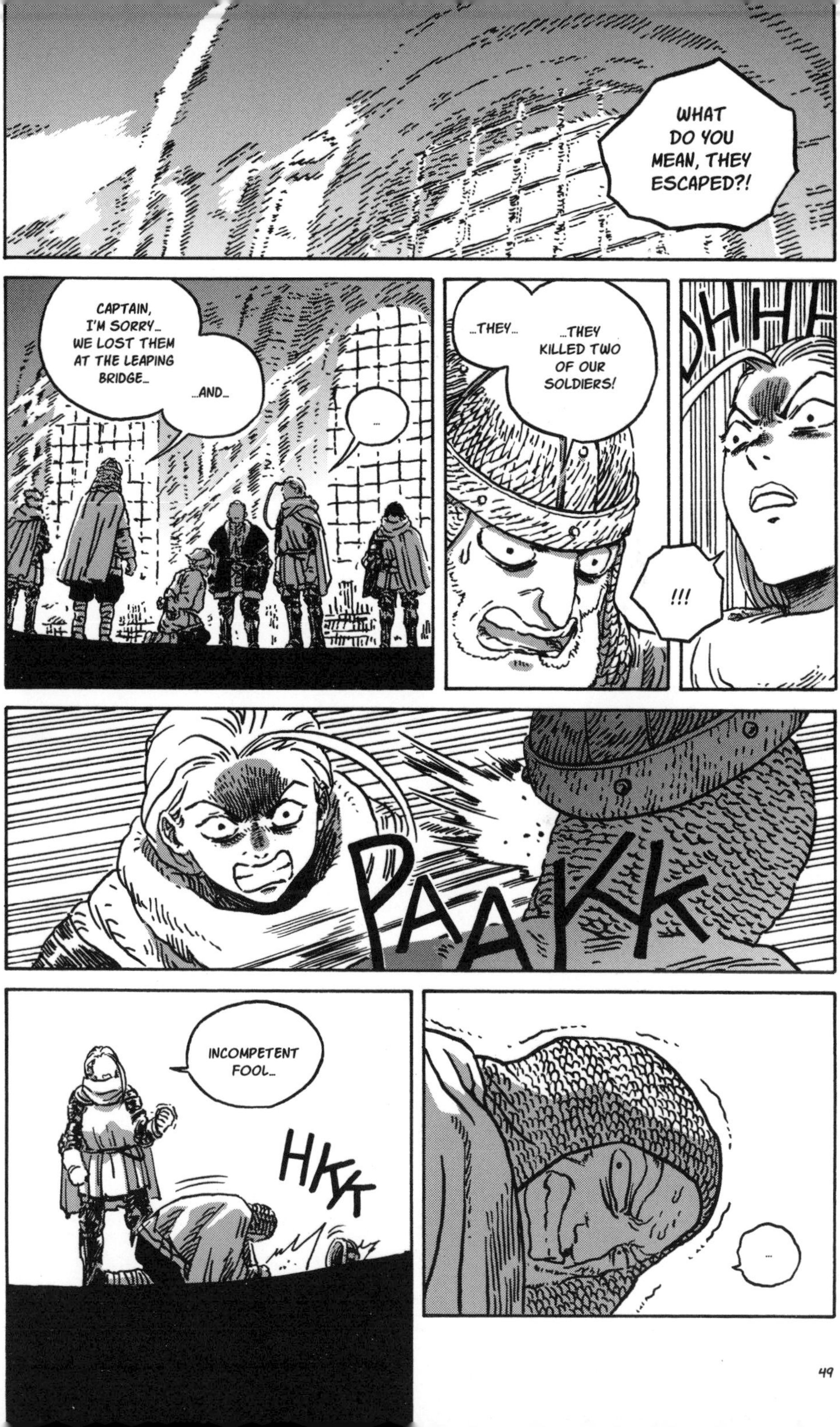
WHAT DO YOU MEAN, THEY ESCAPED?!
CAPTAIN, I'M SORRY... WE LOST THEM AT THE LEAPING BRIDGE...
...AND...
...
...THEY...
...THEY KILLED TWO OF OUR SOLDIERS!
!!!
PAAKK
INCOMPETENT FOOL...
HKK
...

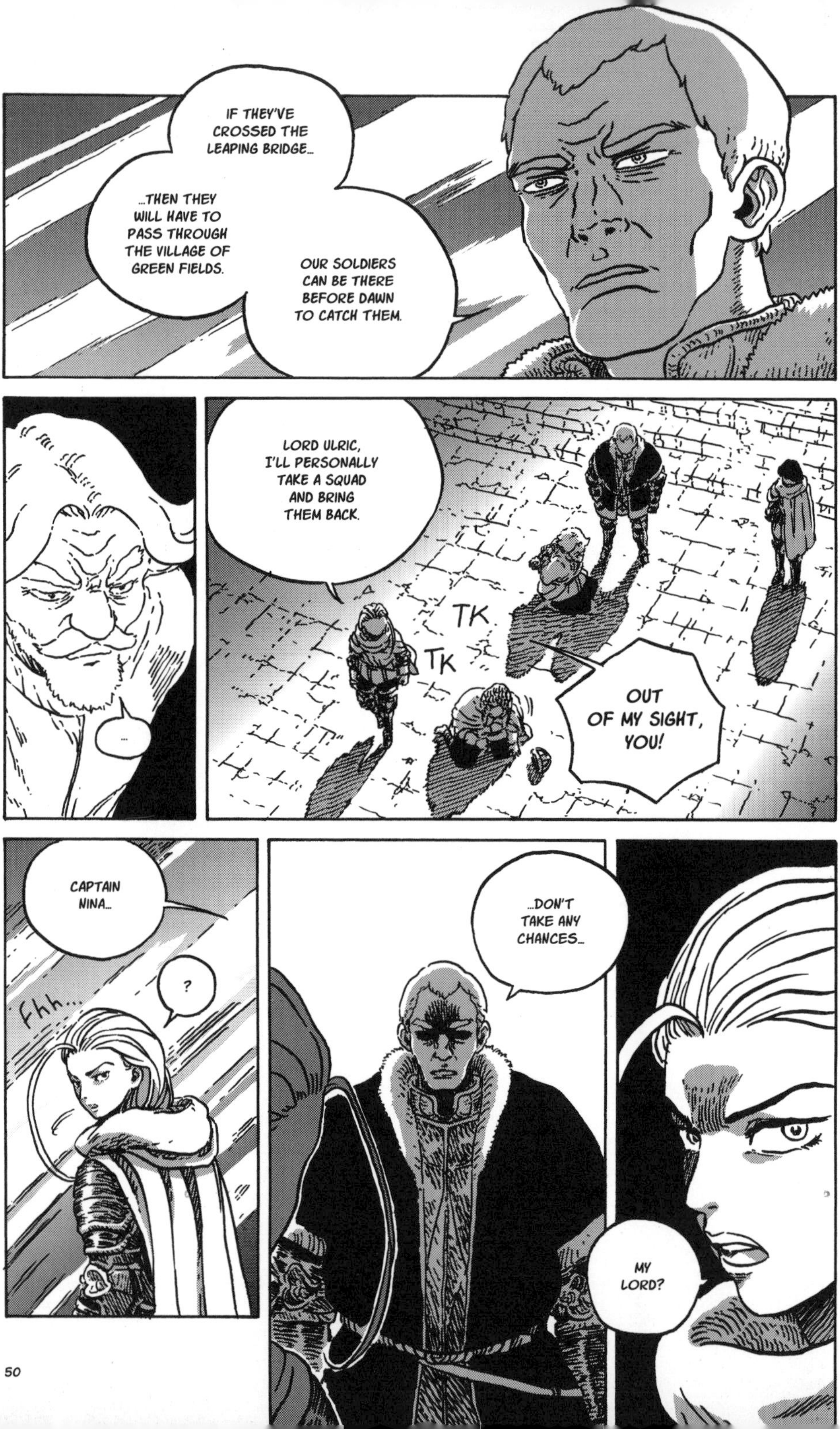
IF THEY'VE CROSSED THE LEAPING BRIDGE...
...THEN THEY WILL HAVE TO PASS THROUGH THE VILLAGE OF GREEN FIELDS.
OUR SOLDIERS CAN BE THERE BEFORE DAWN TO CATCH THEM.
...
LORD ULRIC, I'LL PERSONALLY TAKE A SQUAD AND BRING THEM BACK.
TK
TK
OUT OF MY SIGHT, YOU!
CAPTAIN NINA...
?
Fhh...
...DON'T TAKE ANY CHANCES...
MY LORD?

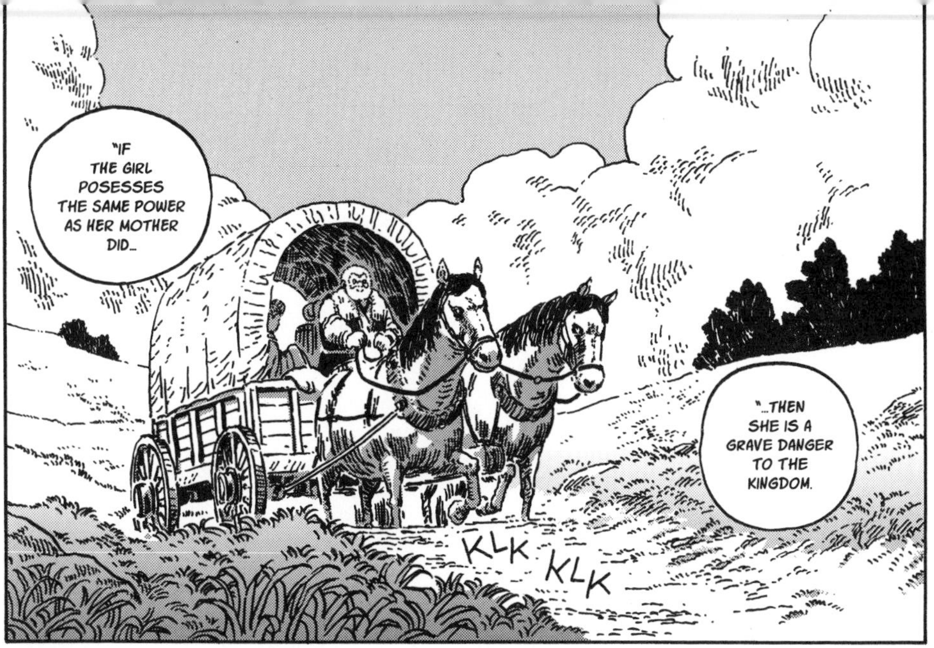
"IF THE GIRL POSESSES THE SAME POWER AS HER MOTHER DID...
"...THEN SHE IS A GRAVE DANGER TO THE KINGDOM.
KLK KLK

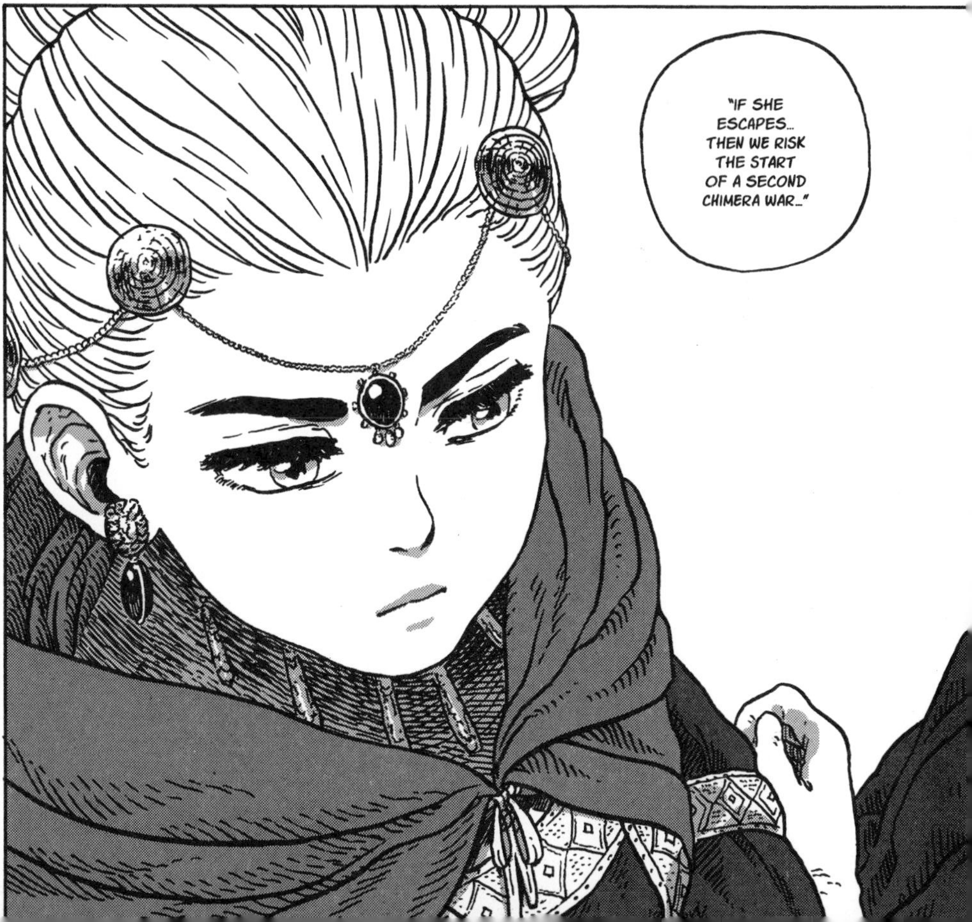
"IF SHE ESCAPES... THEN WE RISK THE START OF A SECOND CHIMERA WAR..."

Chapter 2
A Better Deal

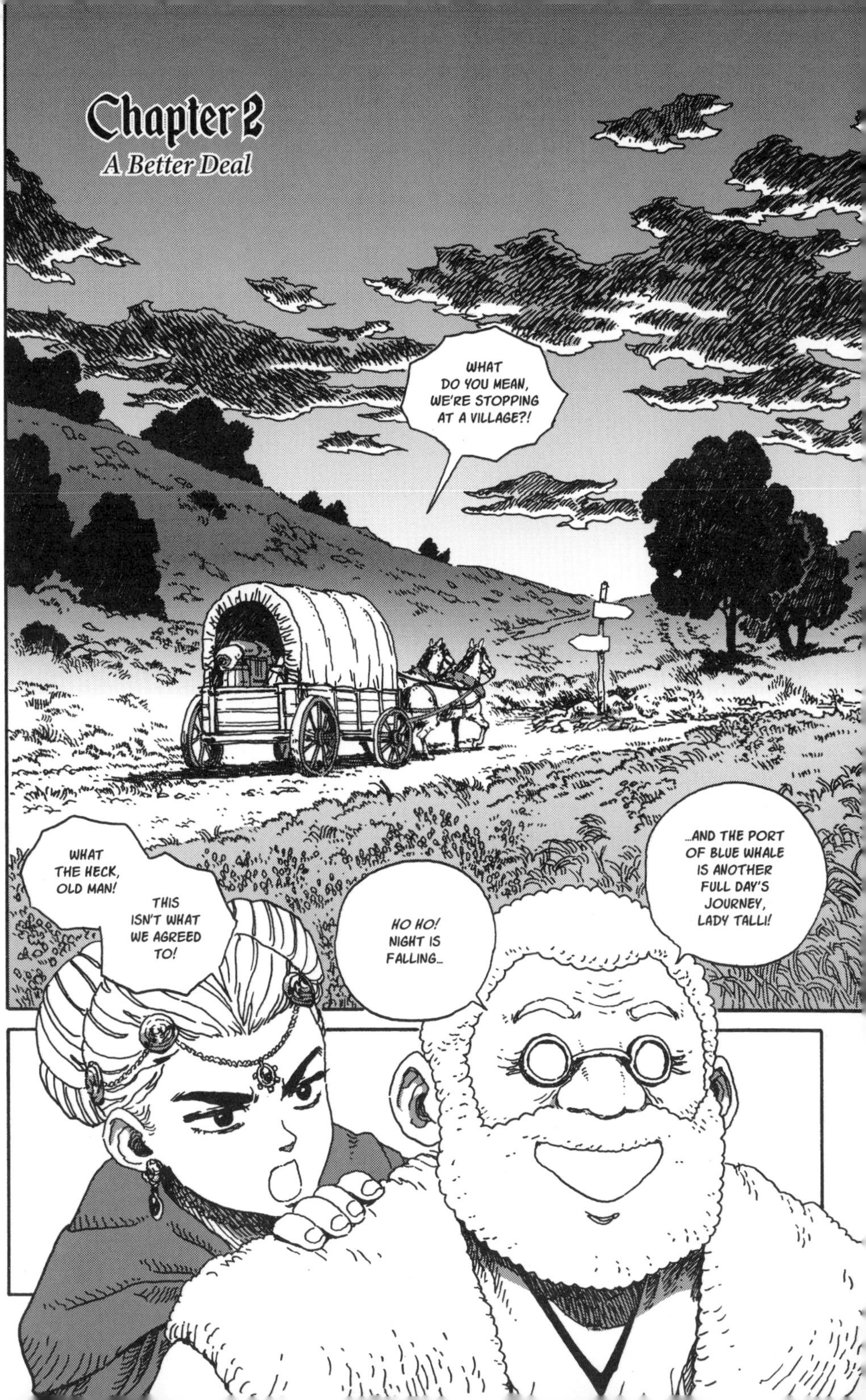
WHAT DO YOU MEAN, WE'RE STOPPING AT A VILLAGE?!
...AND THE PORT OF BLUE WHALE IS ANOTHER FULL DAY'S JOURNEY, LADY TALLI!
HO HO! NIGHT IS FALLING...
WHAT THE HECK, OLD MAN!
THIS ISN'T WHAT WE AGREED TO!

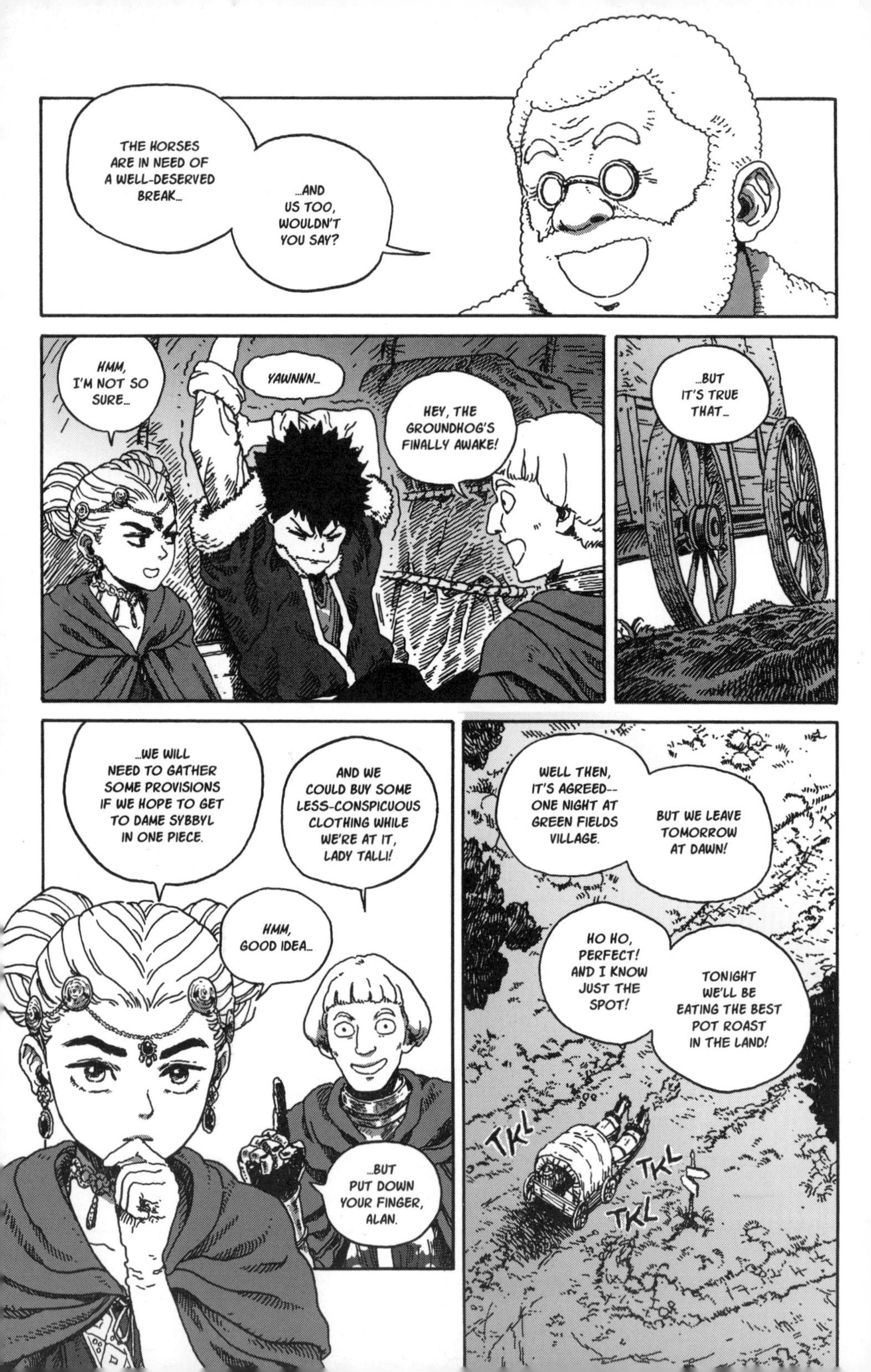
THE HORSES ARE IN NEED OF A WELL-DESERVED BREAK...
...AND US TOO, WOULDN'T YOU SAY?
HMM, I'M NOT SO SURE...
YAWNNN...
HEY, THE GROUNDHOG'S FINALLY AWAKE!
...BUT IT'S TRUE THAT...
...WE WILL NEED TO GATHER SOME PROVISIONS IF WE HOPE TO GET TO DAME SYBBYL IN ONE PIECE.
AND WE COULD BUY SOME LESS-CONSPICUOUS CLOTHING WHILE WE'RE AT IT, LADY TALLI!
HMM, GOOD IDEA...
...BUT PUT DOWN YOUR FINGER, ALAN.
WELL THEN, IT'S AGREED-- ONE NIGHT AT GREEN FIELDS VILLAGE.
BUT WE LEAVE TOMORROW AT DAWN!
HO HO, PERFECT! AND I KNOW JUST THE SPOT!
TONIGHT WE'LL BE EATING THE BEST POT ROAST IN THE LAND!
TKL
TKL
TKL

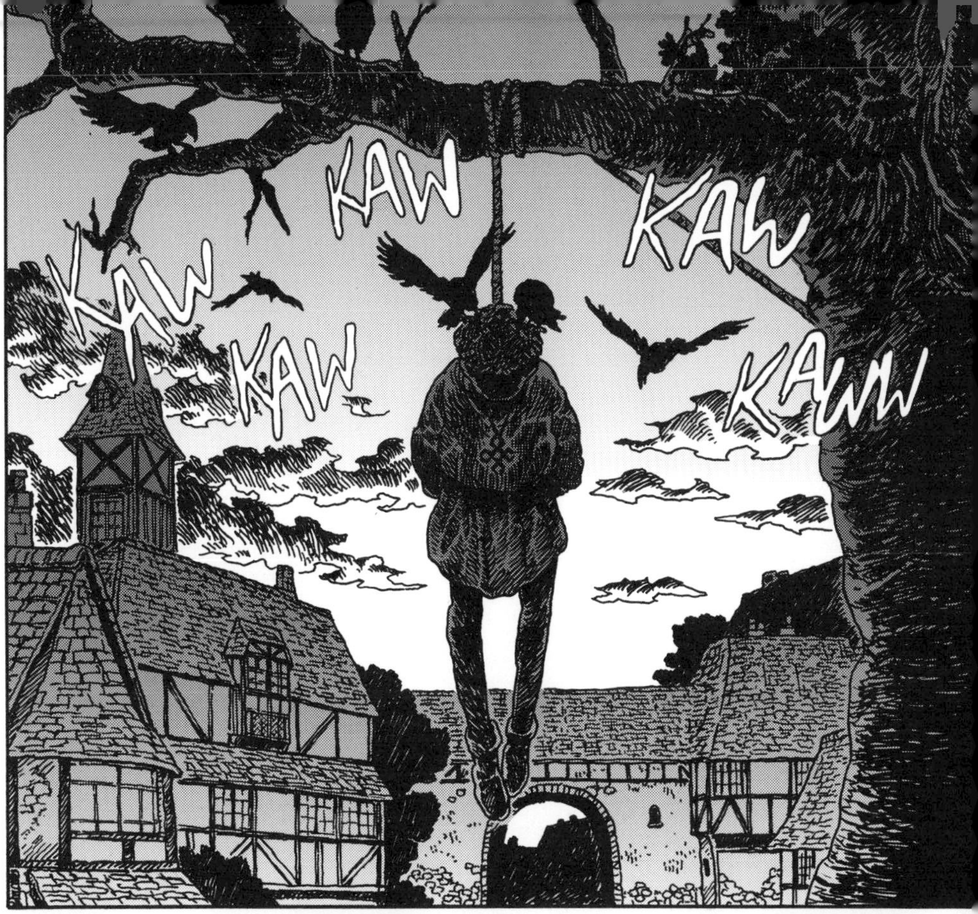
KAW
KAW
KAW
KAW
KAWW

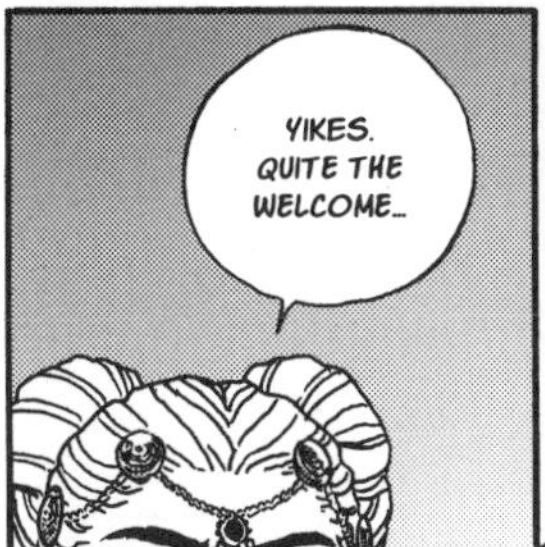
YIKES. QUITE THE WELCOME...

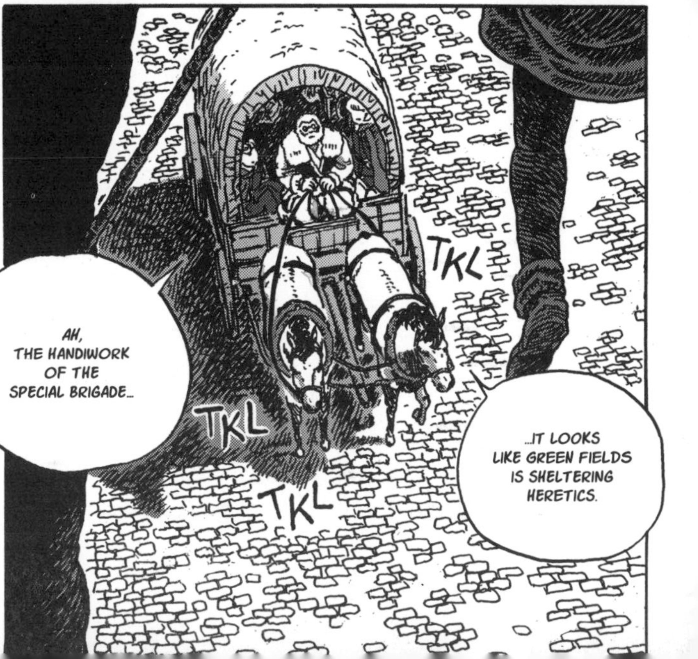
TKL
AH, THE HANDIWORK OF THE SPECIAL BRIGADE...
TKL
TKL
...IT LOOKS LIKE GREEN FIELDS IS SHELTERING HERETICS.

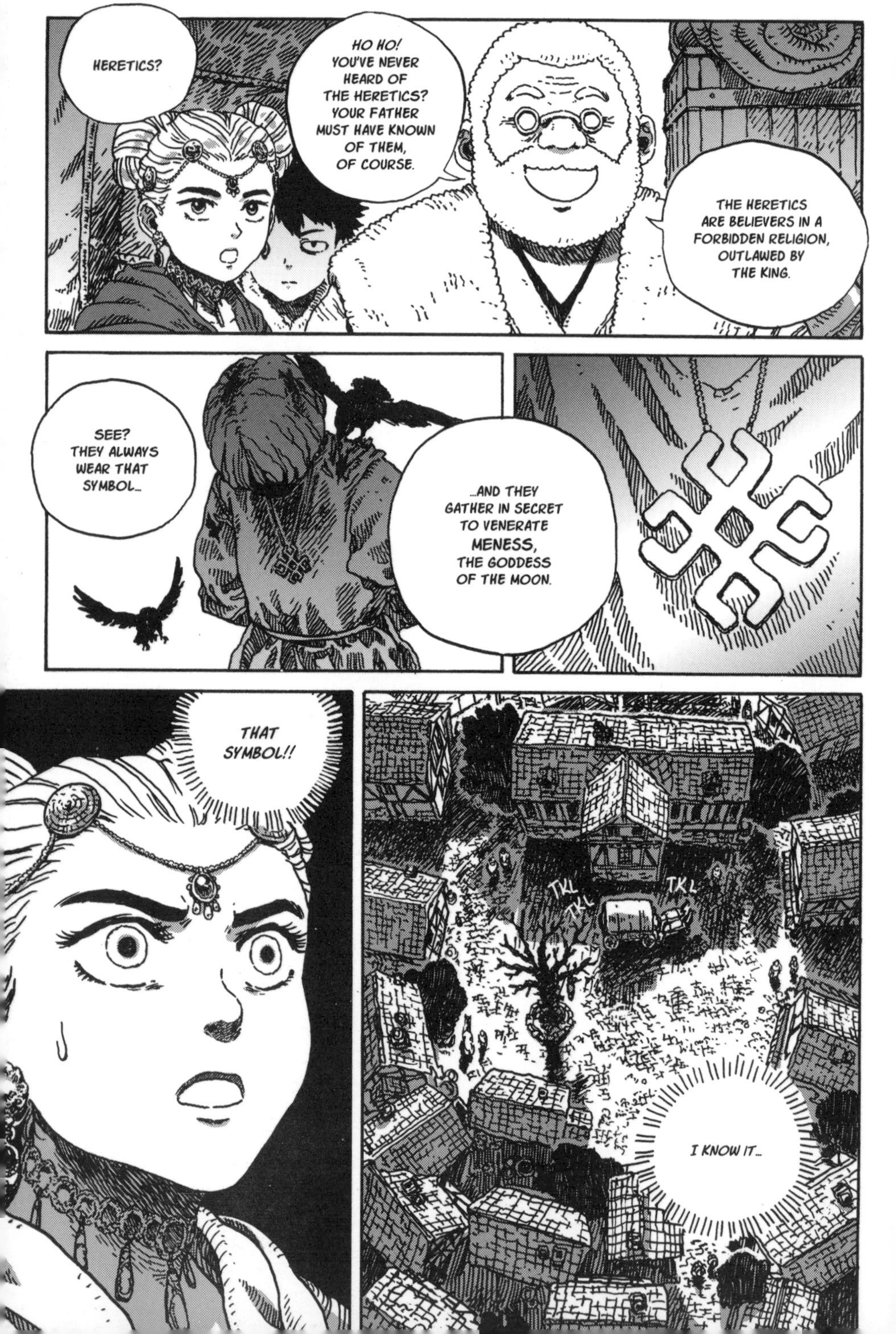
HERETICS?
HO HO! YOU'VE NEVER HEARD OF THE HERETICS? YOUR FATHER MUST HAVE KNOWN OF THEM, OF COURSE.
THE HERETICS ARE BELIEVERS IN A FORBIDDEN RELIGION, OUTLAWED BY THE KING.
SEE? THEY ALWAYS WEAR THAT SYMBOL...
...AND THEY GATHER IN SECRET TO VENERATE MENESS, THE GODDESS OF THE MOON.
THAT SYMBOL!!
TKL TKL TKL
I KNOW IT...

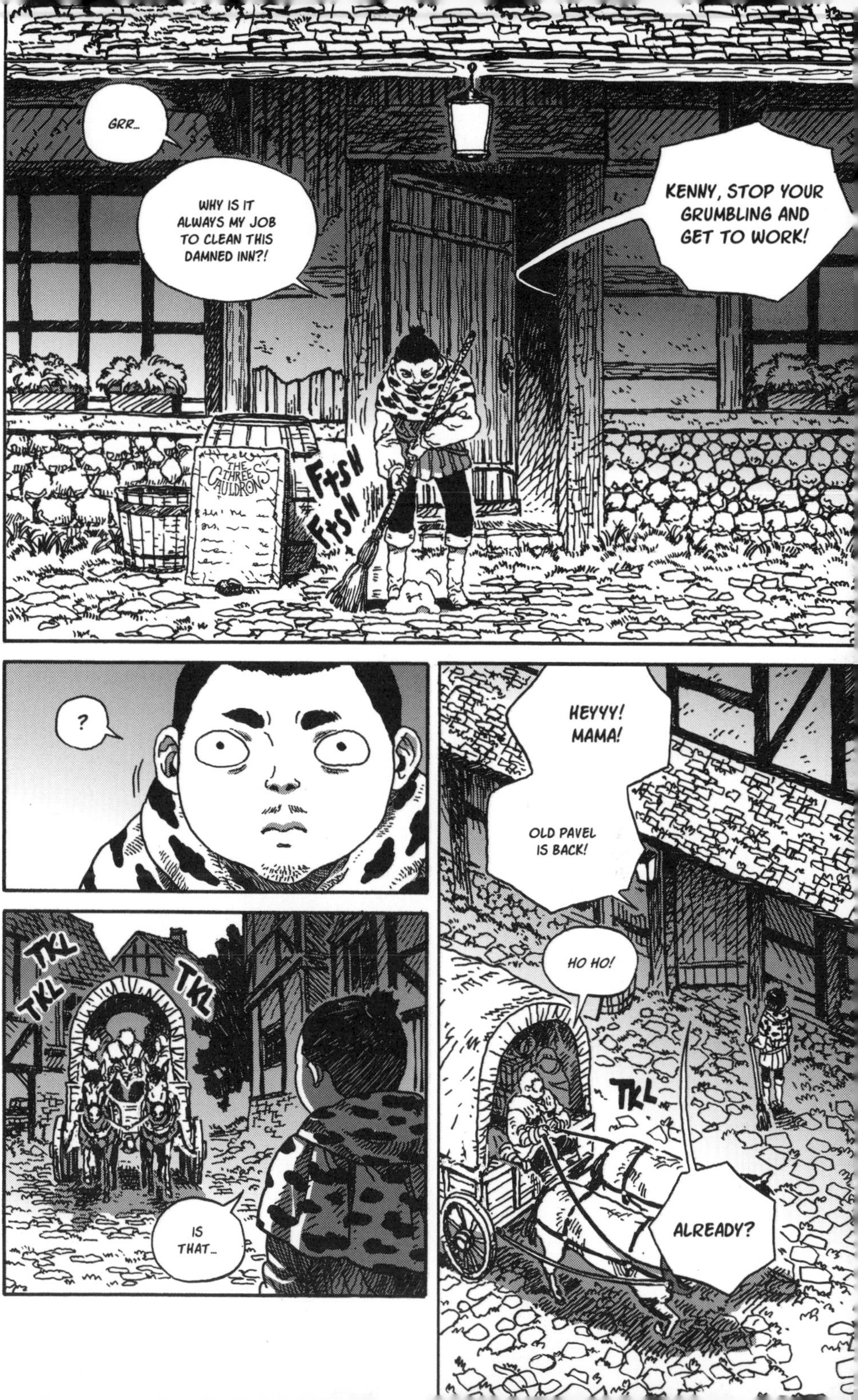
GRR...
WHY IS IT ALWAYS MY JOB TO CLEAN THIS DAMNED INN?!
KENNY, STOP YOUR GRUMBLING AND GET TO WORK!
THE THREE CAULDRONS
FTSH
FTSH
?
TKL
TKL
TKL
IS THAT...
HEYYY! MAMA!
OLD PAVEL IS BACK!
HO HO!
TKL
ALREADY?

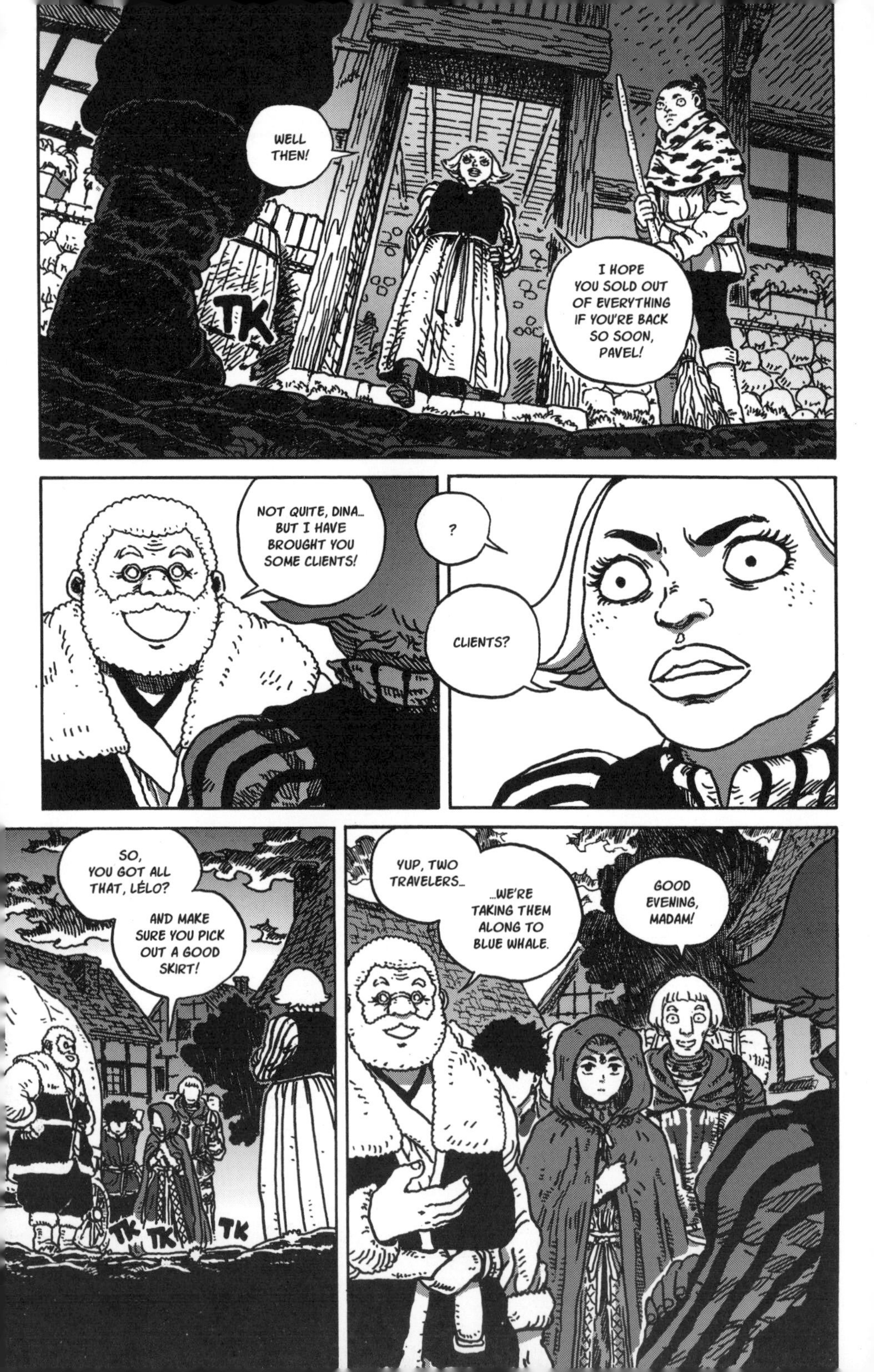
TK
WELL THEN!
I HOPE YOU SOLD OUT OF EVERYTHING IF YOU'RE BACK SO SOON, PAVEL!
NOT QUITE, DINA... BUT I HAVE BROUGHT YOU SOME CLIENTS!
?
CLIENTS?
SO, YOU GOT ALL THAT, LÉLO?
AND MAKE SURE YOU PICK OUT A GOOD SKIRT!
TK TK TK
YUP, TWO TRAVELERS...
...WE'RE TAKING THEM ALONG TO BLUE WHALE.
GOOD EVENING, MADAM!

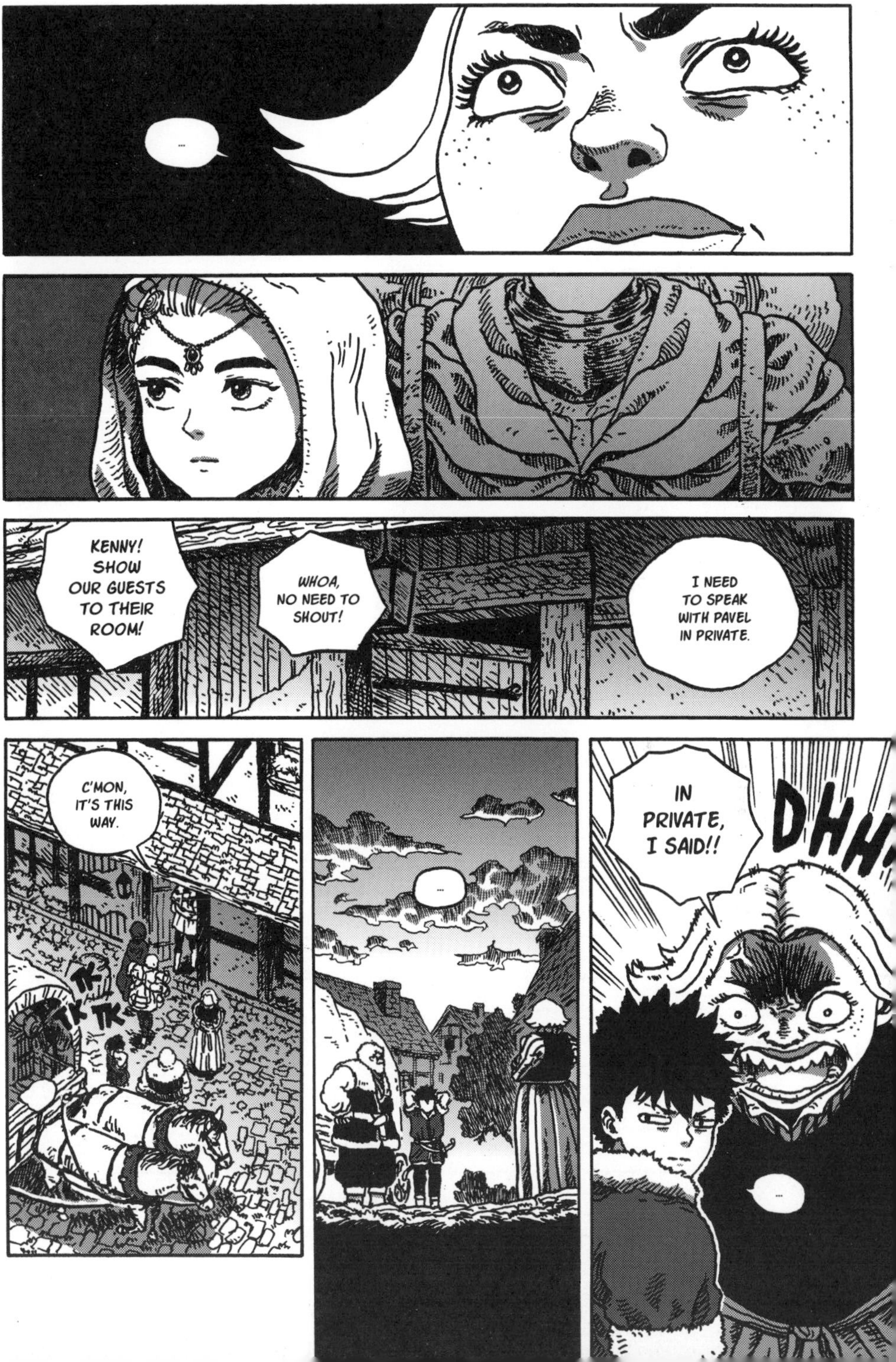
...
KENNY! SHOW OUR GUESTS TO THEIR ROOM!
WHOA, NO NEED TO SHOUT!
I NEED TO SPEAK WITH PAVEL IN PRIVATE.
C'MON, IT'S THIS WAY.
TK TK TK
...
IN PRIVATE, I SAID!!
...

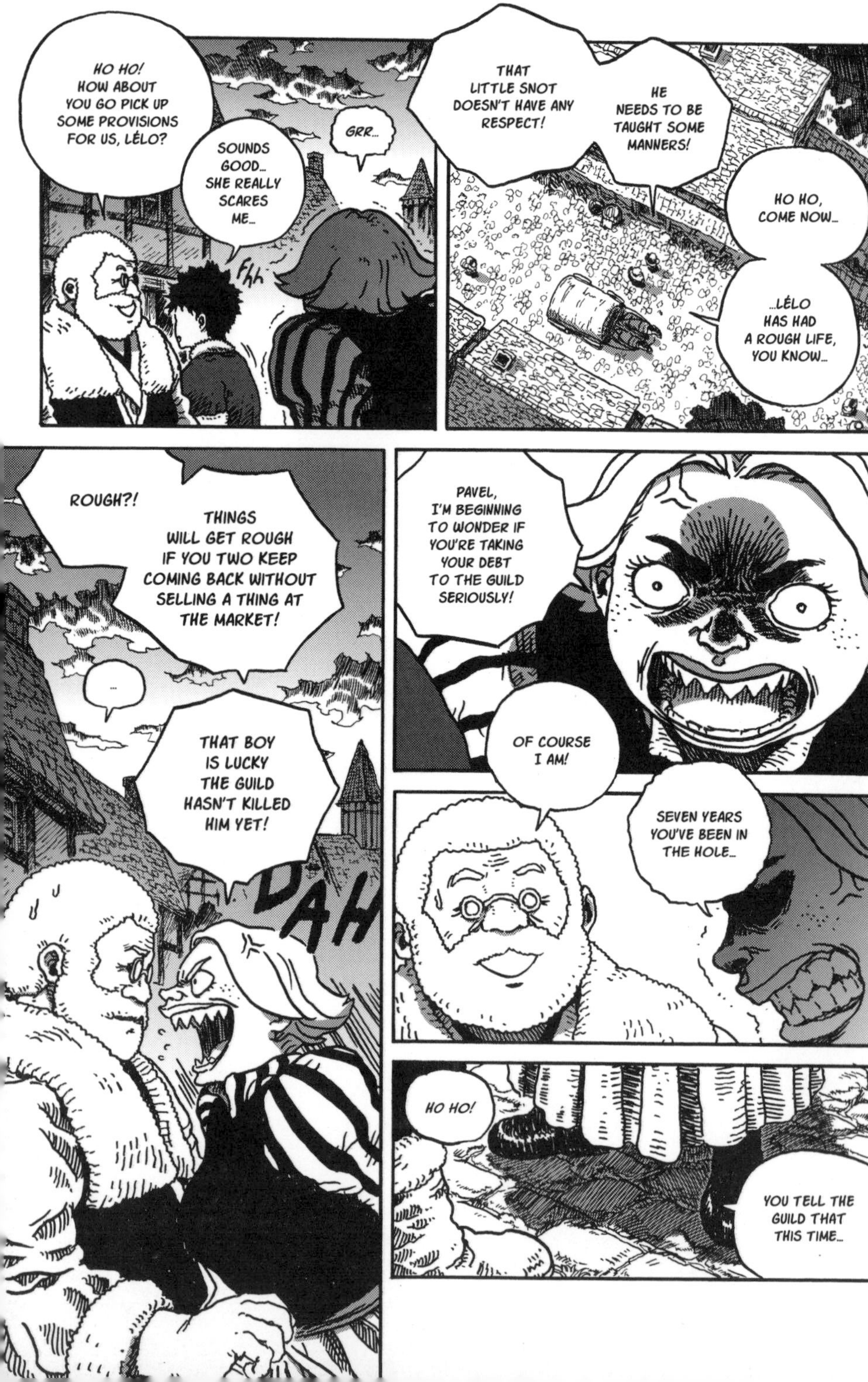
HO HO! HOW ABOUT YOU GO PICK UP SOME PROVISIONS FOR US, LÉLO?
SOUNDS GOOD... SHE REALLY SCARES ME...
GRR...
Fhh
THAT LITTLE SNOT DOESN'T HAVE ANY RESPECT!
HE NEEDS TO BE TAUGHT SOME MANNERS!
HO HO, COME NOW...
...LÉLO HAS HAD A ROUGH LIFE, YOU KNOW...
ROUGH?!
THINGS WILL GET ROUGH IF YOU TWO KEEP COMING BACK WITHOUT SELLING A THING AT THE MARKET!
...
THAT BOY IS LUCKY THE GUILD HASN'T KILLED HIM YET!
DAH
PAVEL, I'M BEGINNING TO WONDER IF YOU'RE TAKING YOUR DEBT TO THE GUILD SERIOUSLY!
OF COURSE I AM!
SEVEN YEARS YOU'VE BEEN IN THE HOLE...
HO HO!
YOU TELL THE GUILD THAT THIS TIME...

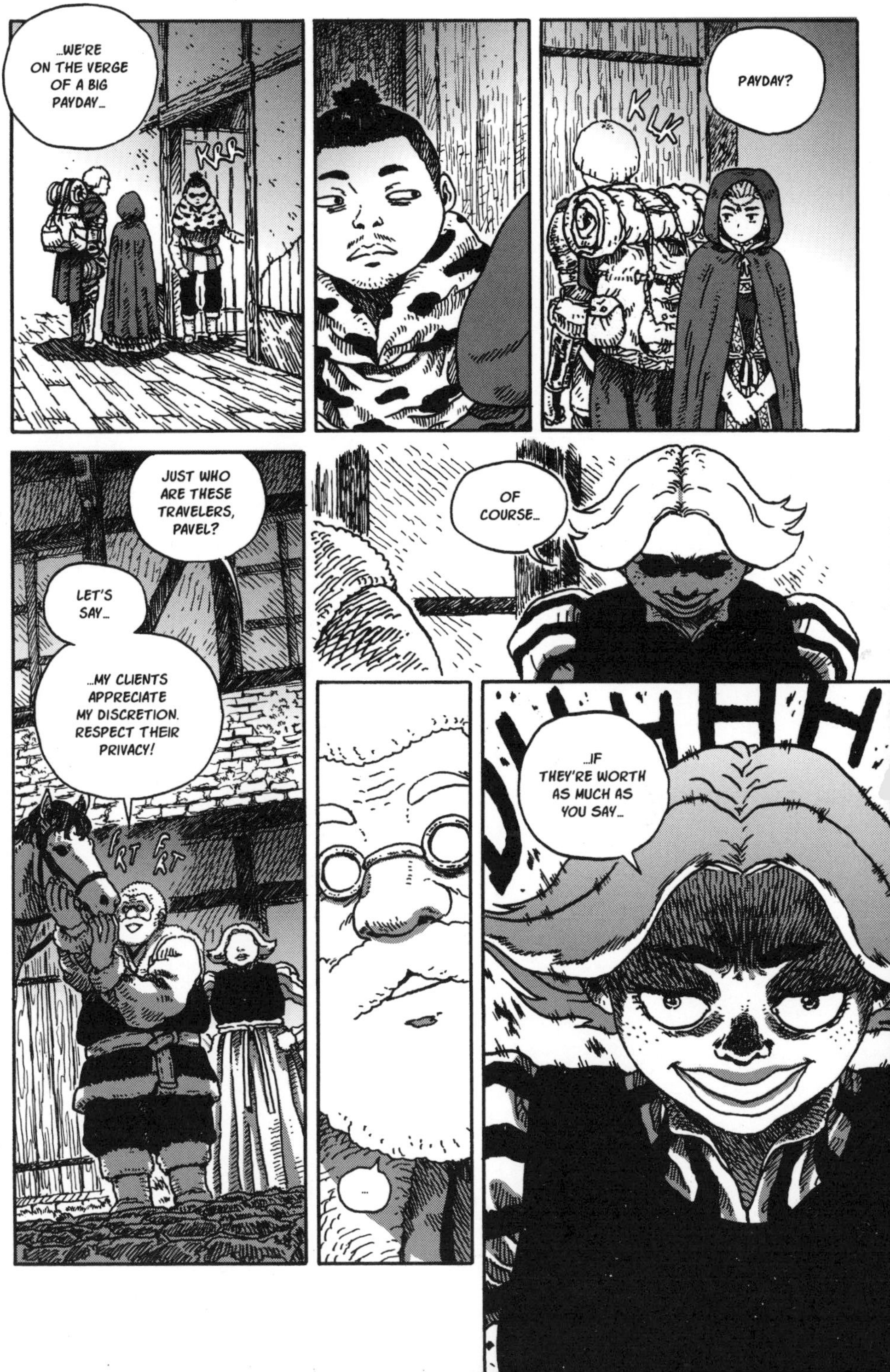
...WE'RE ON THE VERGE OF A BIG PAYDAY...
KRR
KLK
PAYDAY?
JUST WHO ARE THESE TRAVELERS, PAVEL?
LET'S SAY...
...MY CLIENTS APPRECIATE MY DISCRETION. RESPECT THEIR PRIVACY!
FRT
FRT
OF COURSE...
...
...IF THEY'RE WORTH AS MUCH AS YOU SAY...

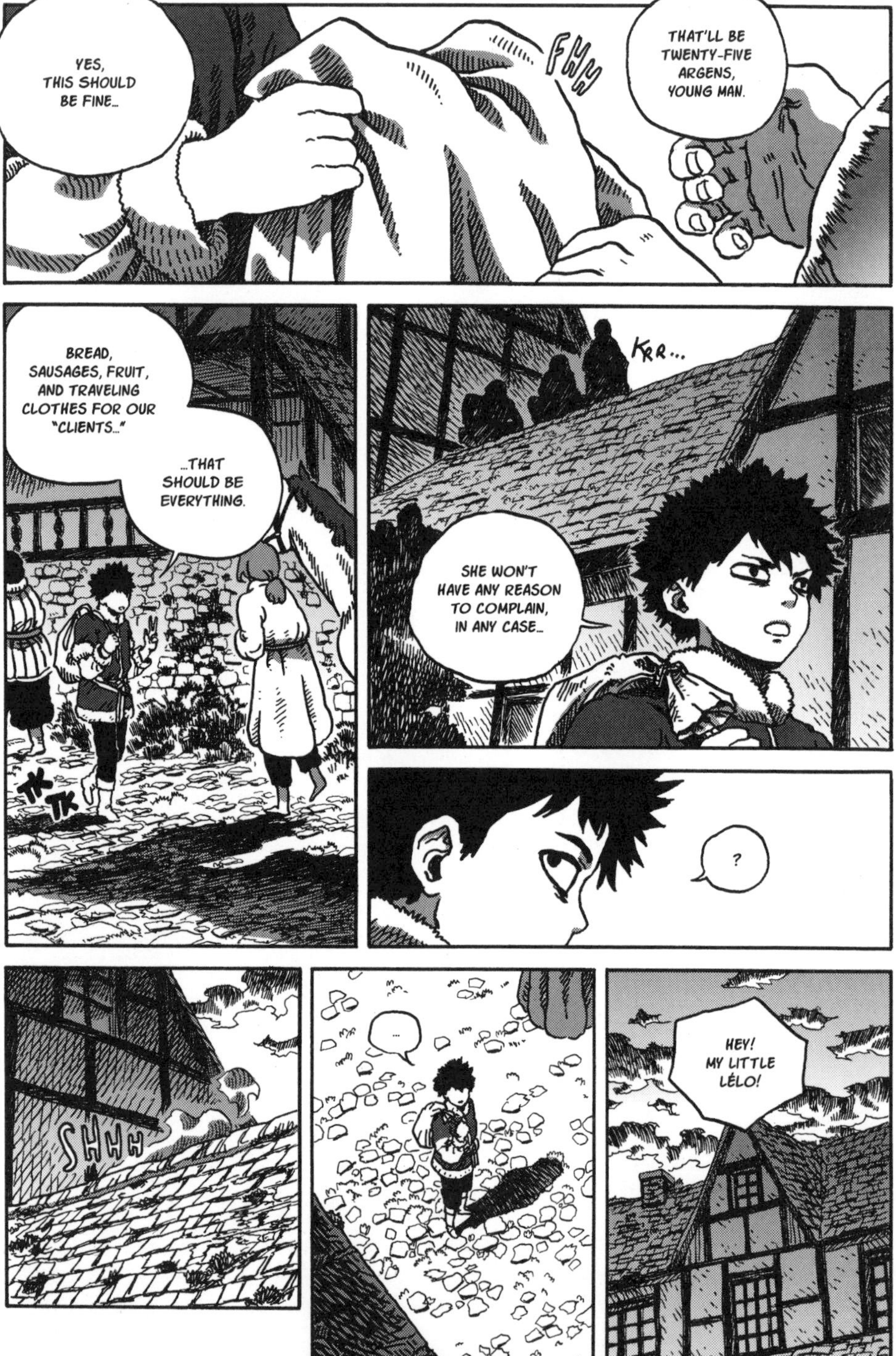
YES, THIS SHOULD BE FINE...
FHH
THAT'LL BE TWENTY-FIVE ARGENS, YOUNG MAN.
BREAD, SAUSAGES, FRUIT, AND TRAVELING CLOTHES FOR OUR "CLIENTS..."
...THAT SHOULD BE EVERYTHING.
TK TK
KRR...
SHE WON'T HAVE ANY REASON TO COMPLAIN, IN ANY CASE...
?
SHHH
...
HEY! MY LITTLE LÉLO!

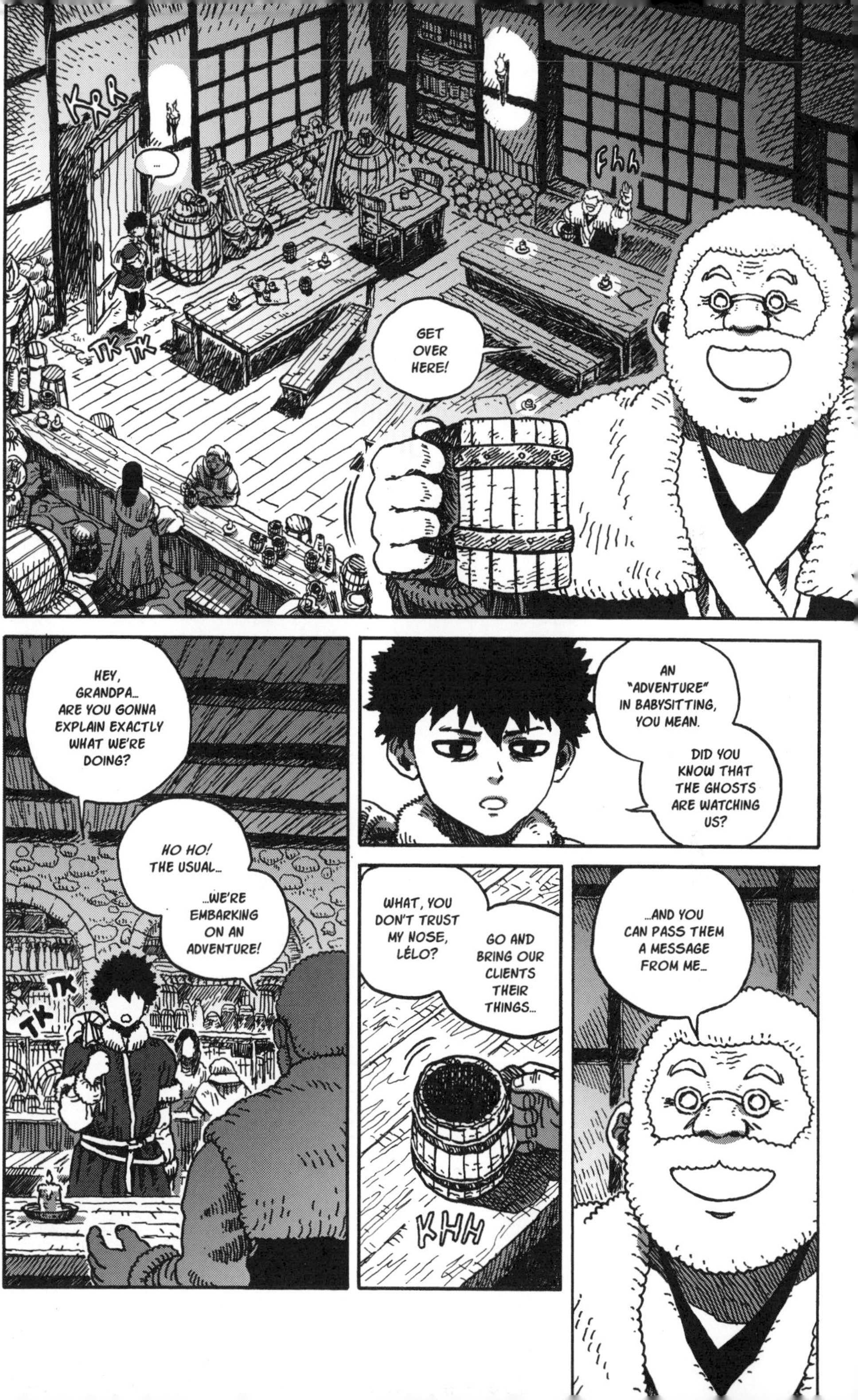
KRR
...
Fhh
TK TK
GET OVER HERE!
HEY, GRANDPA... ARE YOU GONNA EXPLAIN EXACTLY WHAT WE'RE DOING?
HO HO! THE USUAL...
...WE'RE EMBARKING ON AN ADVENTURE!
TK TK
AN "ADVENTURE" IN BABYSITTING, YOU MEAN.
DID YOU KNOW THAT THE GHOSTS ARE WATCHING US?
WHAT, YOU DON'T TRUST MY NOSE, LÉLO?
GO AND BRING OUR CLIENTS THEIR THINGS...
KHH
...AND YOU CAN PASS THEM A MESSAGE FROM ME...

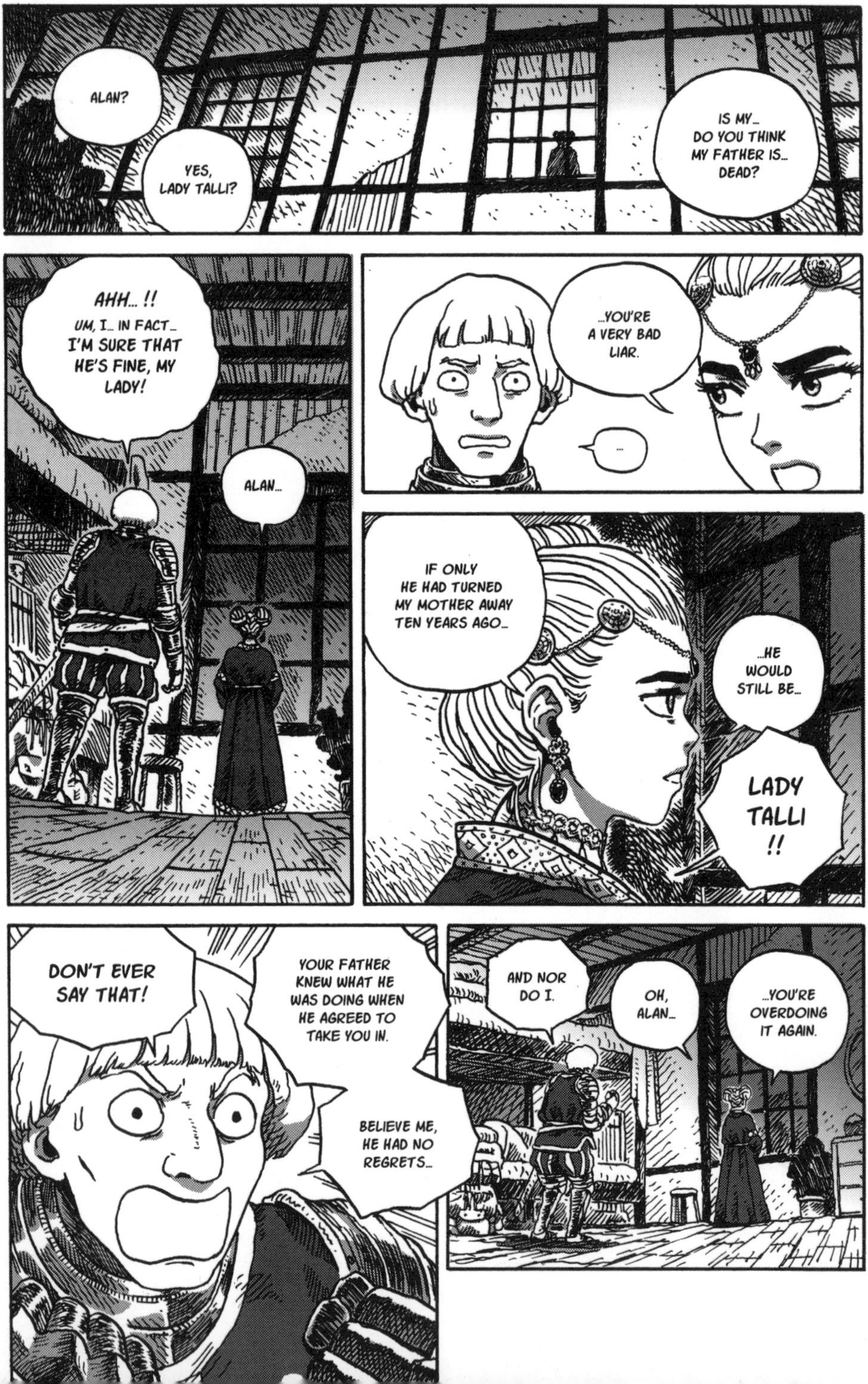
ALAN?
YES, LADY TALLI?
IS MY... DO YOU THINK MY FATHER IS... DEAD?
AHH... !! UM, I... IN FACT... I'M SURE THAT HE'S FINE, MY LADY!
ALAN...
...YOU'RE A VERY BAD LIAR.
...
IF ONLY HE HAD TURNED MY MOTHER AWAY TEN YEARS AGO...
...HE WOULD STILL BE...
LADY TALLI !!
DON'T EVER SAY THAT!
YOUR FATHER KNEW WHAT HE WAS DOING WHEN HE AGREED TO TAKE YOU IN.
BELIEVE ME, HE HAD NO REGRETS...
AND NOR DO I.
OH, ALAN...
...YOU'RE OVERDOING IT AGAIN.

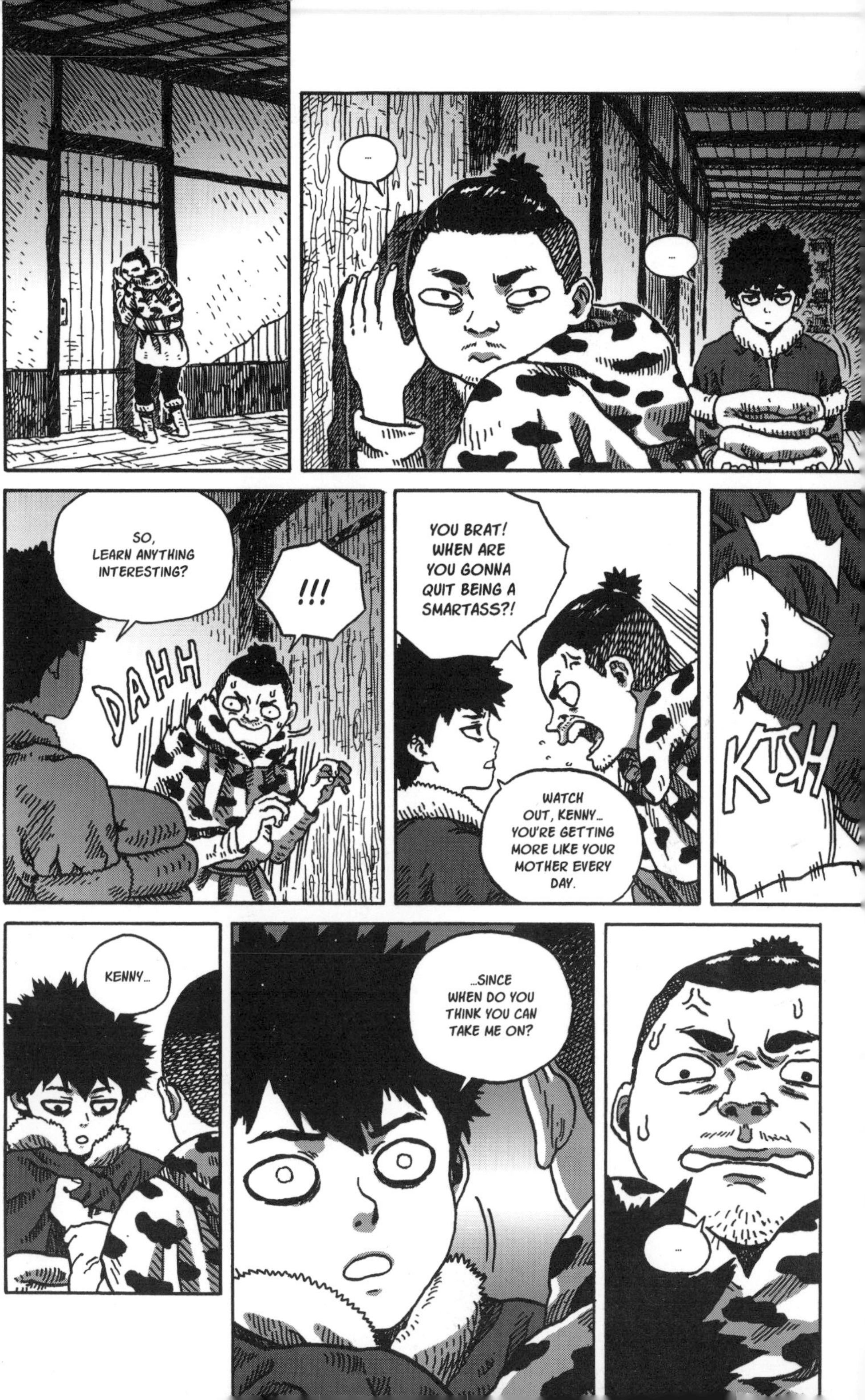
...
...
SO, LEARN ANYTHING INTERESTING?
DAHH
!!!
YOU BRAT! WHEN ARE YOU GONNA QUIT BEING A SMARTASS?!
WATCH OUT, KENNY... YOU'RE GETTING MORE LIKE YOUR MOTHER EVERY DAY.
KTSH
KENNY...
...SINCE WHEN DO YOU THINK YOU CAN TAKE ME ON?
...

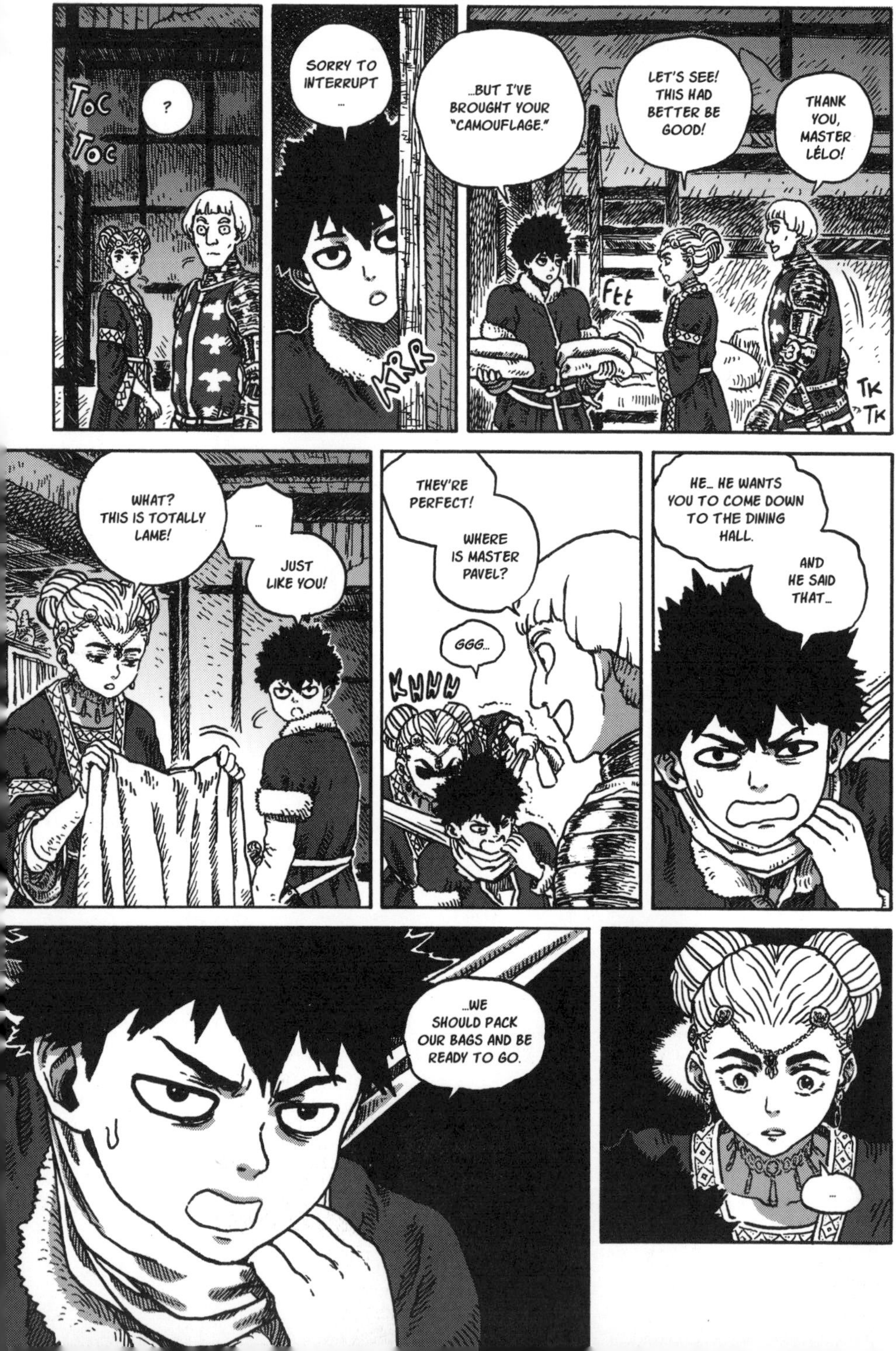
TOC TOC
?
SORRY TO INTERRUPT ...
KRR
...BUT I'VE BROUGHT YOUR "CAMOUFLAGE."
LET'S SEE! THIS HAD BETTER BE GOOD!
THANK YOU, MASTER LÉLO!
FTT
TK TK
WHAT? THIS IS TOTALLY LAME!
...
JUST LIKE YOU!
THEY'RE PERFECT!
WHERE IS MASTER PAVEL?
GGG...
KHHH
HE... HE WANTS YOU TO COME DOWN TO THE DINING HALL.
AND HE SAID THAT...
...WE SHOULD PACK OUR BAGS AND BE READY TO GO.
...

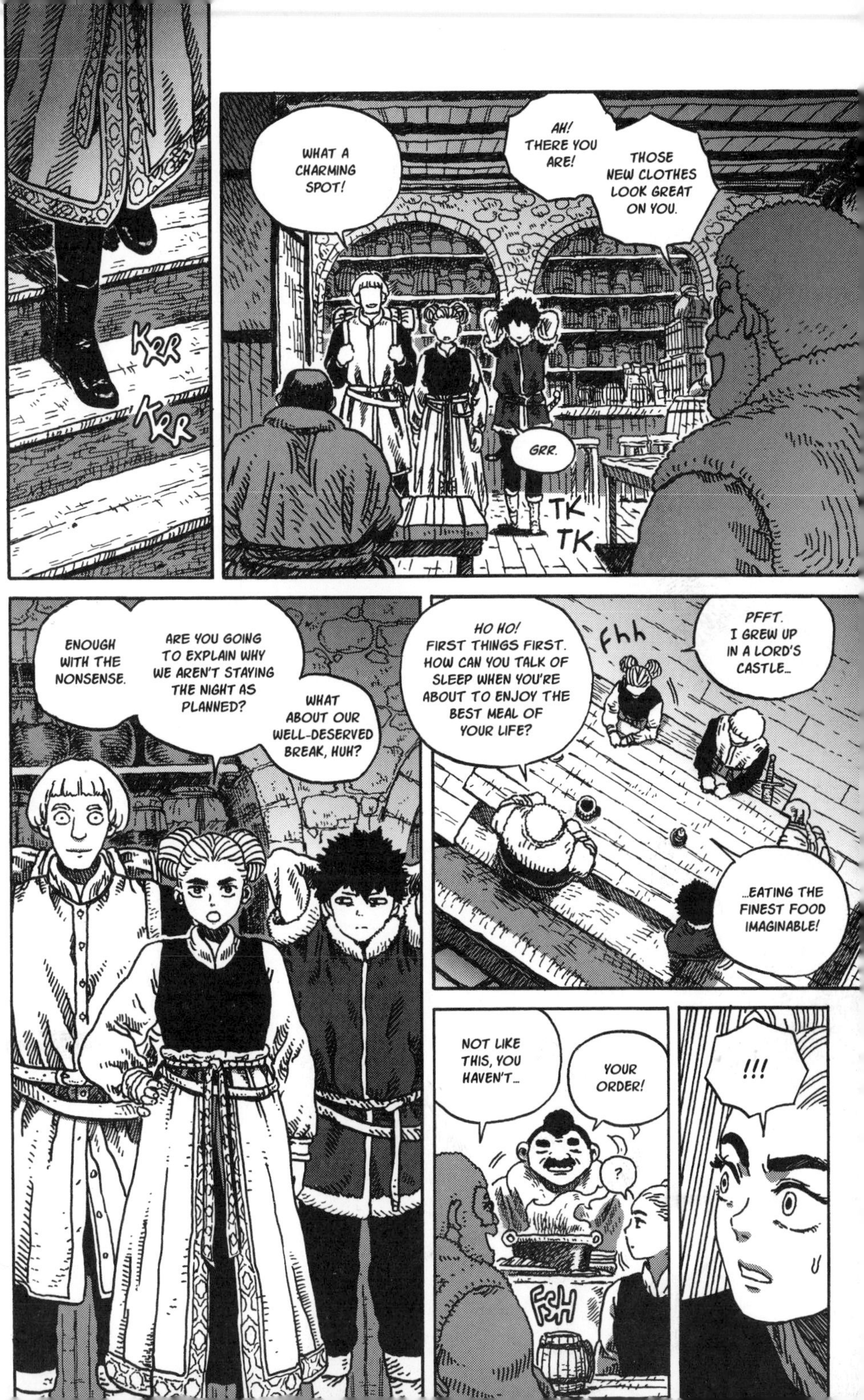
KRR
KRR
WHAT A CHARMING SPOT!
AH! THERE YOU ARE!
THOSE NEW CLOTHES LOOK GREAT ON YOU.
GRR.
TK
TK
ENOUGH WITH THE NONSENSE.
ARE YOU GOING TO EXPLAIN WHY WE AREN'T STAYING THE NIGHT AS PLANNED?
WHAT ABOUT OUR WELL-DESERVED BREAK, HUH?
HO HO! FIRST THINGS FIRST. HOW CAN YOU TALK OF SLEEP WHEN YOU'RE ABOUT TO ENJOY THE BEST MEAL OF YOUR LIFE?
fhh
PFFT. I GREW UP IN A LORD'S CASTLE...
...EATING THE FINEST FOOD IMAGINABLE!
NOT LIKE THIS, YOU HAVEN'T...
YOUR ORDER!
?
FSSH
!!!

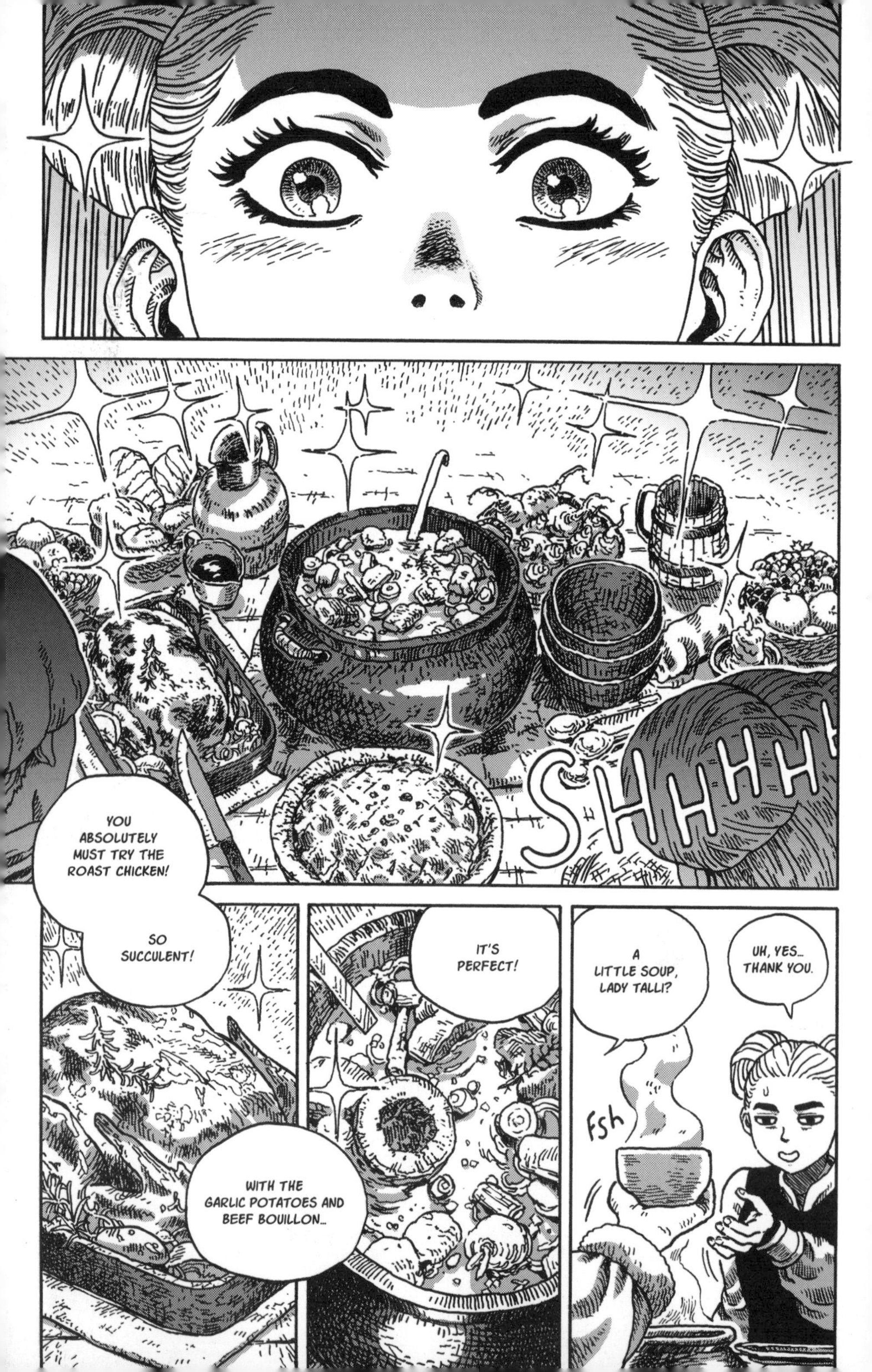
SHHHH
YOU ABSOLUTELY MUST TRY THE ROAST CHICKEN!
SO SUCCULENT!
IT'S PERFECT!
WITH THE GARLIC POTATOES AND BEEF BOUILLON...
A LITTLE SOUP, LADY TALLI?
UH, YES... THANK YOU.
Fsh

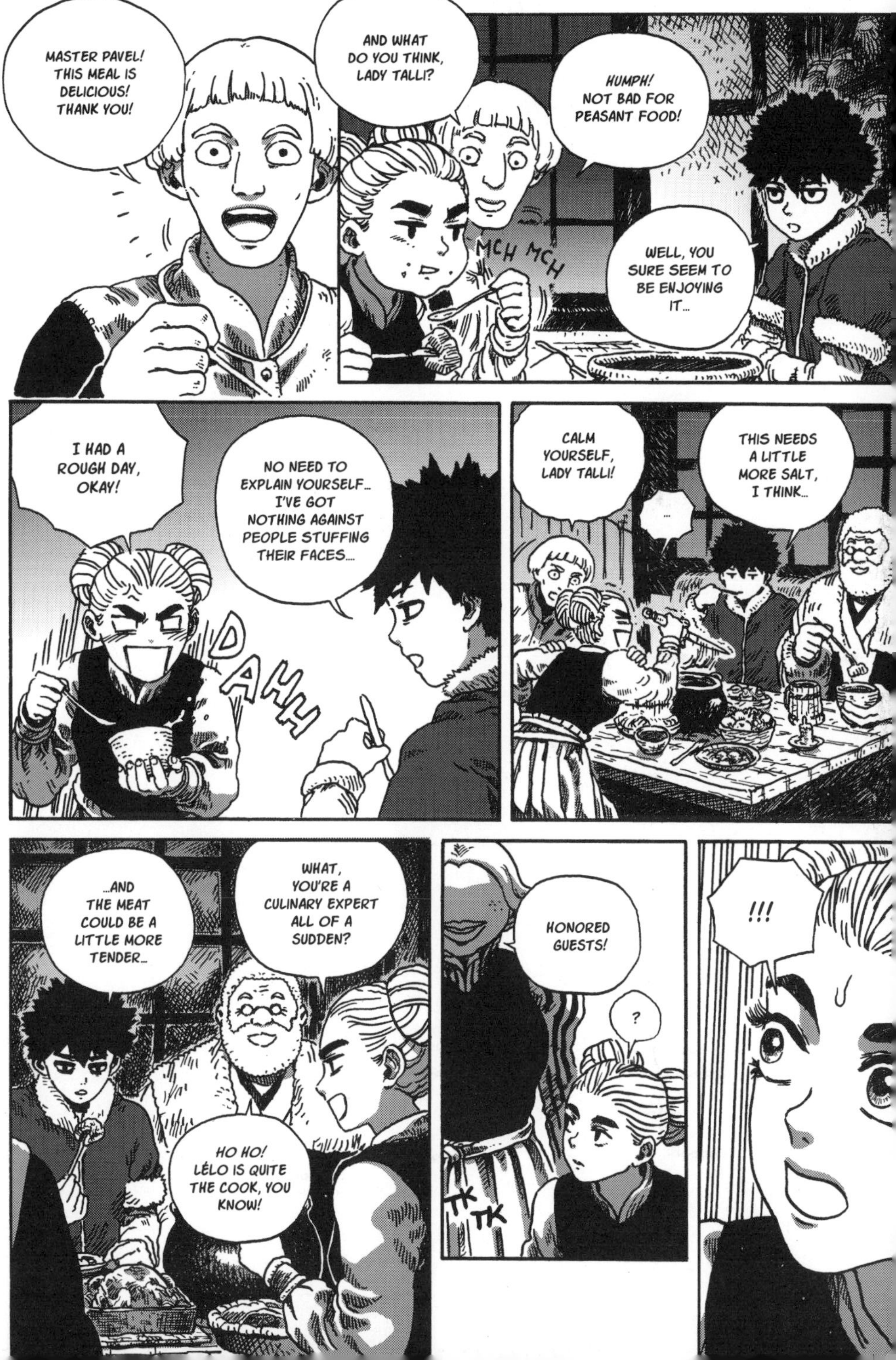
MASTER PAVEL! THIS MEAL IS DELICIOUS! THANK YOU!
AND WHAT DO YOU THINK, LADY TALLI?
HUMPH! NOT BAD FOR PEASANT FOOD!
MCH MCH
WELL, YOU SURE SEEM TO BE ENJOYING IT...
I HAD A ROUGH DAY, OKAY!
NO NEED TO EXPLAIN YOURSELF... I'VE GOT NOTHING AGAINST PEOPLE STUFFING THEIR FACES....
DAHH
CALM YOURSELF, LADY TALLI!
...
THIS NEEDS A LITTLE MORE SALT, I THINK...
...AND THE MEAT COULD BE A LITTLE MORE TENDER...
WHAT, YOU'RE A CULINARY EXPERT ALL OF A SUDDEN?
HO HO! LÉLO IS QUITE THE COOK, YOU KNOW!
HONORED GUESTS!
?
TK TK
!!!

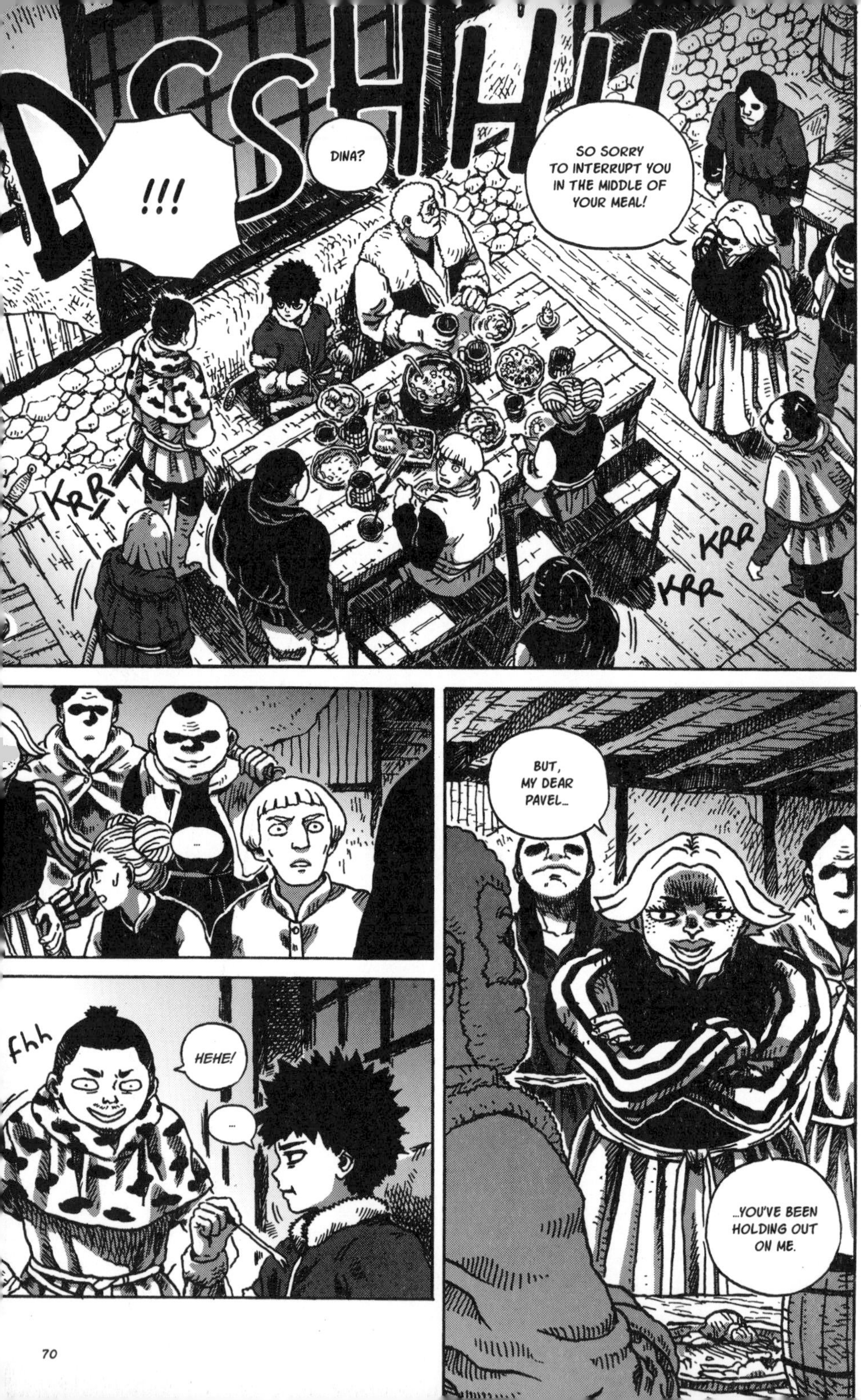
!!!
DINA?
SO SORRY TO INTERRUPT YOU IN THE MIDDLE OF YOUR MEAL!
KRR
KRR
KRR
...
fhh
HEHE!
...
BUT, MY DEAR PAVEL...
...YOU'VE BEEN HOLDING OUT ON ME.

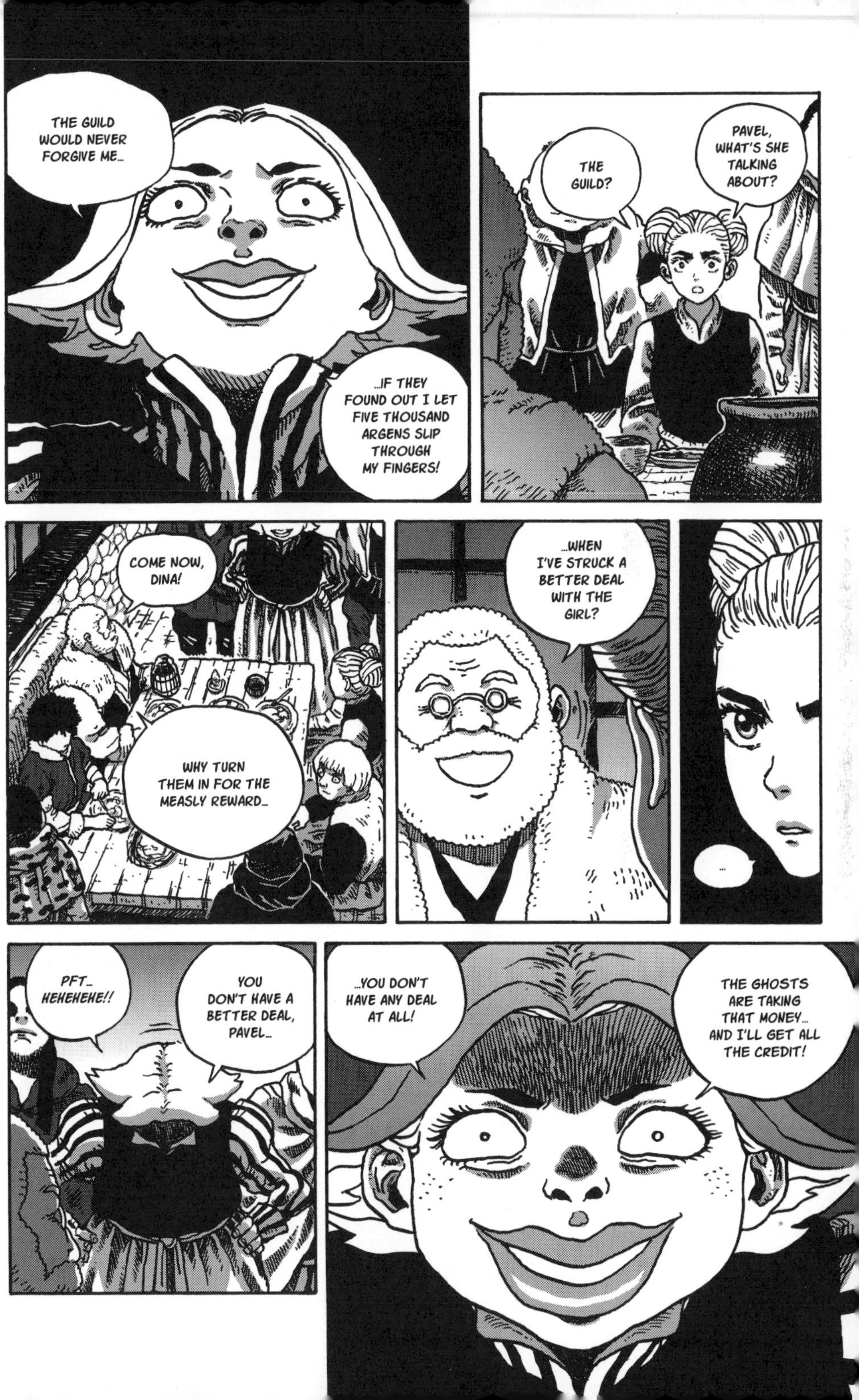
THE GUILD WOULD NEVER FORGIVE ME...
...IF THEY FOUND OUT I LET FIVE THOUSAND ARGENS SLIP THROUGH MY FINGERS!
THE GUILD?
PAVEL, WHAT'S SHE TALKING ABOUT?
COME NOW, DINA!
WHY TURN THEM IN FOR THE MEASLY REWARD...
...WHEN I'VE STRUCK A BETTER DEAL WITH THE GIRL?
...
PFT... HEHEHEHE!!
YOU DON'T HAVE A BETTER DEAL, PAVEL...
...YOU DON'T HAVE ANY DEAL AT ALL!
THE GHOSTS ARE TAKING THAT MONEY... AND I'LL GET ALL THE CREDIT!

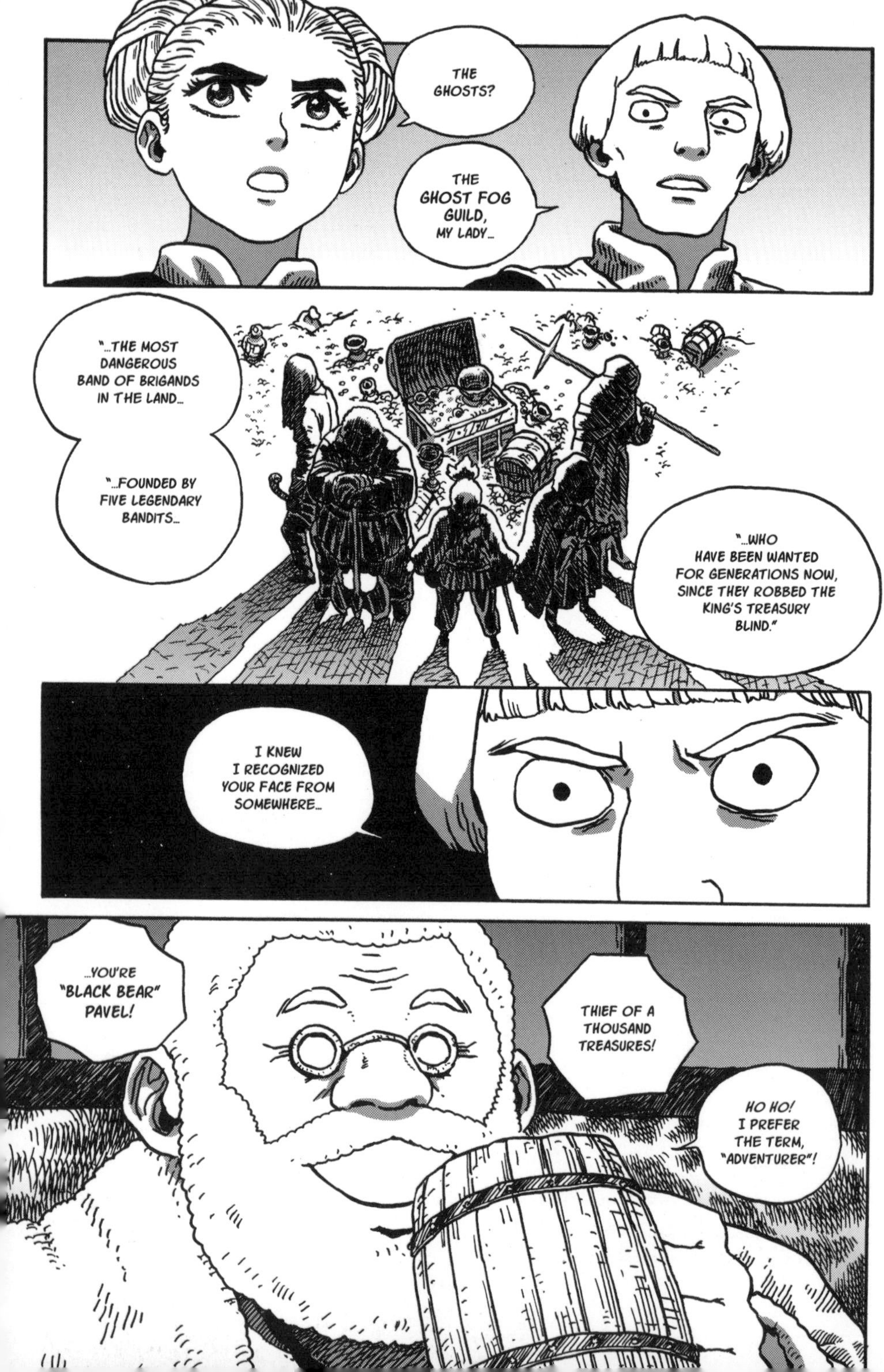
THE GHOSTS?
THE GHOST FOG GUILD, MY LADY...
"...THE MOST DANGEROUS BAND OF BRIGANDS IN THE LAND...
"...FOUNDED BY FIVE LEGENDARY BANDITS...
"...WHO HAVE BEEN WANTED FOR GENERATIONS NOW, SINCE THEY ROBBED THE KING'S TREASURY BLIND."
I KNEW I RECOGNIZED YOUR FACE FROM SOMEWHERE...
...YOU'RE "BLACK BEAR" PAVEL!
THIEF OF A THOUSAND TREASURES!
HO HO! I PREFER THE TERM, "ADVENTURER"!

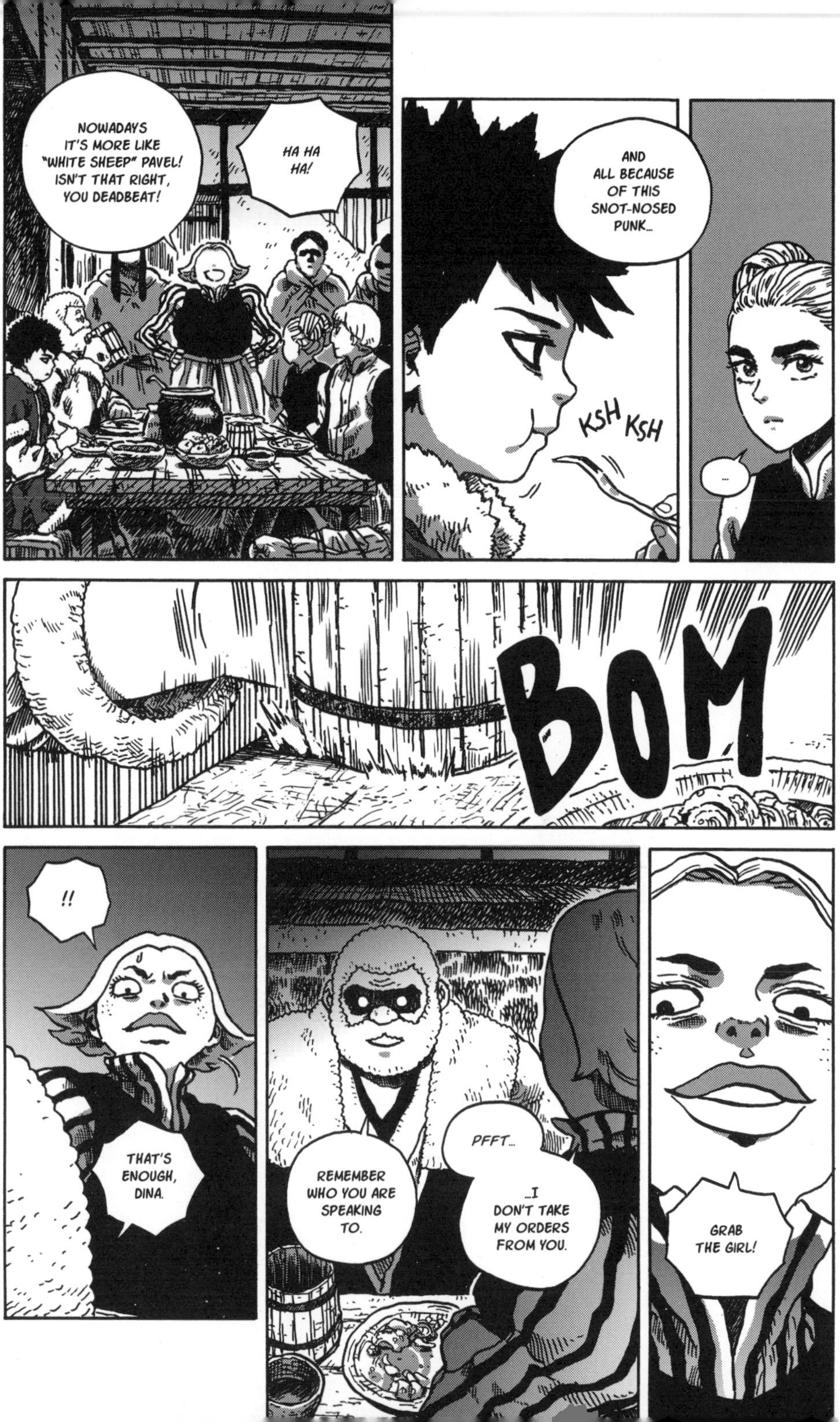
NOWADAYS IT'S MORE LIKE "WHITE SHEEP" PAVEL! ISN'T THAT RIGHT, YOU DEADBEAT!
HA HA HA!
AND ALL BECAUSE OF THIS SNOT-NOSED PUNK...
KSH KSH
...
BOM
!!
THAT'S ENOUGH, DINA.
REMEMBER WHO YOU ARE SPEAKING TO.
PFFT...
...I DON'T TAKE MY ORDERS FROM YOU.
GRAB THE GIRL!

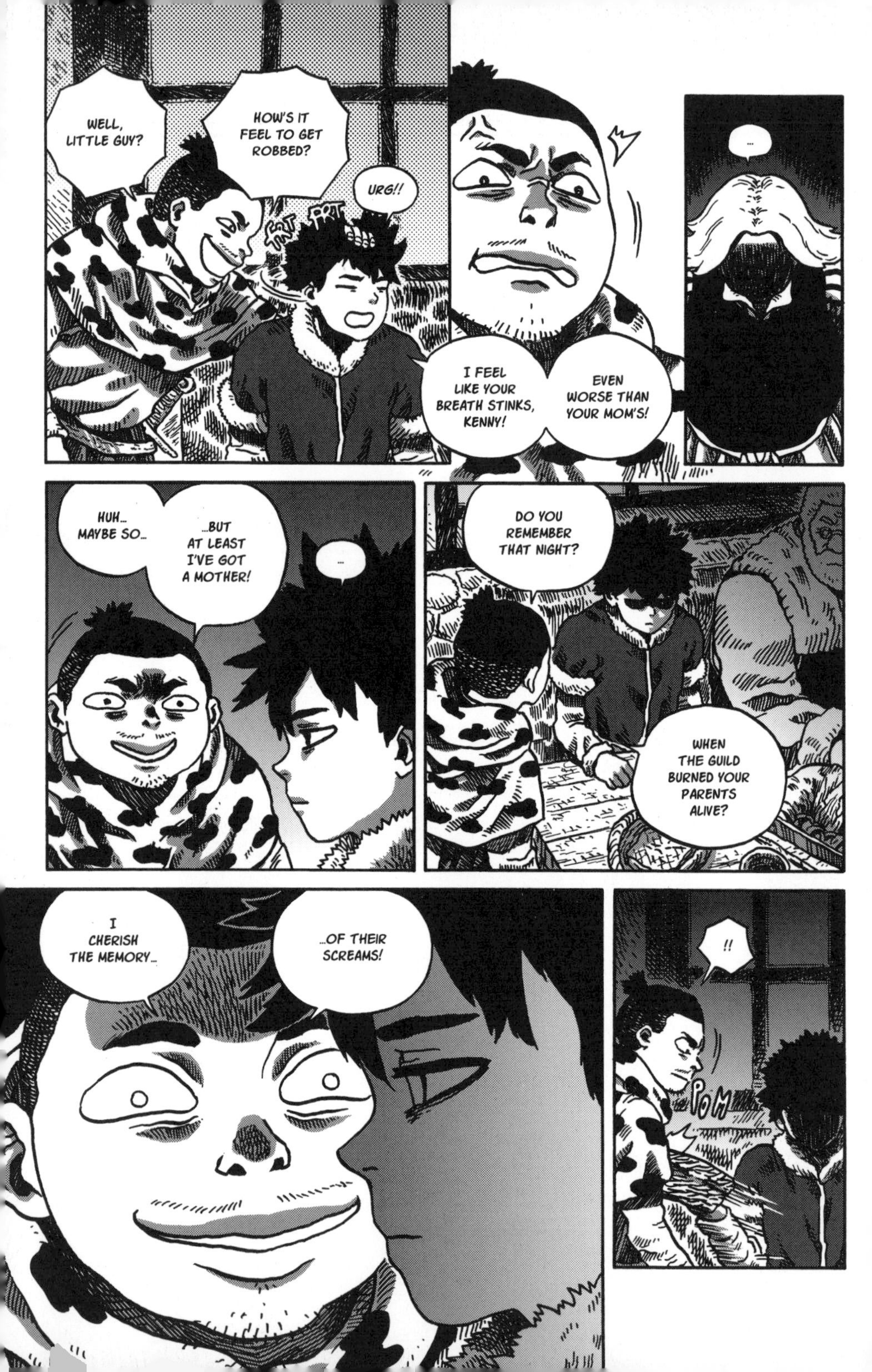
WELL, LITTLE GUY?
HOW'S IT FEEL TO GET ROBBED?
FRT FRT
URG!!
I FEEL LIKE YOUR BREATH STINKS, KENNY!
EVEN WORSE THAN YOUR MOM'S!
...
HUH... MAYBE SO...
...BUT AT LEAST I'VE GOT A MOTHER!
...
DO YOU REMEMBER THAT NIGHT?
WHEN THE GUILD BURNED YOUR PARENTS ALIVE?
I CHERISH THE MEMORY...
...OF THEIR SCREAMS!
!!
POM

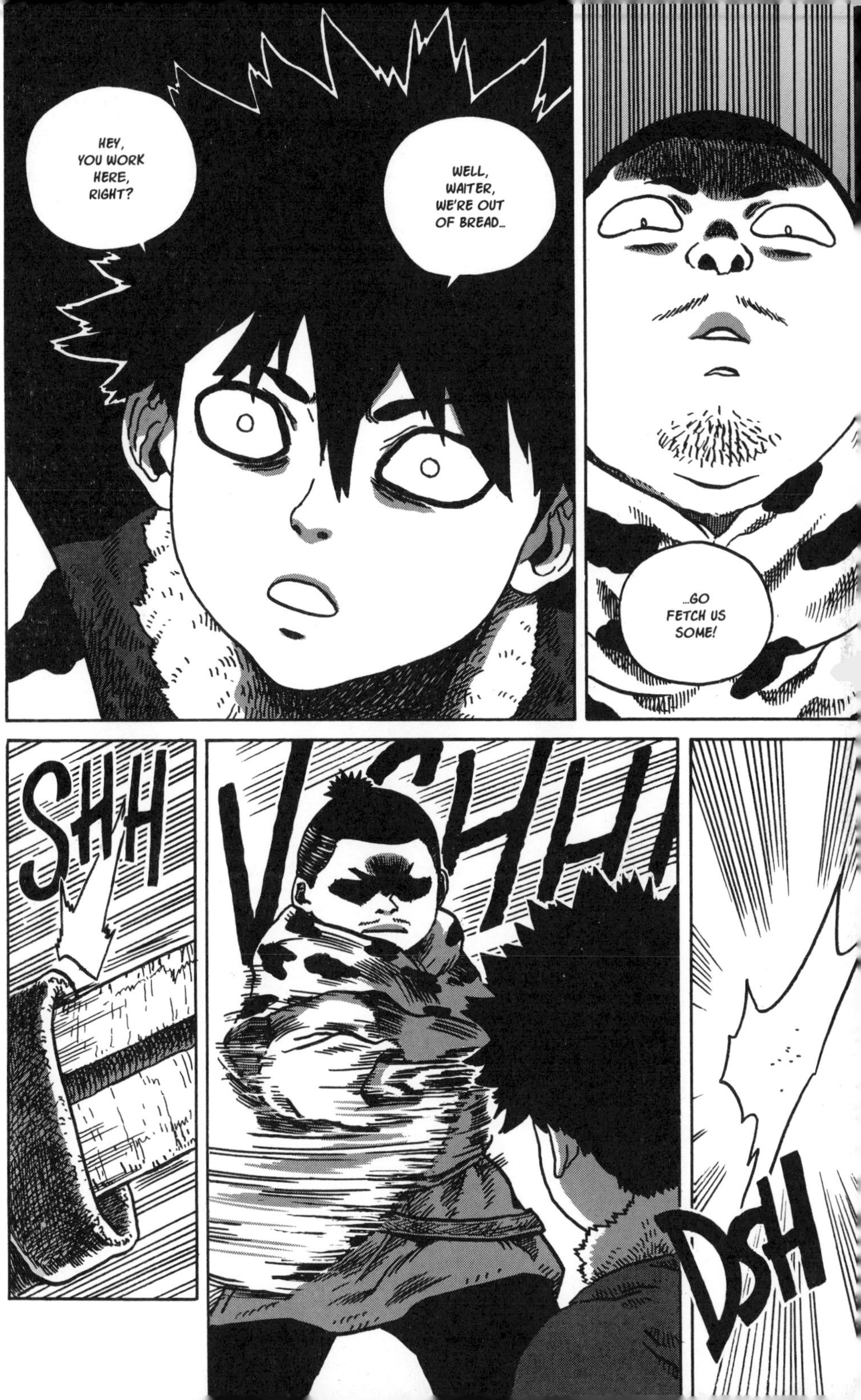
HEY, YOU WORK HERE, RIGHT?
WELL, WAITER, WE'RE OUT OF BREAD...
...GO FETCH US SOME!
SHH
VSHH
DSH

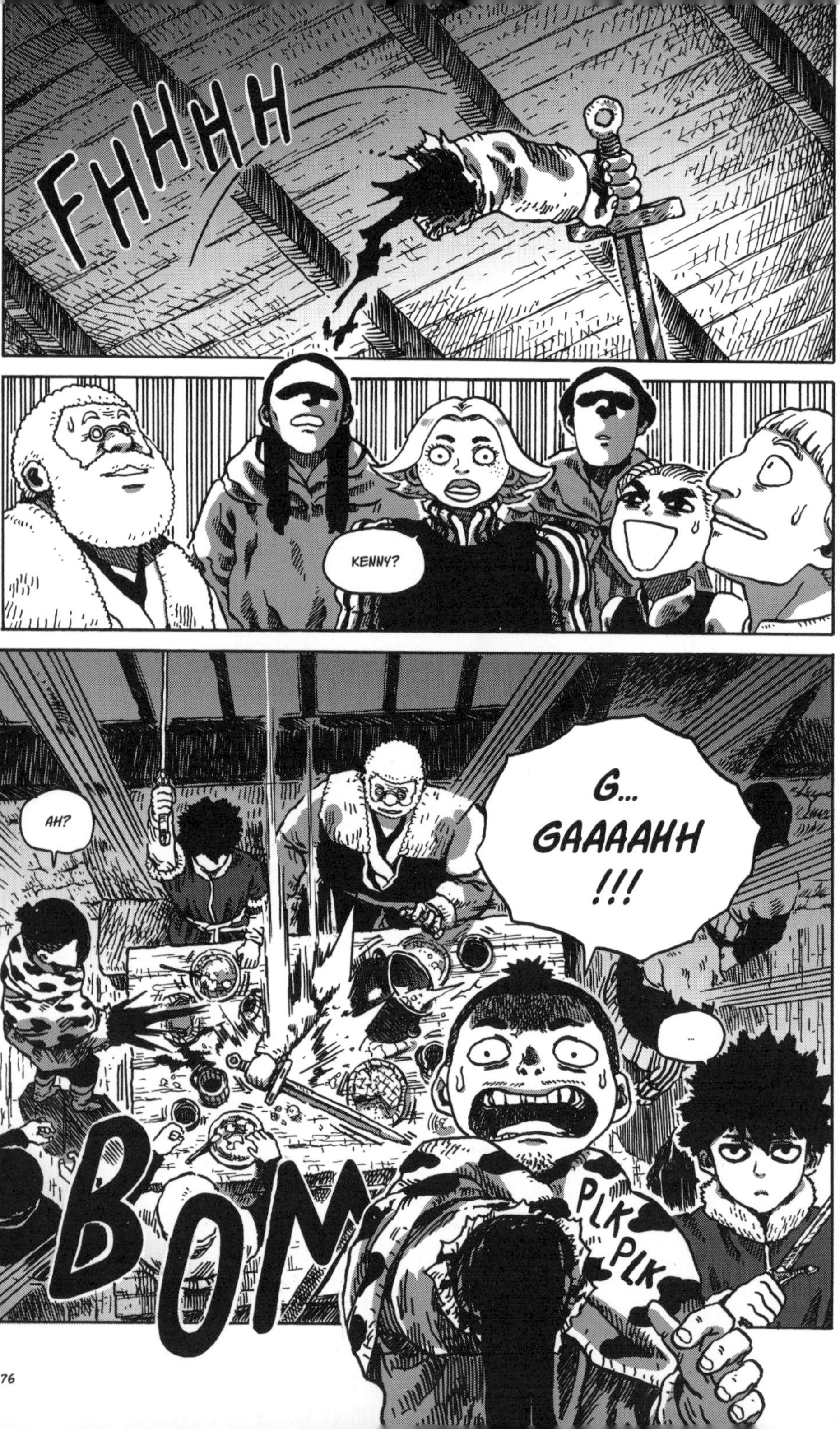
FHHHH
KENNY?
AH?
G... GAAAAHH !!!
...
BOM
PLK PLK PLK

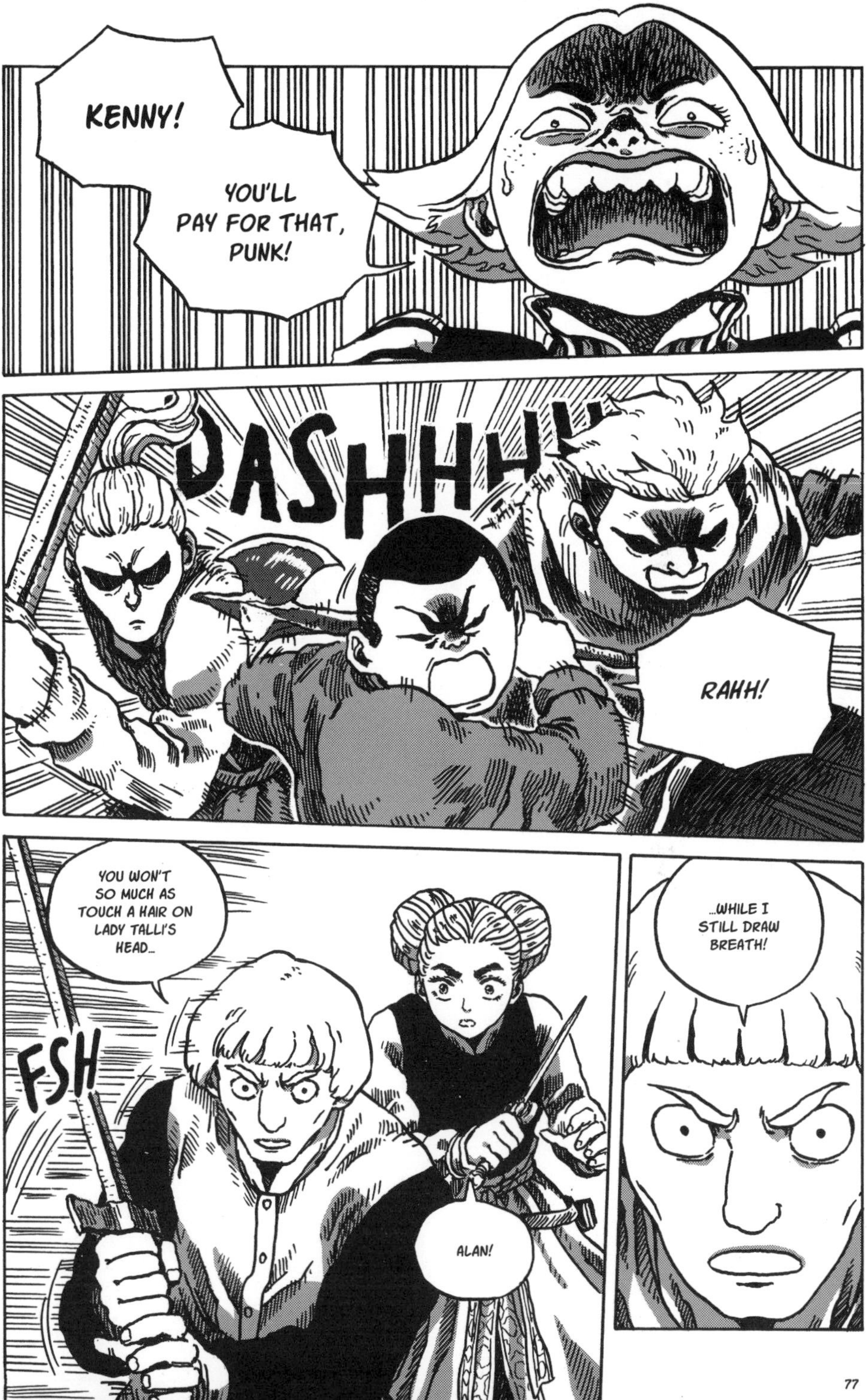
KENNY!
YOU'LL PAY FOR THAT, PUNK!
DASHHH
RAHH!
YOU WON'T SO MUCH AS TOUCH A HAIR ON LADY TALLI'S HEAD...
FSH
ALAN!
...WHILE I STILL DRAW BREATH!

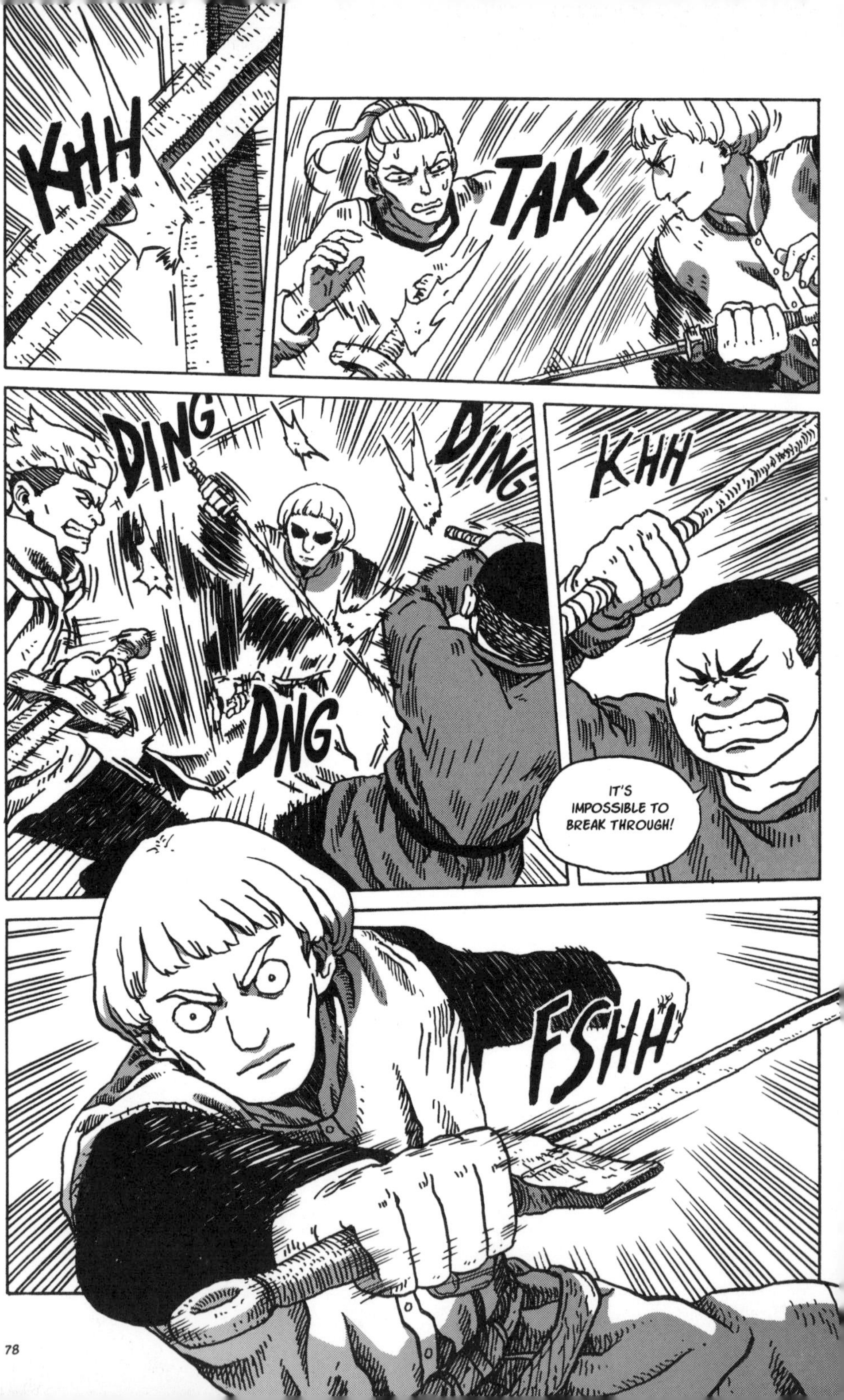
KHH
TAK
DING
DING
DNG
KHH
IT'S IMPOSSIBLE TO BREAK THROUGH!
FSHH

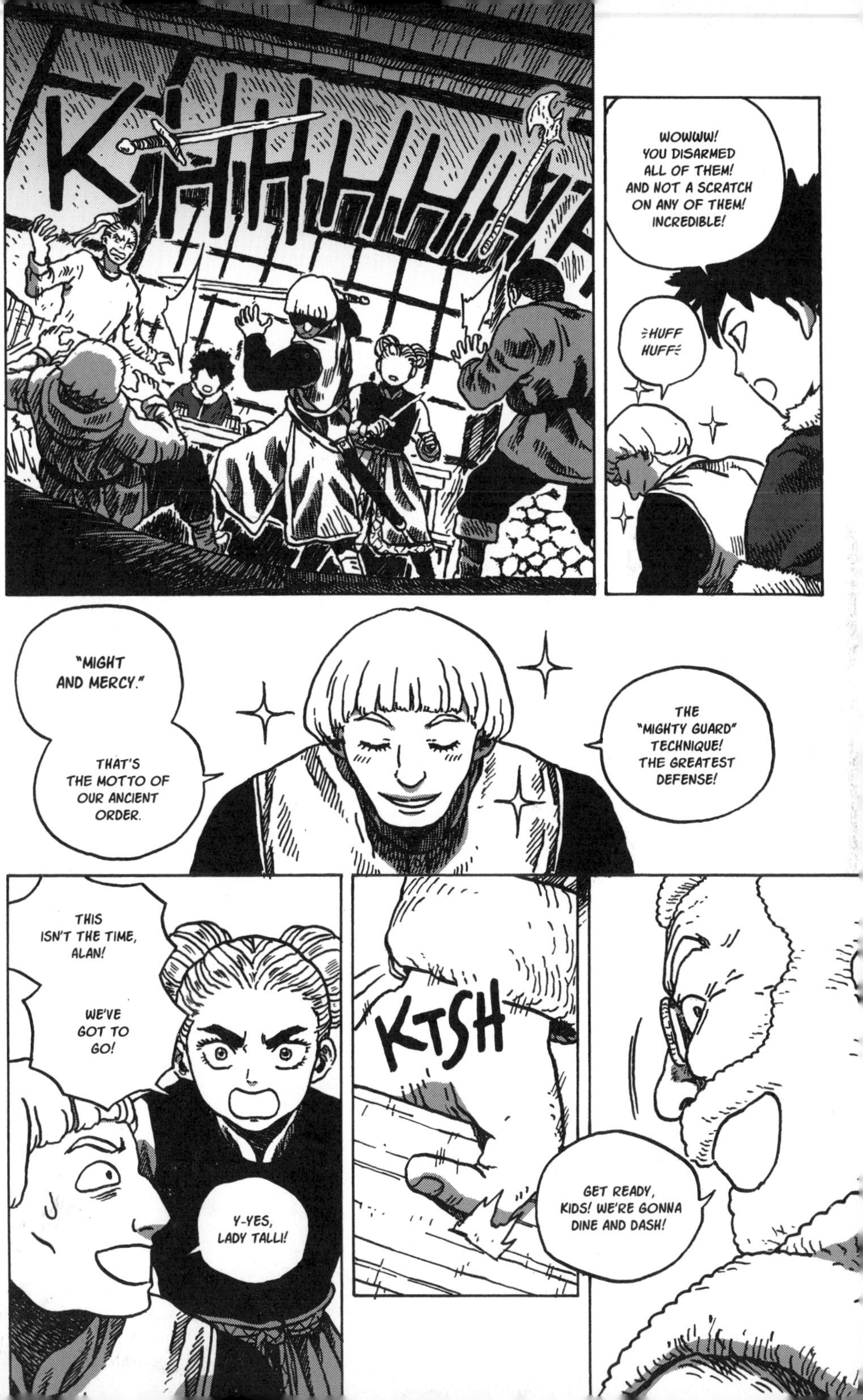
KHHHHHHH
WOWWW! YOU DISARMED ALL OF THEM! AND NOT A SCRATCH ON ANY OF THEM! INCREDIBLE!
HUFF HUFF
"MIGHT AND MERCY."
THAT'S THE MOTTO OF OUR ANCIENT ORDER.
THE "MIGHTY GUARD" TECHNIQUE! THE GREATEST DEFENSE!
THIS ISN'T THE TIME, ALAN!
WE'VE GOT TO GO!
Y-YES, LADY TALLI!
KTSH
GET READY, KIDS! WE'RE GONNA DINE AND DASH!

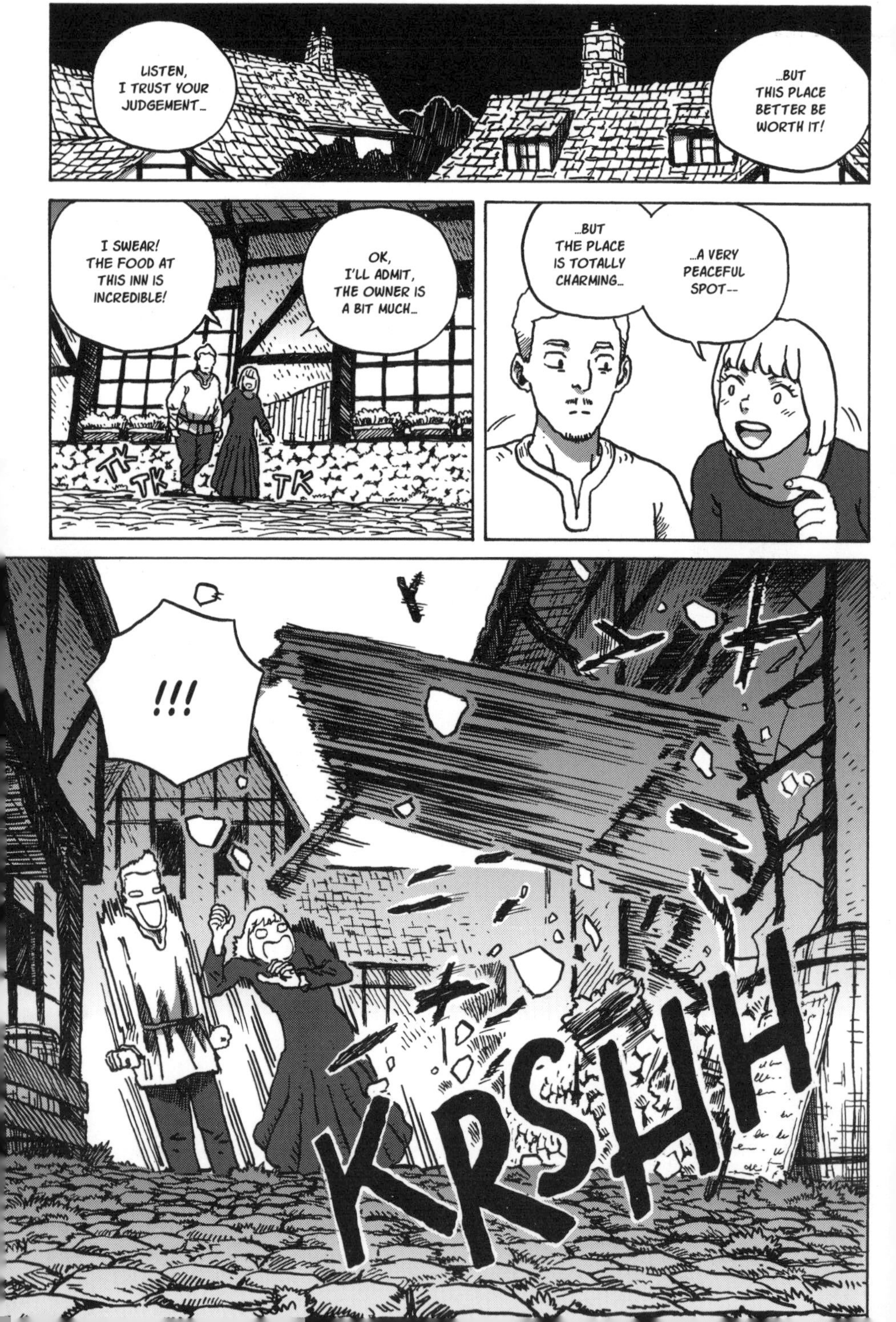
LISTEN, I TRUST YOUR JUDGEMENT...
...BUT THIS PLACE BETTER BE WORTH IT!
I SWEAR! THE FOOD AT THIS INN IS INCREDIBLE!
OK, I'LL ADMIT, THE OWNER IS A BIT MUCH...
TK TK TK
...BUT THE PLACE IS TOTALLY CHARMING...
...A VERY PEACEFUL SPOT--
!!!
KRSHH

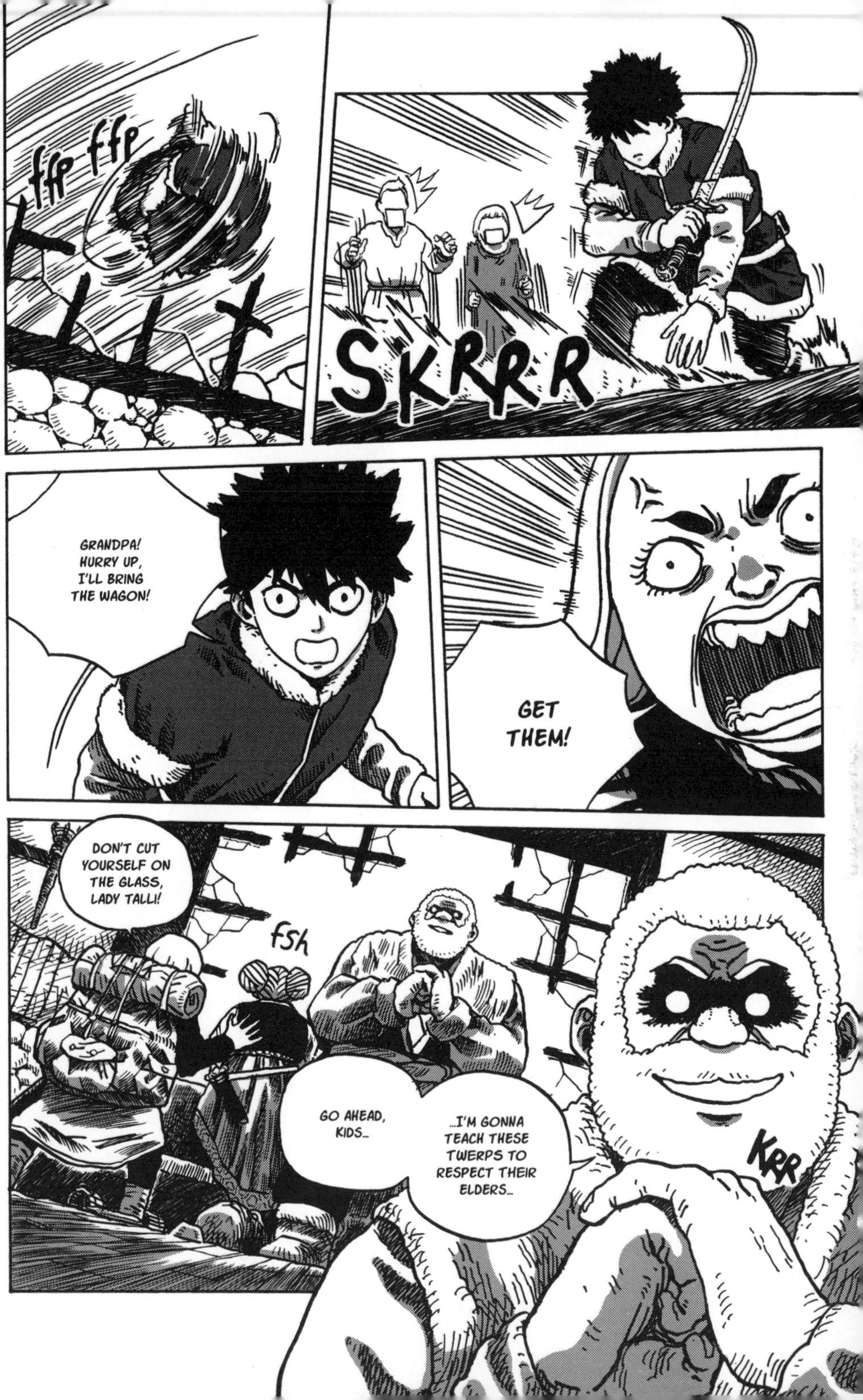
ffp ffp
SKRRR
GRANDPA! HURRY UP, I'LL BRING THE WAGON!
GET THEM!
DON'T CUT YOURSELF ON THE GLASS, LADY TALLI!
fsh
GO AHEAD, KIDS...
...I'M GONNA TEACH THESE TWERPS TO RESPECT THEIR ELDERS...
KRR

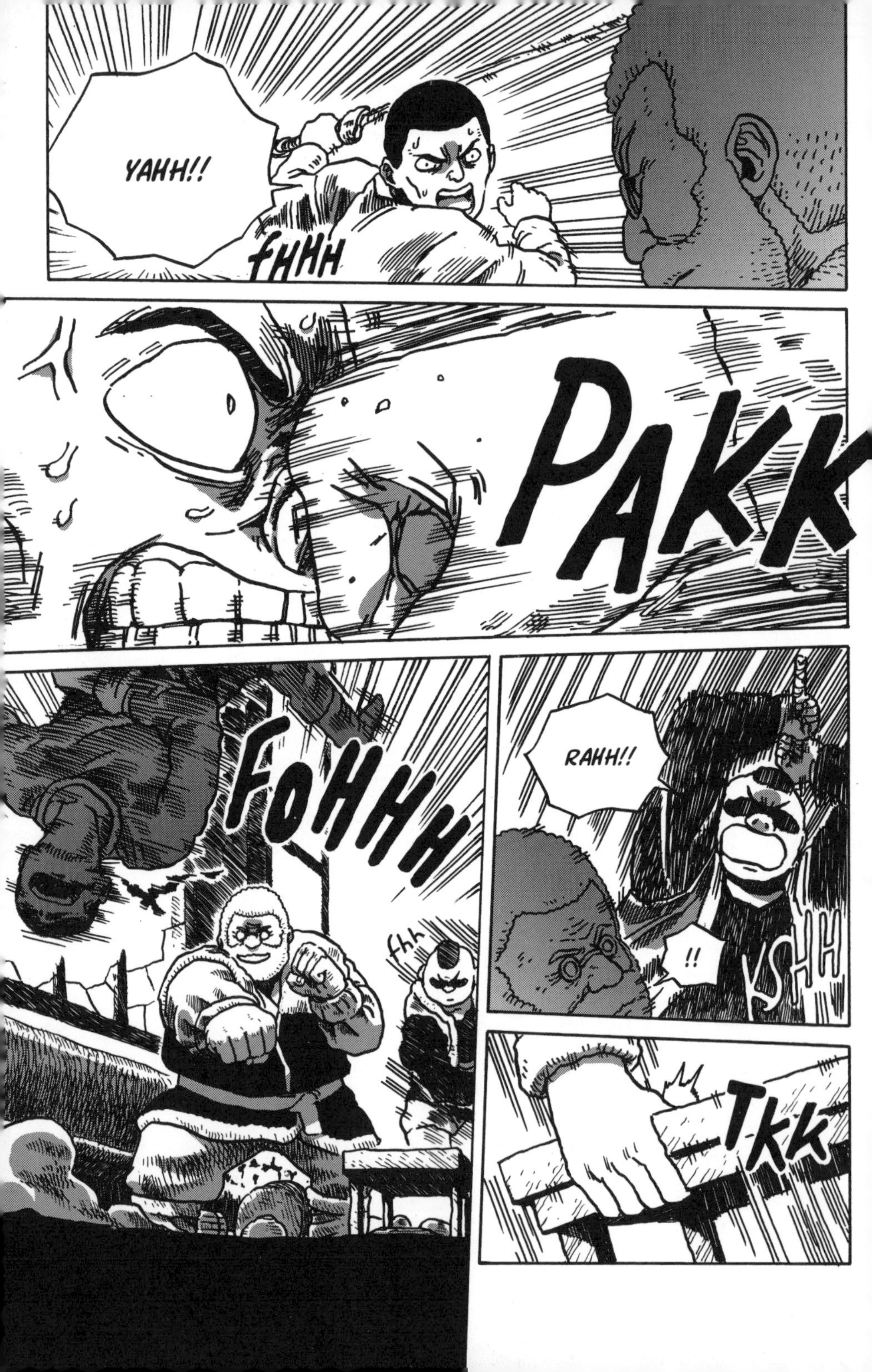
YAHH!!
fHHH
PAKK
FOHHHH
fhh
RAHH!!
!!
KSHH
TKK

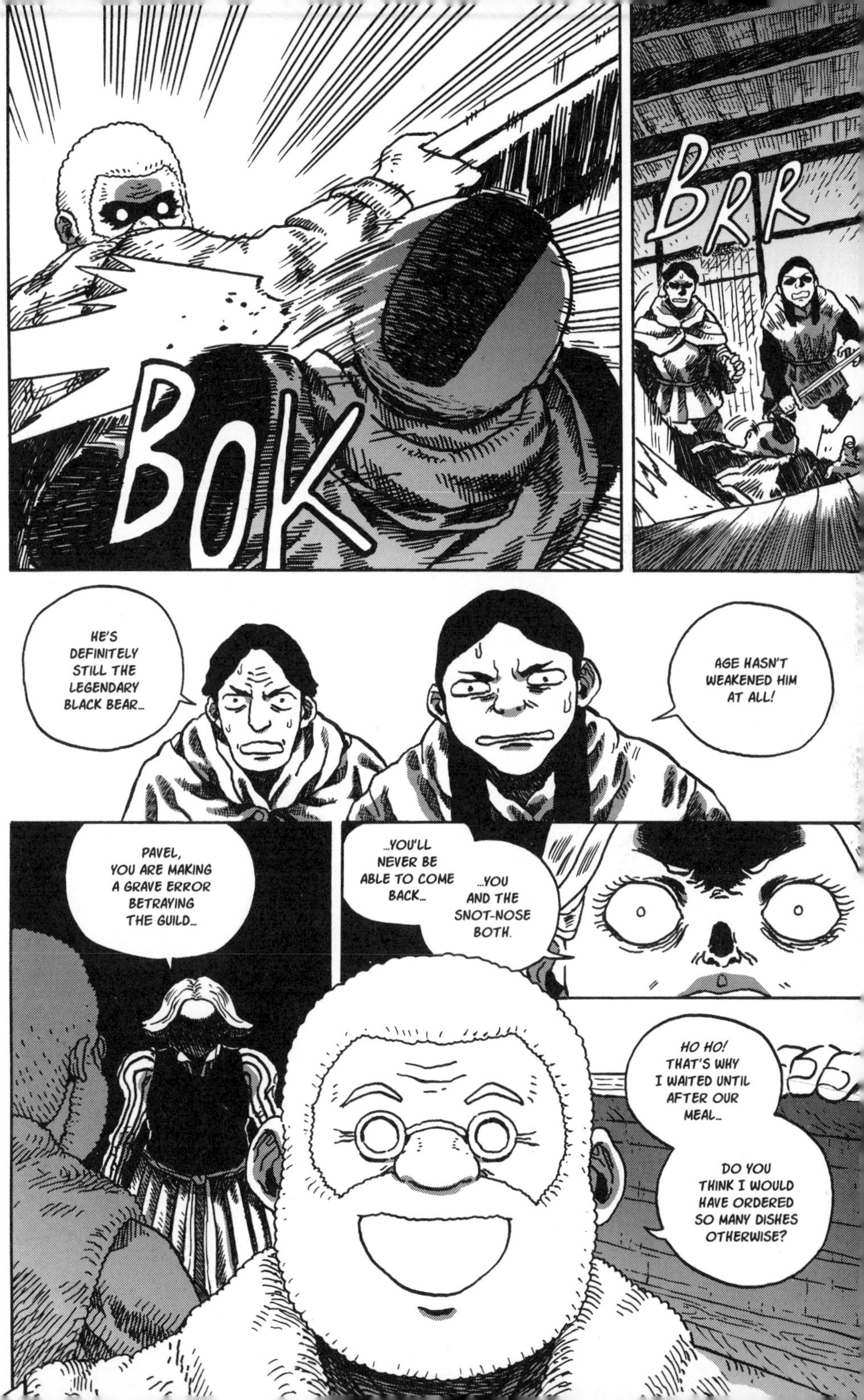
BOK
BRR
HE'S DEFINITELY STILL THE LEGENDARY BLACK BEAR...
AGE HASN'T WEAKENED HIM AT ALL!
PAVEL, YOU ARE MAKING A GRAVE ERROR BETRAYING THE GUILD...
...YOU'LL NEVER BE ABLE TO COME BACK...
...YOU AND THE SNOT-NOSE BOTH.
HO HO! THAT'S WHY I WAITED UNTIL AFTER OUR MEAL...
DO YOU THINK I WOULD HAVE ORDERED SO MANY DISHES OTHERWISE?

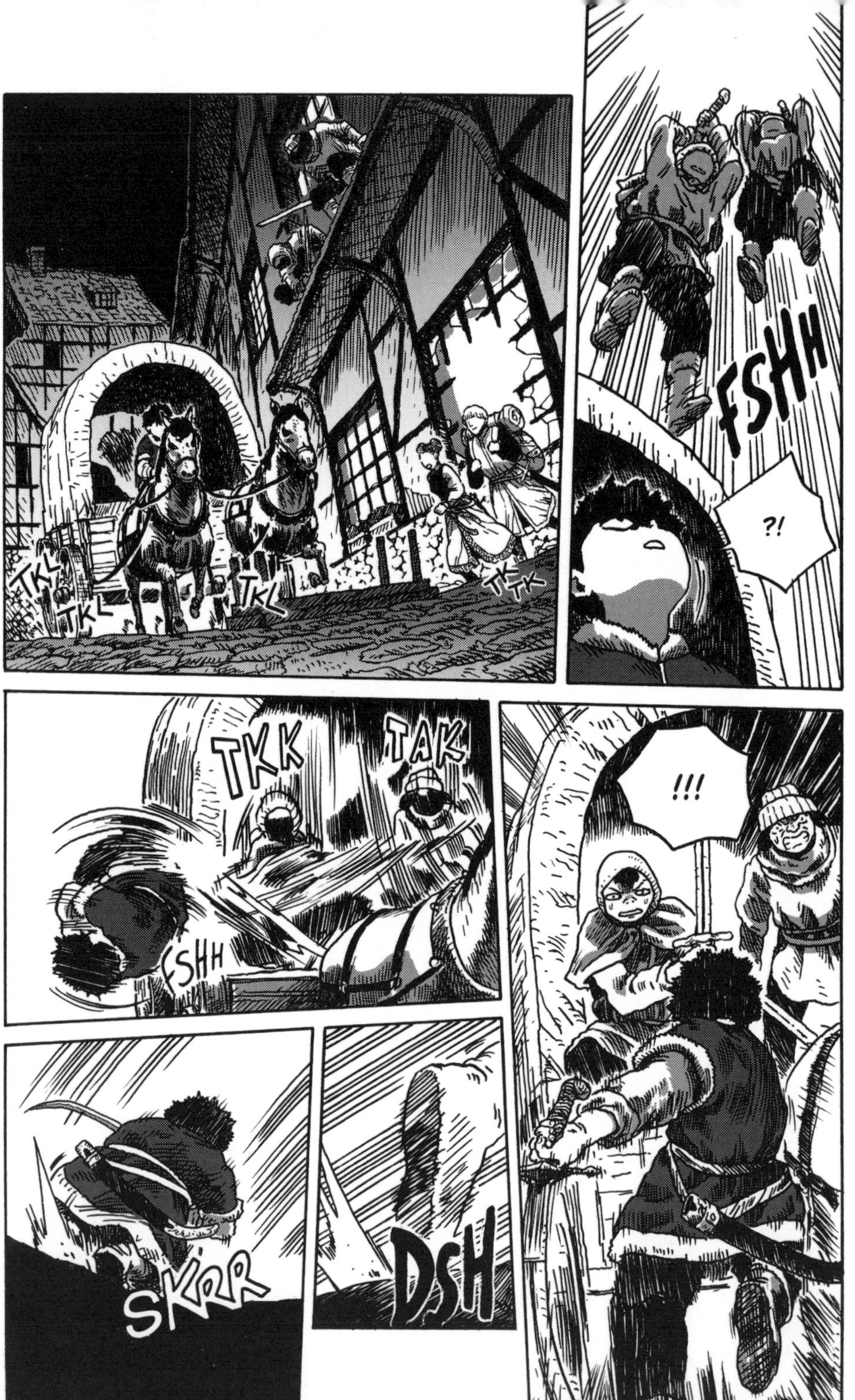
TKL
TKL
TKL
TK TK
FSHH
?!
TKK
TAK
FSHH
SKRR
DSH
!!!

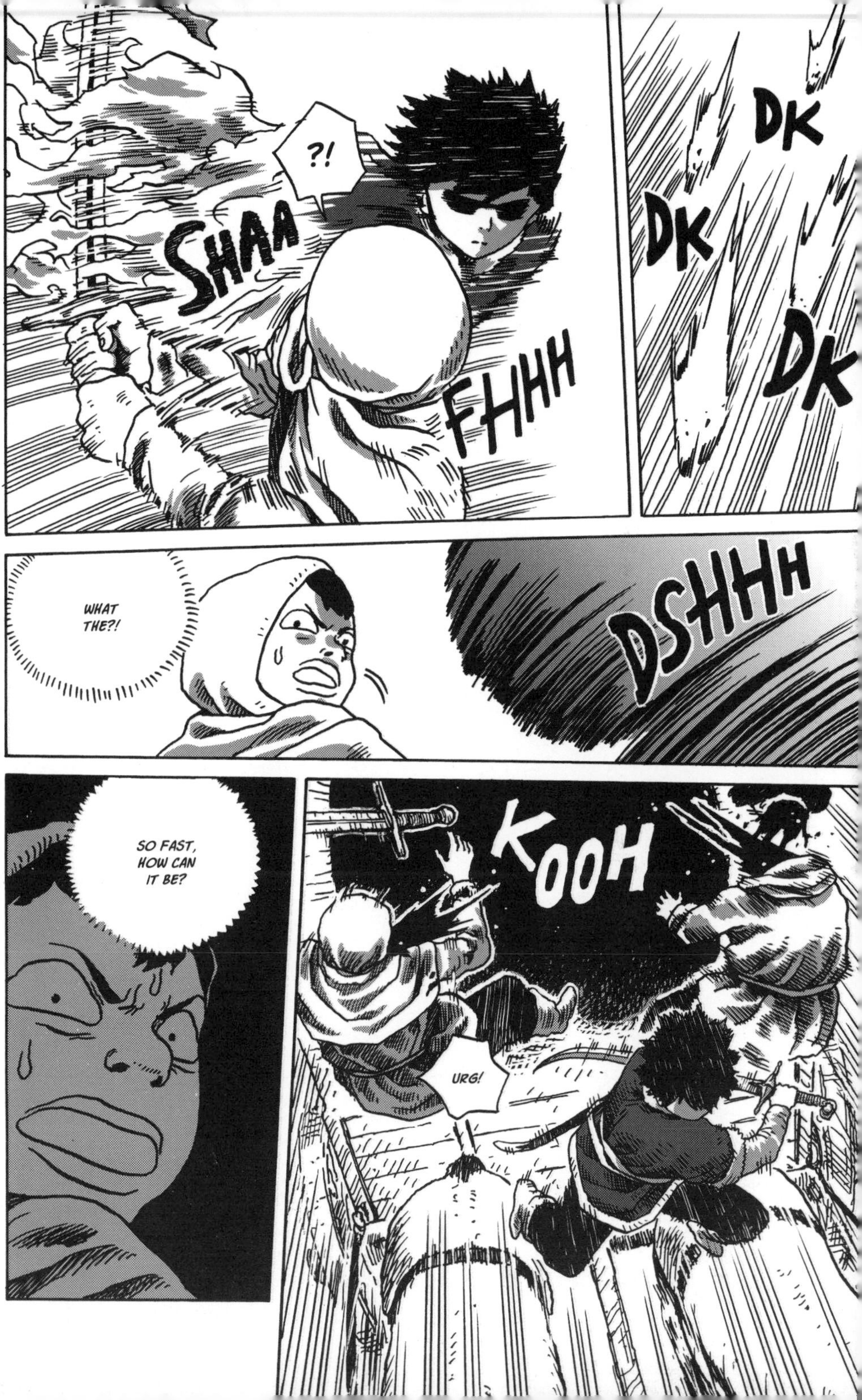
?!
SHAA
FHHH
DK
DK
DK
WHAT THE?!
DSHHH
SO FAST, HOW CAN IT BE?
KOOH
URG!

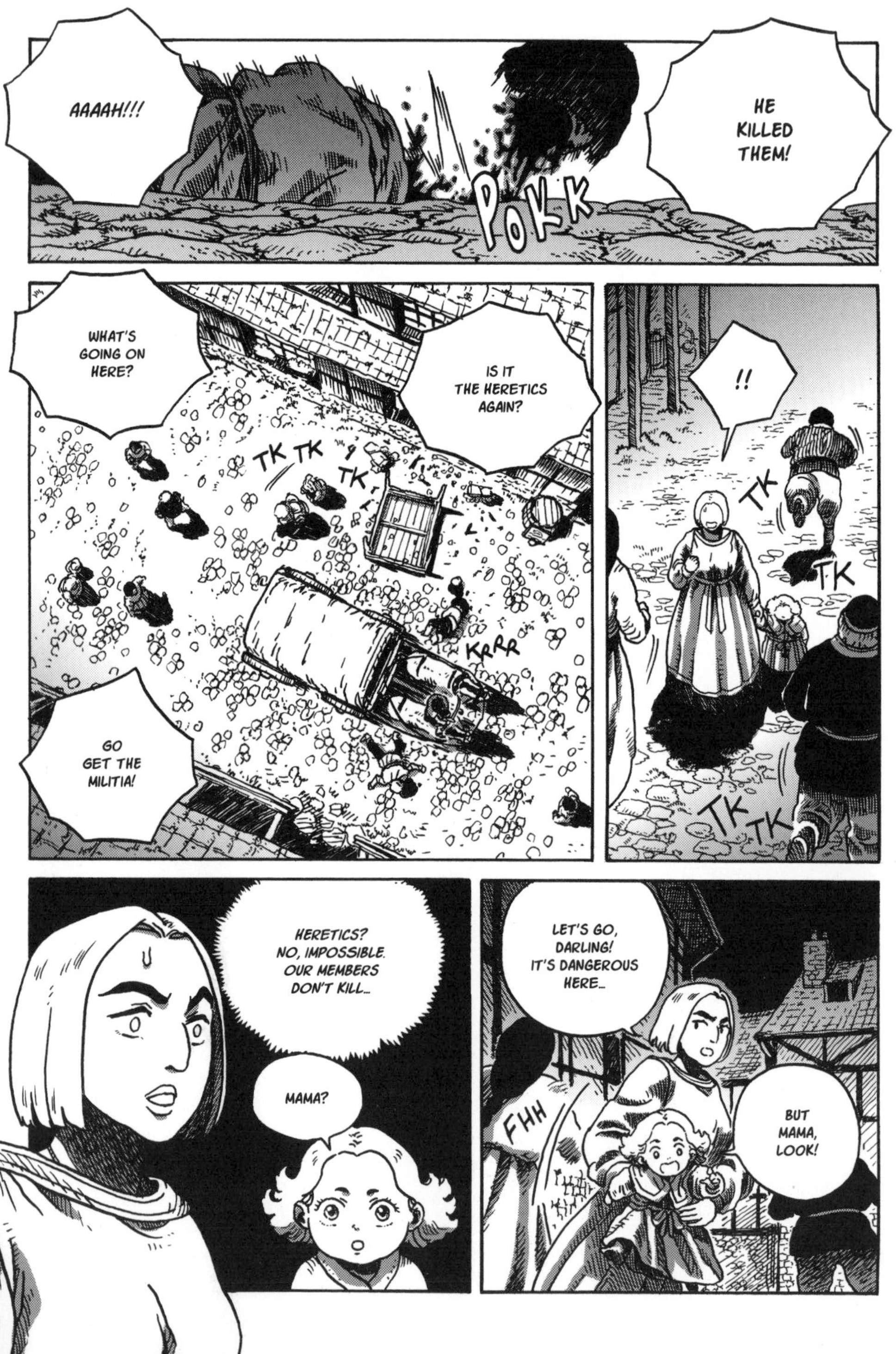
AAAAH!!!
POKK
HE KILLED THEM!
WHAT'S GOING ON HERE?
IS IT THE HERETICS AGAIN?
TK TK TK
KRRR
GO GET THE MILITIA!
!!
TK
TK
TK TK
HERETICS? NO, IMPOSSIBLE. OUR MEMBERS DON'T KILL...
MAMA?
LET'S GO, DARLING! IT'S DANGEROUS HERE...
FHH
BUT MAMA, LOOK!

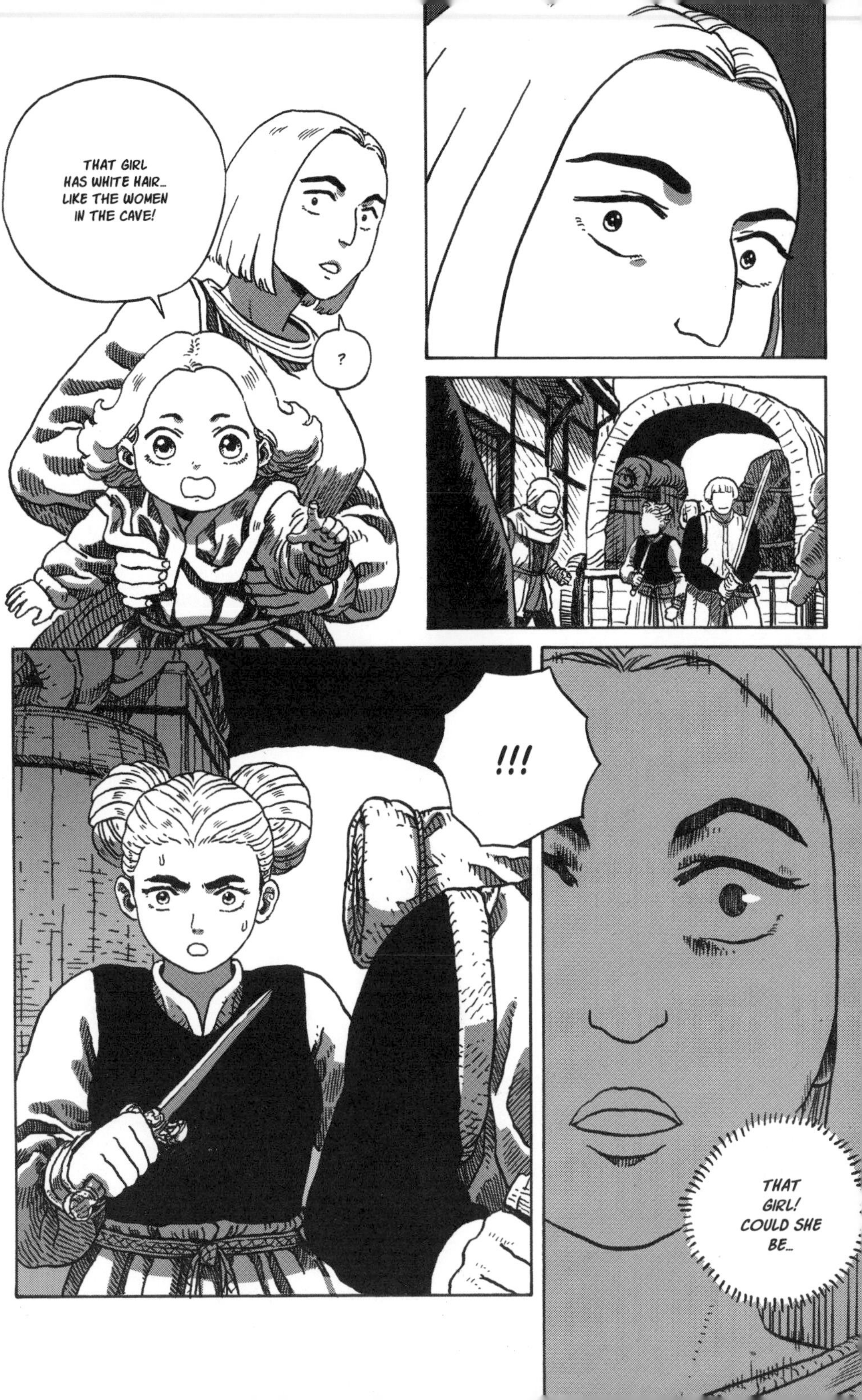
THAT GIRL HAS WHITE HAIR... LIKE THE WOMEN IN THE CAVE!
?
!!!
THAT GIRL! COULD SHE BE...

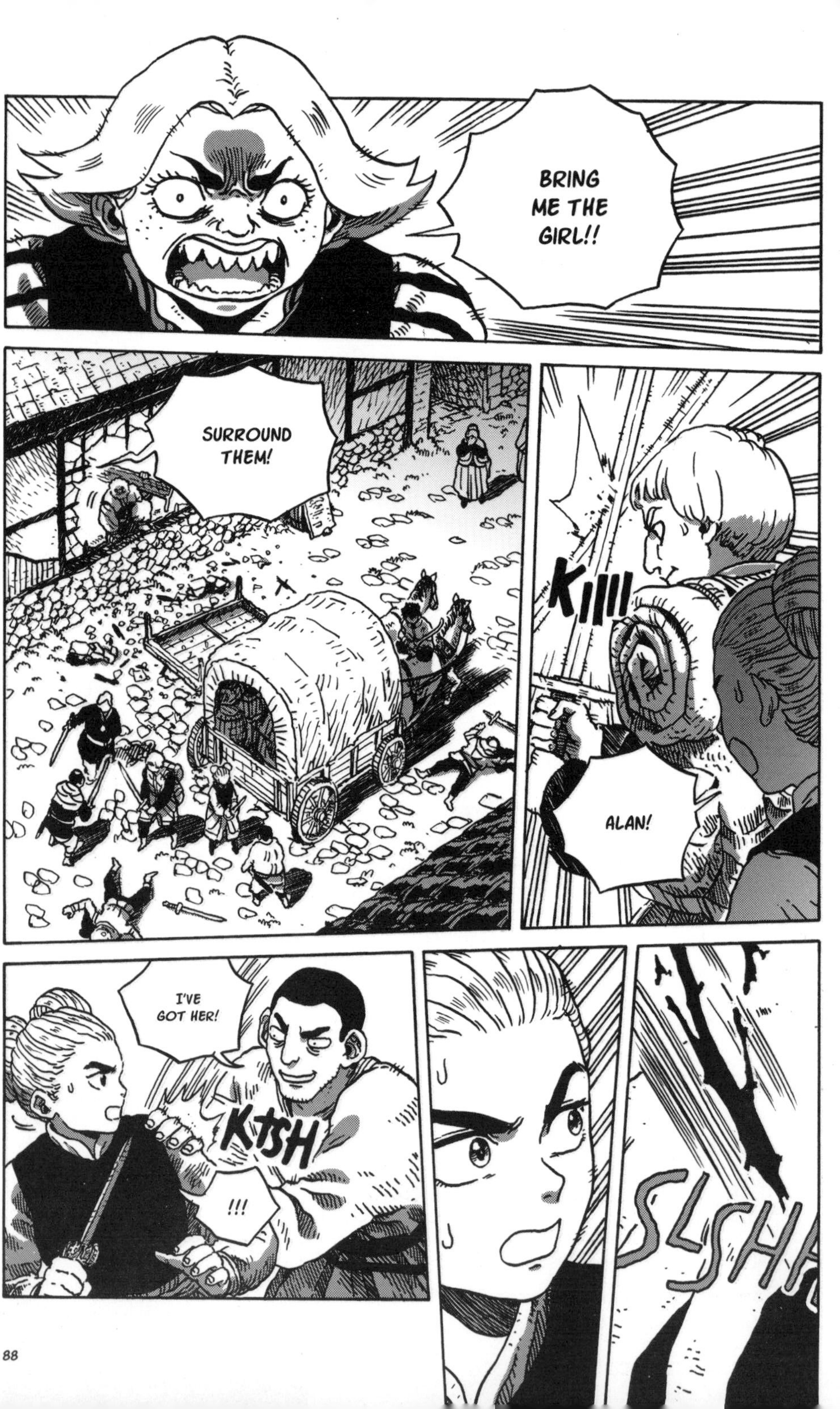
BRING ME THE GIRL!!
SURROUND THEM!
KIIII
ALAN!
I'VE GOT HER!
KISH
!!!
SLSH

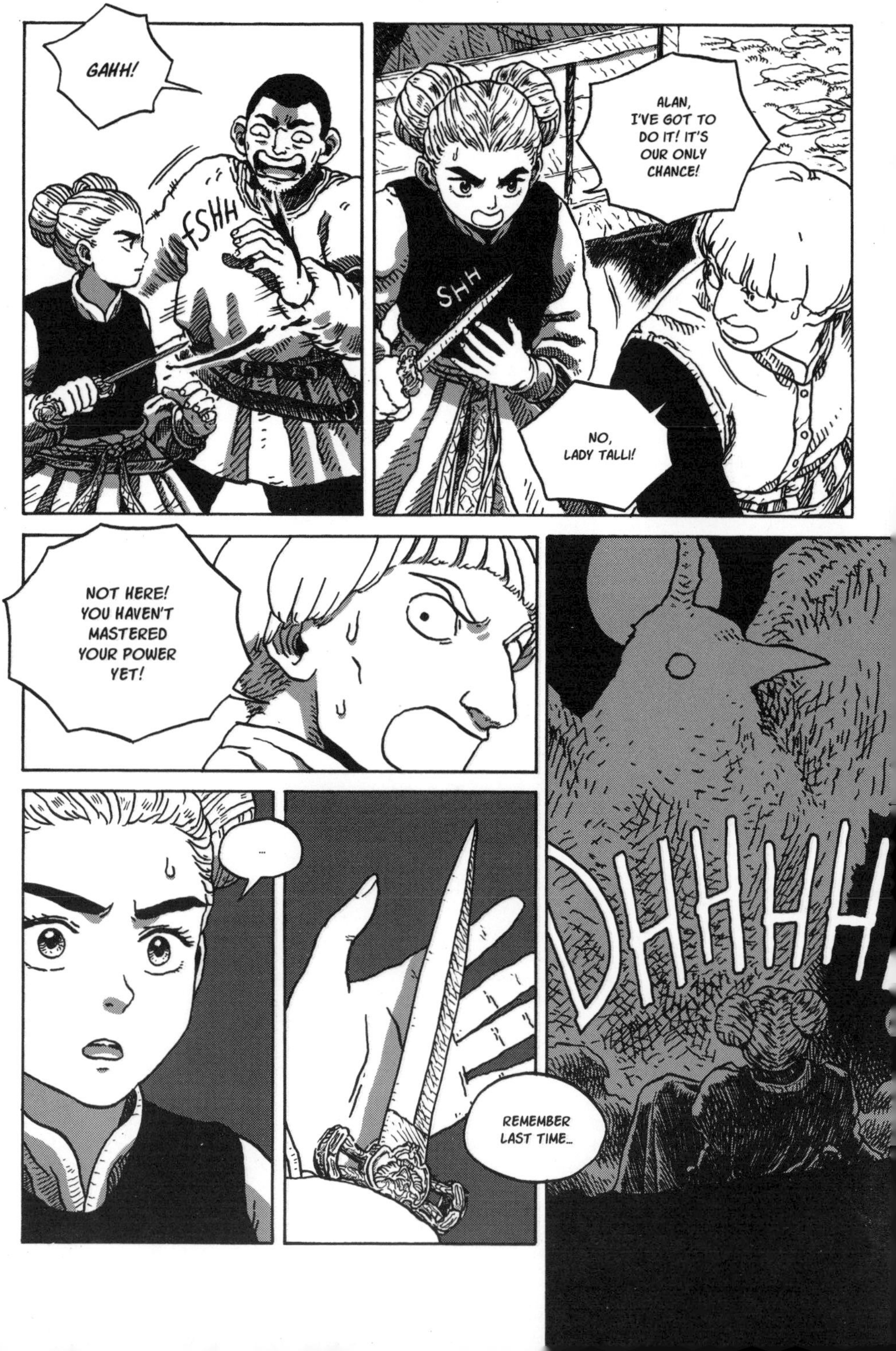
GAHH!
fSHH
SHH
ALAN, I'VE GOT TO DO IT! IT'S OUR ONLY CHANCE!
NO, LADY TALLI!
NOT HERE! YOU HAVEN'T MASTERED YOUR POWER YET!
...
REMEMBER LAST TIME...
DHHHH

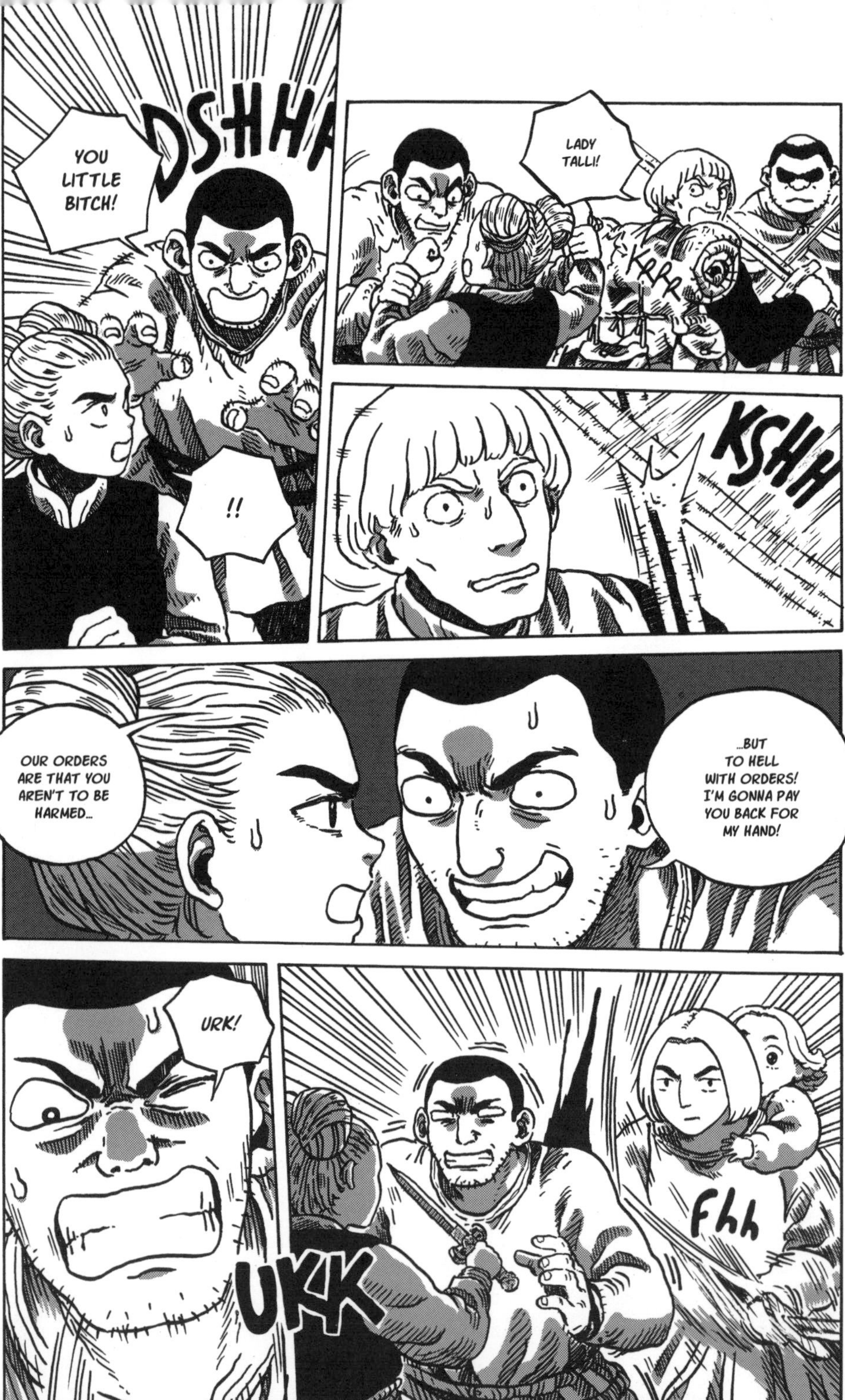
YOU LITTLE BITCH!
DSHHA
!!
LADY TALLI!
KRRR
KSHH
OUR ORDERS ARE THAT YOU AREN'T TO BE HARMED...
...BUT TO HELL WITH ORDERS! I'M GONNA PAY YOU BACK FOR MY HAND!
URK!
UKK
Fhh

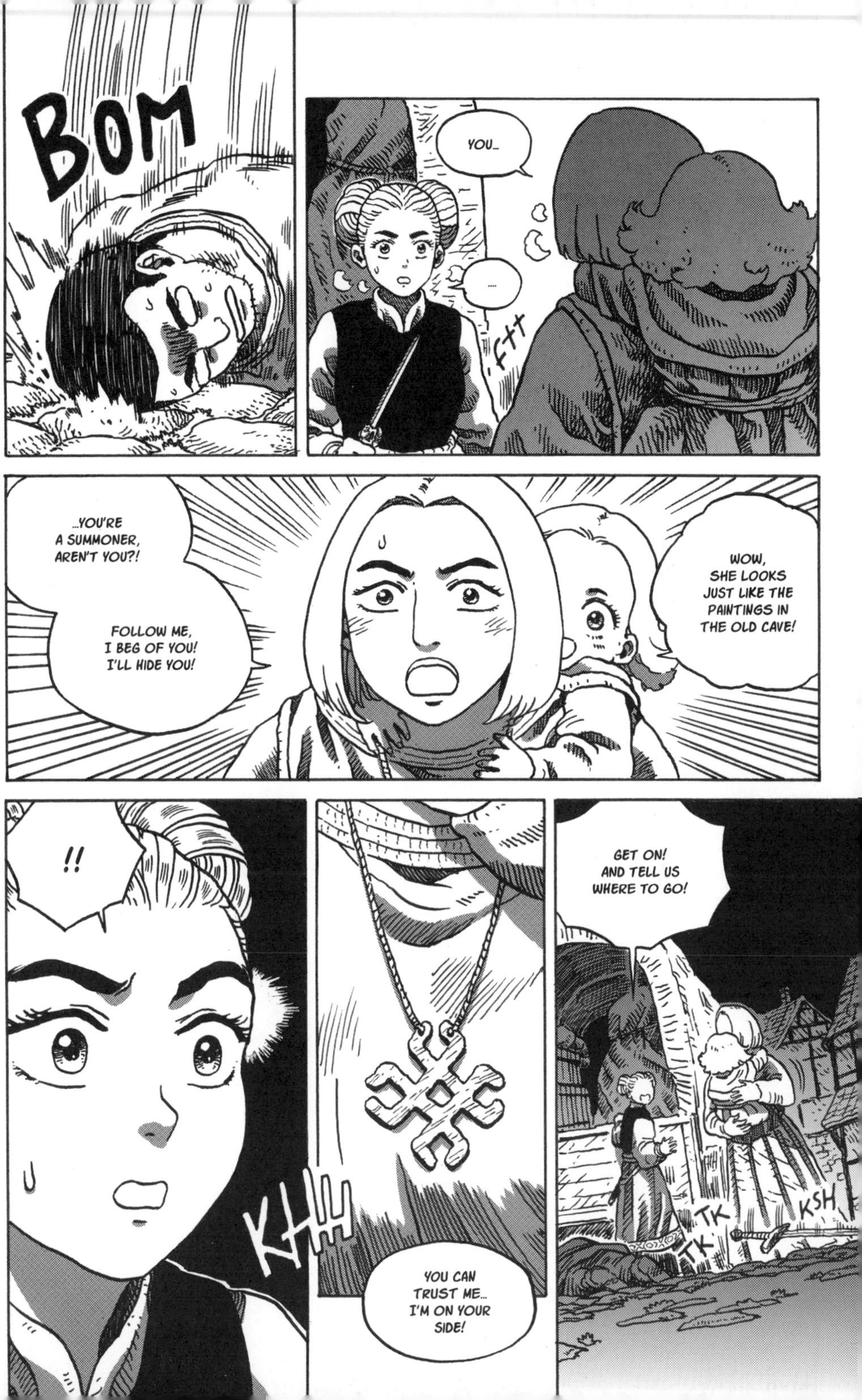
BOM
YOU...
...
FTT
...YOU'RE A SUMMONER, AREN'T YOU?!
FOLLOW ME, I BEG OF YOU! I'LL HIDE YOU!
WOW, SHE LOOKS JUST LIKE THE PAINTINGS IN THE OLD CAVE!
!!
KHH
YOU CAN TRUST ME... I'M ON YOUR SIDE!
GET ON! AND TELL US WHERE TO GO!
TK
TK
KSH

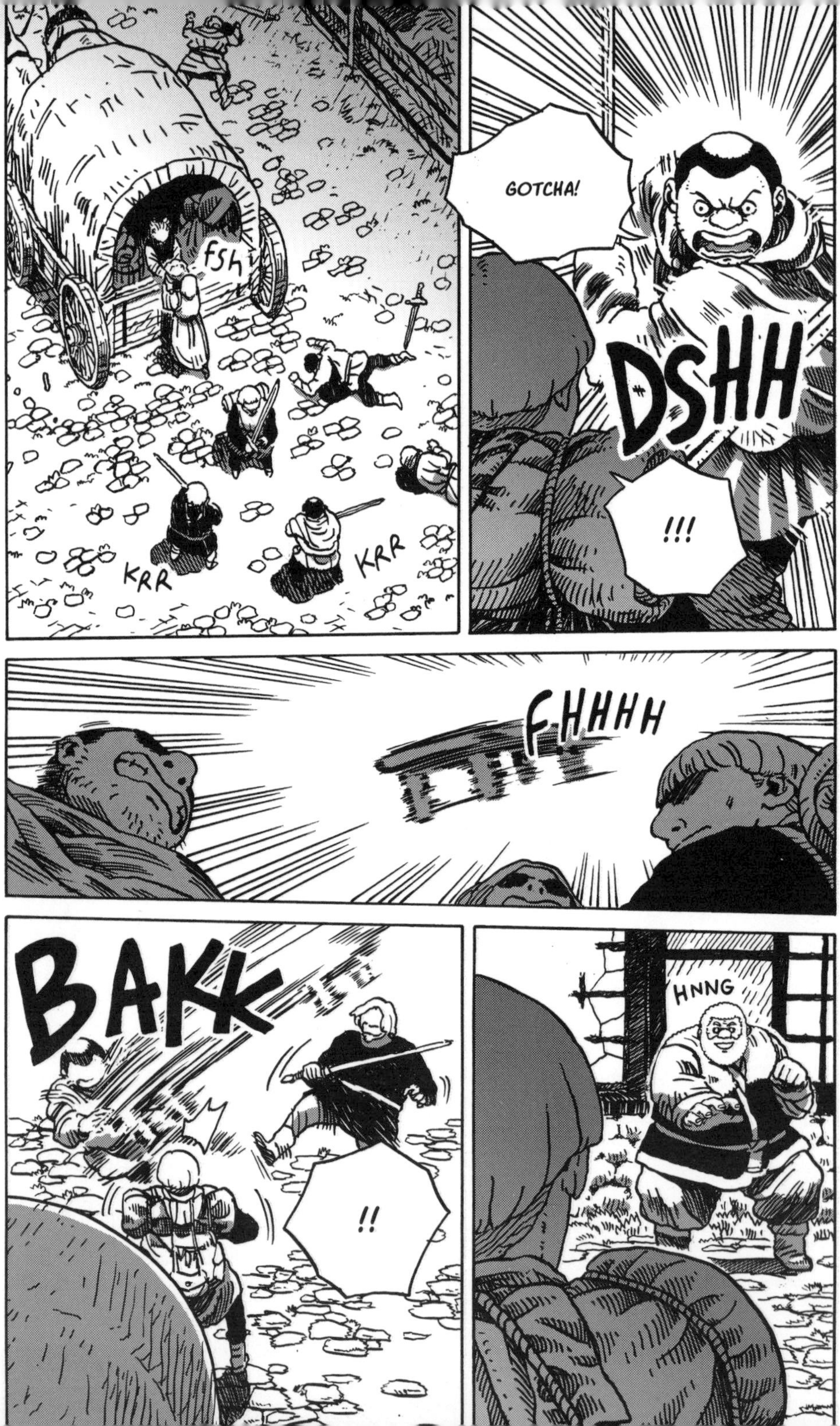
FSH
KRR
KRR
GOTCHA!
DSHH
!!!
FHHHH
BAKK
!!
HNNG

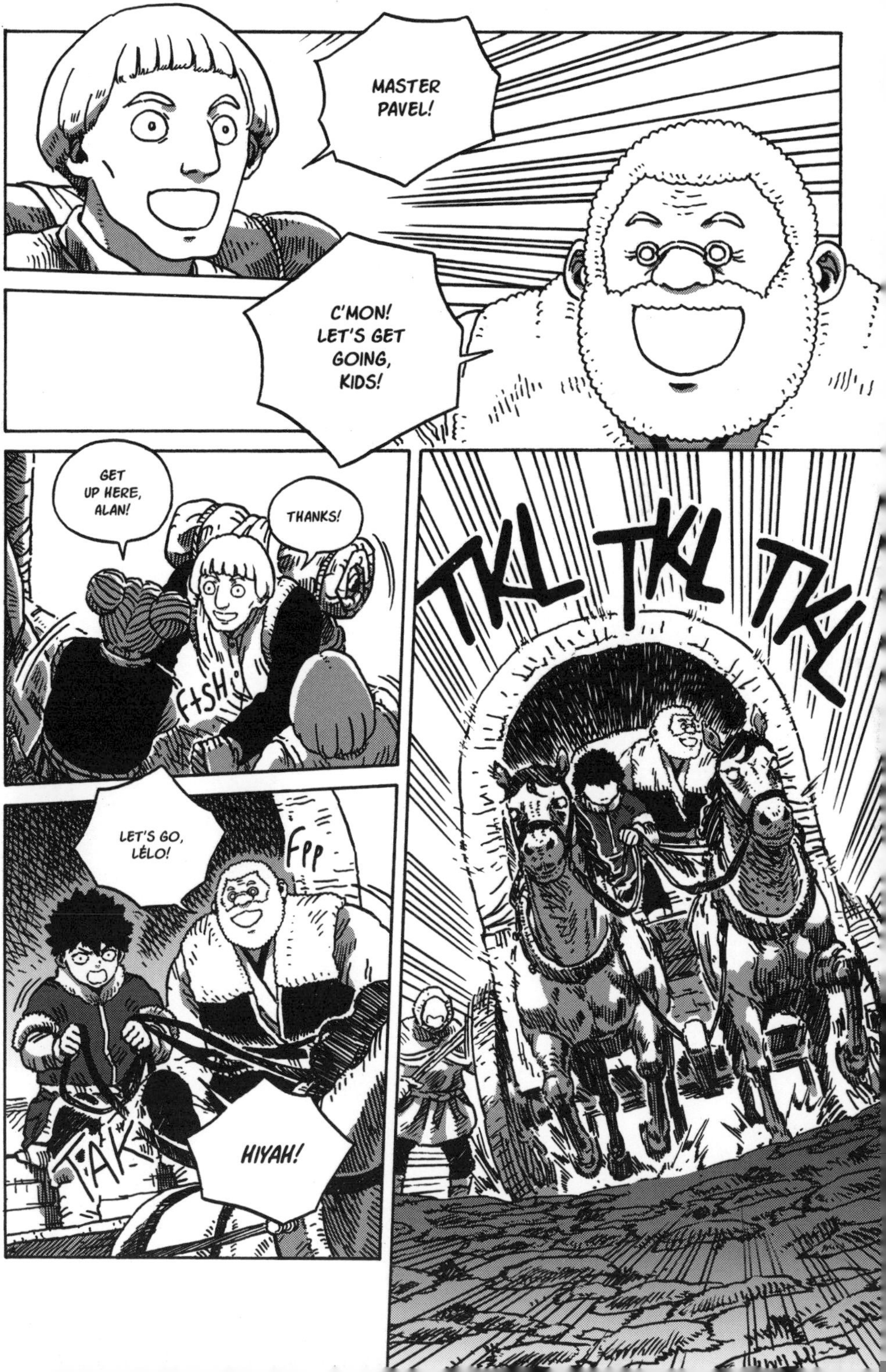
MASTER PAVEL!
C'MON! LET'S GET GOING, KIDS!
GET UP HERE, ALAN!
THANKS!
LET'S GO, LÉLO!
FPP
TAK
HIYAH!
TKL TKL TKL

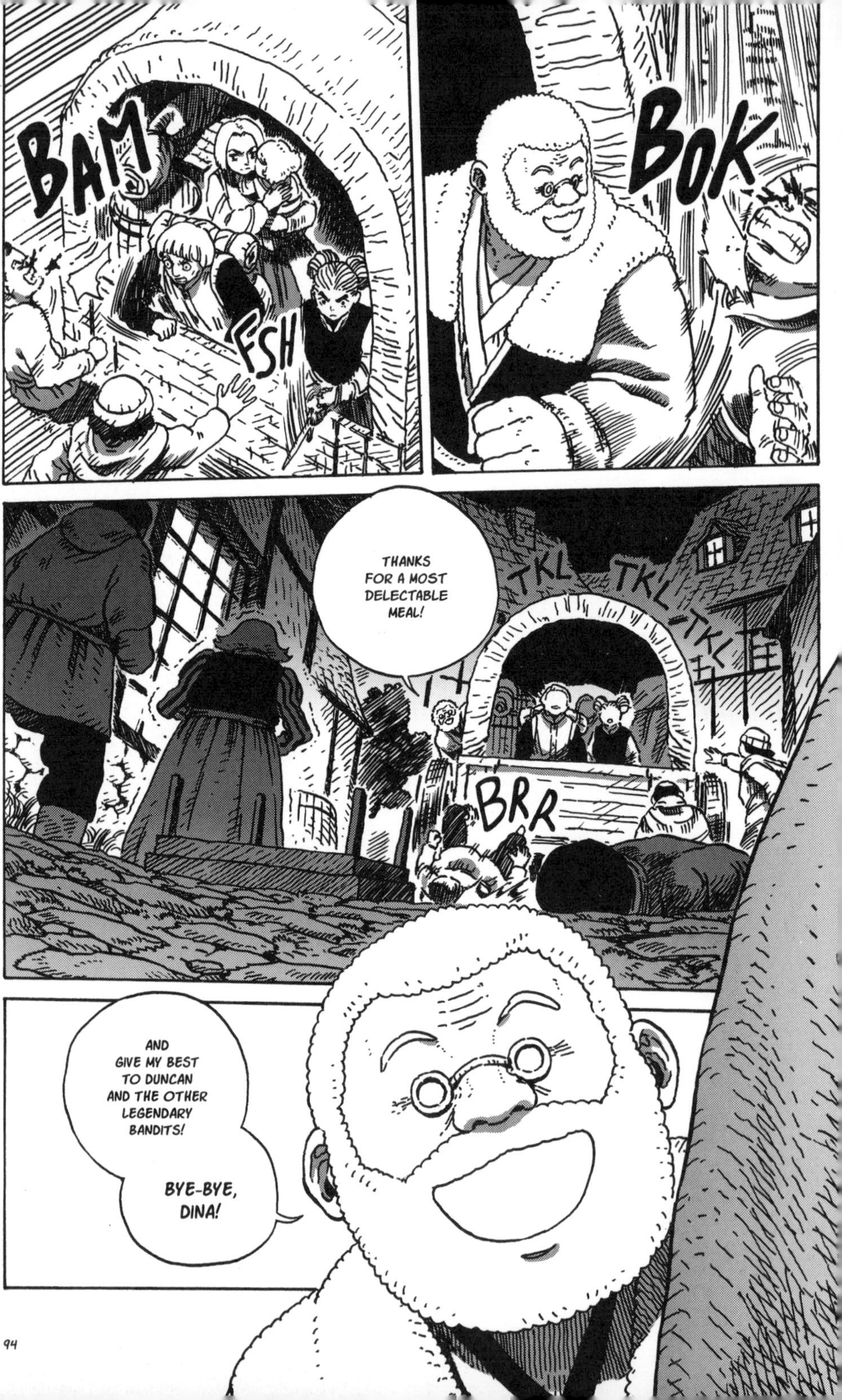

BAM
FSH
BOK
THANKS FOR A MOST DELECTABLE MEAL!
TKL TKL TKL
BRR
AND GIVE MY BEST TO DUNCAN AND THE OTHER LEGENDARY BANDITS!
BYE-BYE, DINA!

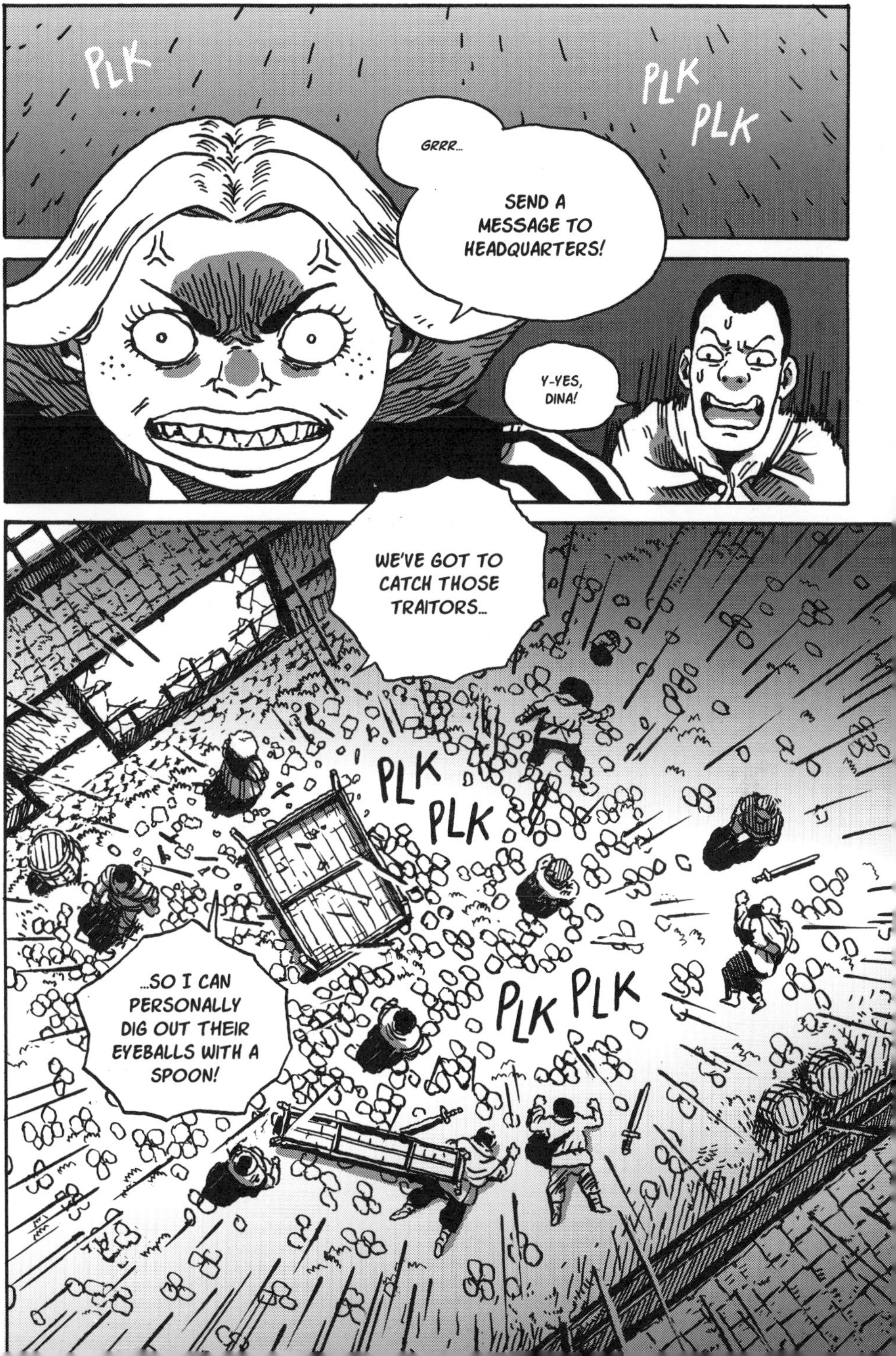
PLK
GRRR...
SEND A MESSAGE TO HEADQUARTERS!
PLK PLK
Y-YES, DINA!
WE'VE GOT TO CATCH THOSE TRAITORS...
PLK PLK
...SO I CAN PERSONALLY DIG OUT THEIR EYEBALLS WITH A SPOON!
PLK PLK

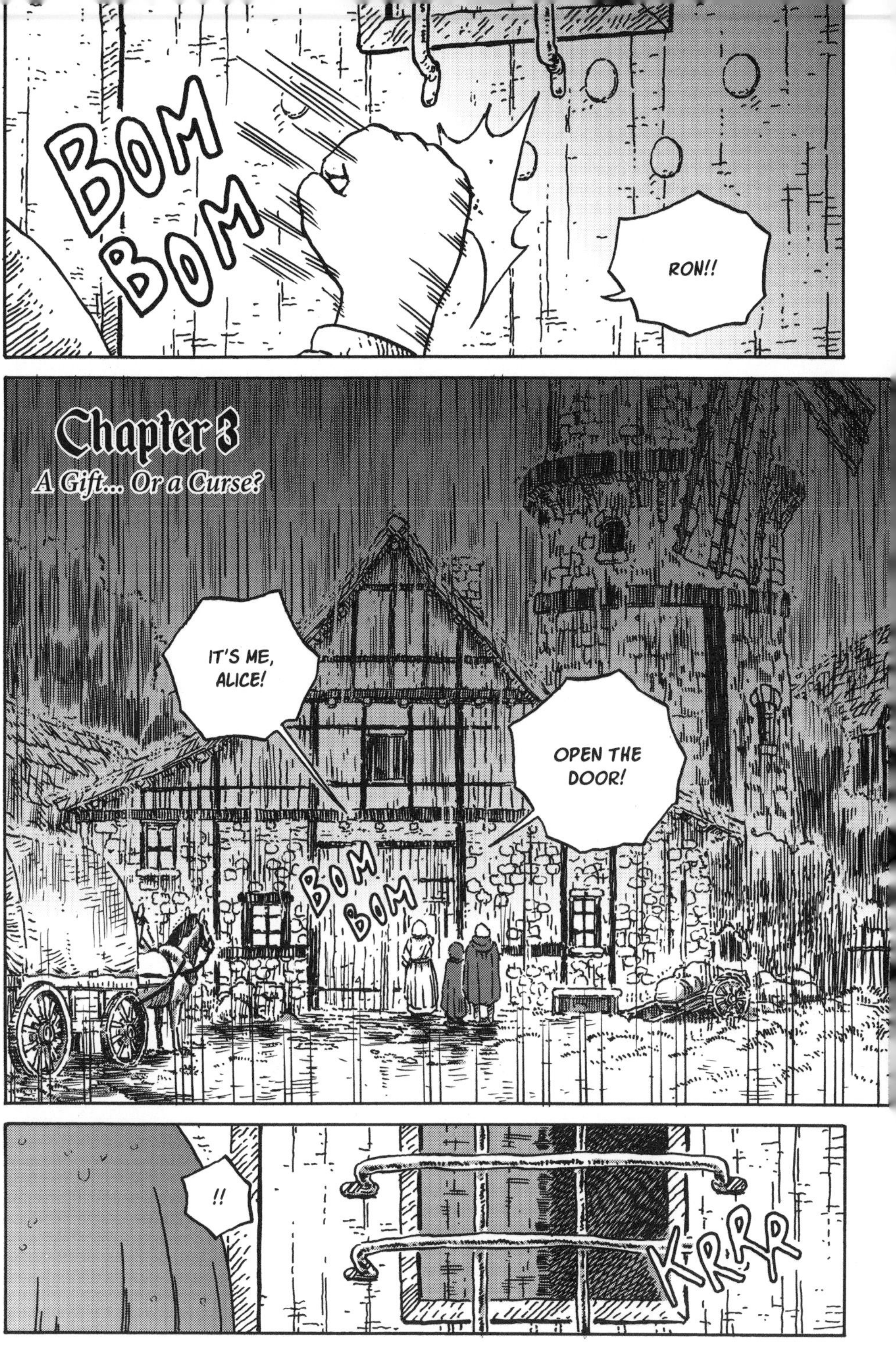
BOM
BOM
RON!!
Chapter 3
A Gift... Or a Curse?
IT'S ME, ALICE!
OPEN THE DOOR!
BOM BOM
!!
KRRR

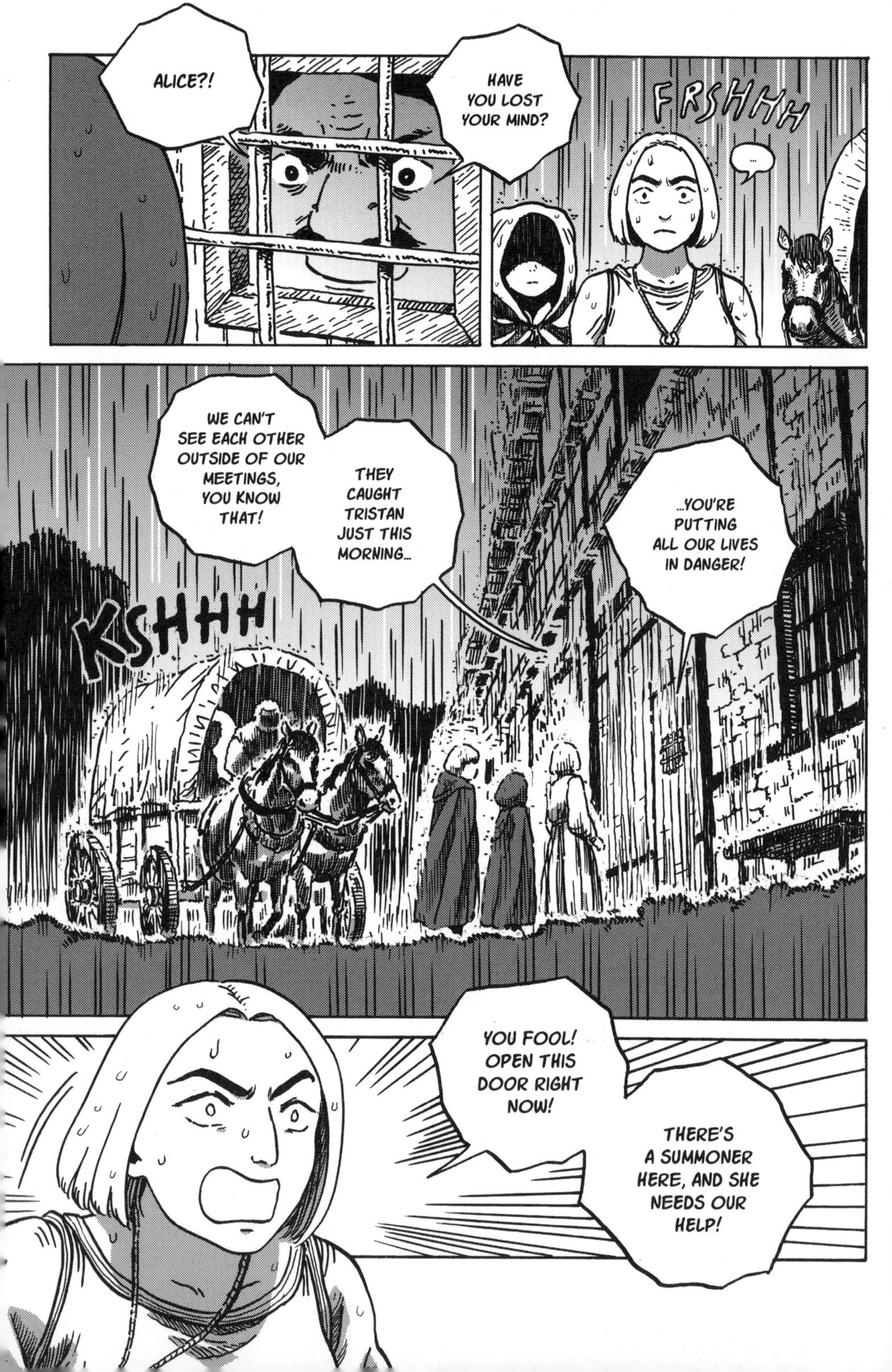
ALICE?!
HAVE YOU LOST YOUR MIND?
FRSHHH
...
WE CAN'T SEE EACH OTHER OUTSIDE OF OUR MEETINGS, YOU KNOW THAT!
THEY CAUGHT TRISTAN JUST THIS MORNING...
...YOU'RE PUTTING ALL OUR LIVES IN DANGER!
KSHHH
YOU FOOL! OPEN THIS DOOR RIGHT NOW!
THERE'S A SUMMONER HERE, AND SHE NEEDS OUR HELP!

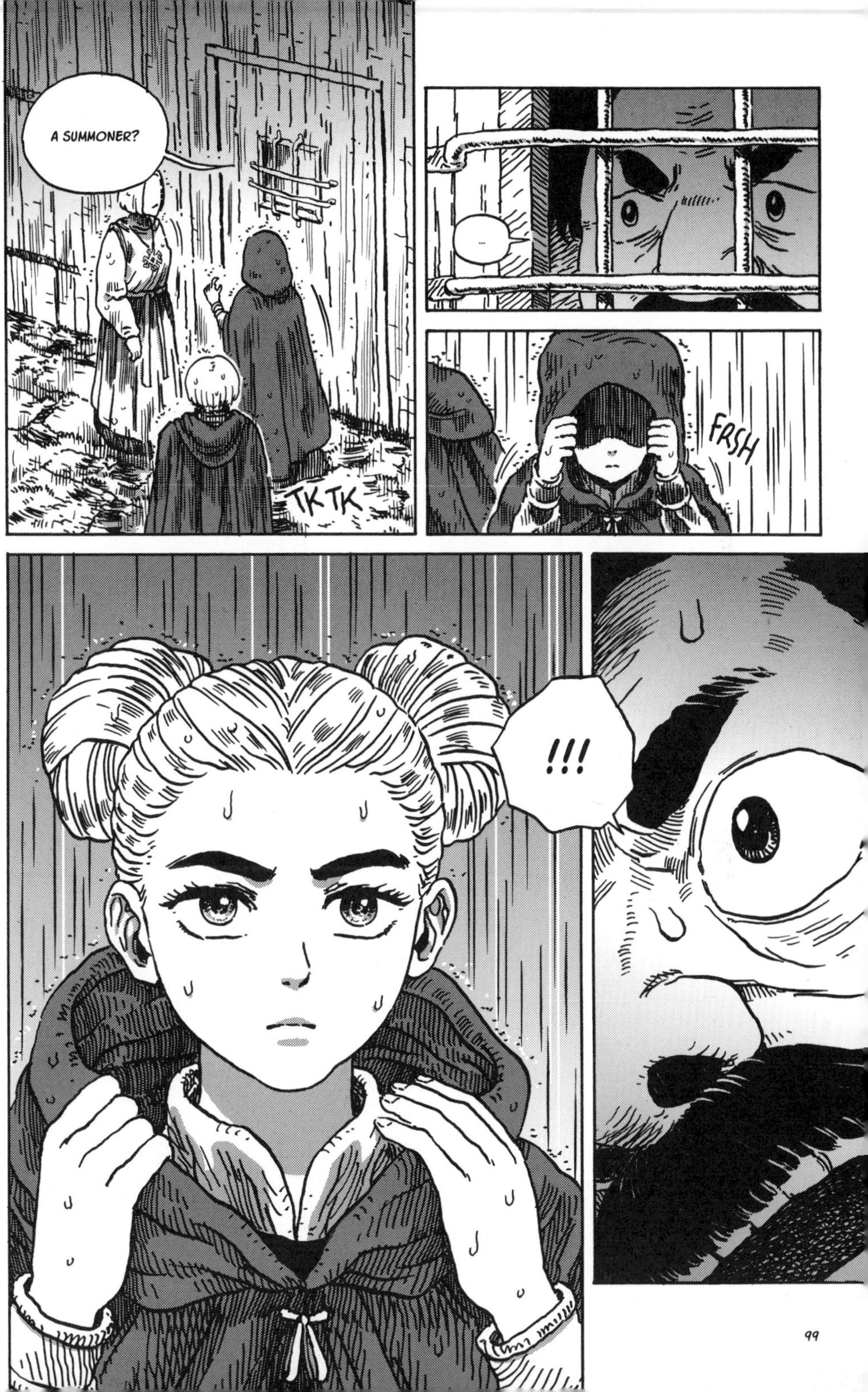
A SUMMONER?
TK TK
...
FRSH
!!!

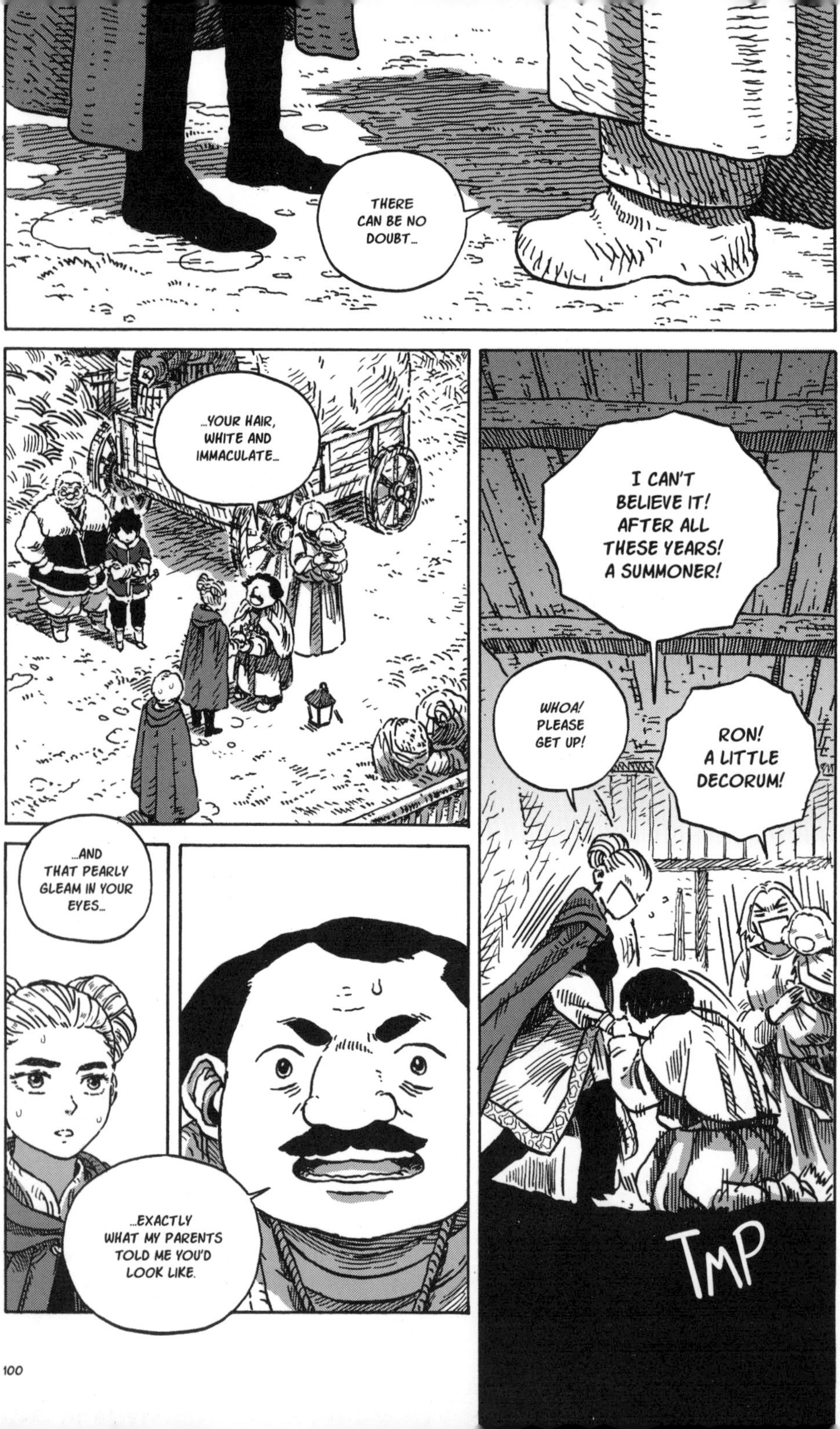

THERE CAN BE NO DOUBT...
...YOUR HAIR, WHITE AND IMMACULATE...
...AND THAT PEARLY GLEAM IN YOUR EYES...
...EXACTLY WHAT MY PARENTS TOLD ME YOU'D LOOK LIKE.
I CAN'T BELIEVE IT! AFTER ALL THESE YEARS! A SUMMONER!
WHOA! PLEASE GET UP!
RON! A LITTLE DECORUM!
TMP

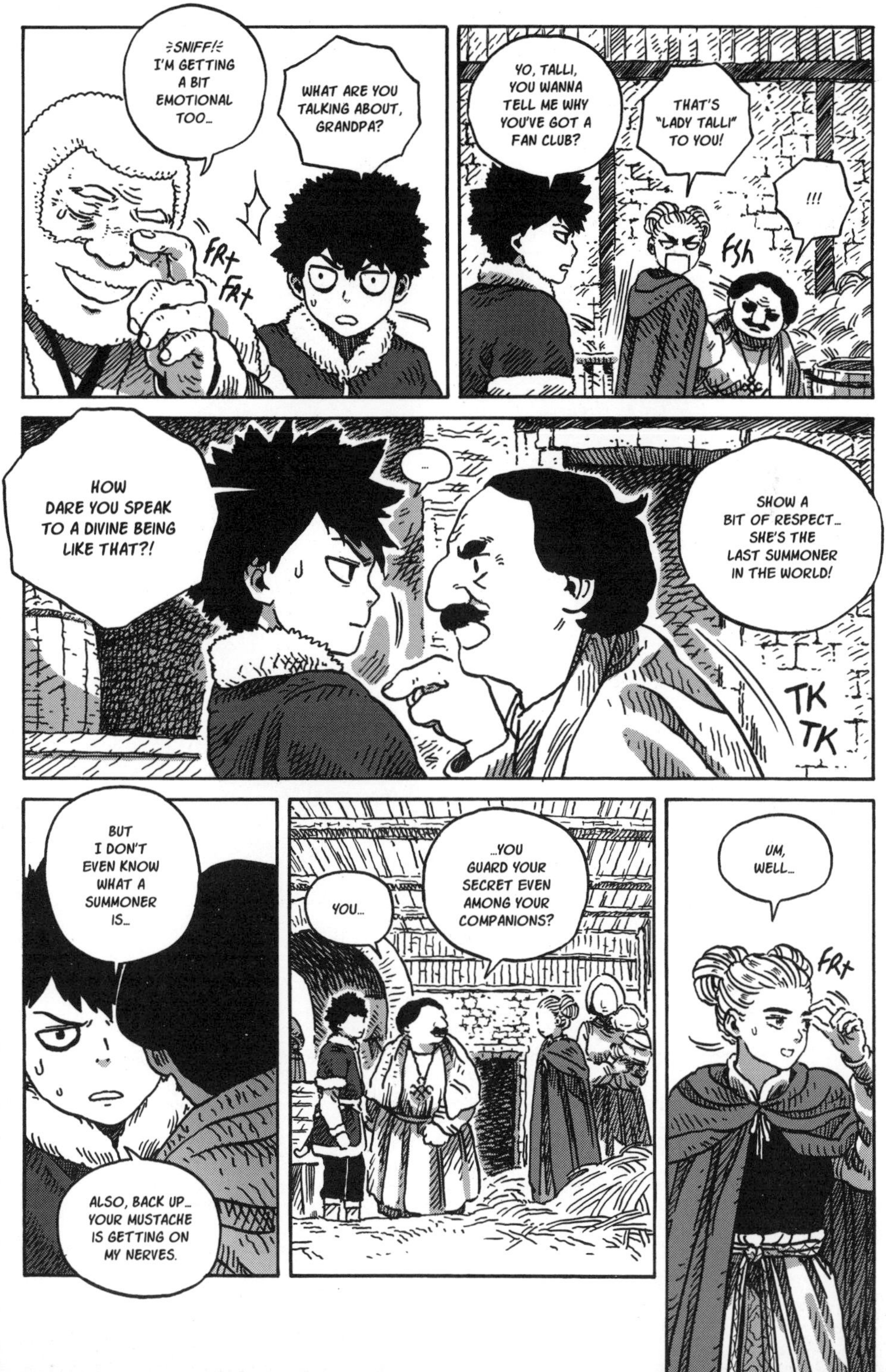

≑SNIFF!≑ I'M GETTING A BIT EMOTIONAL TOO...
FRt FRt
WHAT ARE YOU TALKING ABOUT, GRANDPA?
YO, TALLI, YOU WANNA TELL ME WHY YOU'VE GOT A FAN CLUB?
THAT'S "LADY TALLI" TO YOU!
!!!
FSh
HOW DARE YOU SPEAK TO A DIVINE BEING LIKE THAT?!
...
SHOW A BIT OF RESPECT... SHE'S THE LAST SUMMONER IN THE WORLD!
TK TK
BUT I DON'T EVEN KNOW WHAT A SUMMONER IS...
ALSO, BACK UP... YOUR MUSTACHE IS GETTING ON MY NERVES.
YOU...
...YOU GUARD YOUR SECRET EVEN AMONG YOUR COMPANIONS?
UM, WELL...
FRt

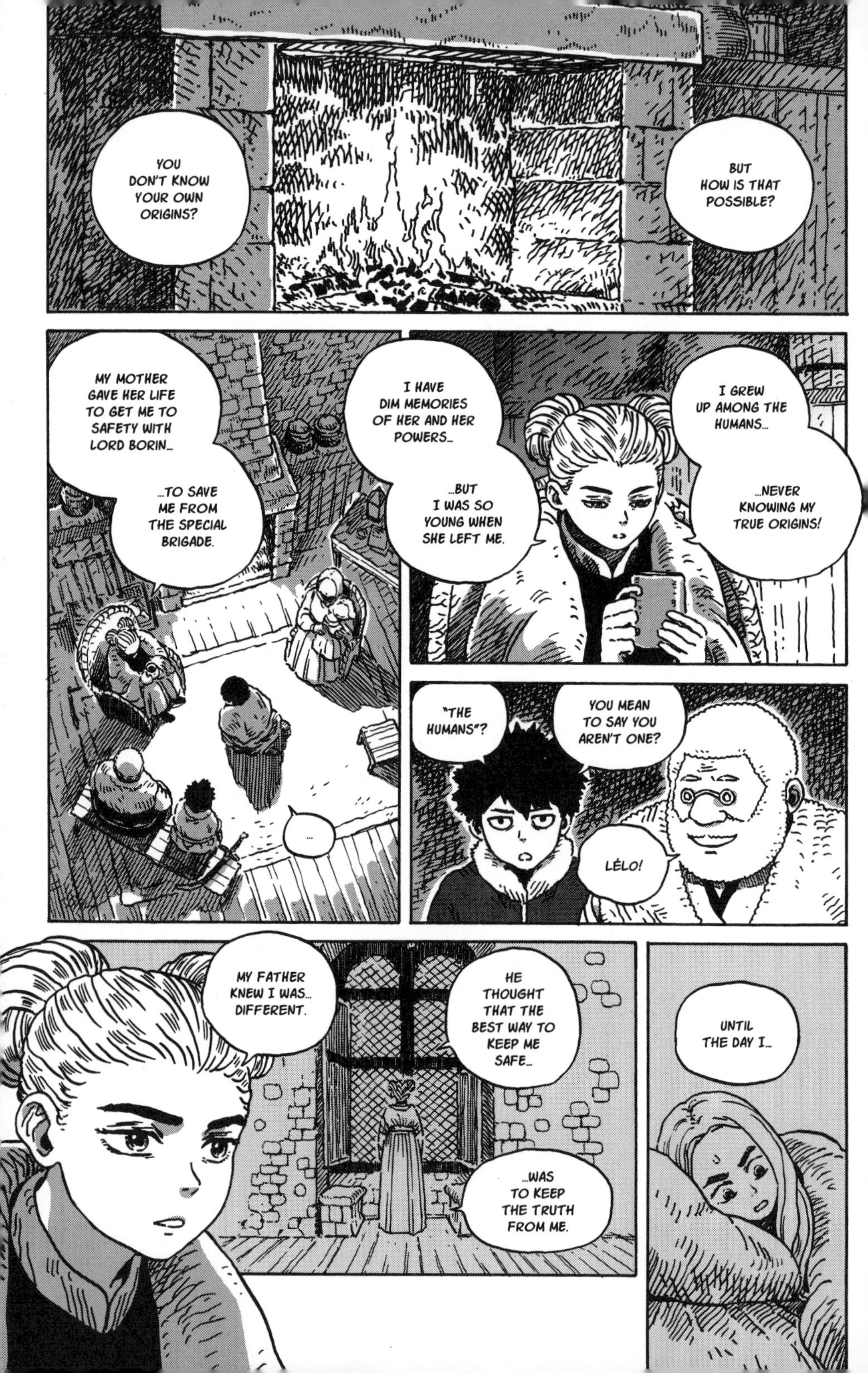
YOU DON'T KNOW YOUR OWN ORIGINS?
BUT HOW IS THAT POSSIBLE?
MY MOTHER GAVE HER LIFE TO GET ME TO SAFETY WITH LORD BORIN...
...TO SAVE ME FROM THE SPECIAL BRIGADE.
...
I HAVE DIM MEMORIES OF HER AND HER POWERS...
...BUT I WAS SO YOUNG WHEN SHE LEFT ME.
I GREW UP AMONG THE HUMANS...
...NEVER KNOWING MY TRUE ORIGINS!
"THE HUMANS"?
YOU MEAN TO SAY YOU AREN'T ONE?
LÉLO!
MY FATHER KNEW I WAS... DIFFERENT.
HE THOUGHT THAT THE BEST WAY TO KEEP ME SAFE...
...WAS TO KEEP THE TRUTH FROM ME.
UNTIL THE DAY I...

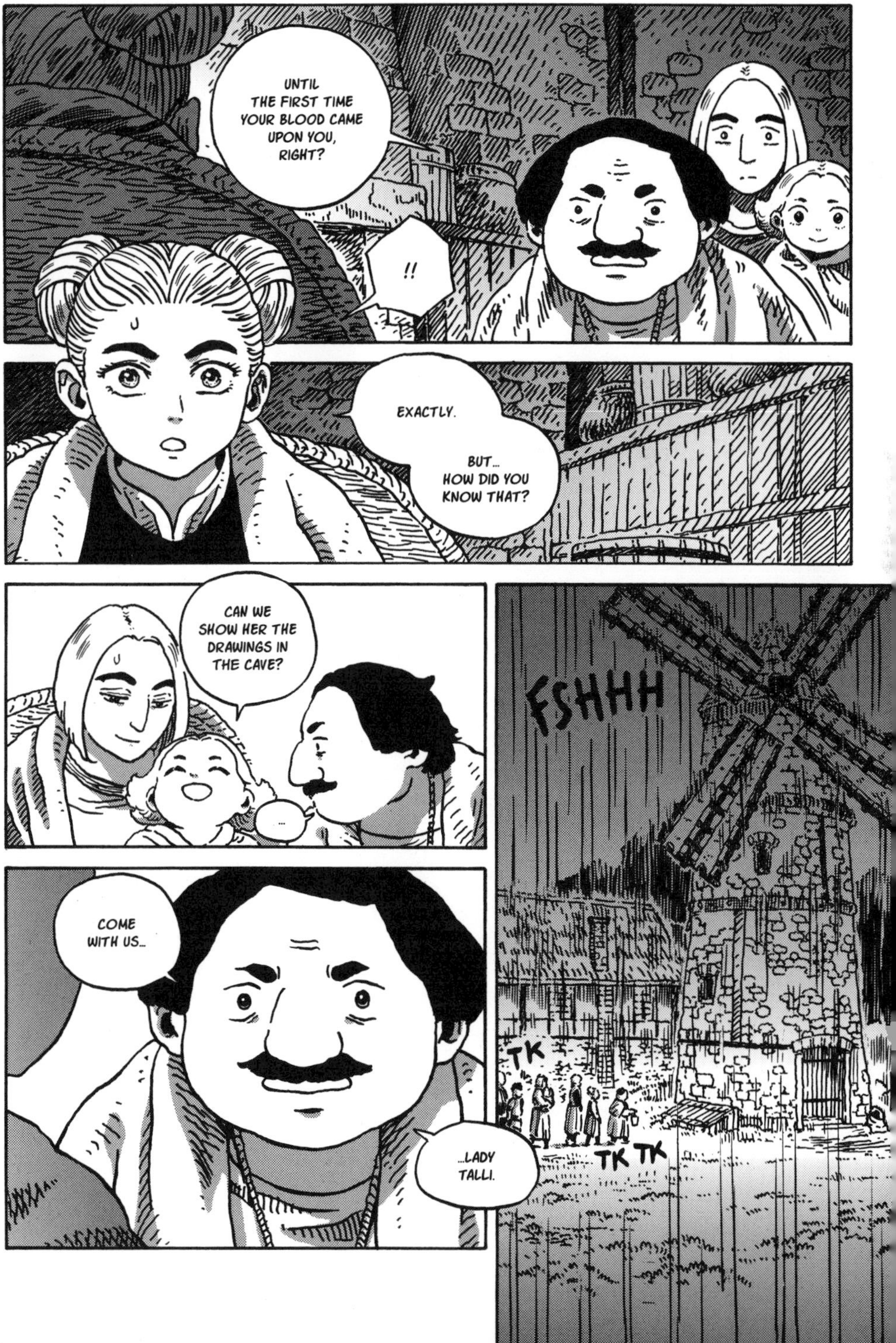
UNTIL THE FIRST TIME YOUR BLOOD CAME UPON YOU, RIGHT?
!!
EXACTLY.
BUT... HOW DID YOU KNOW THAT?
CAN WE SHOW HER THE DRAWINGS IN THE CAVE?
...
COME WITH US...
...LADY TALLI.
FSHHH
TK
TK TK

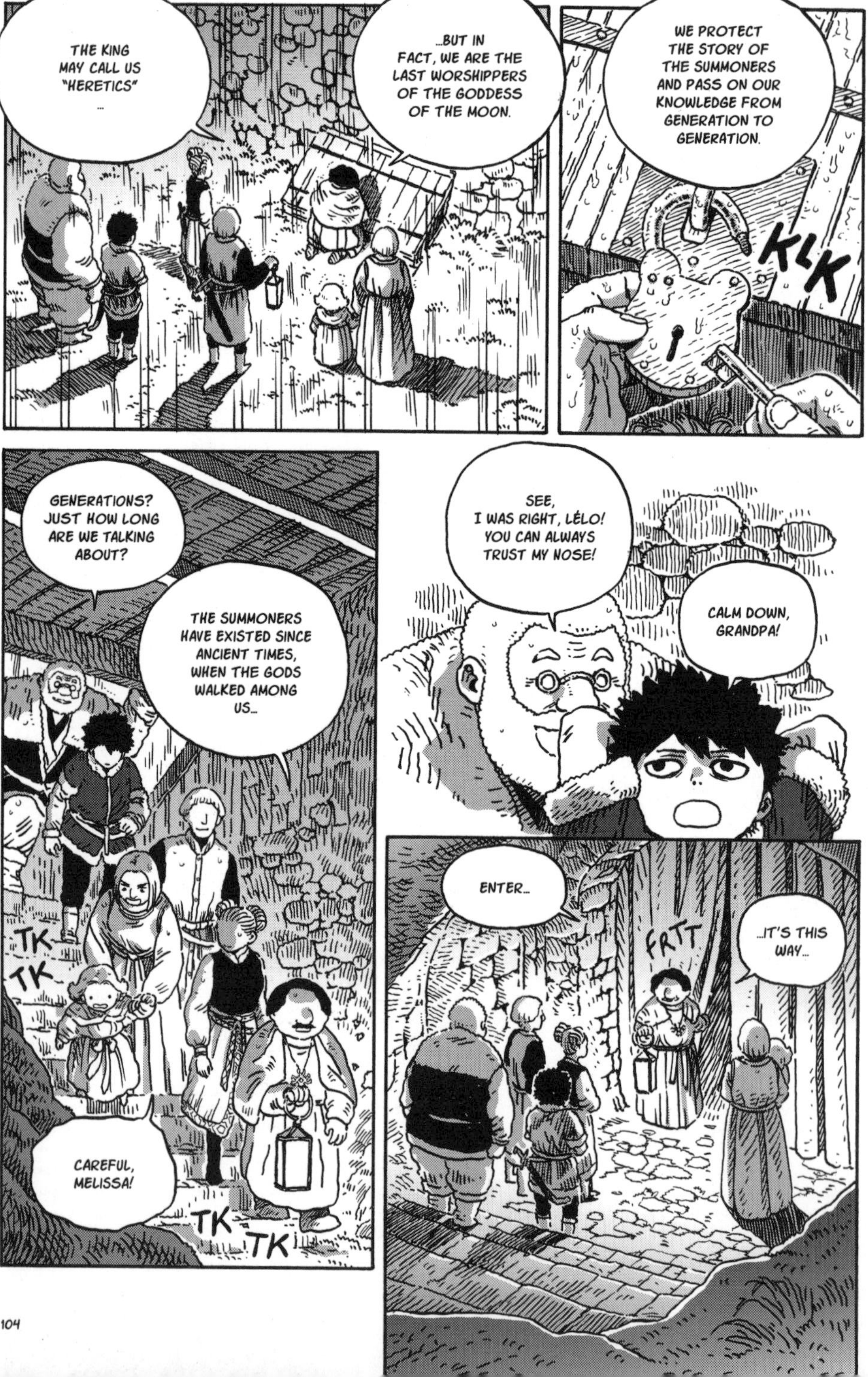
THE KING MAY CALL US "HERETICS" ...
...BUT IN FACT, WE ARE THE LAST WORSHIPPERS OF THE GODDESS OF THE MOON.
WE PROTECT THE STORY OF THE SUMMONERS AND PASS ON OUR KNOWLEDGE FROM GENERATION TO GENERATION.
KLK
GENERATIONS? JUST HOW LONG ARE WE TALKING ABOUT?
THE SUMMONERS HAVE EXISTED SINCE ANCIENT TIMES, WHEN THE GODS WALKED AMONG US...
TK
TK
CAREFUL, MELISSA!
TK
TK
SEE, I WAS RIGHT, LÉLO! YOU CAN ALWAYS TRUST MY NOSE!
CALM DOWN, GRANDPA!
ENTER...
FRTT
...IT'S THIS WAY...

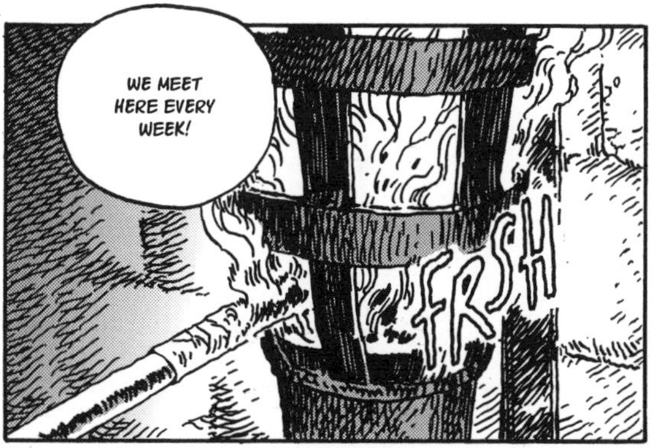
WE MEET HERE EVERY WEEK!
FRSH

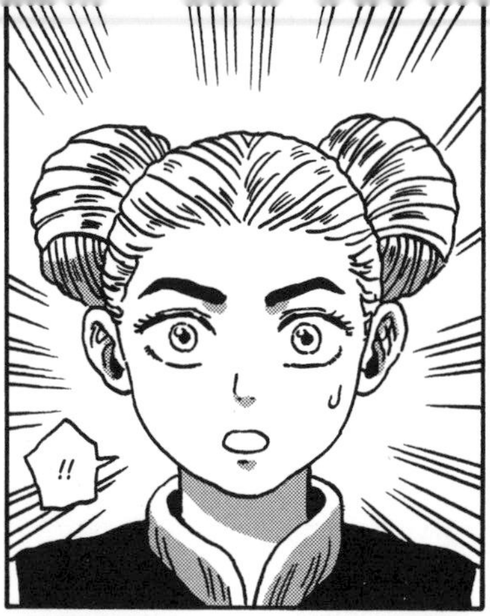
!!

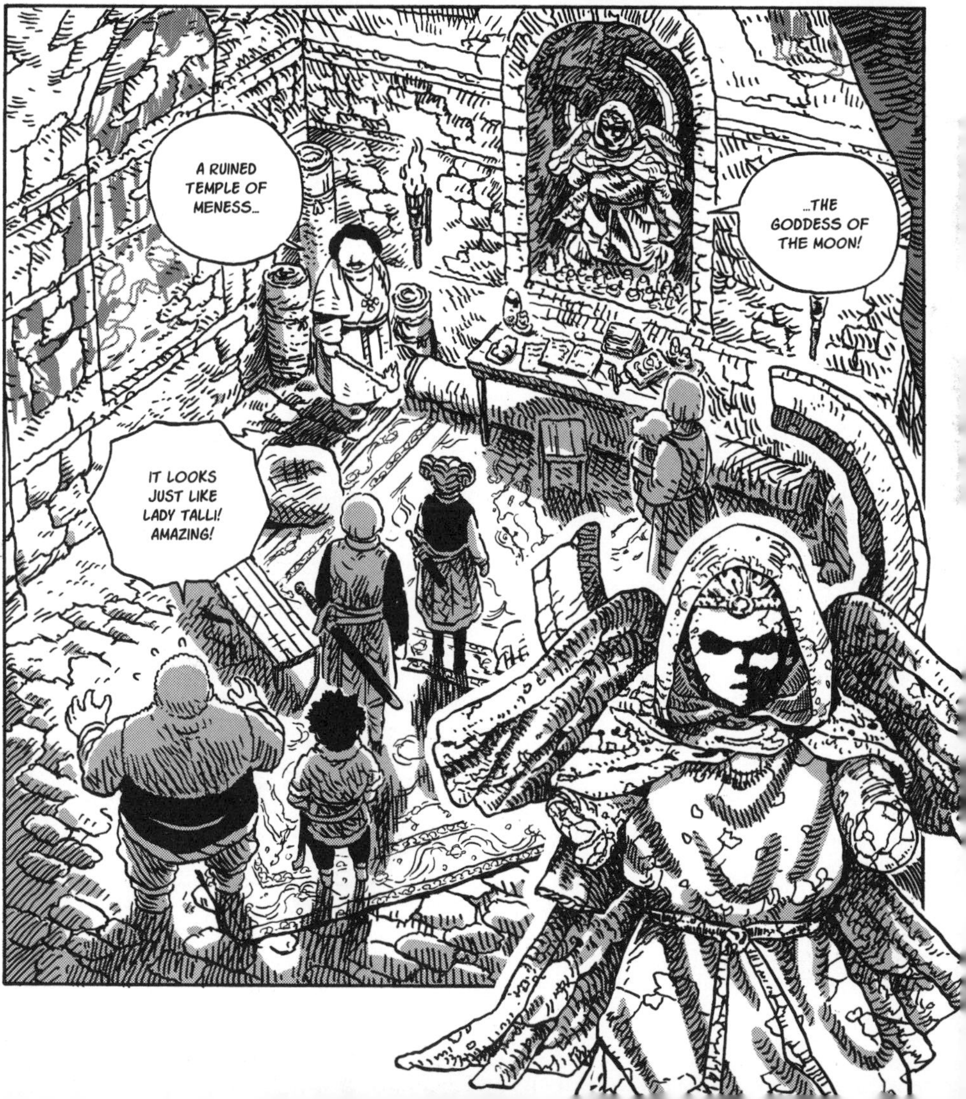
A RUINED TEMPLE OF MENESS...
...THE GODDESS OF THE MOON!
IT LOOKS JUST LIKE LADY TALLI! AMAZING!

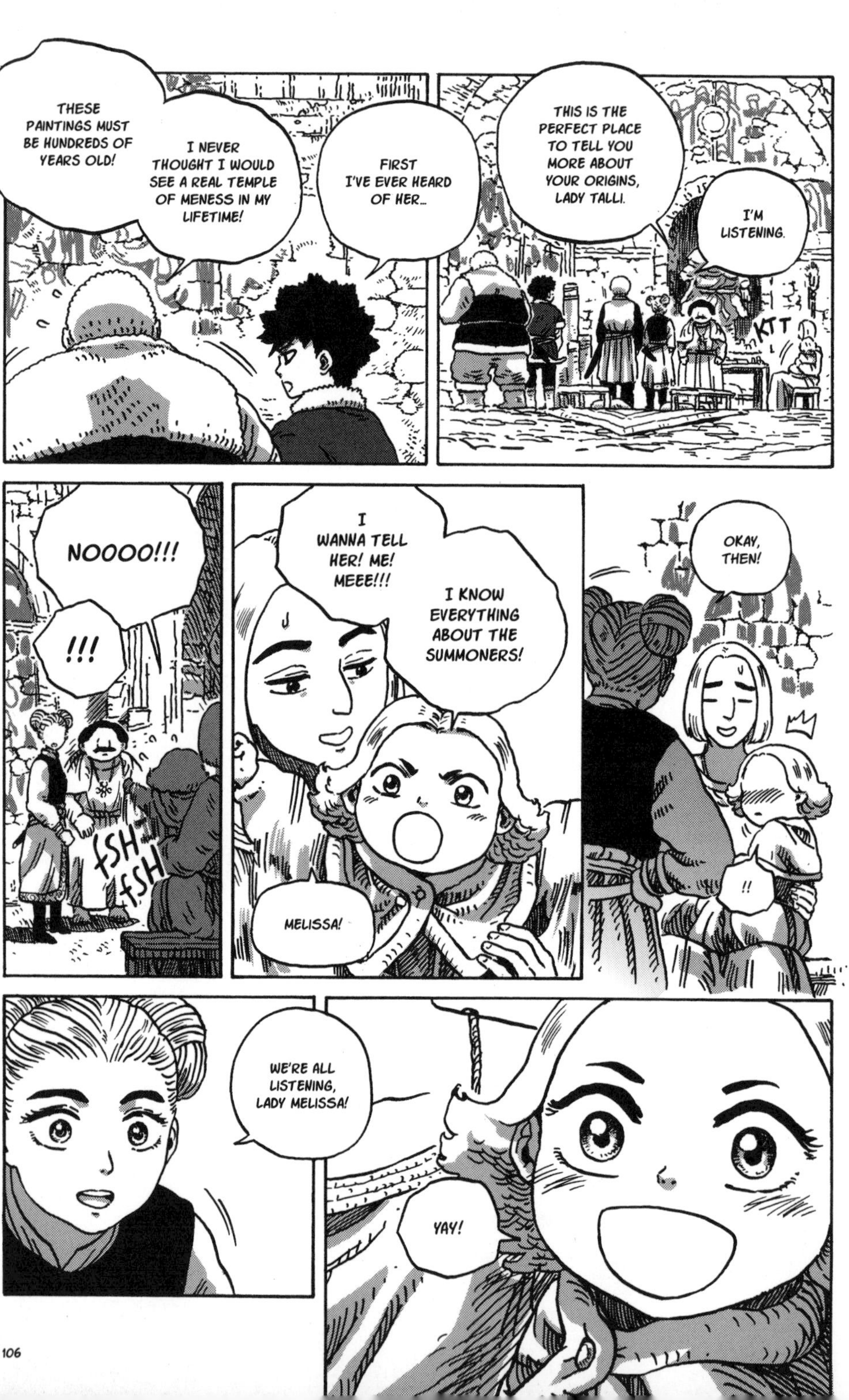
THESE PAINTINGS MUST BE HUNDREDS OF YEARS OLD!
I NEVER THOUGHT I WOULD SEE A REAL TEMPLE OF MENESS IN MY LIFETIME!
FIRST I'VE EVER HEARD OF HER...
THIS IS THE PERFECT PLACE TO TELL YOU MORE ABOUT YOUR ORIGINS, LADY TALLI.
I'M LISTENING.
KTT
NOOOO!!!
!!!
fSH fSH
I WANNA TELL HER! ME! MEEE!!!
I KNOW EVERYTHING ABOUT THE SUMMONERS!
MELISSA!
OKAY, THEN!
!!
WE'RE ALL LISTENING, LADY MELISSA!
YAY!

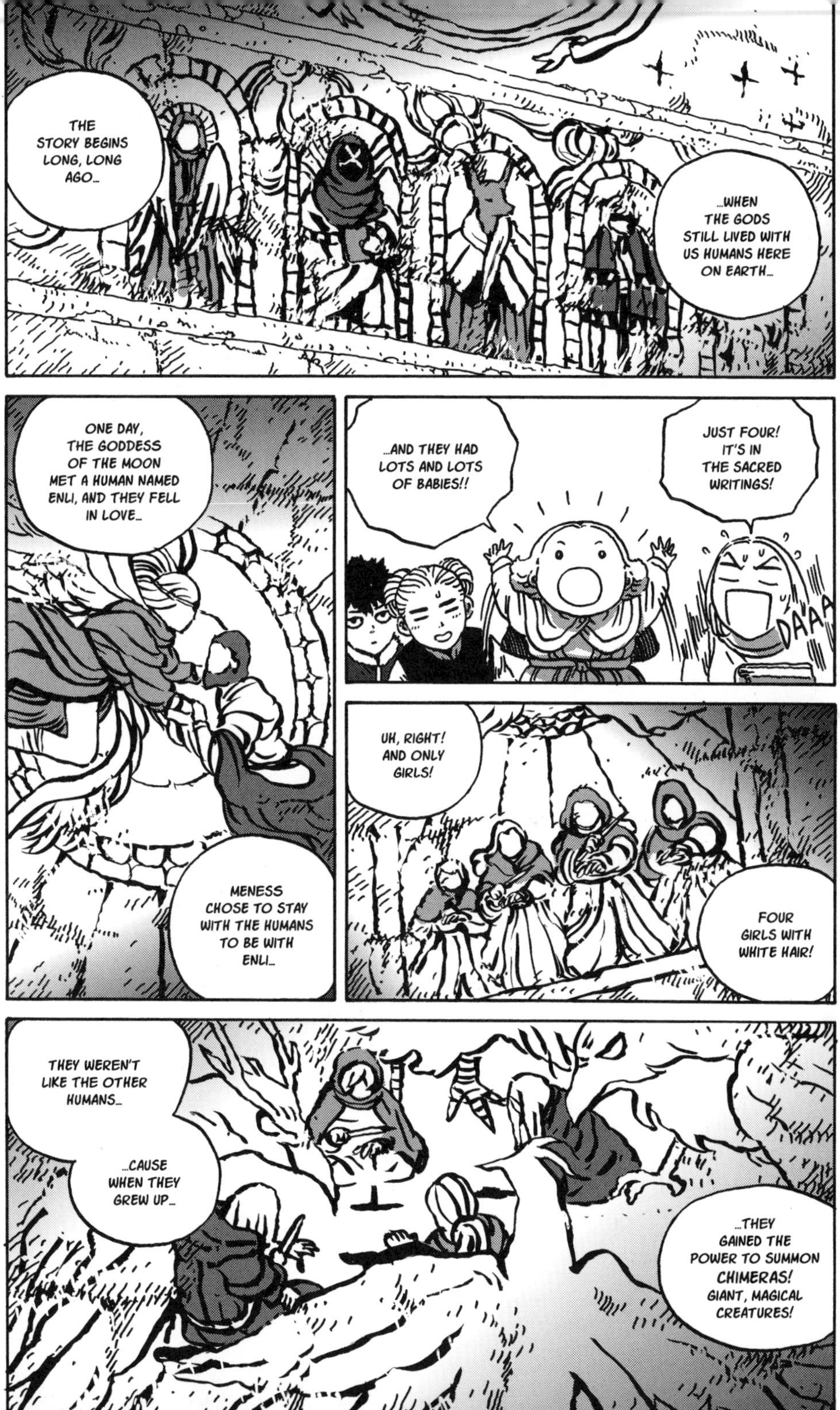
THE STORY BEGINS LONG, LONG AGO...
...WHEN THE GODS STILL LIVED WITH US HUMANS HERE ON EARTH...
ONE DAY, THE GODDESS OF THE MOON MET A HUMAN NAMED ENLI, AND THEY FELL IN LOVE...
MENESS CHOSE TO STAY WITH THE HUMANS TO BE WITH ENLI...
...AND THEY HAD LOTS AND LOTS OF BABIES!!
JUST FOUR! IT'S IN THE SACRED WRITINGS!
DAAA
UH, RIGHT! AND ONLY GIRLS!
FOUR GIRLS WITH WHITE HAIR!
THEY WEREN'T LIKE THE OTHER HUMANS...
...CAUSE WHEN THEY GREW UP...
...THEY GAINED THE POWER TO SUMMON CHIMERAS! GIANT, MAGICAL CREATURES!

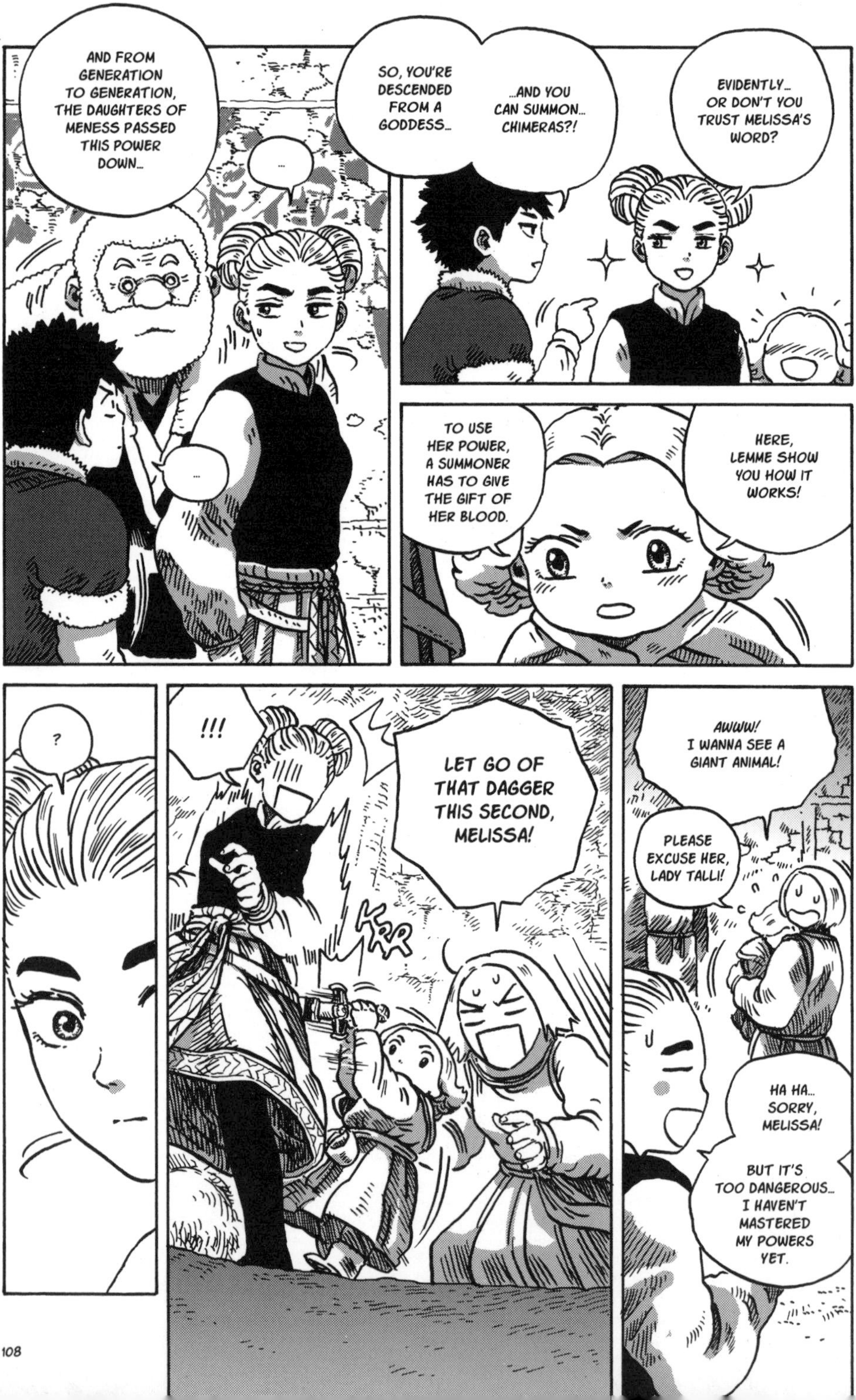
AND FROM GENERATION TO GENERATION, THE DAUGHTERS OF MENESS PASSED THIS POWER DOWN...
...
...
SO, YOU'RE DESCENDED FROM A GODDESS...
...AND YOU CAN SUMMON... CHIMERAS?!
EVIDENTLY... OR DON'T YOU TRUST MELISSA'S WORD?
TO USE HER POWER, A SUMMONER HAS TO GIVE THE GIFT OF HER BLOOD.
HERE, LEMME SHOW YOU HOW IT WORKS!
?
!!!
LET GO OF THAT DAGGER THIS SECOND, MELISSA!
KRR
AWWW! I WANNA SEE A GIANT ANIMAL!
PLEASE EXCUSE HER, LADY TALLI!
HA HA... SORRY, MELISSA!
BUT IT'S TOO DANGEROUS... I HAVEN'T MASTERED MY POWERS YET.

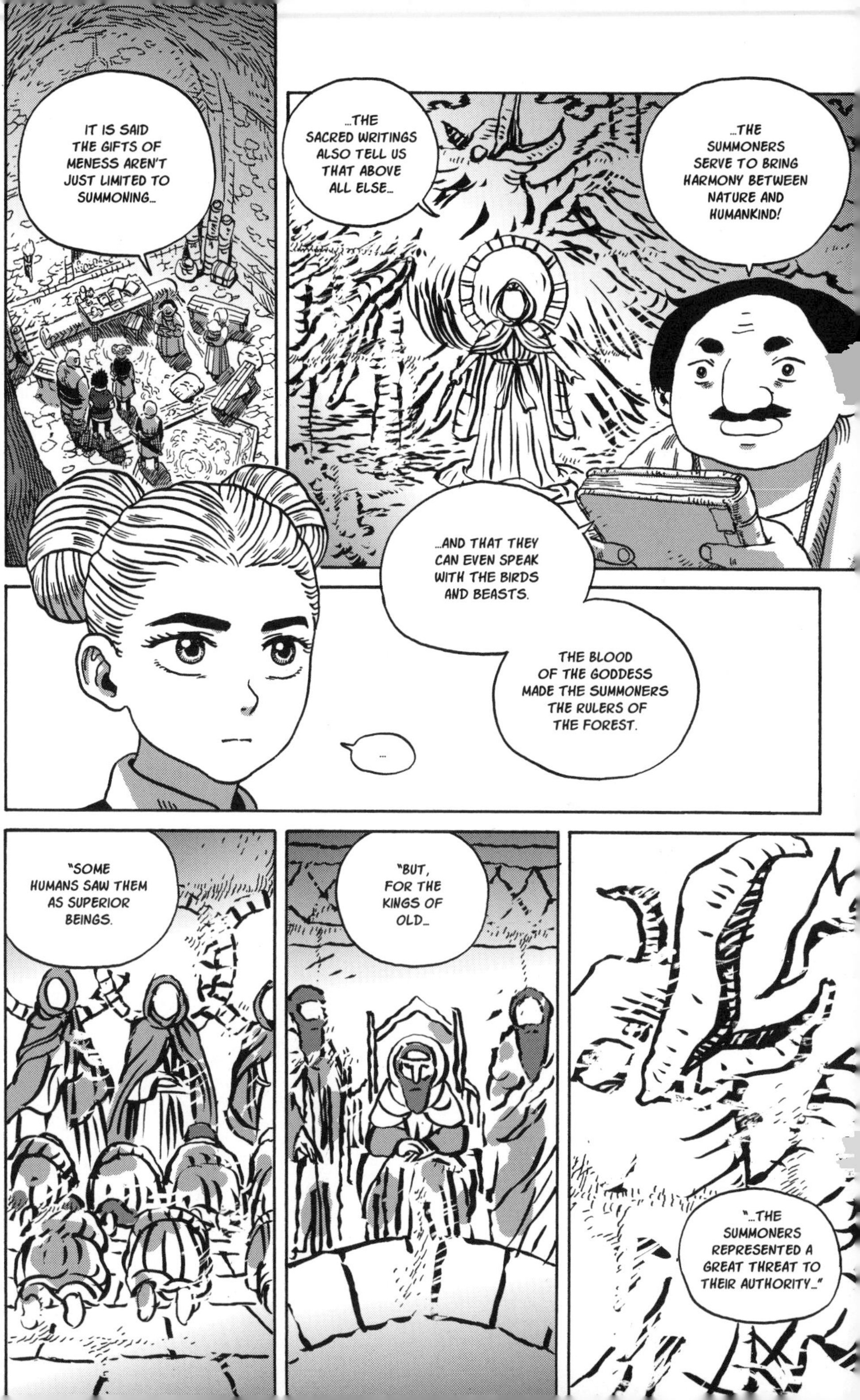
IT IS SAID THE GIFTS OF MENESS AREN'T JUST LIMITED TO SUMMONING...
...THE SACRED WRITINGS ALSO TELL US THAT ABOVE ALL ELSE...
...THE SUMMONERS SERVE TO BRING HARMONY BETWEEN NATURE AND HUMANKIND!
...AND THAT THEY CAN EVEN SPEAK WITH THE BIRDS AND BEASTS.
THE BLOOD OF THE GODDESS MADE THE SUMMONERS THE RULERS OF THE FOREST.
...
"SOME HUMANS SAW THEM AS SUPERIOR BEINGS.
"BUT, FOR THE KINGS OF OLD...
"...THE SUMMONERS REPRESENTED A GREAT THREAT TO THEIR AUTHORITY..."

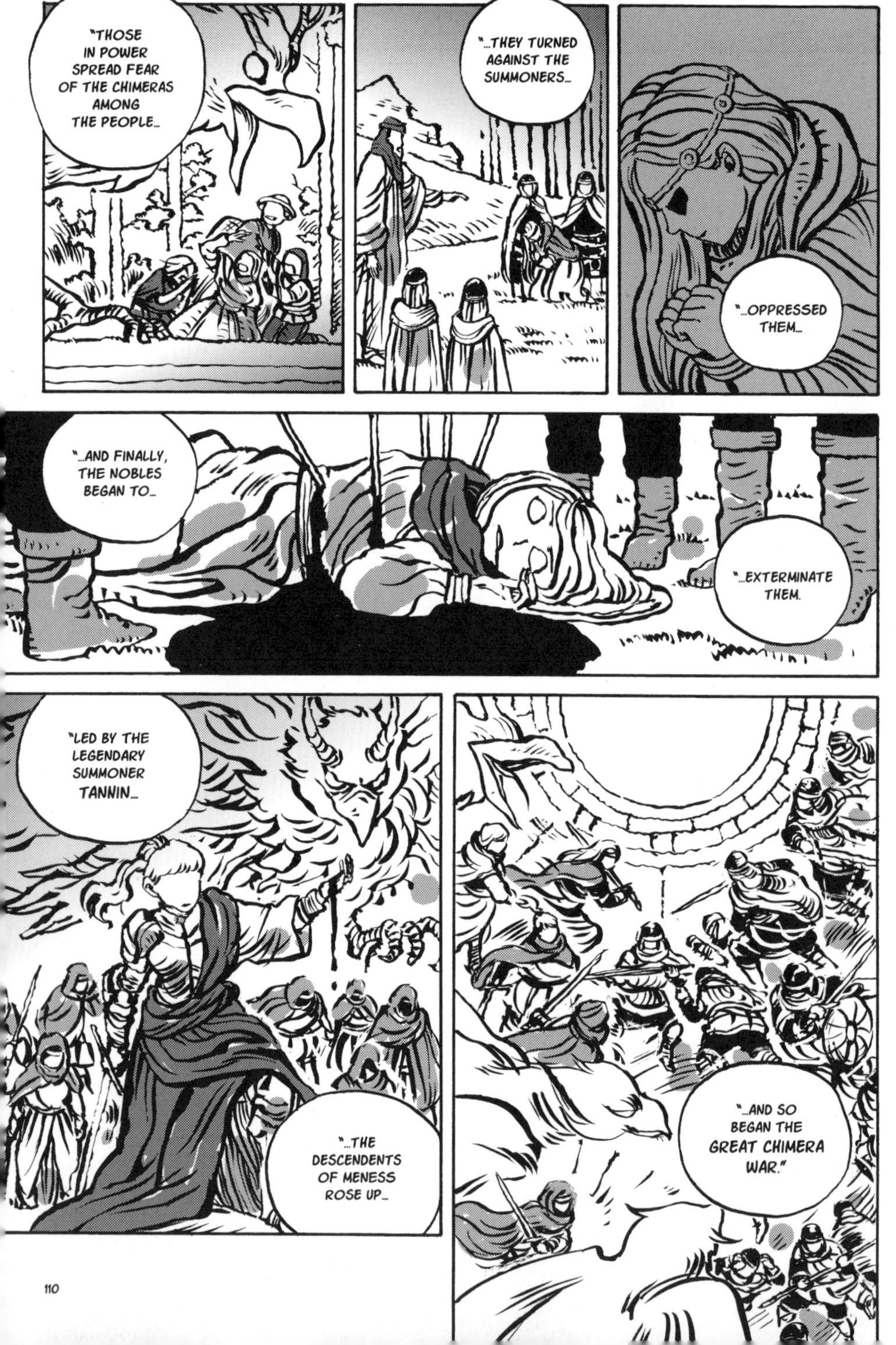
"THOSE IN POWER SPREAD FEAR OF THE CHIMERAS AMONG THE PEOPLE...
"...THEY TURNED AGAINST THE SUMMONERS...
"...OPPRESSED THEM...
"...AND FINALLY, THE NOBLES BEGAN TO...
"...EXTERMINATE THEM.
"LED BY THE LEGENDARY SUMMONER TANNIN...
"...THE DESCENDENTS OF MENESS ROSE UP...
"...AND SO BEGAN THE GREAT CHIMERA WAR."

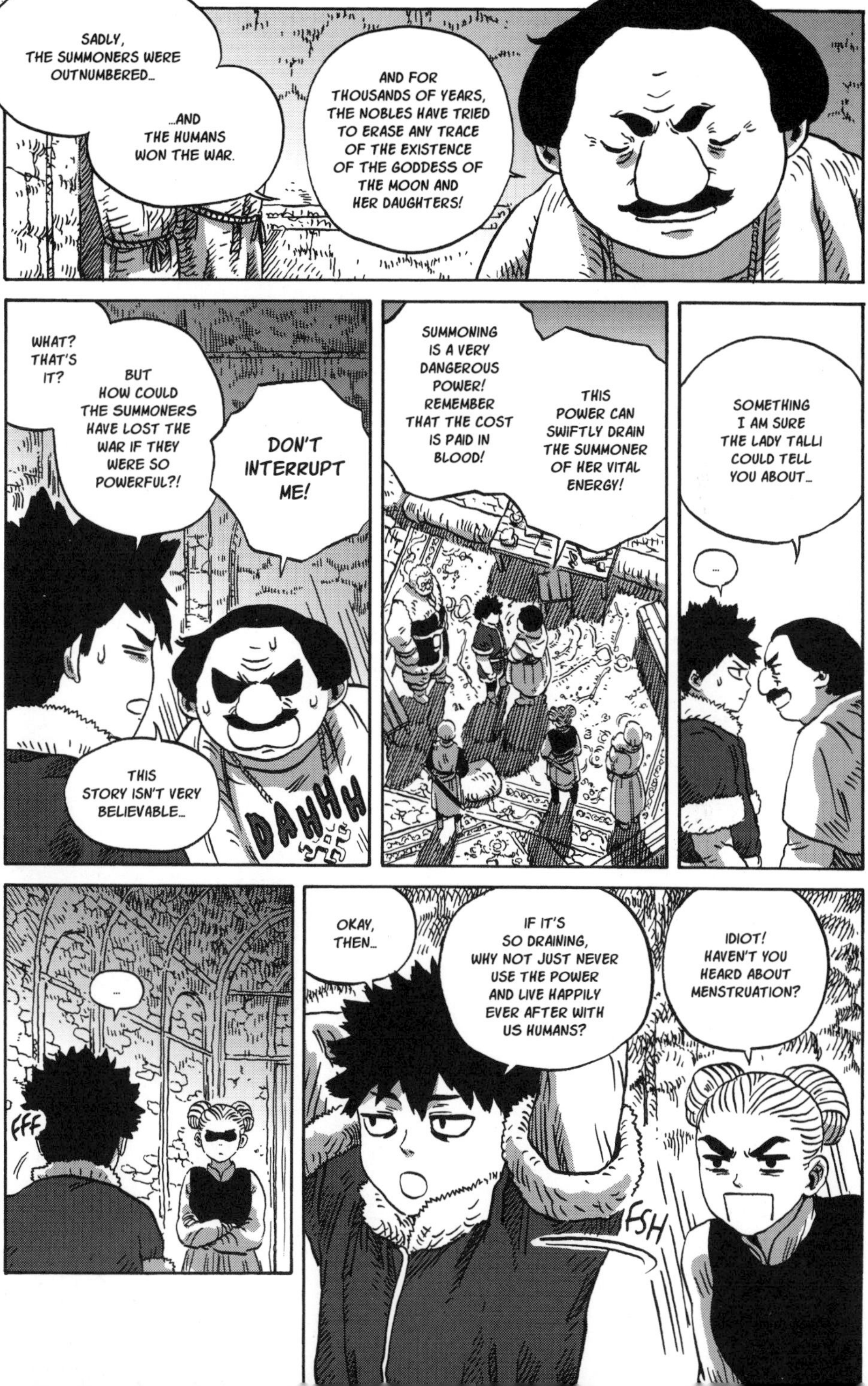
SADLY, THE SUMMONERS WERE OUTNUMBERED...
...AND THE HUMANS WON THE WAR.
AND FOR THOUSANDS OF YEARS, THE NOBLES HAVE TRIED TO ERASE ANY TRACE OF THE EXISTENCE OF THE GODDESS OF THE MOON AND HER DAUGHTERS!
WHAT? THAT'S IT?
BUT HOW COULD THE SUMMONERS HAVE LOST THE WAR IF THEY WERE SO POWERFUL?!
DON'T INTERRUPT ME!
THIS STORY ISN'T VERY BELIEVABLE...
DAHHH
SUMMONING IS A VERY DANGEROUS POWER! REMEMBER THAT THE COST IS PAID IN BLOOD!
THIS POWER CAN SWIFTLY DRAIN THE SUMMONER OF HER VITAL ENERGY!
...
SOMETHING I AM SURE THE LADY TALLI COULD TELL YOU ABOUT...
...
FFF
OKAY, THEN...
IF IT'S SO DRAINING, WHY NOT JUST NEVER USE THE POWER AND LIVE HAPPILY EVER AFTER WITH US HUMANS?
IDIOT! HAVEN'T YOU HEARD ABOUT MENSTRUATION?
FSH

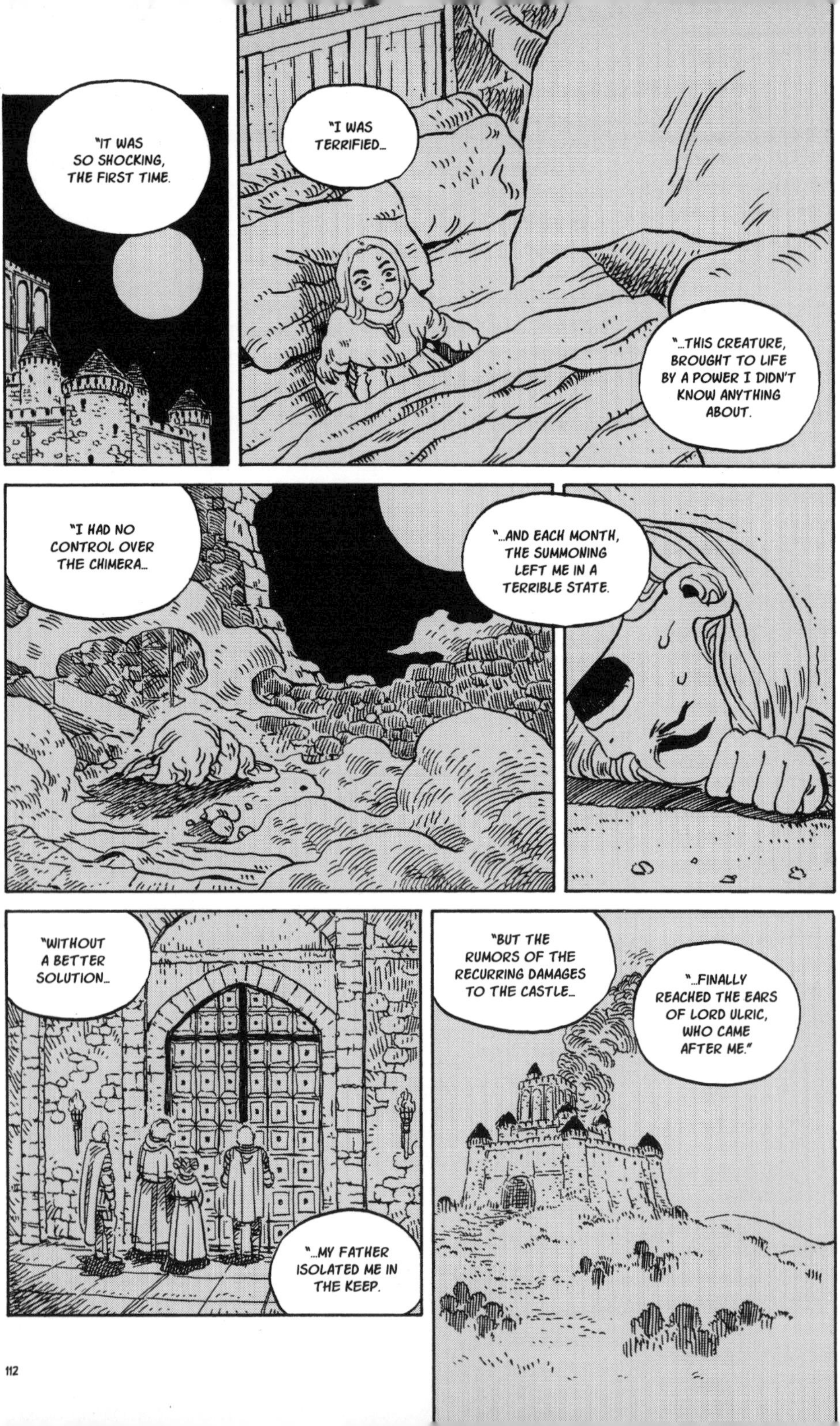
"IT WAS SO SHOCKING, THE FIRST TIME.
"I WAS TERRIFIED...
"...THIS CREATURE, BROUGHT TO LIFE BY A POWER I DIDN'T KNOW ANYTHING ABOUT.
"I HAD NO CONTROL OVER THE CHIMERA...
"...AND EACH MONTH, THE SUMMONING LEFT ME IN A TERRIBLE STATE.
"WITHOUT A BETTER SOLUTION...
"...MY FATHER ISOLATED ME IN THE KEEP.
"BUT THE RUMORS OF THE RECURRING DAMAGES TO THE CASTLE...
"...FINALLY REACHED THE EARS OF LORD ULRIC, WHO CAME AFTER ME."

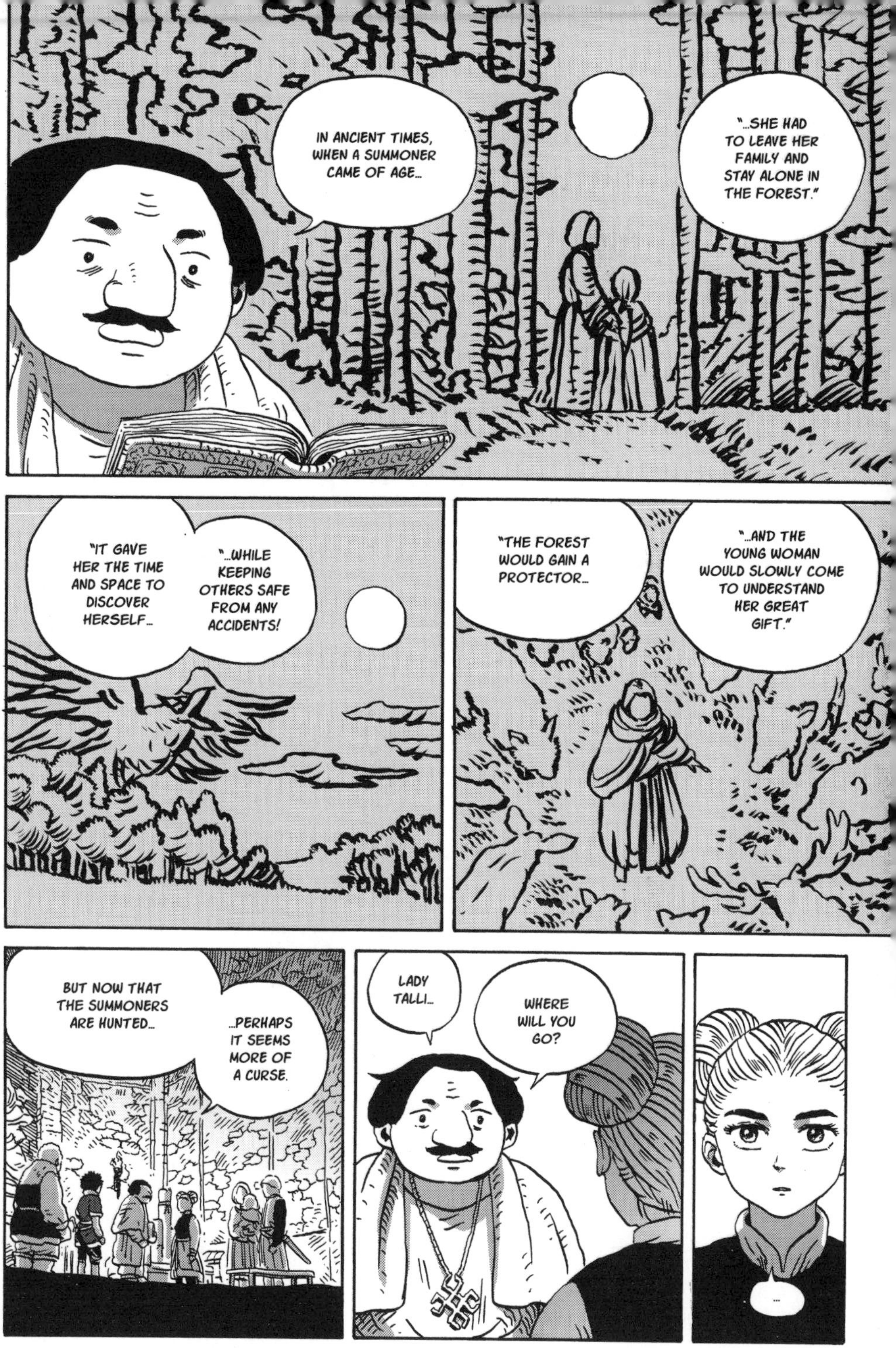
IN ANCIENT TIMES, WHEN A SUMMONER CAME OF AGE...
"...SHE HAD TO LEAVE HER FAMILY AND STAY ALONE IN THE FOREST."
"IT GAVE HER THE TIME AND SPACE TO DISCOVER HERSELF...
"...WHILE KEEPING OTHERS SAFE FROM ANY ACCIDENTS!
"THE FOREST WOULD GAIN A PROTECTOR...
"...AND THE YOUNG WOMAN WOULD SLOWLY COME TO UNDERSTAND HER GREAT GIFT."
BUT NOW THAT THE SUMMONERS ARE HUNTED...
...PERHAPS IT SEEMS MORE OF A CURSE.
LADY TALLI...
WHERE WILL YOU GO?
...

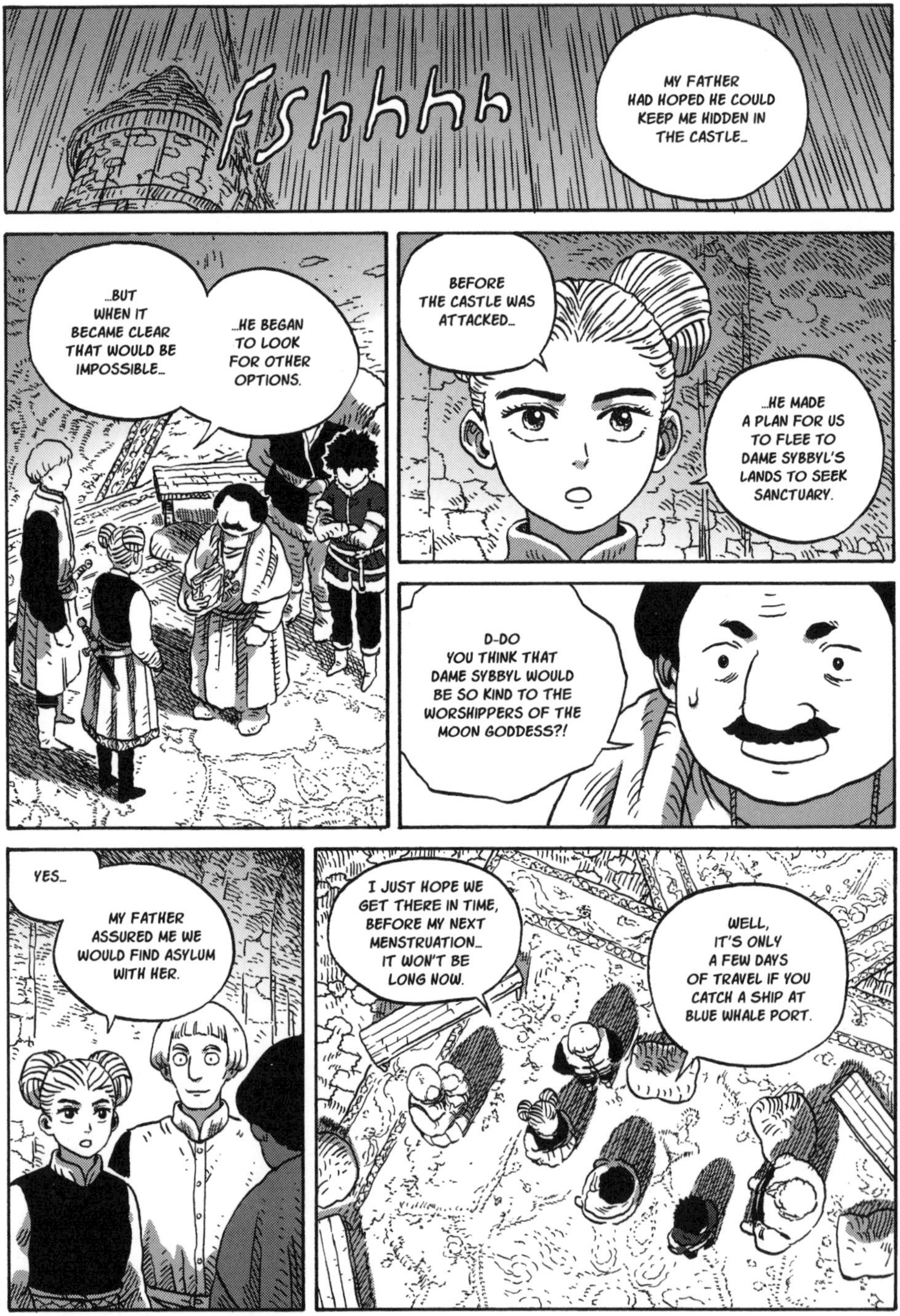
FSHHHH
MY FATHER HAD HOPED HE COULD KEEP ME HIDDEN IN THE CASTLE...
...BUT WHEN IT BECAME CLEAR THAT WOULD BE IMPOSSIBLE...
...HE BEGAN TO LOOK FOR OTHER OPTIONS.
BEFORE THE CASTLE WAS ATTACKED...
...HE MADE A PLAN FOR US TO FLEE TO DAME SYBBYL'S LANDS TO SEEK SANCTUARY.
D-DO YOU THINK THAT DAME SYBBYL WOULD BE SO KIND TO THE WORSHIPPERS OF THE MOON GODDESS?!
YES...
MY FATHER ASSURED ME WE WOULD FIND ASYLUM WITH HER.
I JUST HOPE WE GET THERE IN TIME, BEFORE MY NEXT MENSTRUATION... IT WON'T BE LONG NOW.
WELL, IT'S ONLY A FEW DAYS OF TRAVEL IF YOU CATCH A SHIP AT BLUE WHALE PORT.

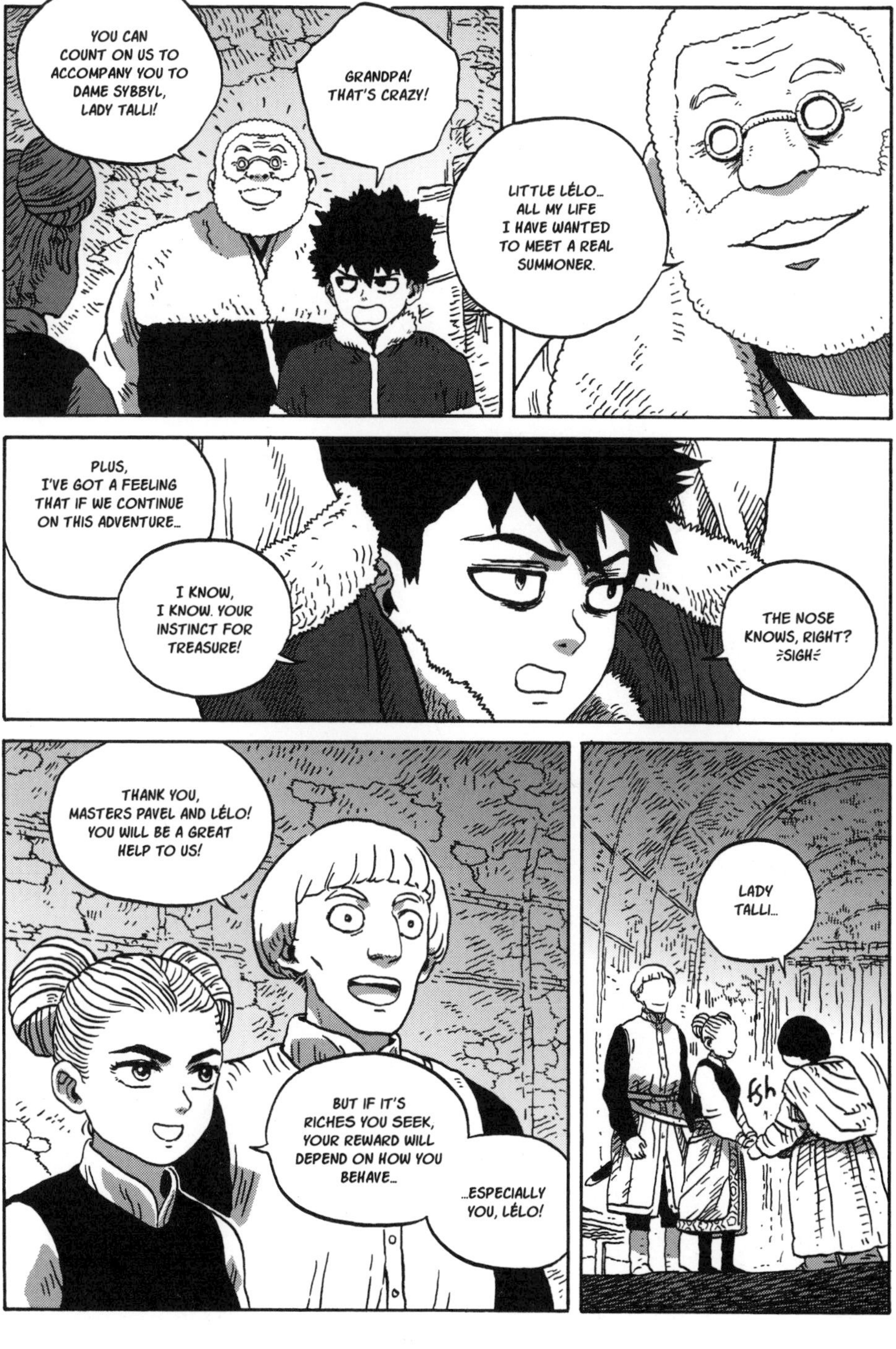
YOU CAN COUNT ON US TO ACCOMPANY YOU TO DAME SYBBYL, LADY TALLI!
GRANDPA! THAT'S CRAZY!
LITTLE LÉLO... ALL MY LIFE I HAVE WANTED TO MEET A REAL SUMMONER.
PLUS, I'VE GOT A FEELING THAT IF WE CONTINUE ON THIS ADVENTURE...
I KNOW, I KNOW. YOUR INSTINCT FOR TREASURE!
THE NOSE KNOWS, RIGHT? SIGH
THANK YOU, MASTERS PAVEL AND LÉLO! YOU WILL BE A GREAT HELP TO US!
BUT IF IT'S RICHES YOU SEEK, YOUR REWARD WILL DEPEND ON HOW YOU BEHAVE...
...ESPECIALLY YOU, LÉLO!
LADY TALLI...
fsh

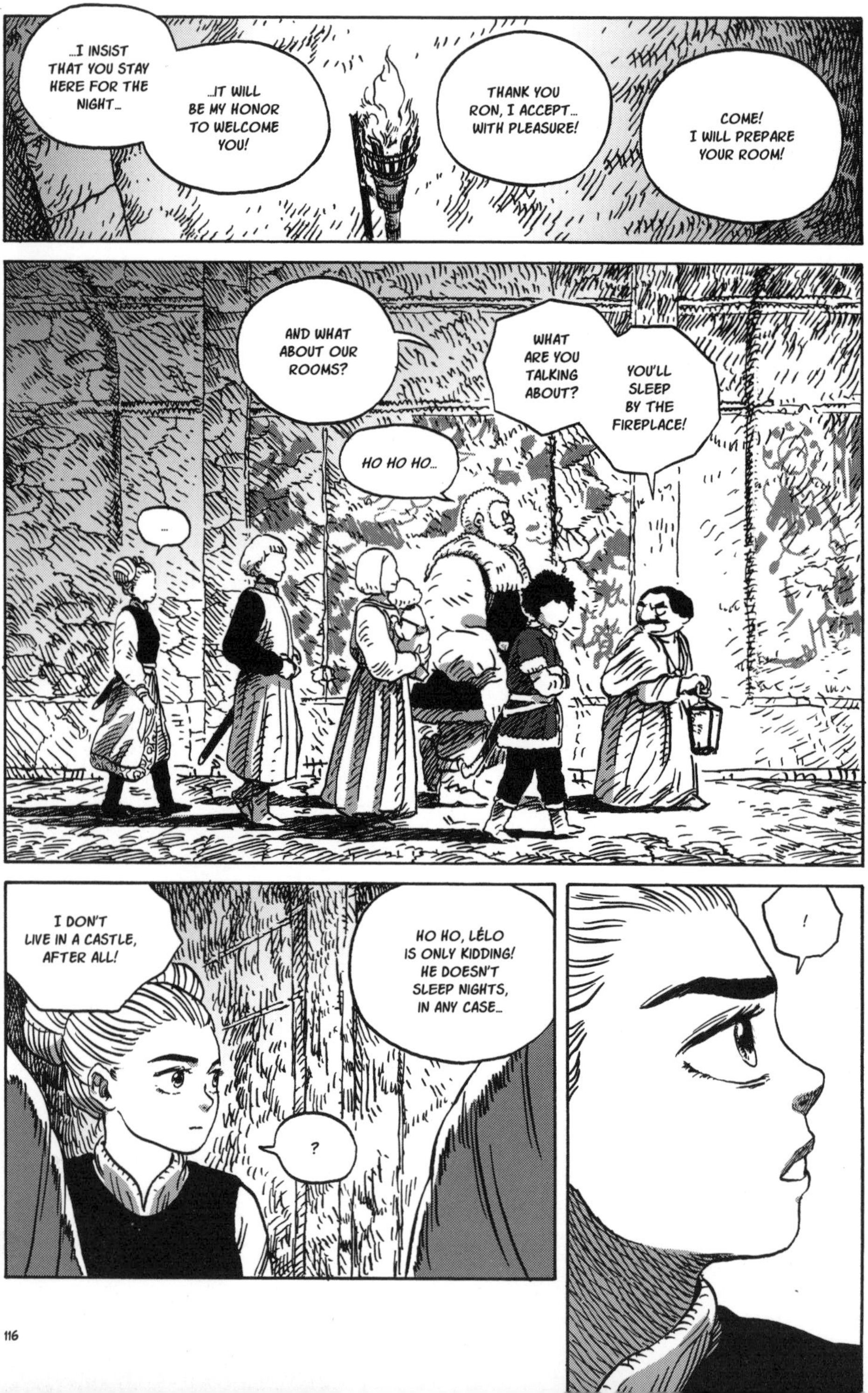
...I INSIST THAT YOU STAY HERE FOR THE NIGHT...
...IT WILL BE MY HONOR TO WELCOME YOU!
THANK YOU RON, I ACCEPT... WITH PLEASURE!
COME! I WILL PREPARE YOUR ROOM!
AND WHAT ABOUT OUR ROOMS?
WHAT ARE YOU TALKING ABOUT?
YOU'LL SLEEP BY THE FIREPLACE!
HO HO HO...
...
I DON'T LIVE IN A CASTLE, AFTER ALL!
HO HO, LÉLO IS ONLY KIDDING! HE DOESN'T SLEEP NIGHTS, IN ANY CASE...
?
!

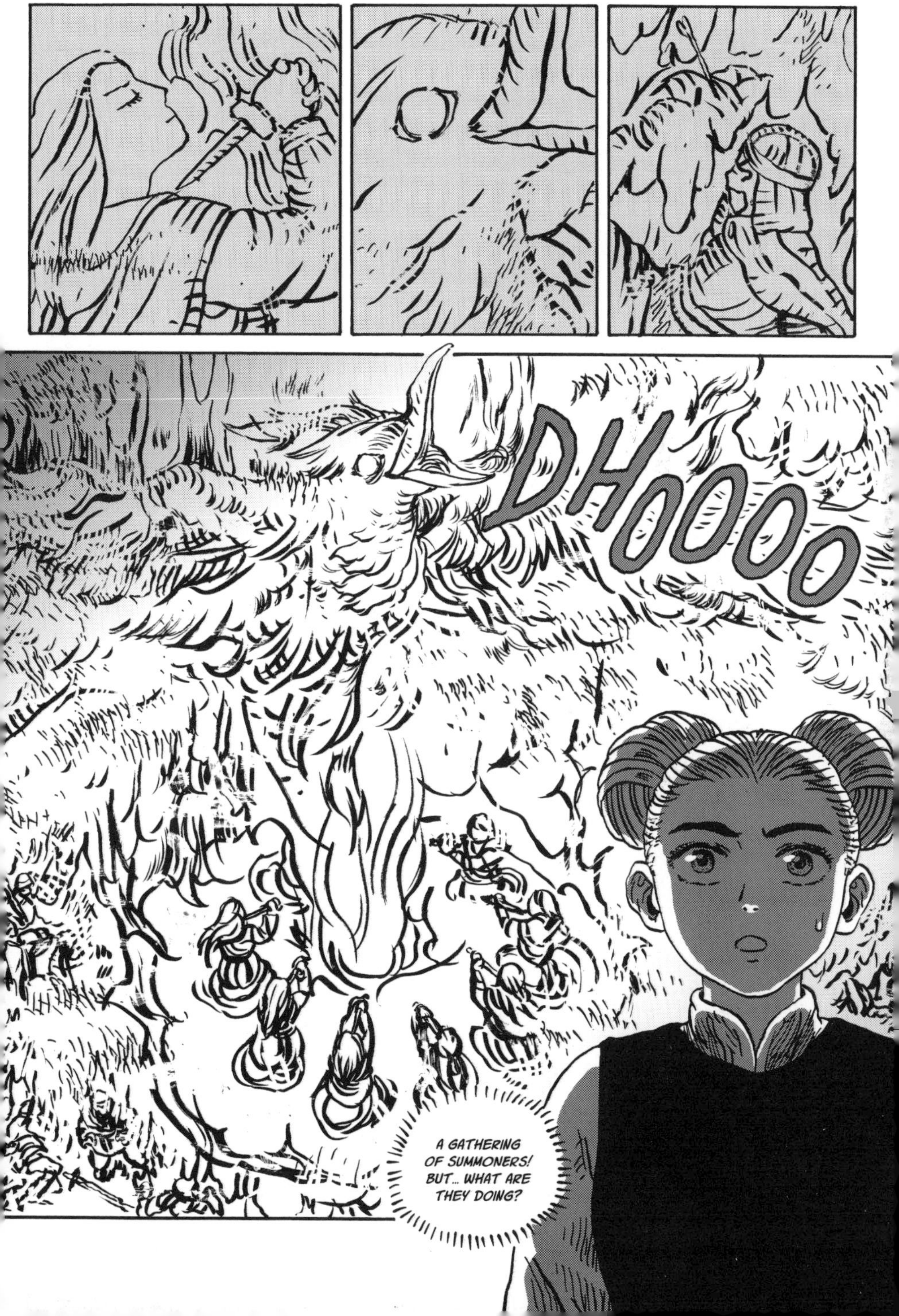
DHOOOO
A GATHERING OF SUMMONERS! BUT... WHAT ARE THEY DOING?

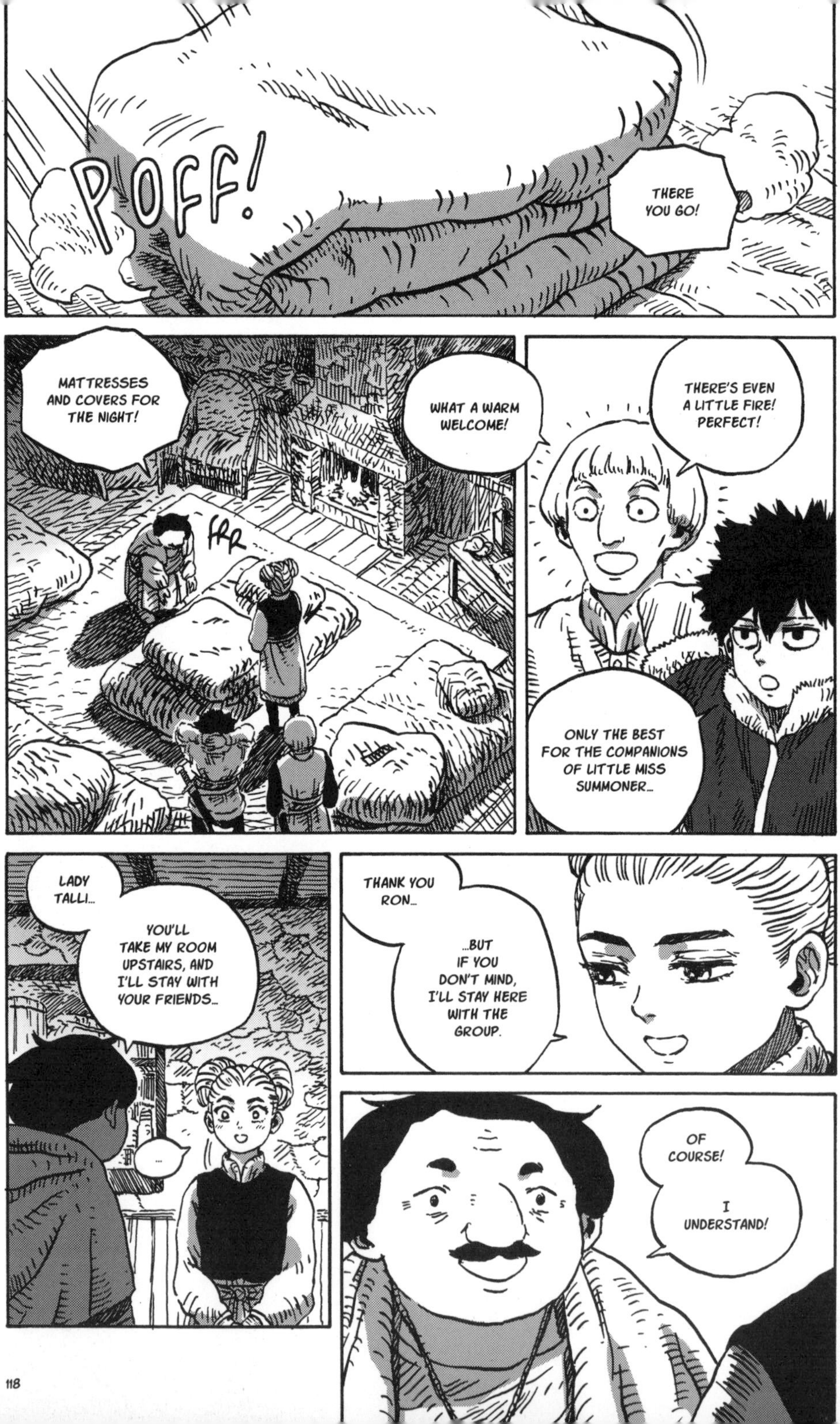
POFF!
THERE YOU GO!
MATTRESSES AND COVERS FOR THE NIGHT!
WHAT A WARM WELCOME!
FRR
THERE'S EVEN A LITTLE FIRE! PERFECT!
ONLY THE BEST FOR THE COMPANIONS OF LITTLE MISS SUMMONER...
LADY TALLI...
YOU'LL TAKE MY ROOM UPSTAIRS, AND I'LL STAY WITH YOUR FRIENDS...
...
THANK YOU RON...
...BUT IF YOU DON'T MIND, I'LL STAY HERE WITH THE GROUP.
OF COURSE!
I UNDERSTAND!

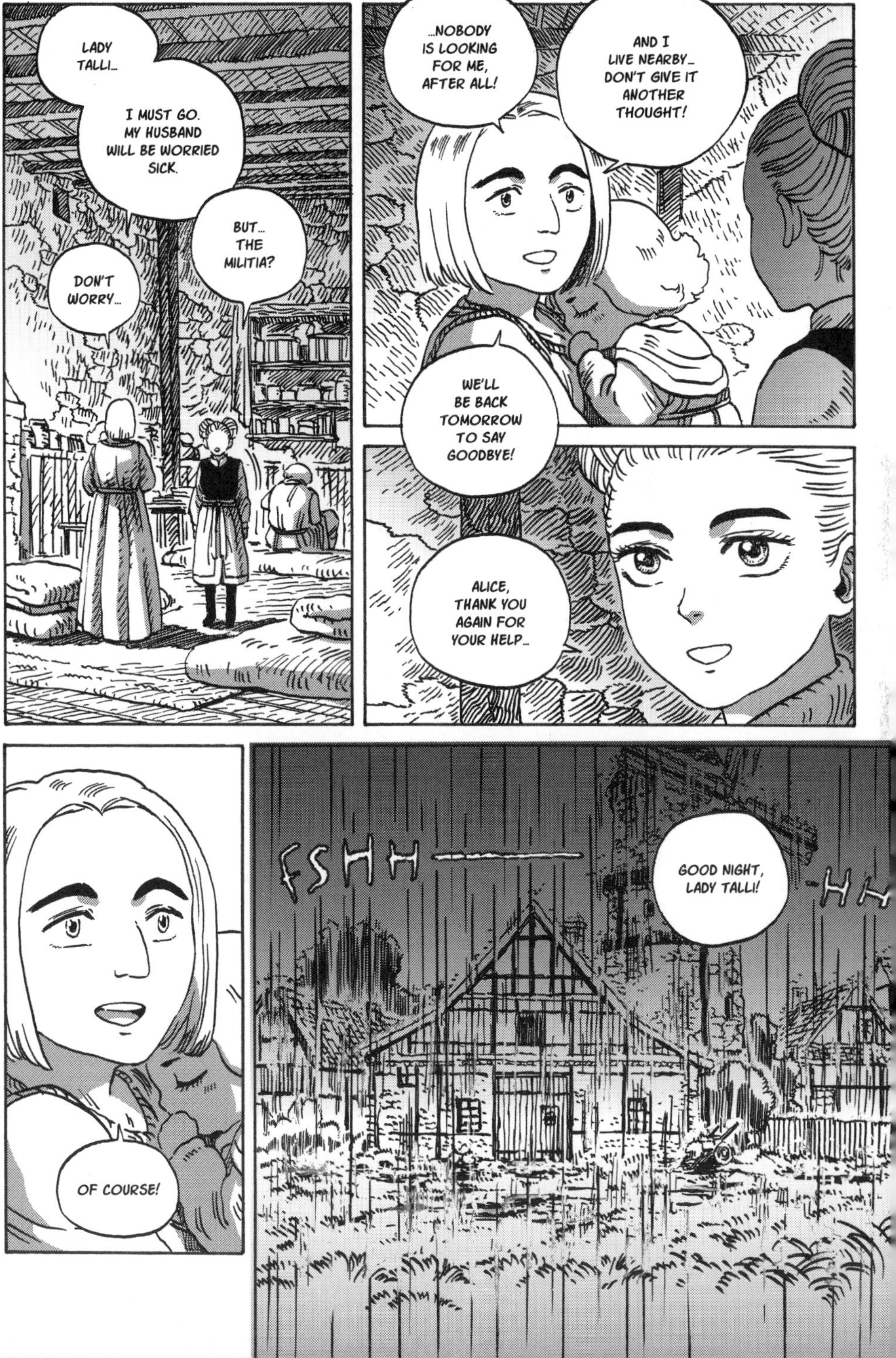
LADY TALLI...
I MUST GO. MY HUSBAND WILL BE WORRIED SICK.
BUT... THE MILITIA?
DON'T WORRY...
...NOBODY IS LOOKING FOR ME, AFTER ALL!
AND I LIVE NEARBY... DON'T GIVE IT ANOTHER THOUGHT!
WE'LL BE BACK TOMORROW TO SAY GOODBYE!
ALICE, THANK YOU AGAIN FOR YOUR HELP...
OF COURSE!
FSHH——
GOOD NIGHT, LADY TALLI!
-HH

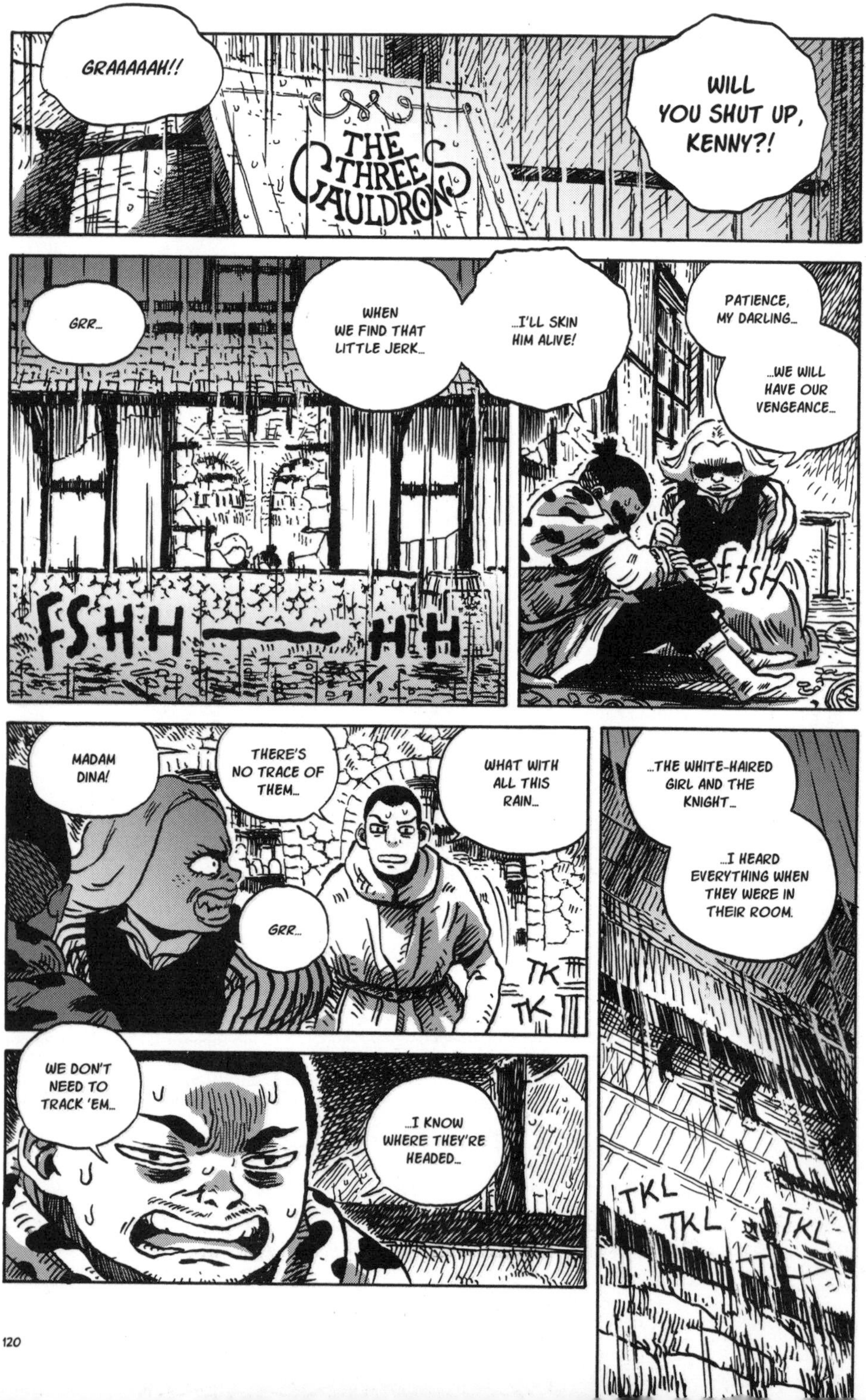
GRAAAAAH!!
THE THREE CAULDRONS
WILL YOU SHUT UP, KENNY?!
GRR...
FSHH—HH
WHEN WE FIND THAT LITTLE JERK...
...I'LL SKIN HIM ALIVE!
PATIENCE, MY DARLING...
...WE WILL HAVE OUR VENGEANCE...
FTSH
MADAM DINA!
THERE'S NO TRACE OF THEM...
GRR...
WHAT WITH ALL THIS RAIN...
TK TK
...THE WHITE-HAIRED GIRL AND THE KNIGHT...
...I HEARD EVERYTHING WHEN THEY WERE IN THEIR ROOM.
WE DON'T NEED TO TRACK 'EM...
...I KNOW WHERE THEY'RE HEADED...
TKL TKL TKL

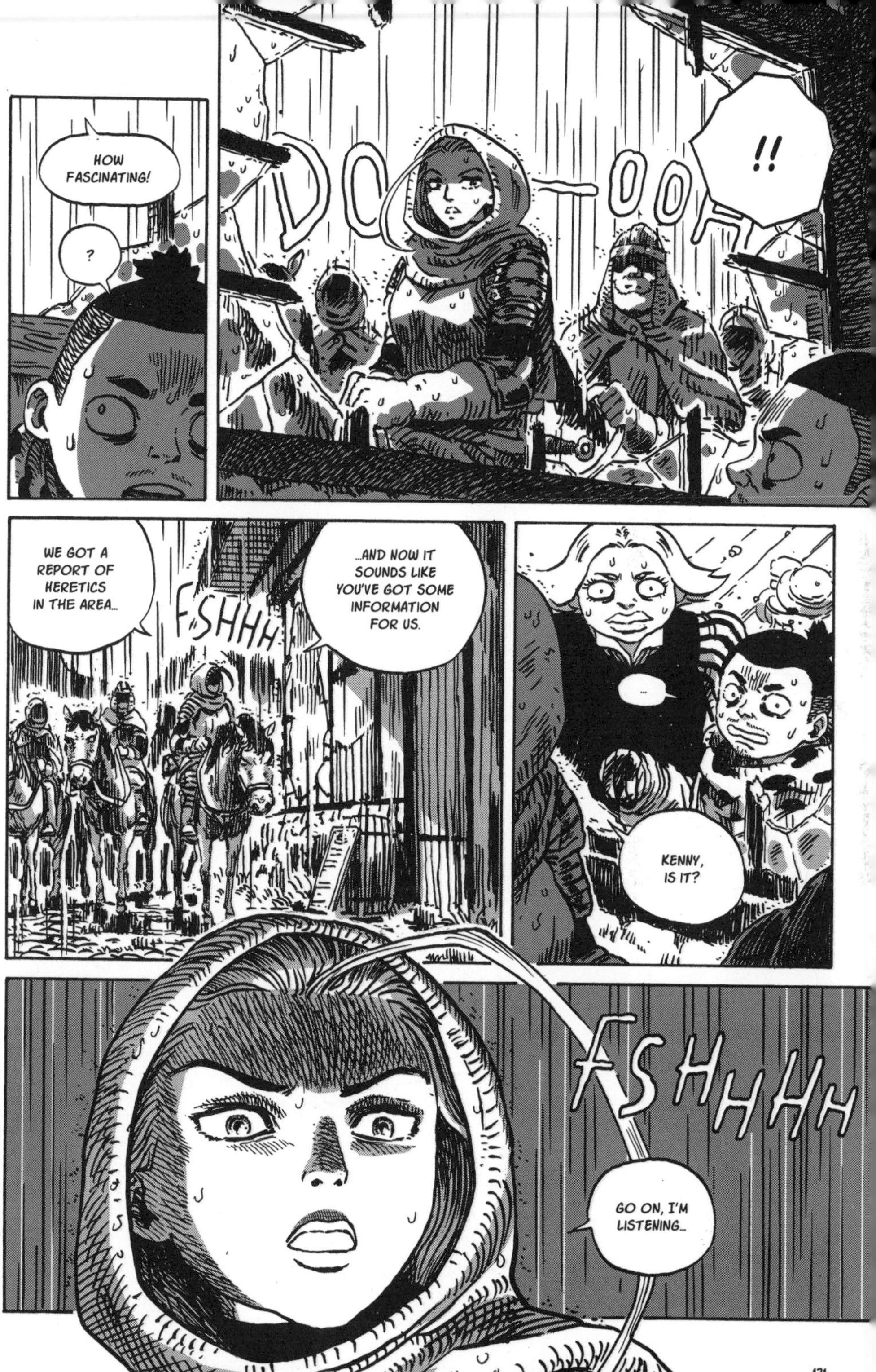

HOW FASCINATING!
?
DO-OOH
!!
WE GOT A REPORT OF HERETICS IN THE AREA...
FSHHH
...AND NOW IT SOUNDS LIKE YOU'VE GOT SOME INFORMATION FOR US.
...
KENNY, IS IT?
FSHHHH
GO ON, I'M LISTENING...

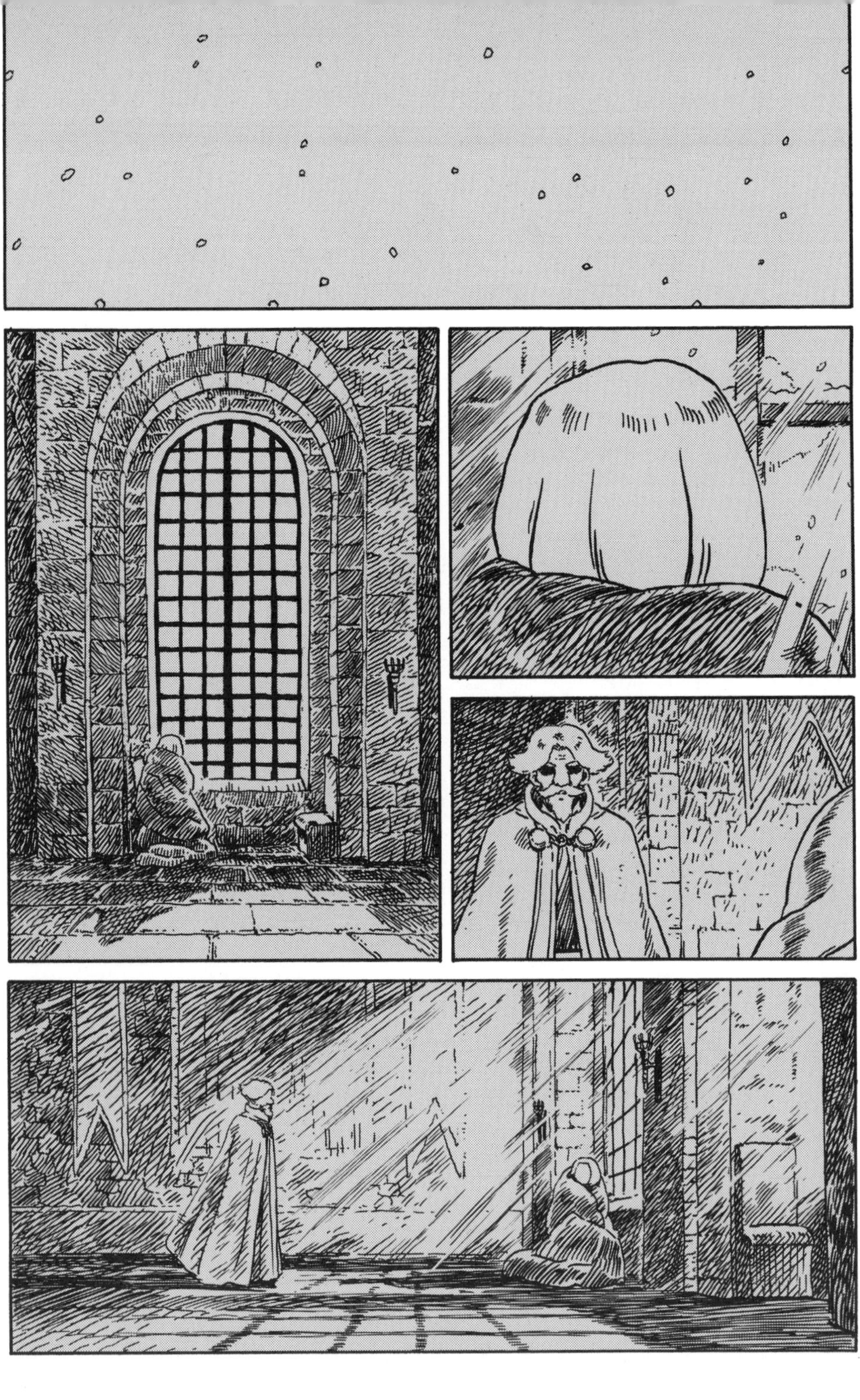

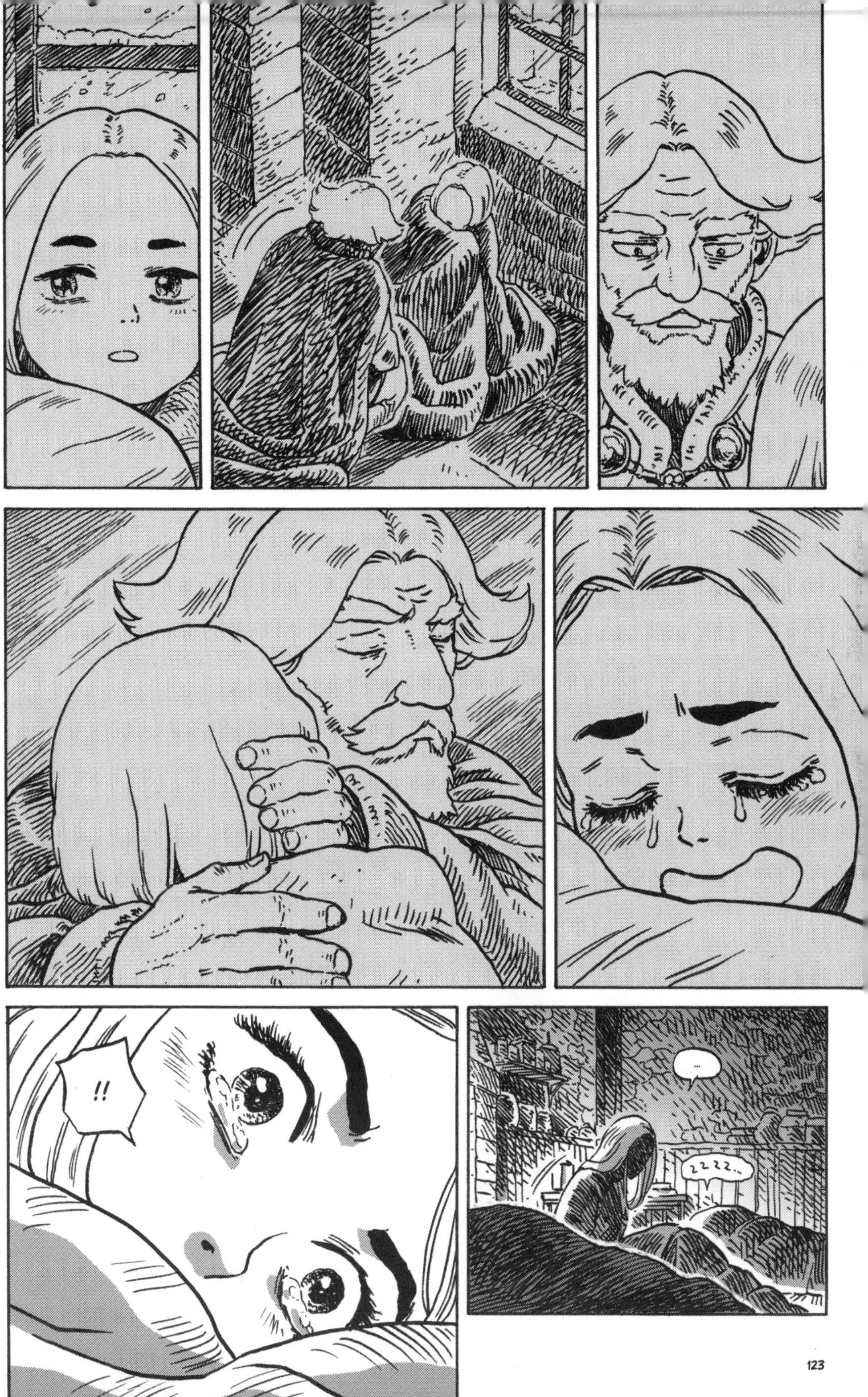
!!
...
zzzz...

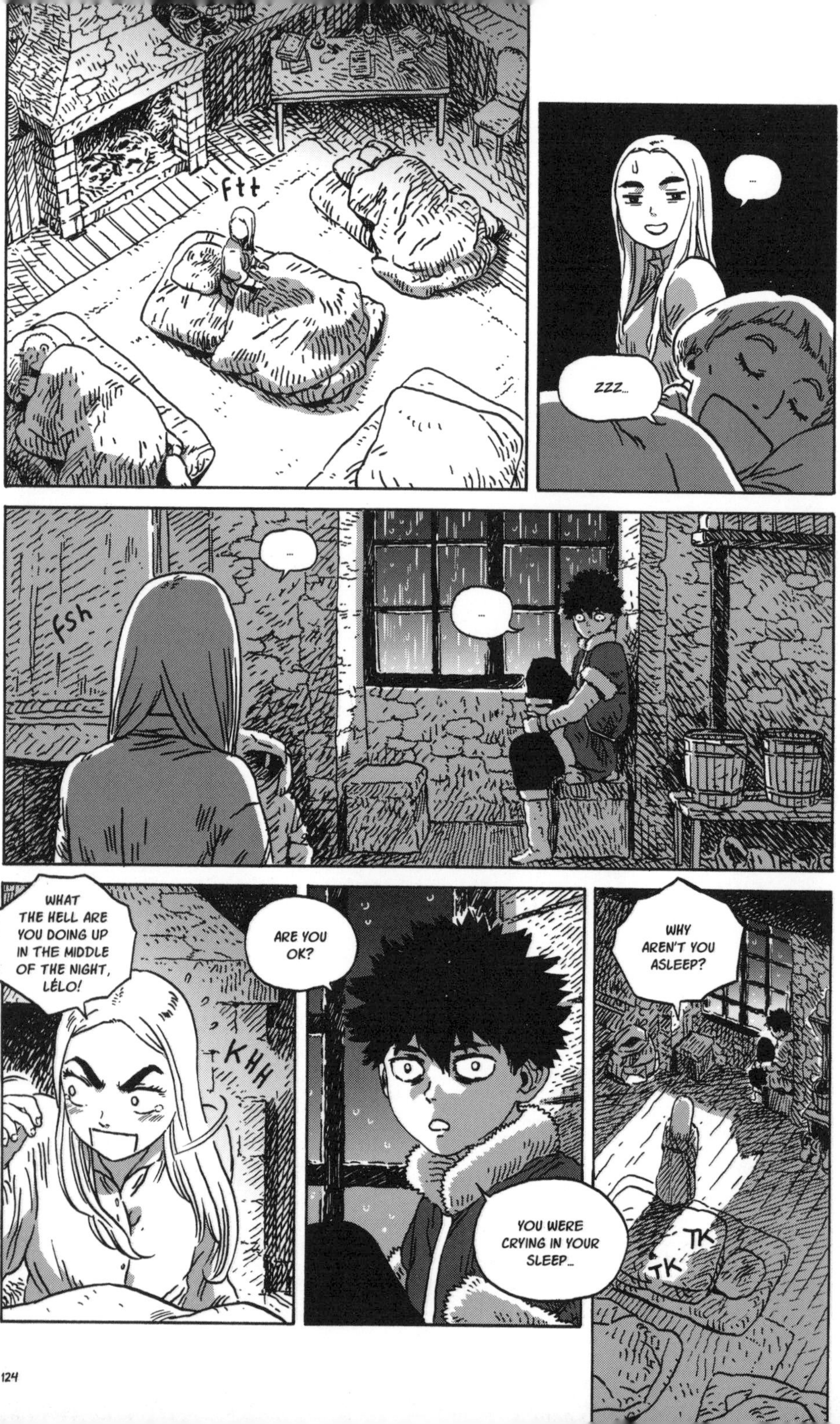
Ftt
...
ZZZ...
fsh
...
...
WHAT THE HELL ARE YOU DOING UP IN THE MIDDLE OF THE NIGHT, LÉLO!
KHH
ARE YOU OK?
YOU WERE CRYING IN YOUR SLEEP...
WHY AREN'T YOU ASLEEP?
TK
TK

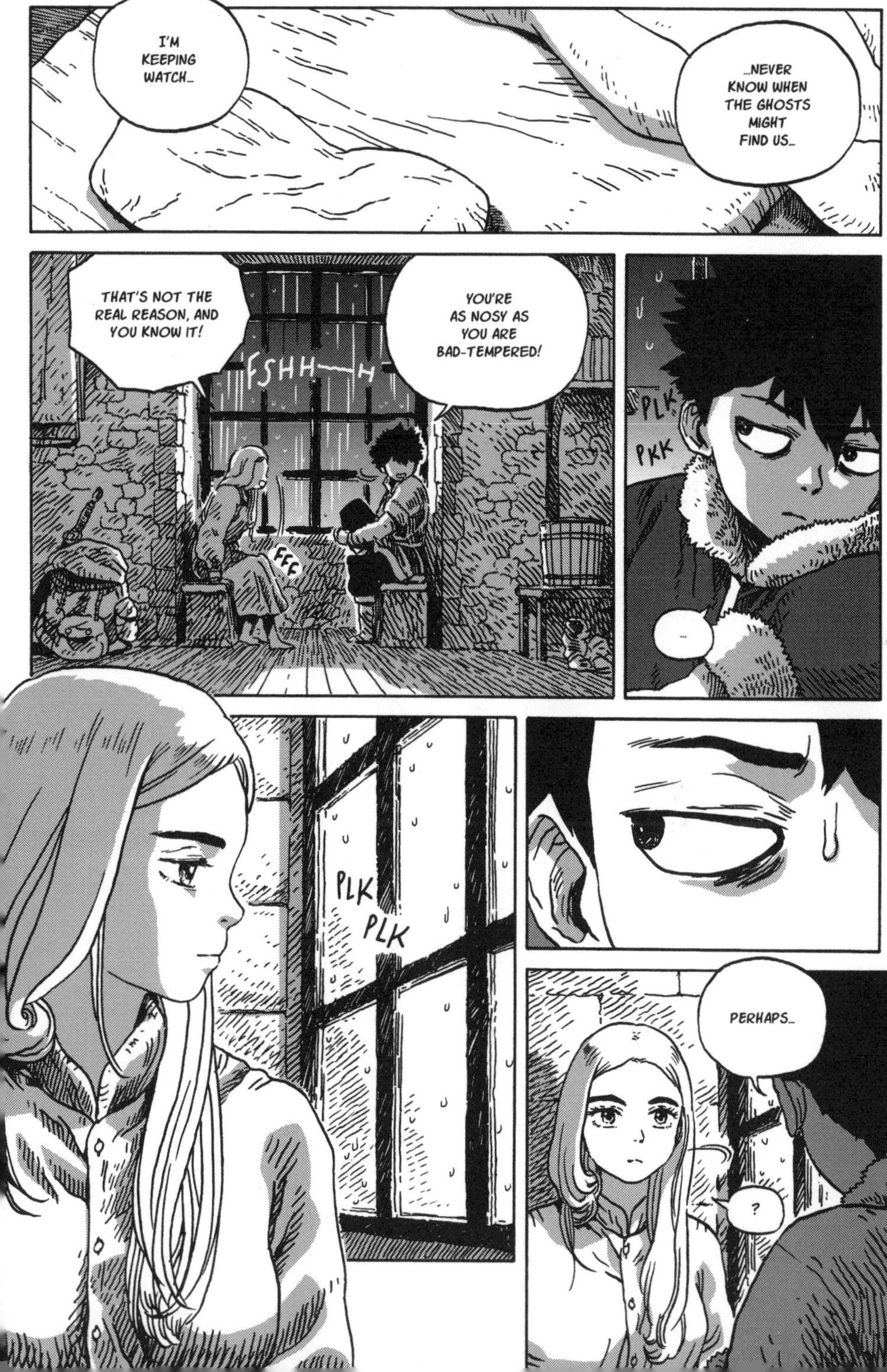
I'M KEEPING WATCH...
...NEVER KNOW WHEN THE GHOSTS MIGHT FIND US...
THAT'S NOT THE REAL REASON, AND YOU KNOW IT!
FSHH—H
YOU'RE AS NOSY AS YOU ARE BAD-TEMPERED!
FFF
PLK
PKK
...
PLK
PLK
PERHAPS...
?

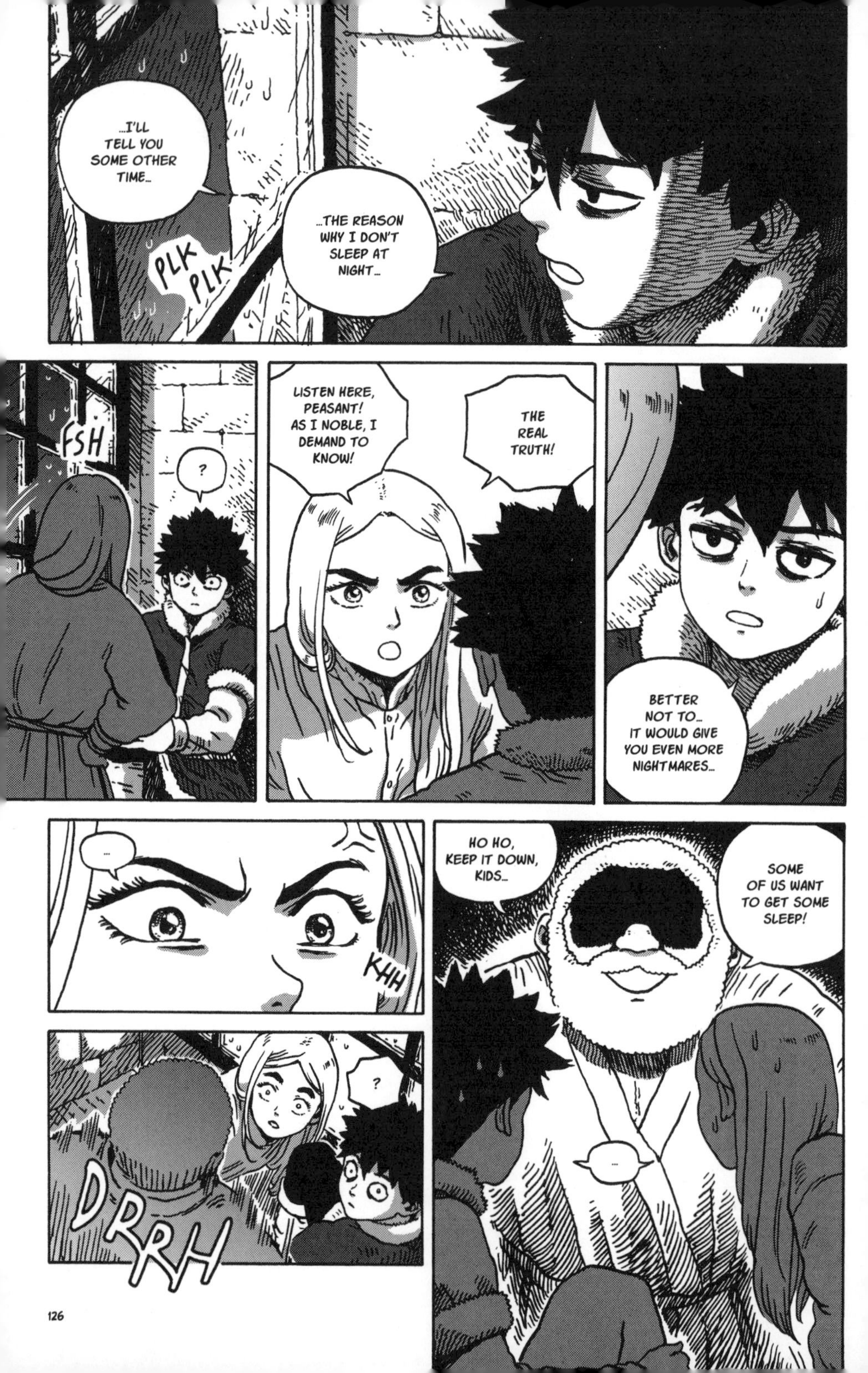
...I'LL TELL YOU SOME OTHER TIME...
PLK PLK
...THE REASON WHY I DON'T SLEEP AT NIGHT...
FSH
?
LISTEN HERE, PEASANT! AS I NOBLE, I DEMAND TO KNOW!
THE REAL TRUTH!
BETTER NOT TO... IT WOULD GIVE YOU EVEN MORE NIGHTMARES...
...
KHH
?
DRRH
HO HO, KEEP IT DOWN, KIDS...
SOME OF US WANT TO GET SOME SLEEP!
...

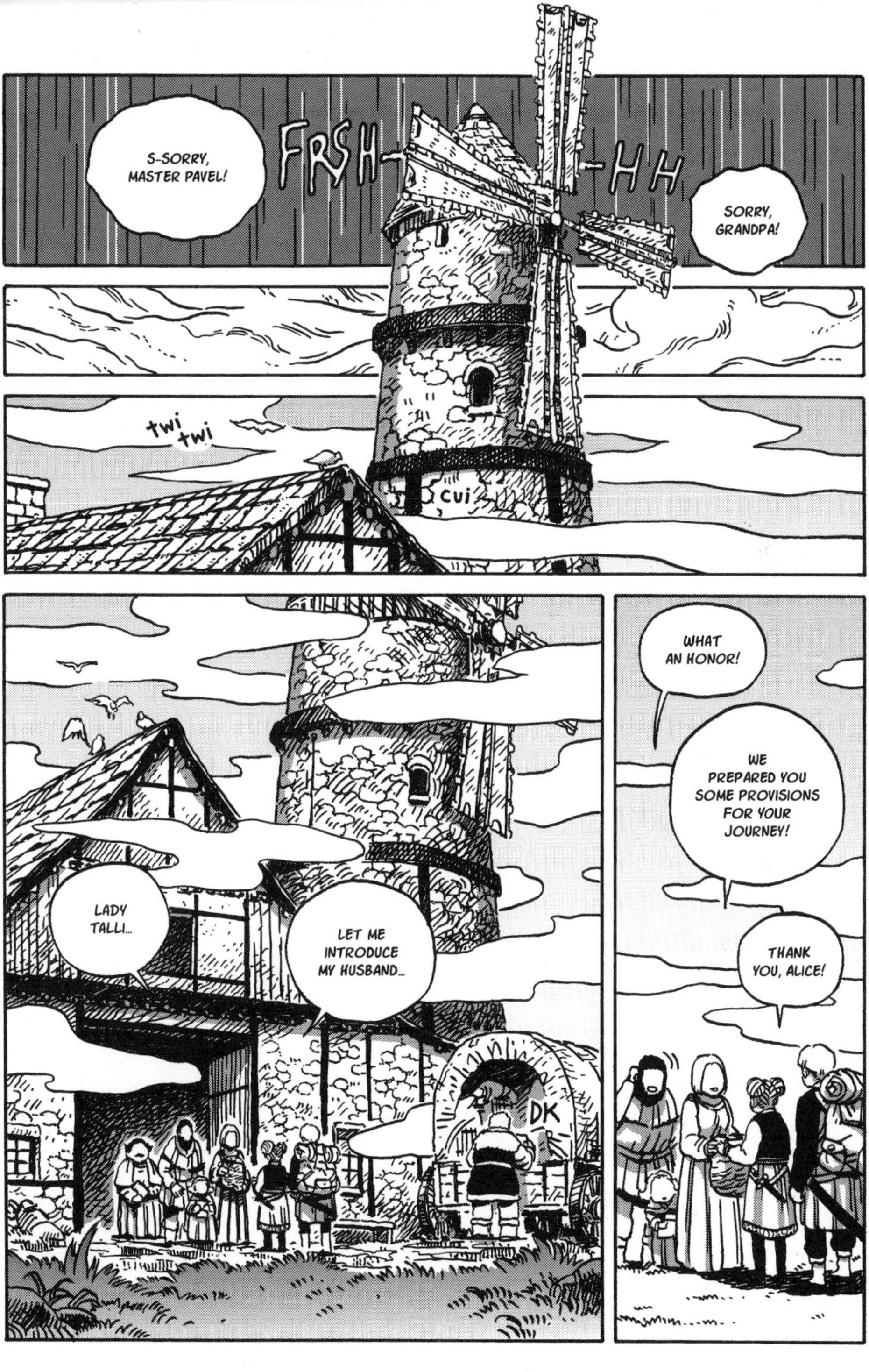
S-SORRY, MASTER PAVEL!
FRSH--HH
SORRY, GRANDPA!
twi twi
CUI
LADY TALLI...
LET ME INTRODUCE MY HUSBAND...
DK
WHAT AN HONOR!
WE PREPARED YOU SOME PROVISIONS FOR YOUR JOURNEY!
THANK YOU, ALICE!

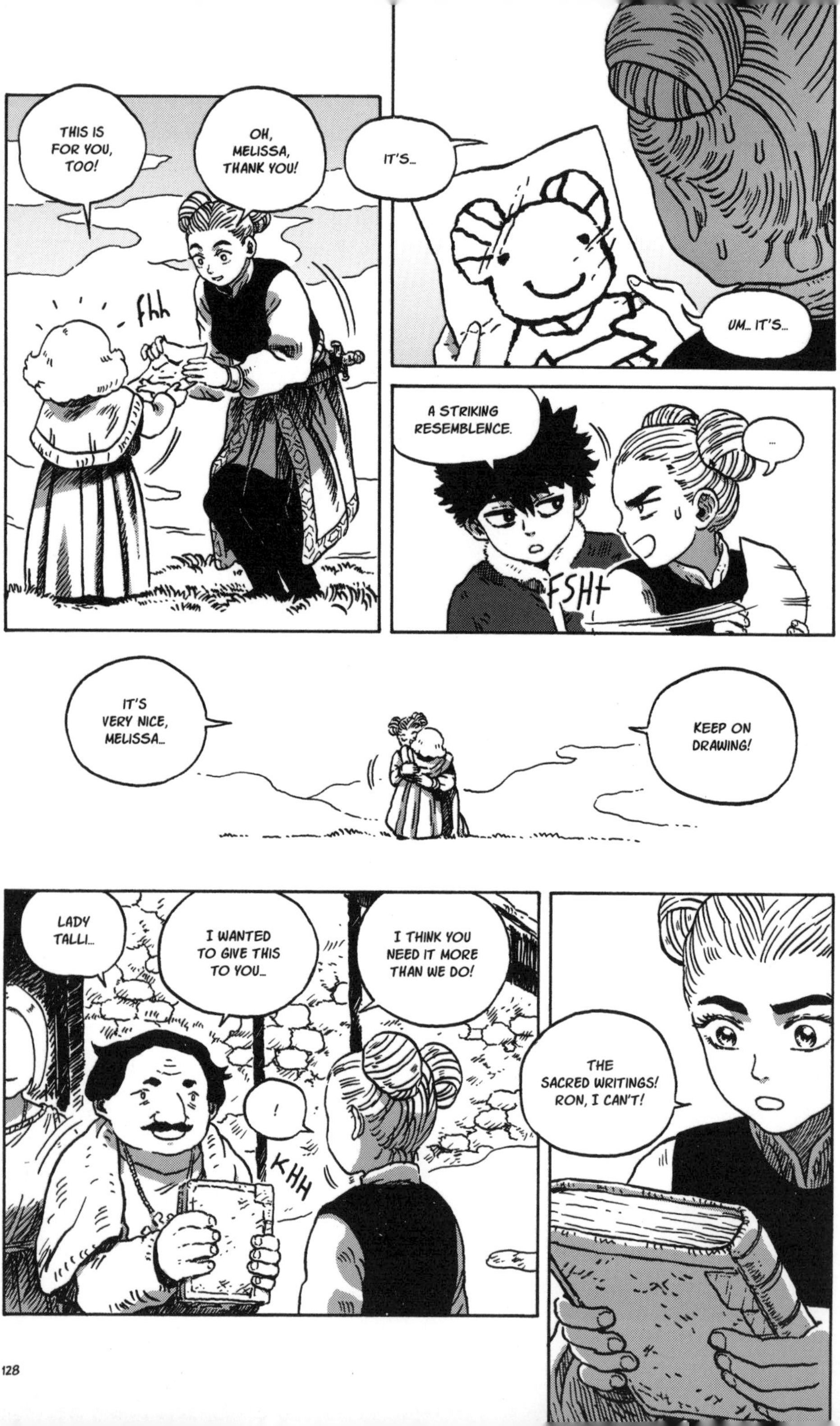
THIS IS FOR YOU, TOO!
OH, MELISSA, THANK YOU!
fhh
IT'S...
UM... IT'S...
A STRIKING RESEMBLENCE.
...
FSHT
IT'S VERY NICE, MELISSA...
KEEP ON DRAWING!
LADY TALLI...
I WANTED TO GIVE THIS TO YOU...
I THINK YOU NEED IT MORE THAN WE DO!
!
KHH
THE SACRED WRITINGS! RON, I CAN'T!

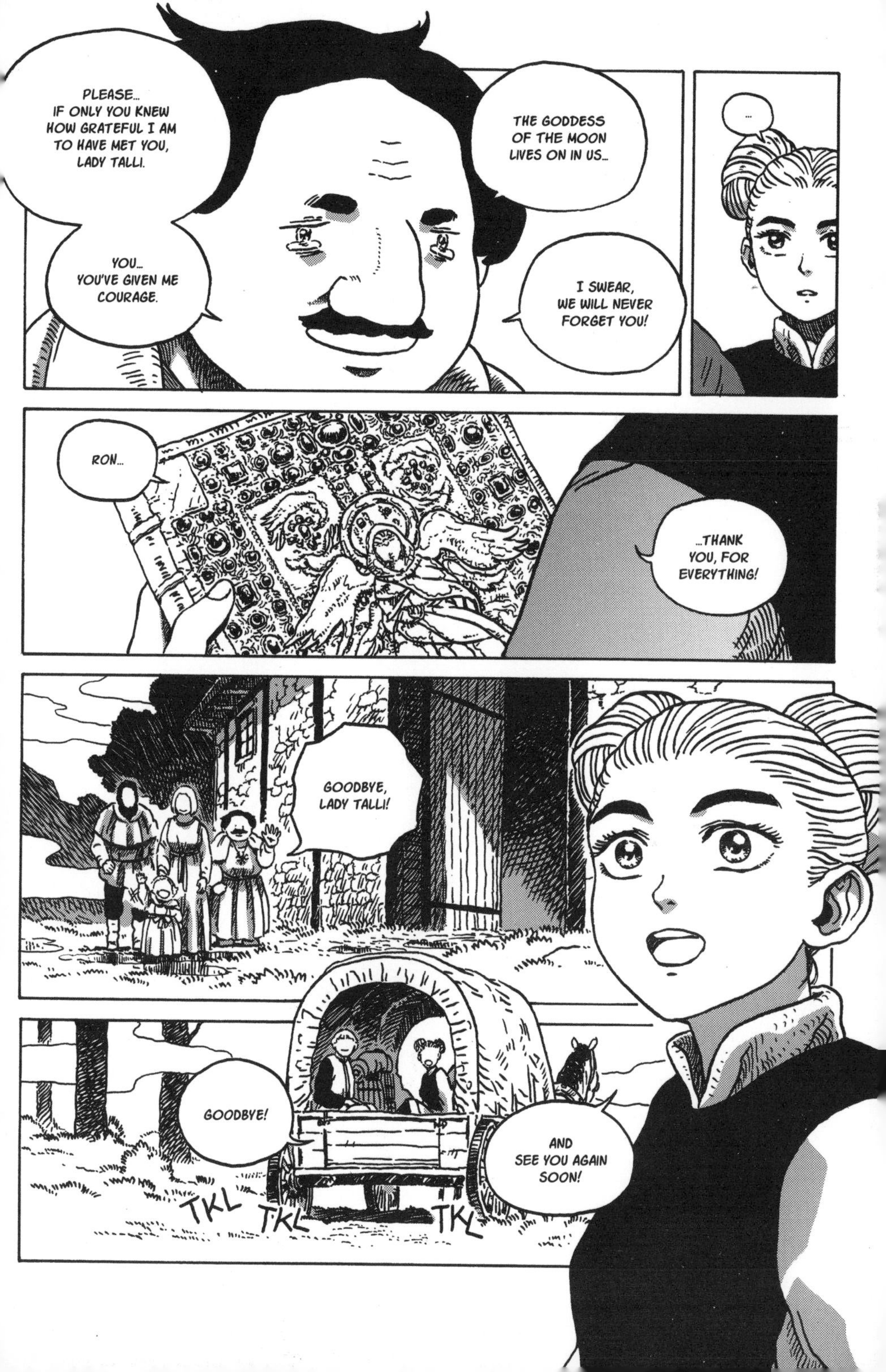
PLEASE... IF ONLY YOU KNEW HOW GRATEFUL I AM TO HAVE MET YOU, LADY TALLI.
YOU... YOU'VE GIVEN ME COURAGE.
THE GODDESS OF THE MOON LIVES ON IN US...
I SWEAR, WE WILL NEVER FORGET YOU!
...
RON...
...THANK YOU, FOR EVERYTHING!
GOODBYE, LADY TALLI!
GOODBYE!
AND SEE YOU AGAIN SOON!
TKL TKL TKL

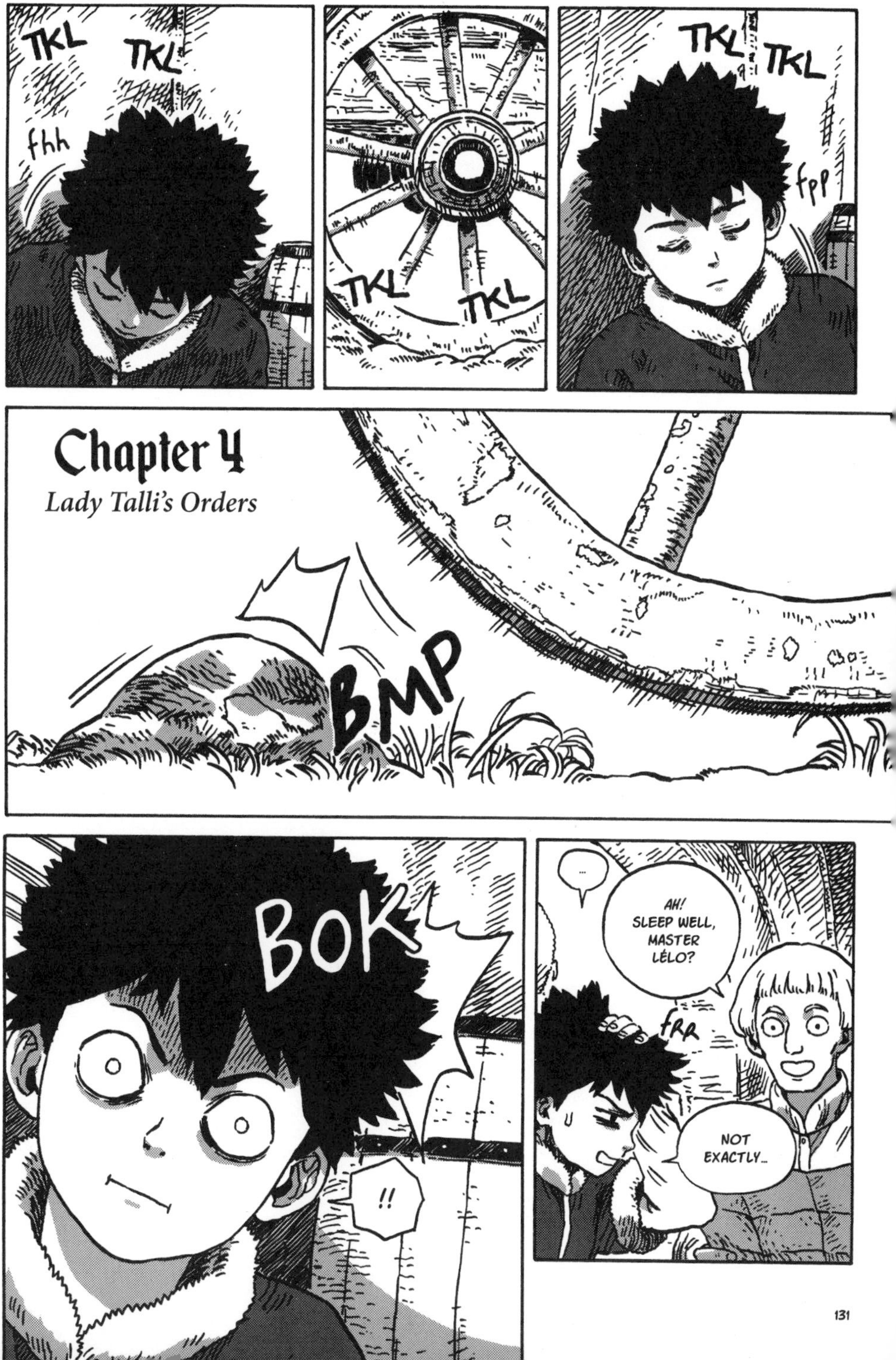
TKL
TKL
fhh
TKL
TKL
TKL
TKL
fpp
Chapter 4
Lady Talli's Orders
BMP
BOK
!!
...
AH! SLEEP WELL, MASTER LÉLO?
frr
NOT EXACTLY...

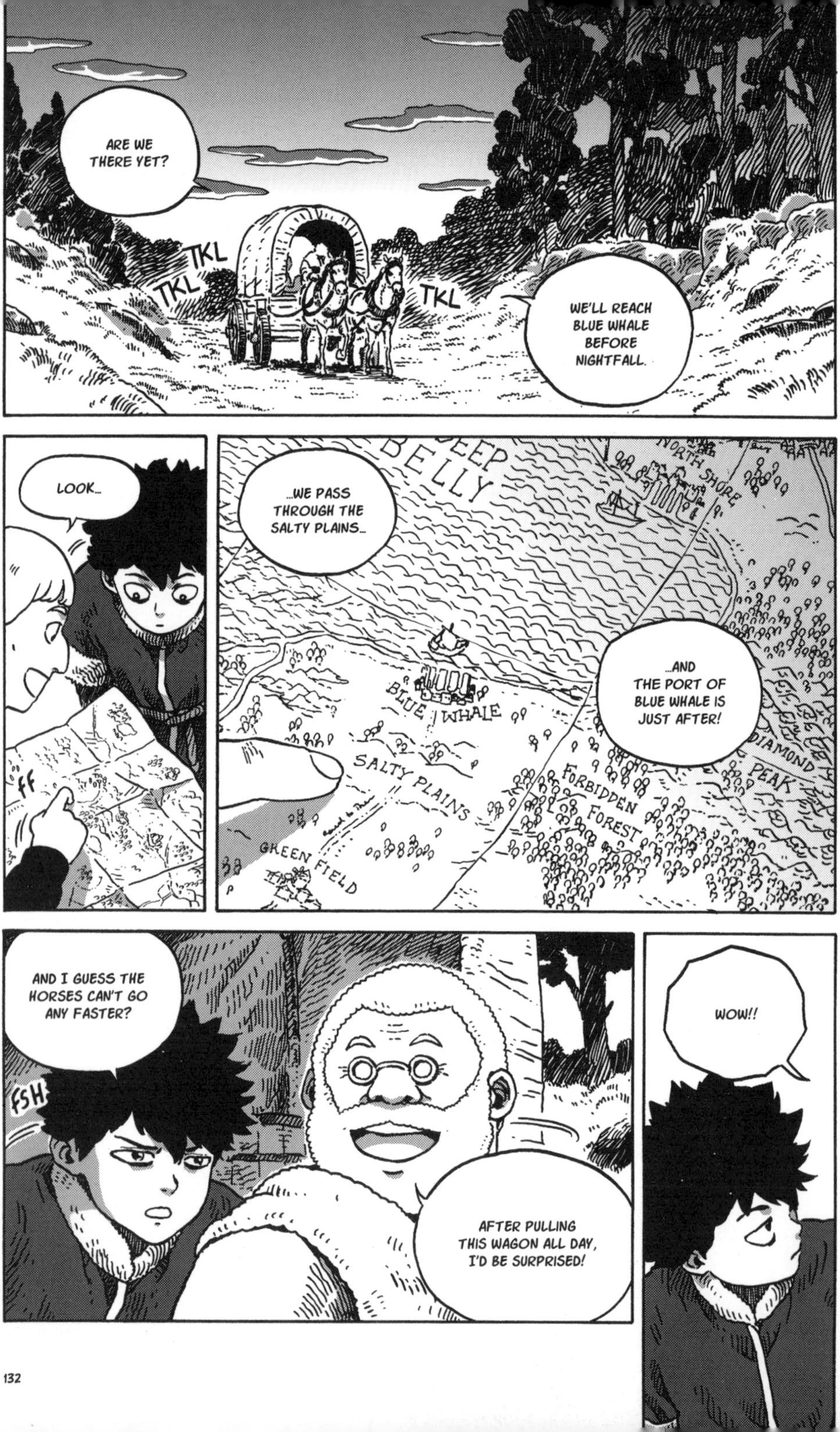
ARE WE THERE YET?
TKL
TKL
TKL
WE'LL REACH BLUE WHALE BEFORE NIGHTFALL.
LOOK...
FF
...WE PASS THROUGH THE SALTY PLAINS...
BELLY
NORTH SHORE
BLUE WHALE
SALTY PLAINS
GREEN FIELD
FORBIDDEN FOREST
DIAMOND PEAK
...AND THE PORT OF BLUE WHALE IS JUST AFTER!
AND I GUESS THE HORSES CAN'T GO ANY FASTER?
FSH
AFTER PULLING THIS WAGON ALL DAY, I'D BE SURPRISED!
WOW!!

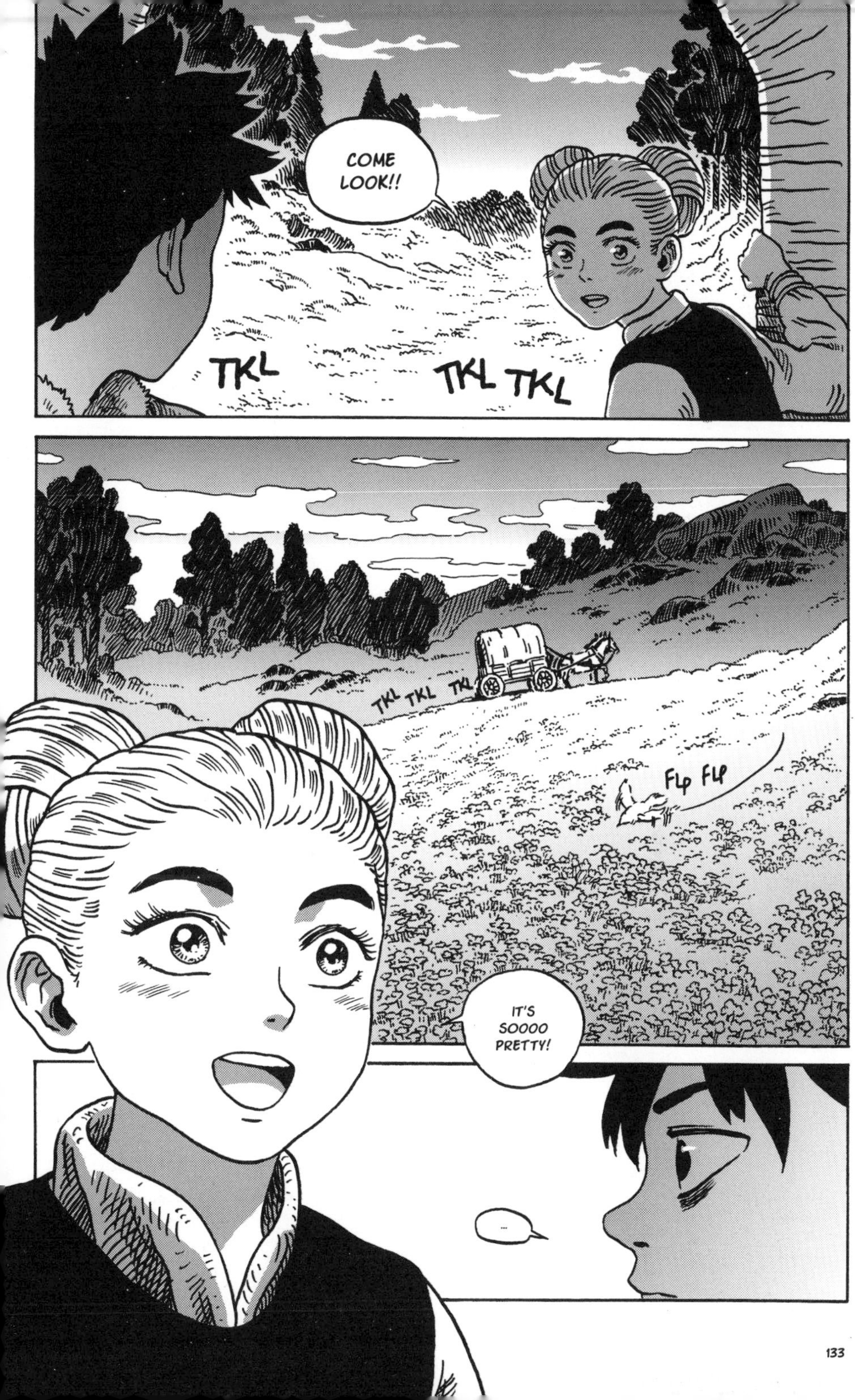
COME LOOK!!
TKL
TKL TKL
TKL TKL TKL
FLP FLP
IT'S SOOOO PRETTY!
...

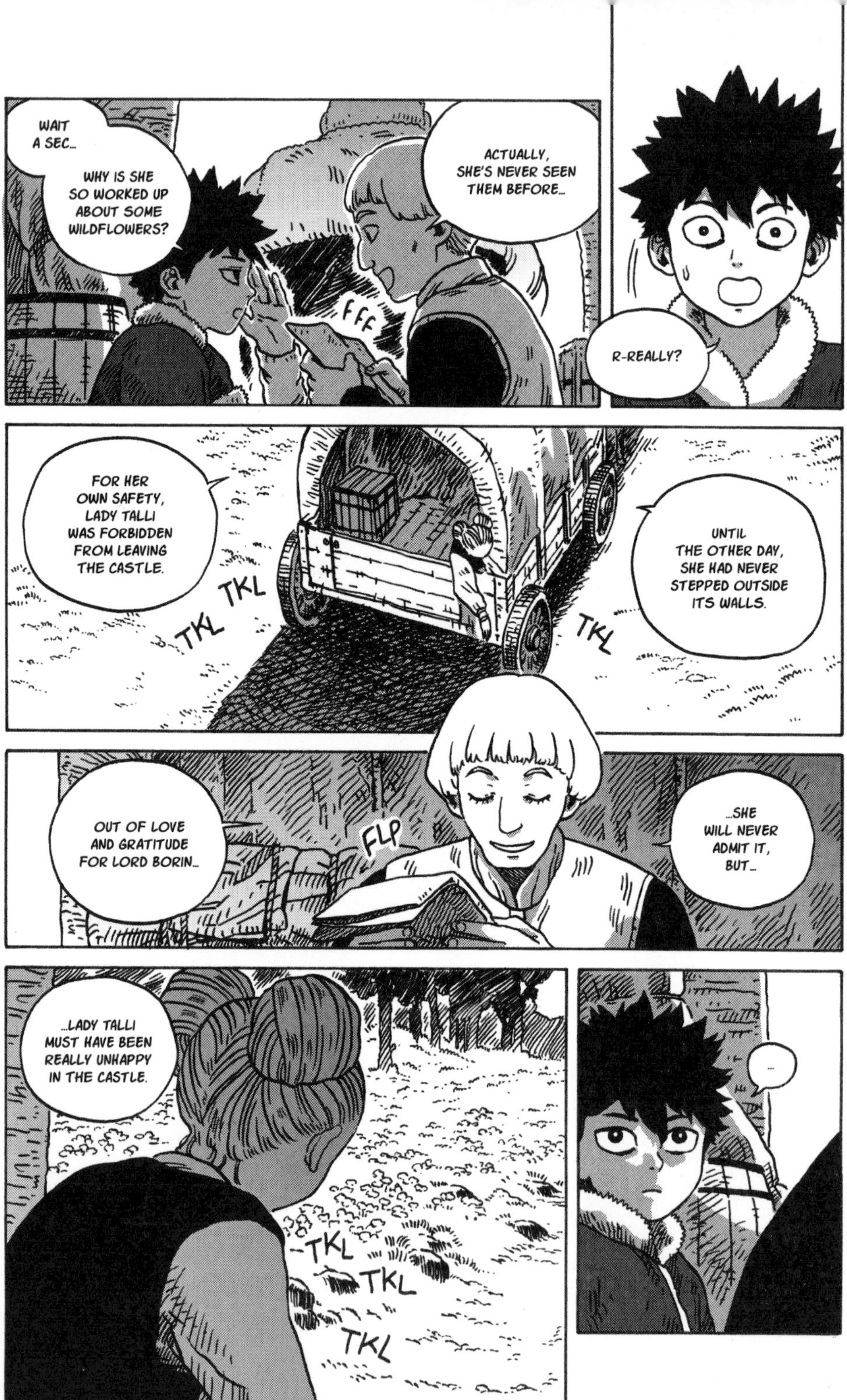
WAIT A SEC...
WHY IS SHE SO WORKED UP ABOUT SOME WILDFLOWERS?
FFF
ACTUALLY, SHE'S NEVER SEEN THEM BEFORE...
R-REALLY?
FOR HER OWN SAFETY, LADY TALLI WAS FORBIDDEN FROM LEAVING THE CASTLE.
TKL TKL
TKL
TKL
UNTIL THE OTHER DAY, SHE HAD NEVER STEPPED OUTSIDE ITS WALLS.
OUT OF LOVE AND GRATITUDE FOR LORD BORIN...
FLP
...SHE WILL NEVER ADMIT IT, BUT...
...LADY TALLI MUST HAVE BEEN REALLY UNHAPPY IN THE CASTLE.
TKL
TKL
TKL
...

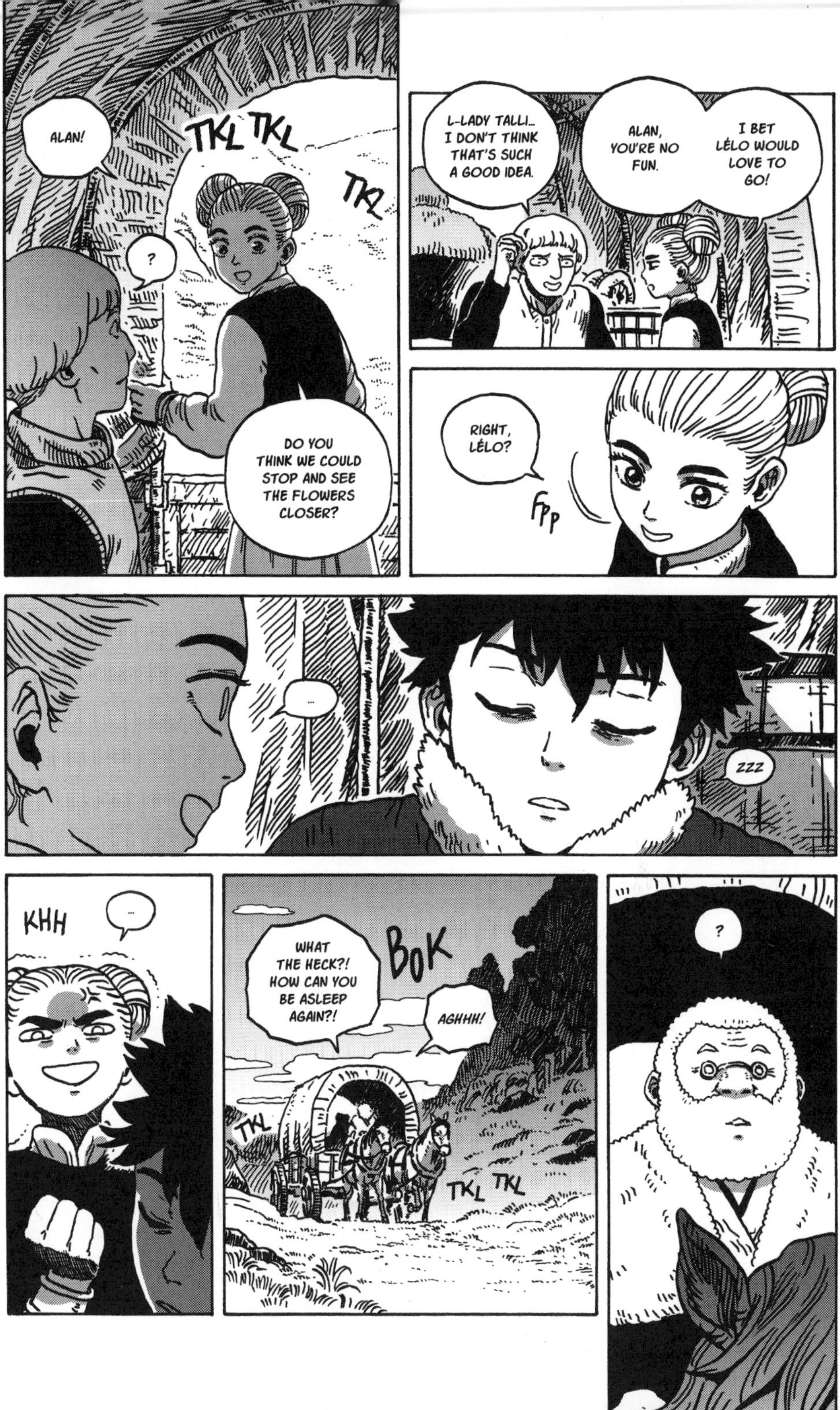
ALAN!
TKL TKL
TKL
?
DO YOU THINK WE COULD STOP AND SEE THE FLOWERS CLOSER?
L-LADY TALLI... I DON'T THINK THAT'S SUCH A GOOD IDEA.
ALAN, YOU'RE NO FUN.
I BET LÉLO WOULD LOVE TO GO!
RIGHT, LÉLO?
FPP
...
ZZZ
KHH
...
WHAT THE HECK?! HOW CAN YOU BE ASLEEP AGAIN?!
BOK
AGHHH!
TKL
TKL TKL
?

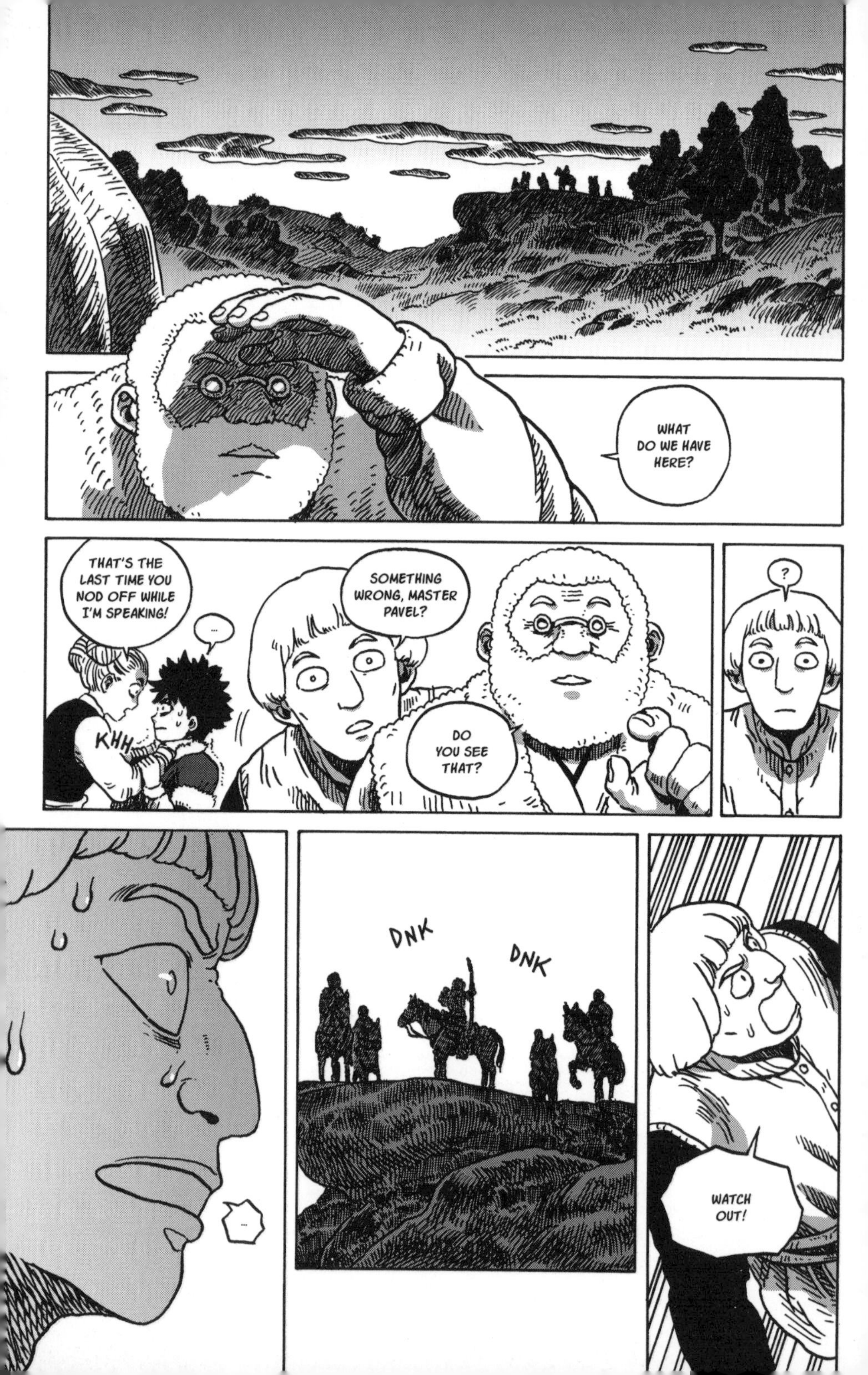

WHAT DO WE HAVE HERE?
THAT'S THE LAST TIME YOU NOD OFF WHILE I'M SPEAKING!
...
KHH
SOMETHING WRONG, MASTER PAVEL?
DO YOU SEE THAT?
?
...
DNK
DNK
WATCH OUT!

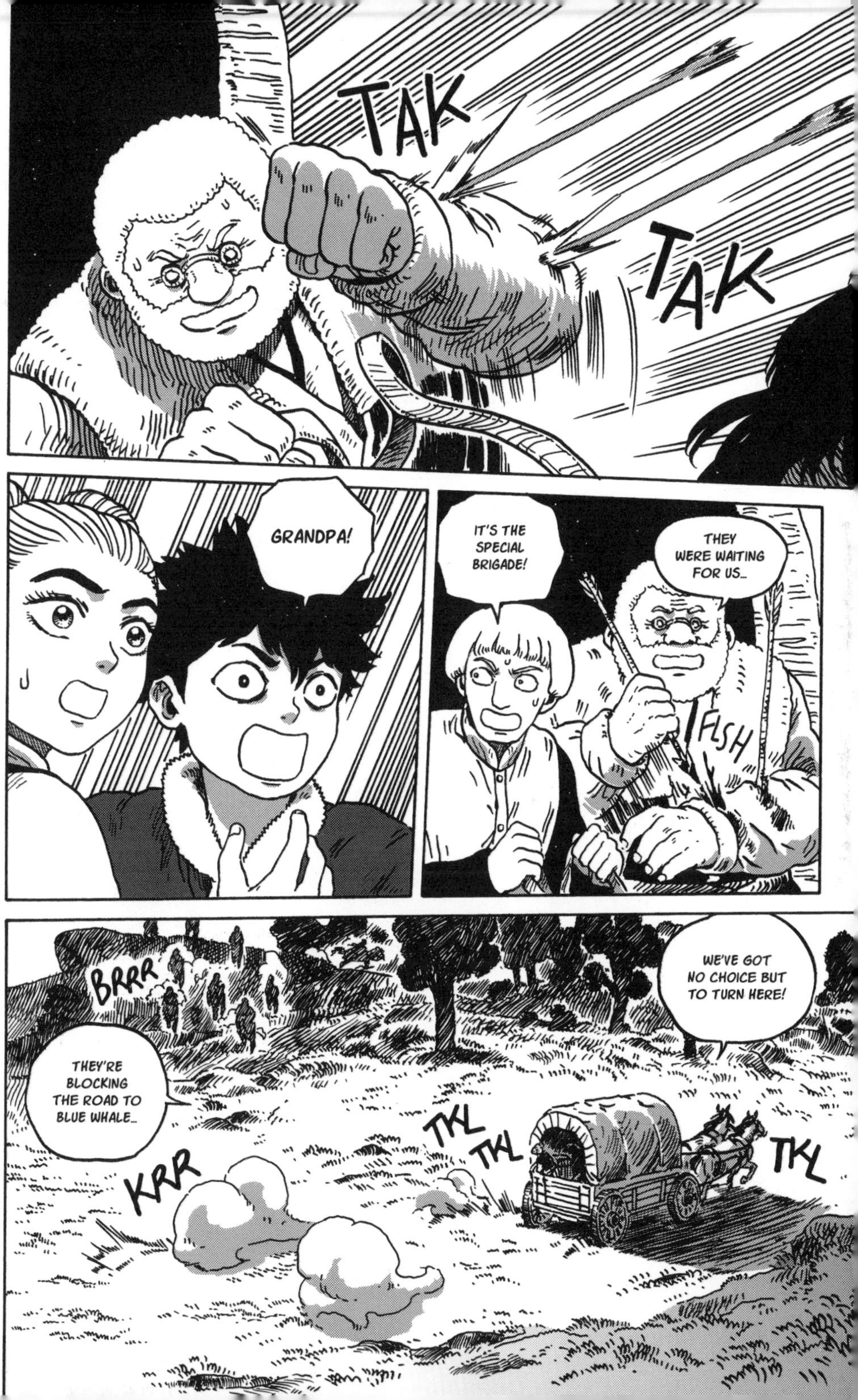
TAK
TAK
GRANDPA!
IT'S THE SPECIAL BRIGADE!
THEY WERE WAITING FOR US...
FLSH
BRRR
THEY'RE BLOCKING THE ROAD TO BLUE WHALE...
WE'VE GOT NO CHOICE BUT TO TURN HERE!
TKL
TKL
TKL
KRR

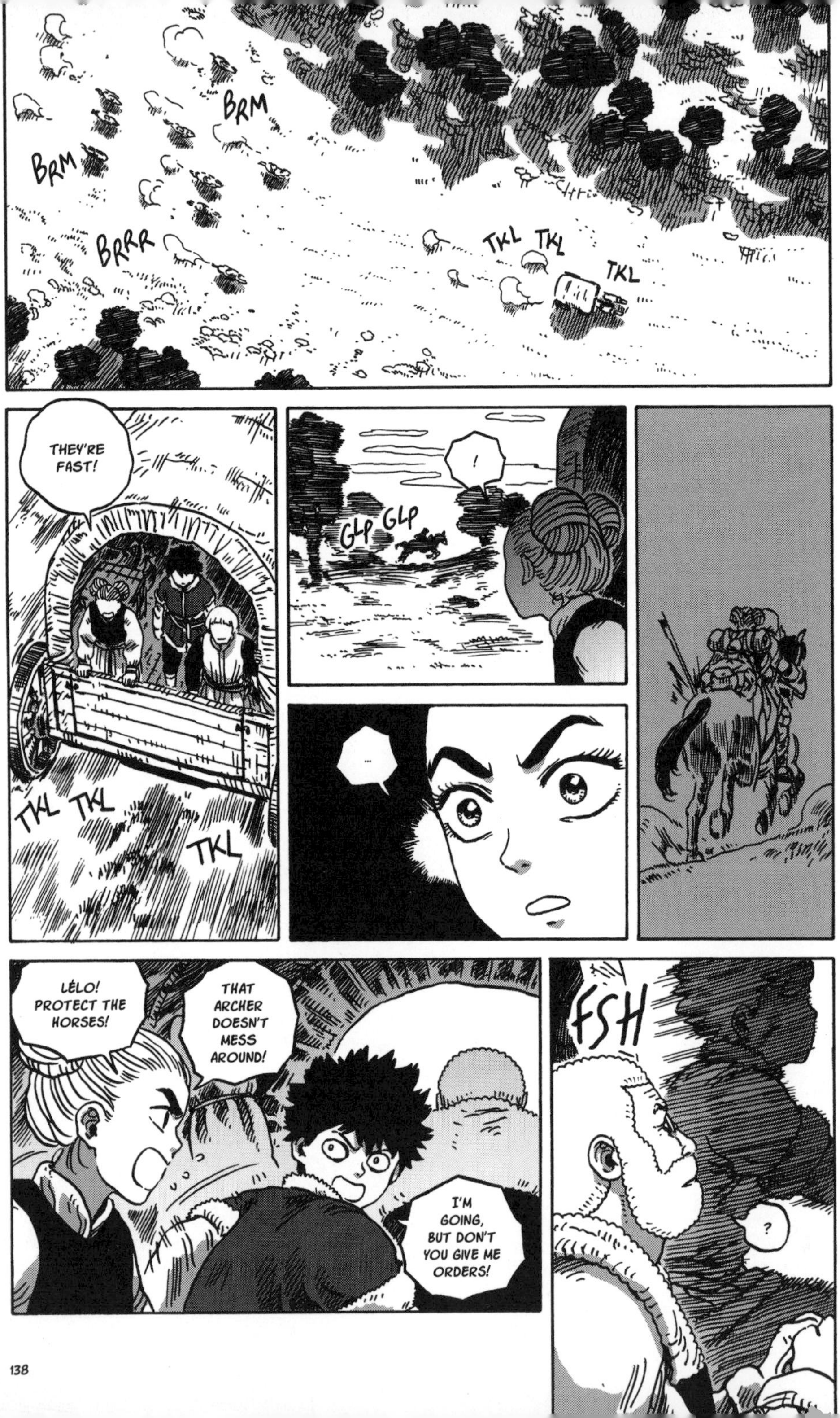
BRM
BRM
BRRR
TKL TKL
TKL
THEY'RE FAST!
TKL TKL
TKL
!
GLP GLP
...
LÉLO! PROTECT THE HORSES!
THAT ARCHER DOESN'T MESS AROUND!
I'M GOING, BUT DON'T YOU GIVE ME ORDERS!
FSH
?

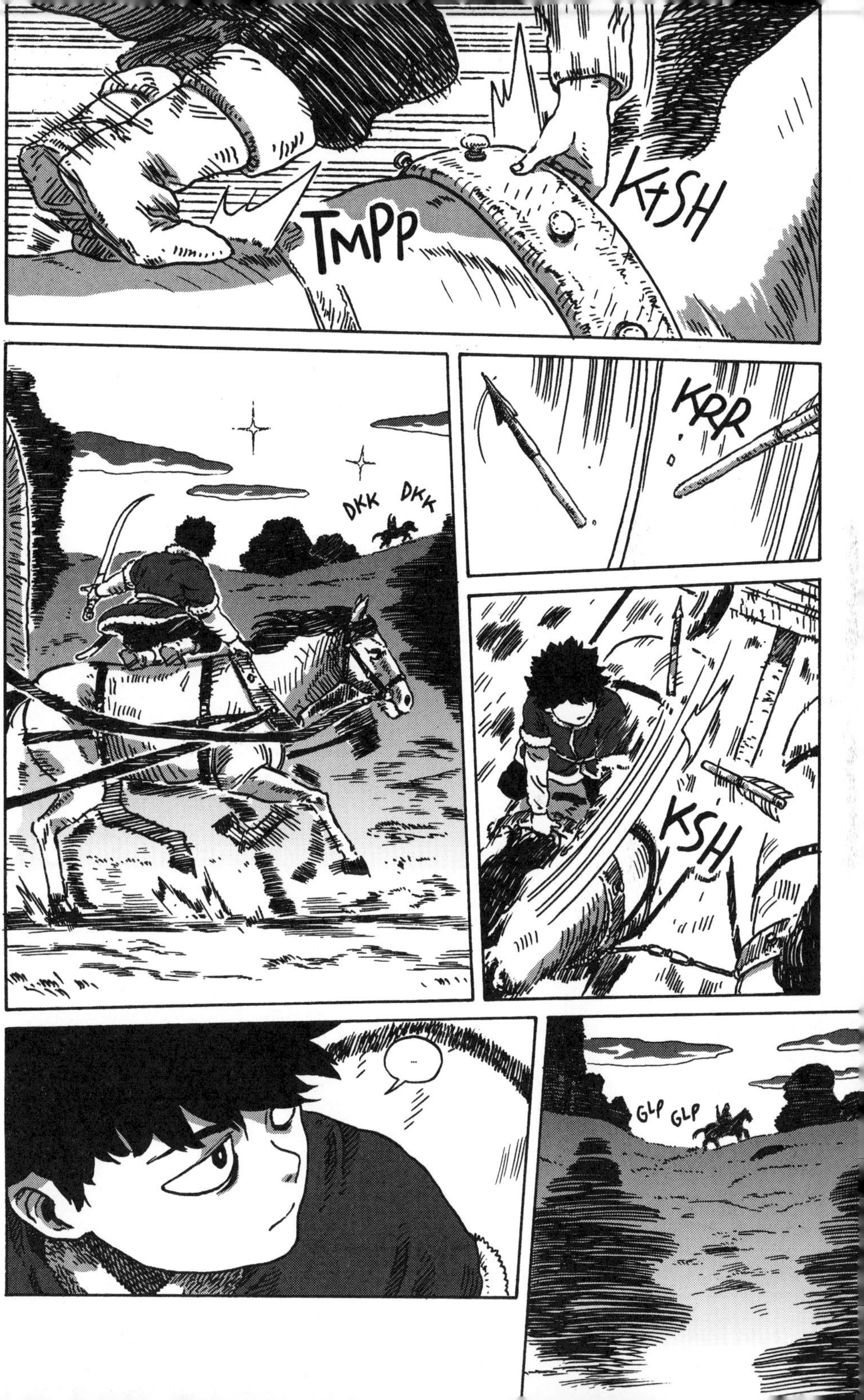
TMPP
KtSH
DKK DKK
KRR
KSH
...
GLP GLP

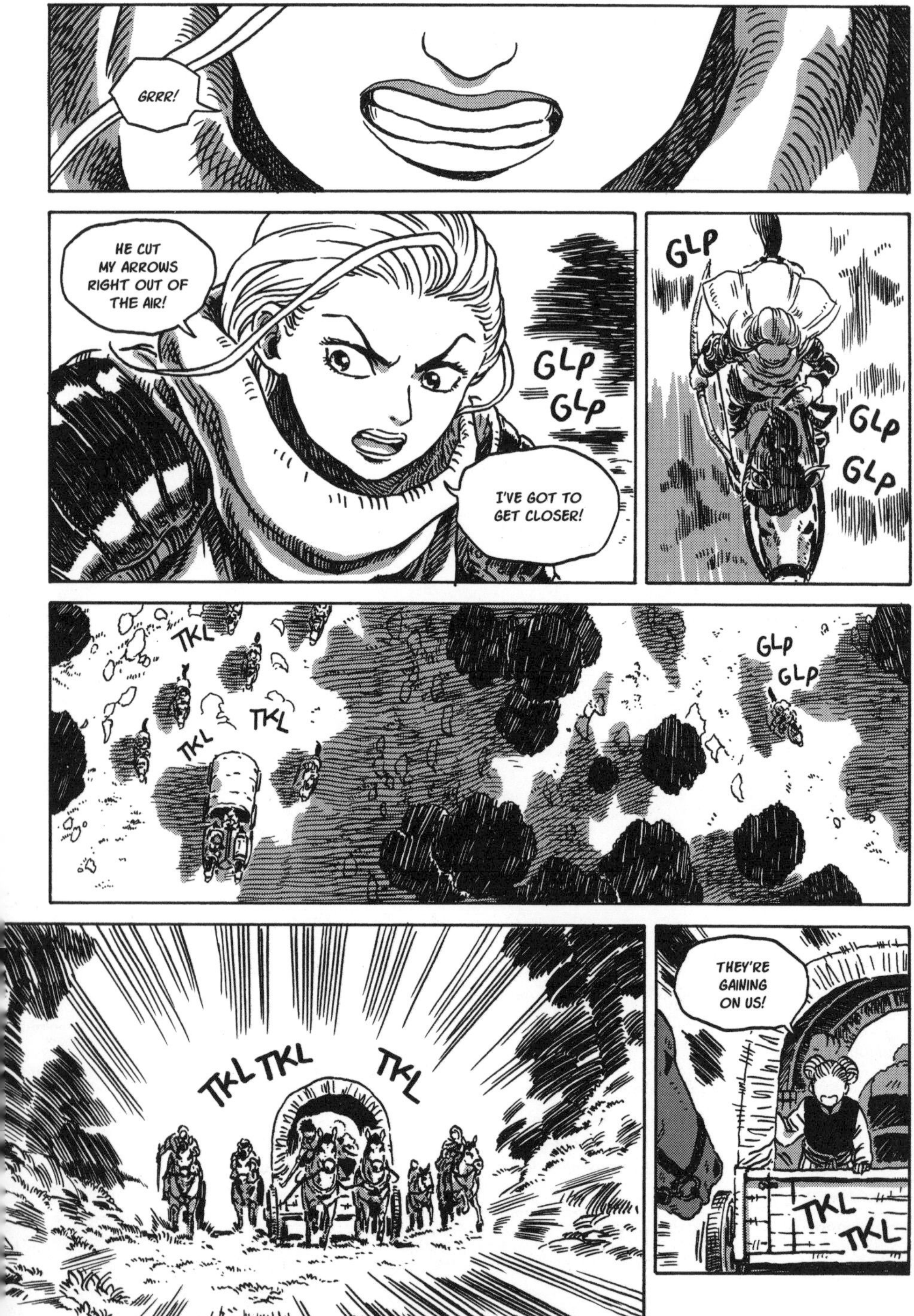
GRRR!
HE CUT MY ARROWS RIGHT OUT OF THE AIR!
GLP GLP
I'VE GOT TO GET CLOSER!
GLP
GLP
GLP
TKL
TKL
TKL
GLP GLP
TKL TKL
TKL
THEY'RE GAINING ON US!
TKL
TKL

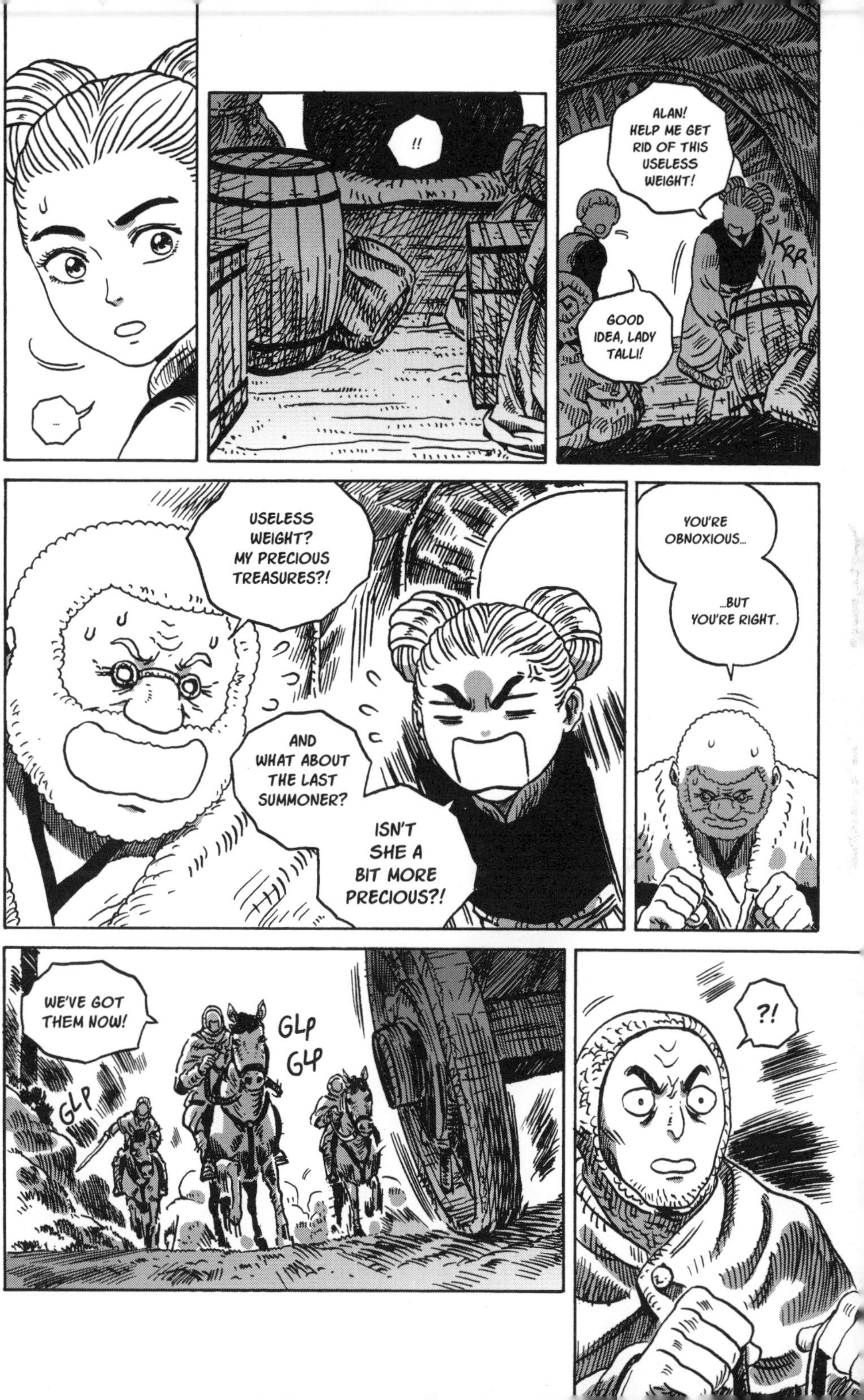
...
!!
ALAN! HELP ME GET RID OF THIS USELESS WEIGHT!
GOOD IDEA, LADY TALLI!
KRR
USELESS WEIGHT? MY PRECIOUS TREASURES?!
AND WHAT ABOUT THE LAST SUMMONER?
ISN'T SHE A BIT MORE PRECIOUS?!
YOU'RE OBNOXIOUS...
...BUT YOU'RE RIGHT.
WE'VE GOT THEM NOW!
GLP GLP
GLP
?!

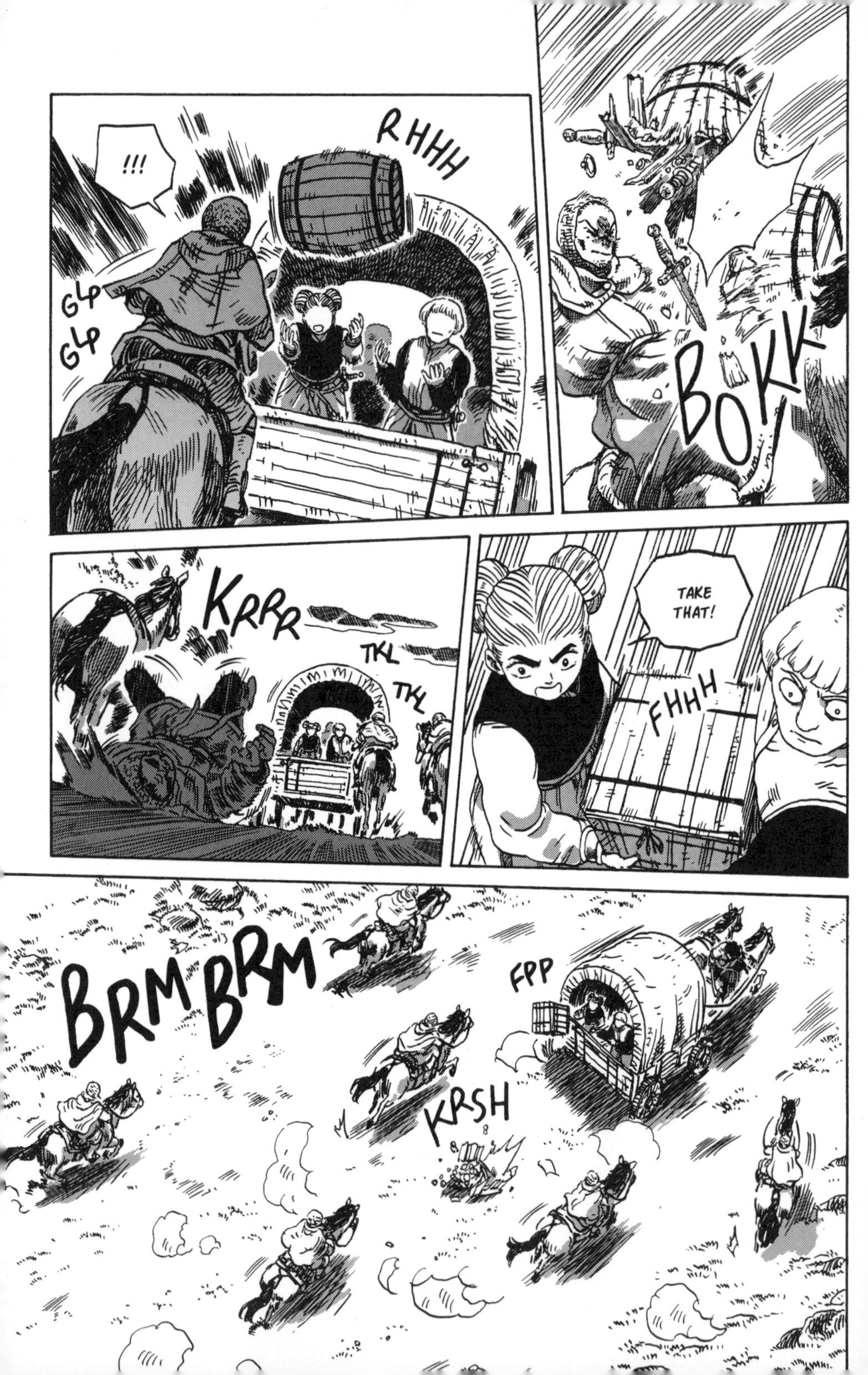

!!!
RHHH
GLP
GLP
BOKK
KRRR
TKL
TKL
TAKE THAT!
FHHH
BRM BRM
FPP
KRSH

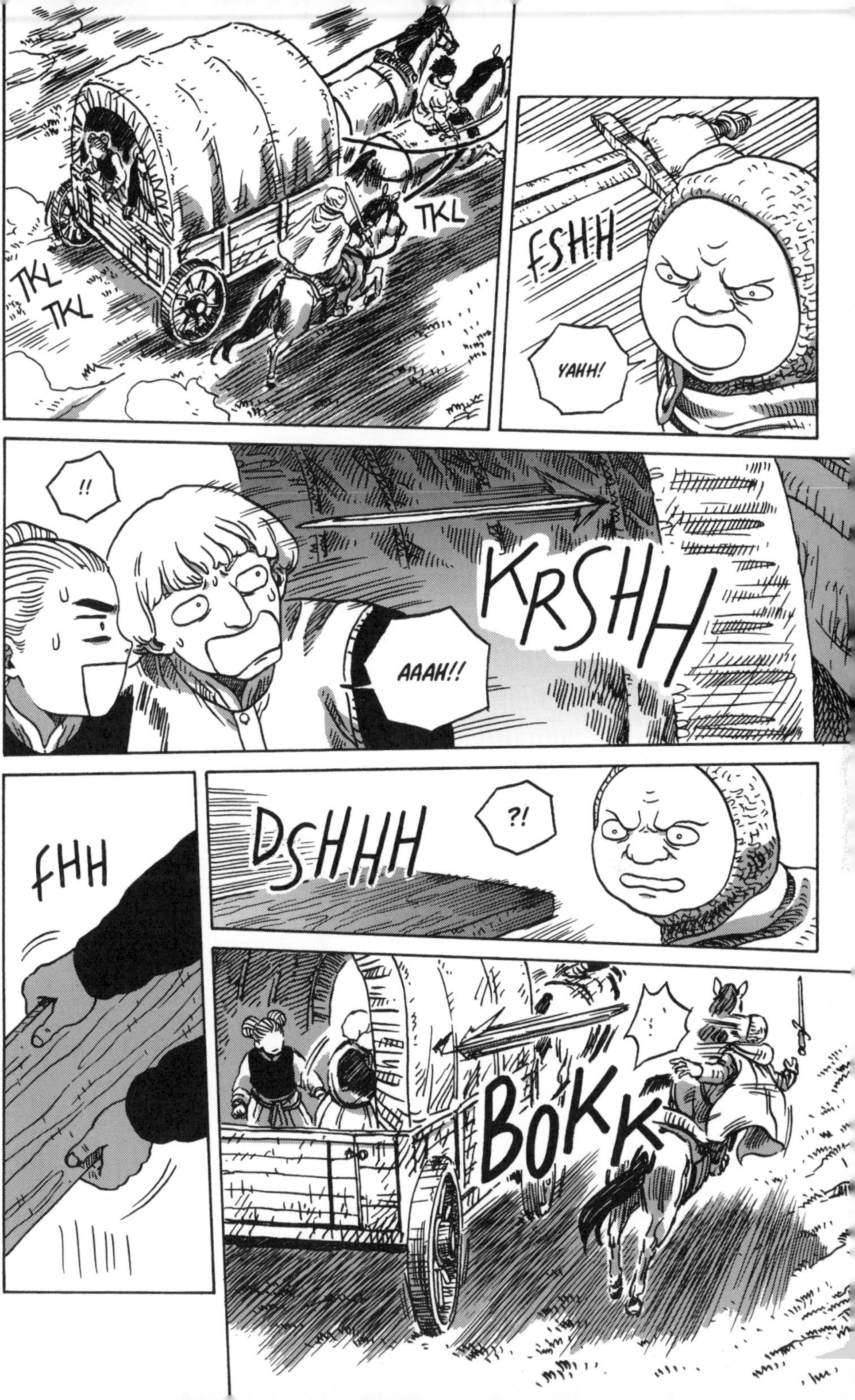
TKL
TKL
TKL
FSHH
YAHH!
!!
AAAH!!
KRSHH
FHH
DSHHH
?!
BOKK

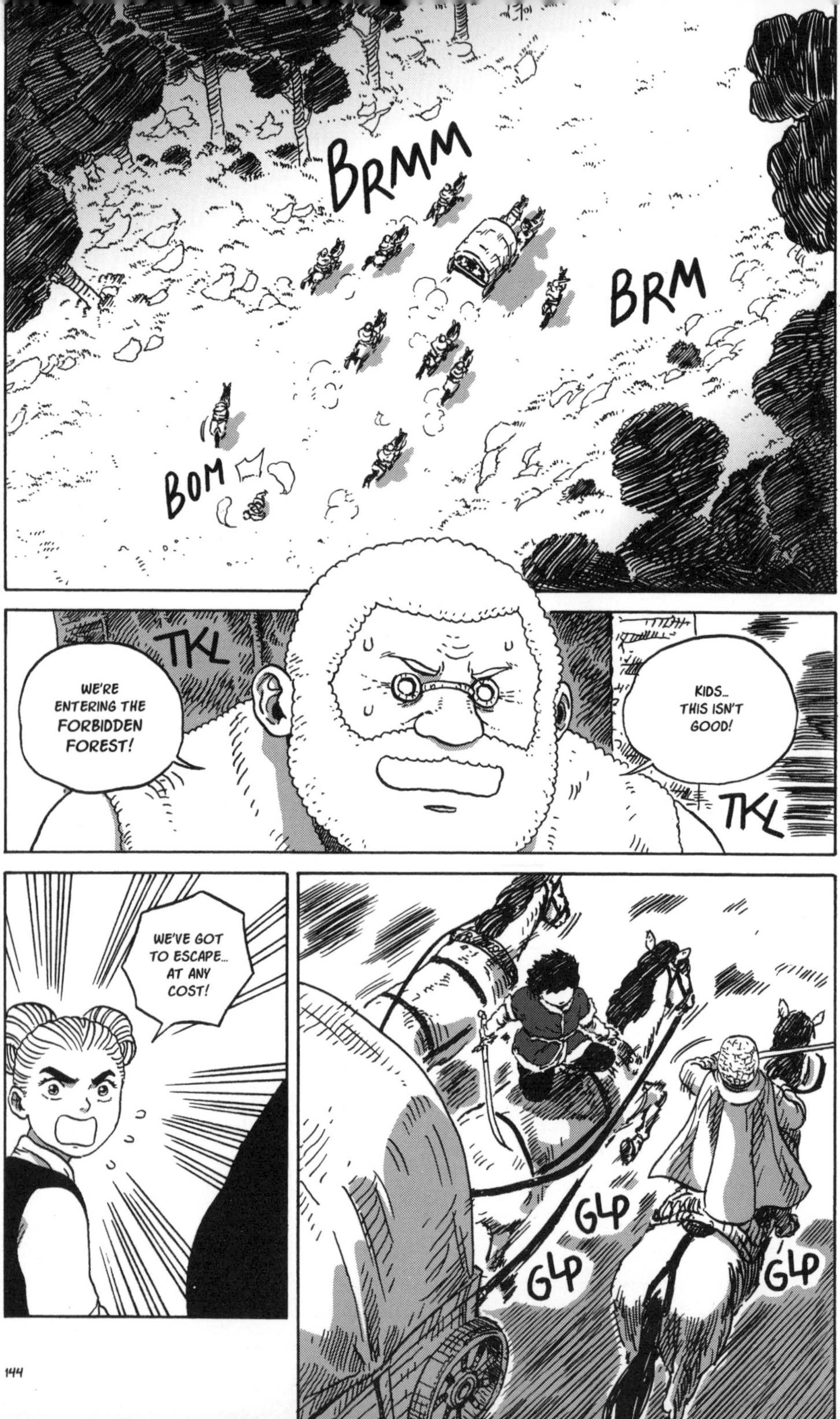
BRMM
BRM
BOM
TKL
WE'RE ENTERING THE FORBIDDEN FOREST!
KIDS... THIS ISN'T GOOD!
TKL
WE'VE GOT TO ESCAPE... AT ANY COST!
GLP
GLP
GLP
GLP

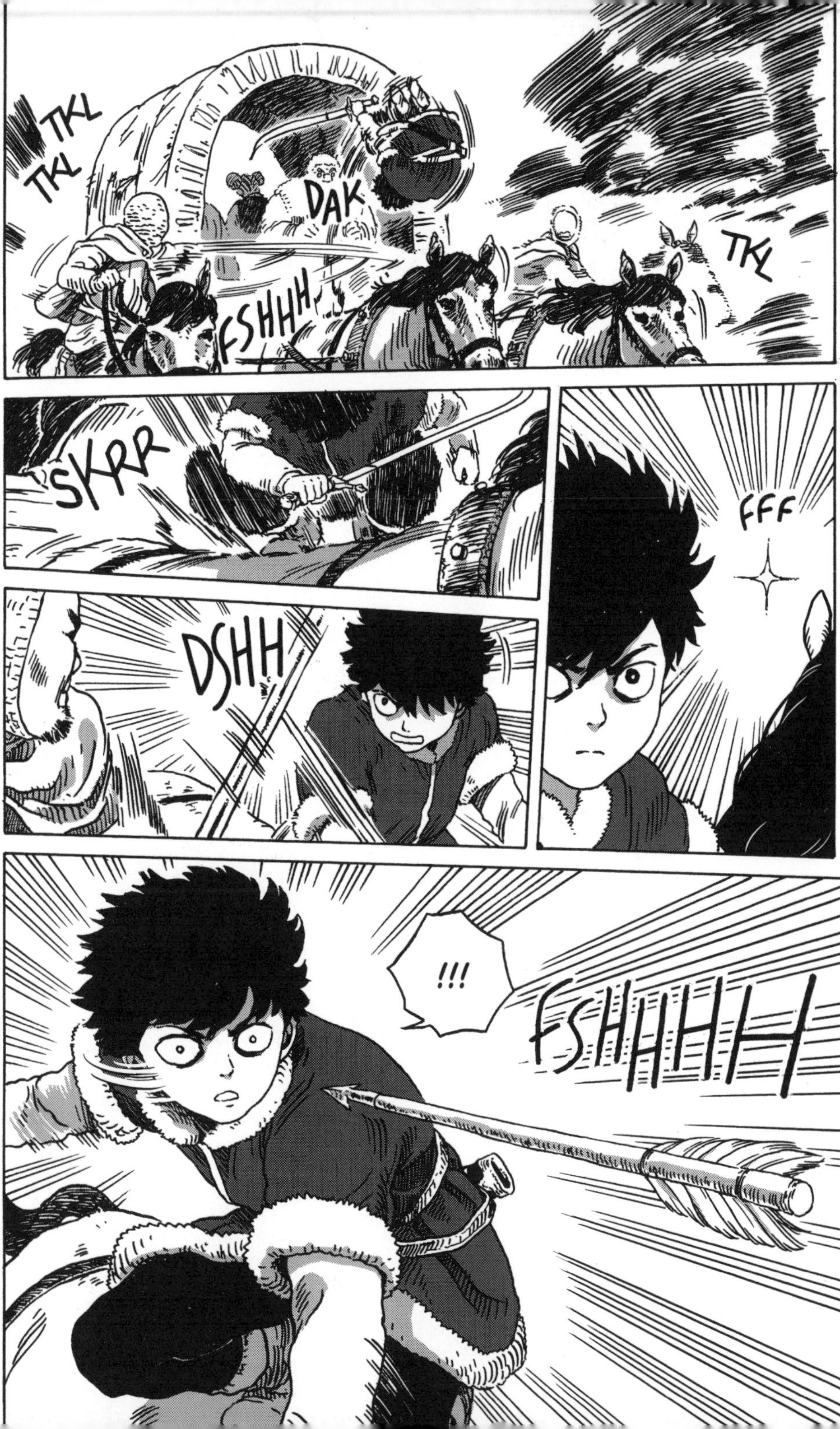
TKL
TKL
DAK
TKL
FSHHH
SKRR
FFF
DSHH
!!!
FSHHHH

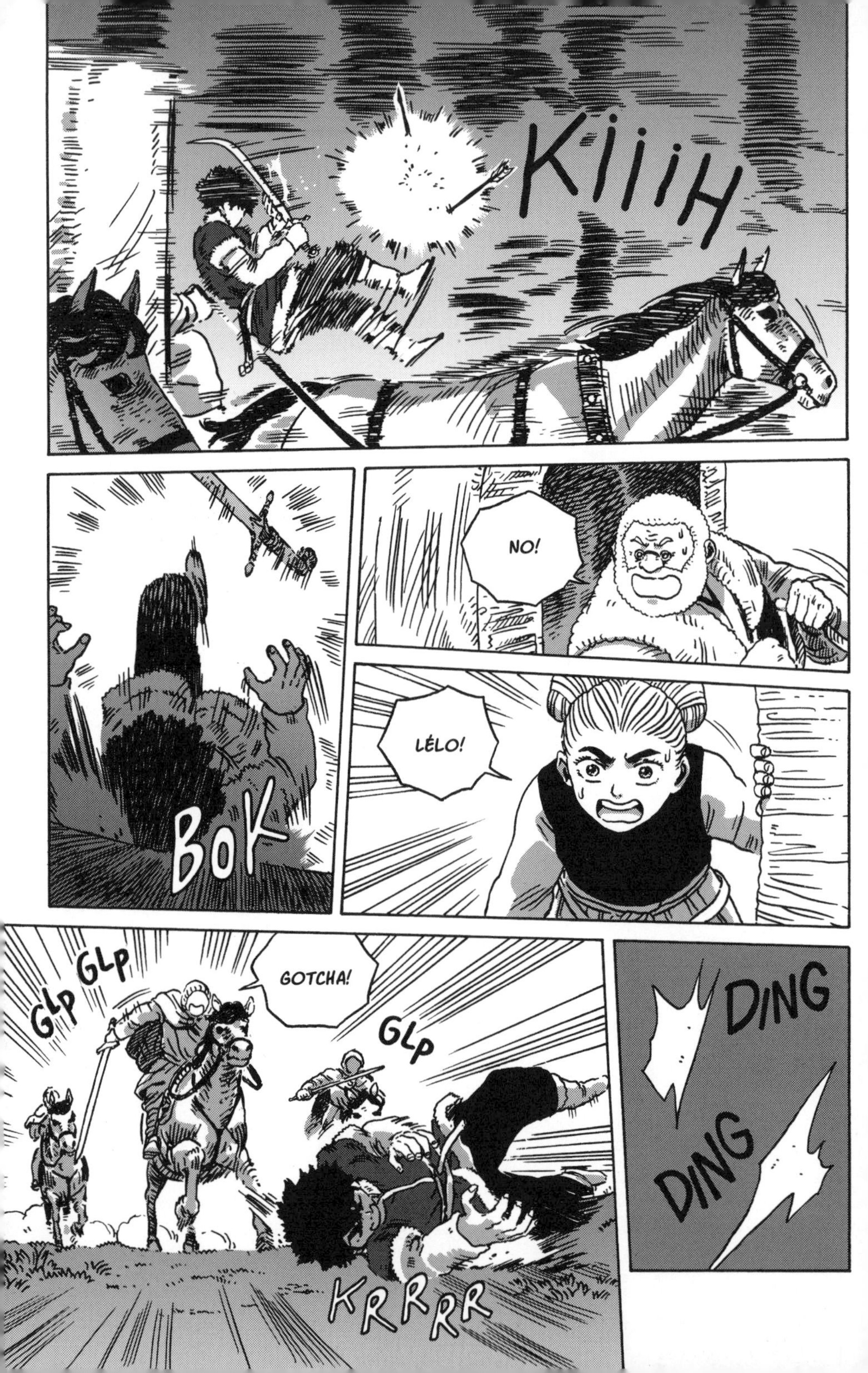
KIIIH
BOK
NO!
LÉLO!
GLP GLP
GOTCHA!
GLP
KRRRR
DING
DING

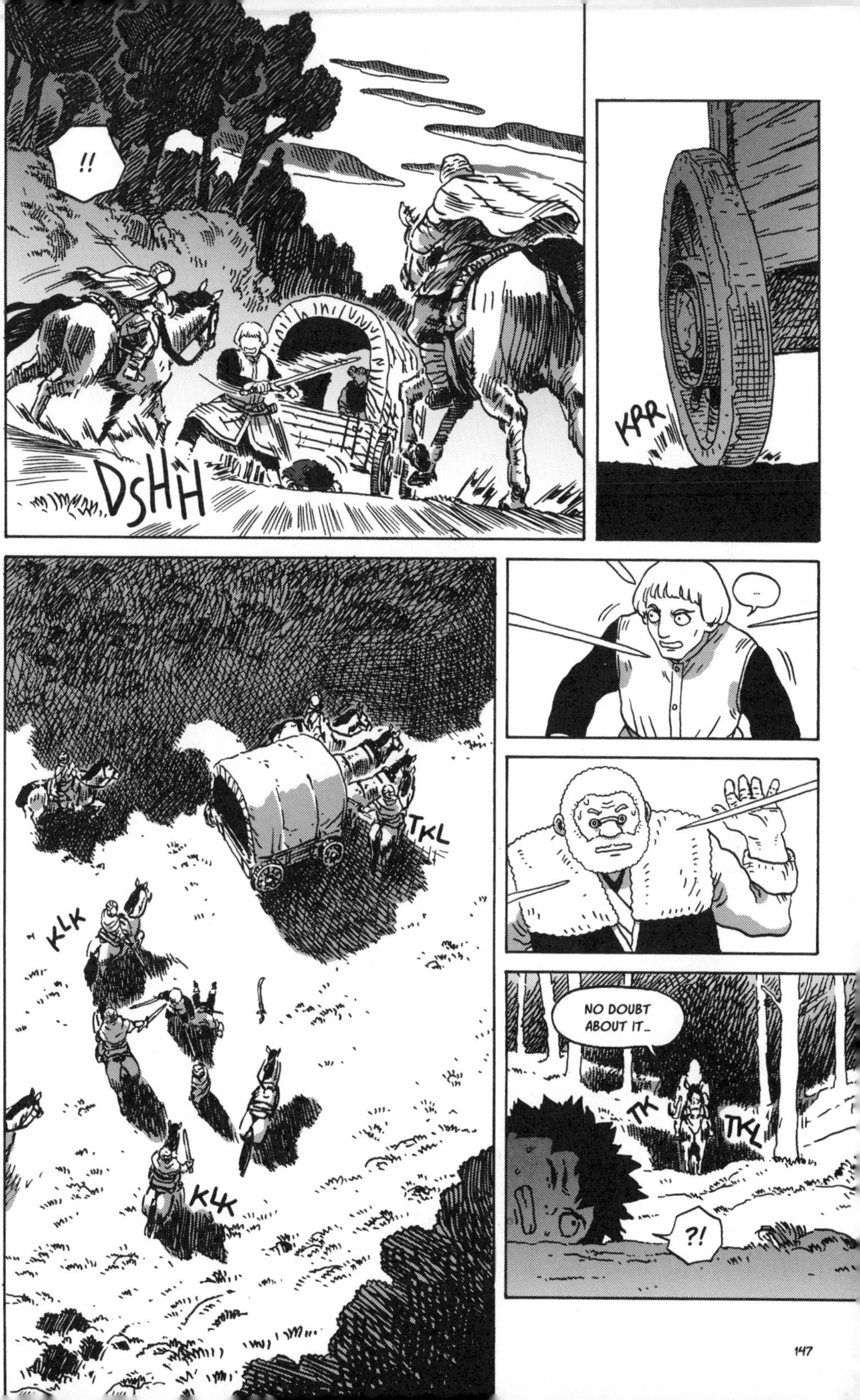
!!
DSHH
KRR
TKL
KLK
KLK
...
NO DOUBT ABOUT IT...
TK
TKL
?!

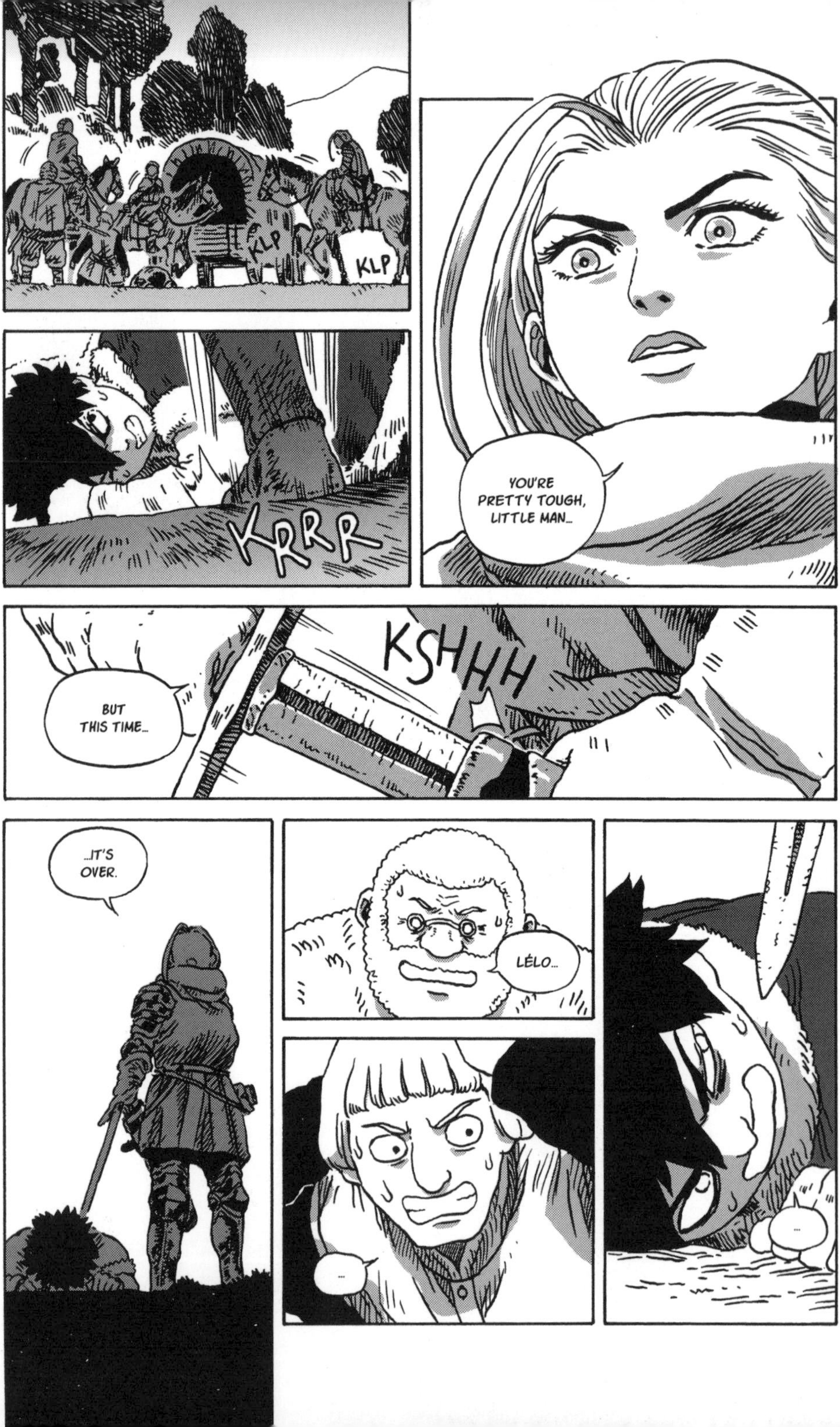
KLP
KLP
KRRR
YOU'RE PRETTY TOUGH, LITTLE MAN...
BUT THIS TIME...
KSHHH
...IT'S OVER.
LÉLO...
...
...

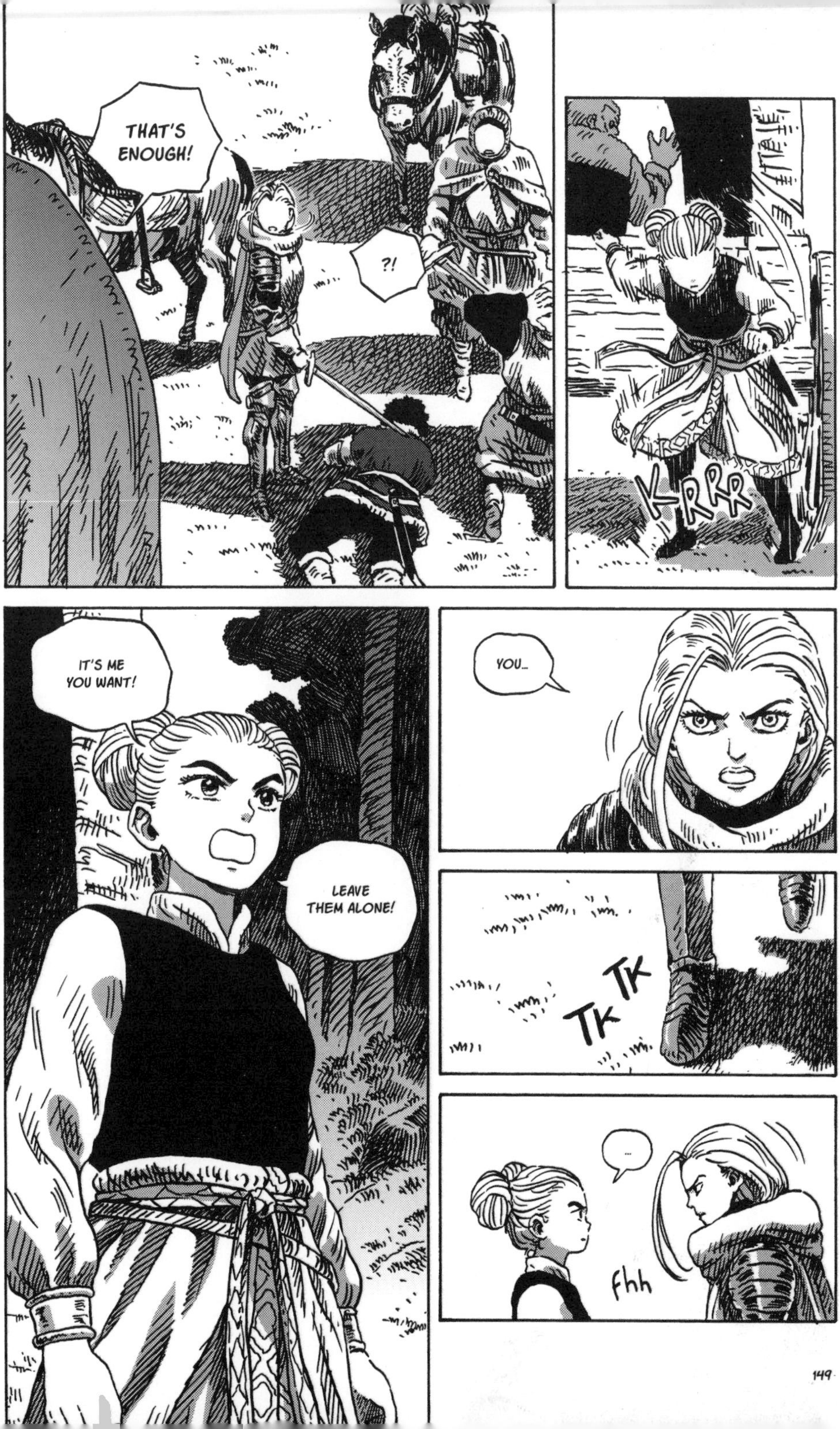
THAT'S ENOUGH!
?!
KRRR
IT'S ME YOU WANT!
LEAVE THEM ALONE!
YOU...
TK TK
...
fhh

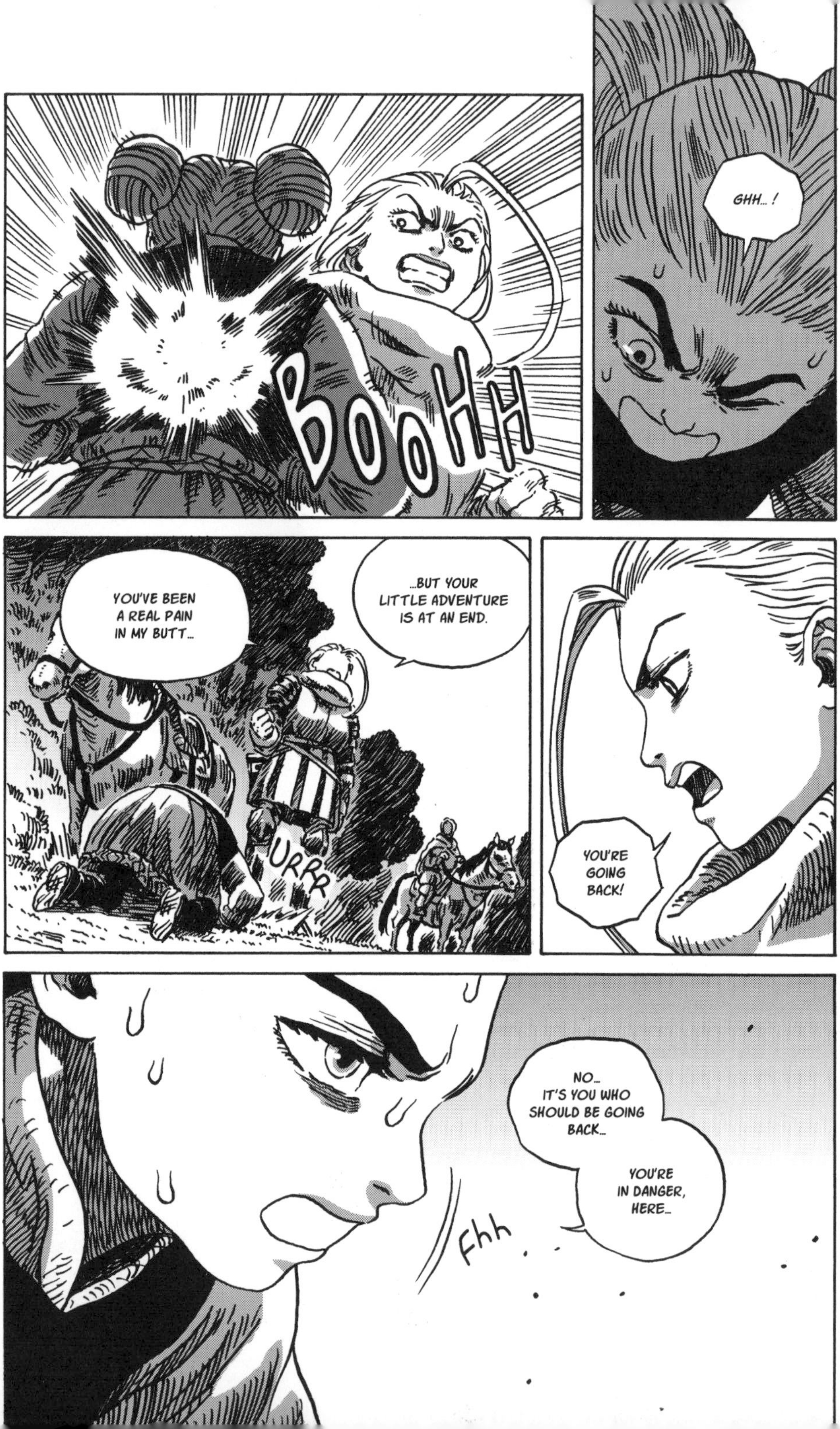
BOOHH
GHH... !
YOU'VE BEEN A REAL PAIN IN MY BUTT...
...BUT YOUR LITTLE ADVENTURE IS AT AN END.
URRR
YOU'RE GOING BACK!
NO... IT'S YOU WHO SHOULD BE GOING BACK...
YOU'RE IN DANGER, HERE...
Fhh

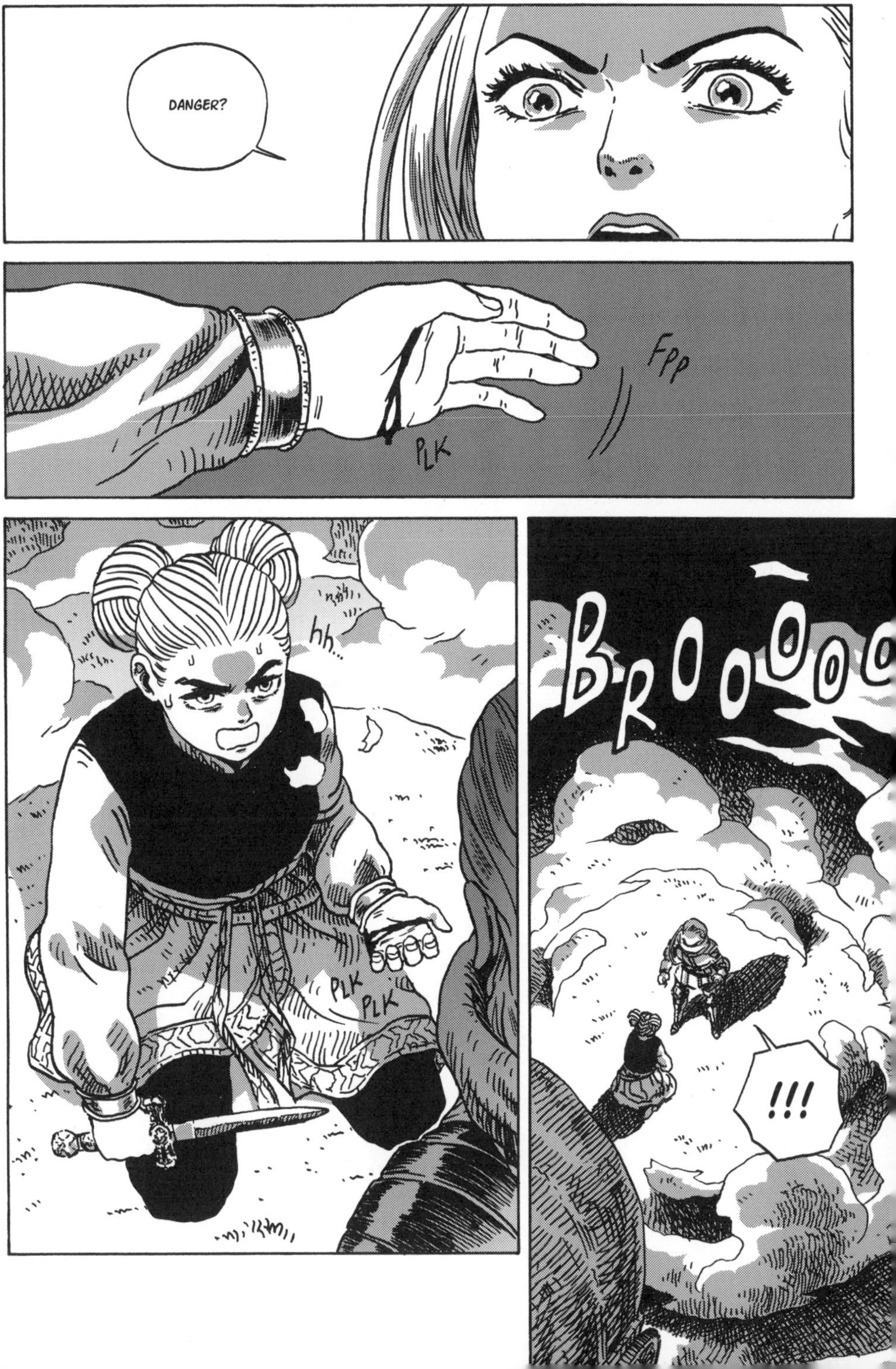
DANGER?
FPP
PLK
hh...
PLK
PLK
BROOOOO
!!!

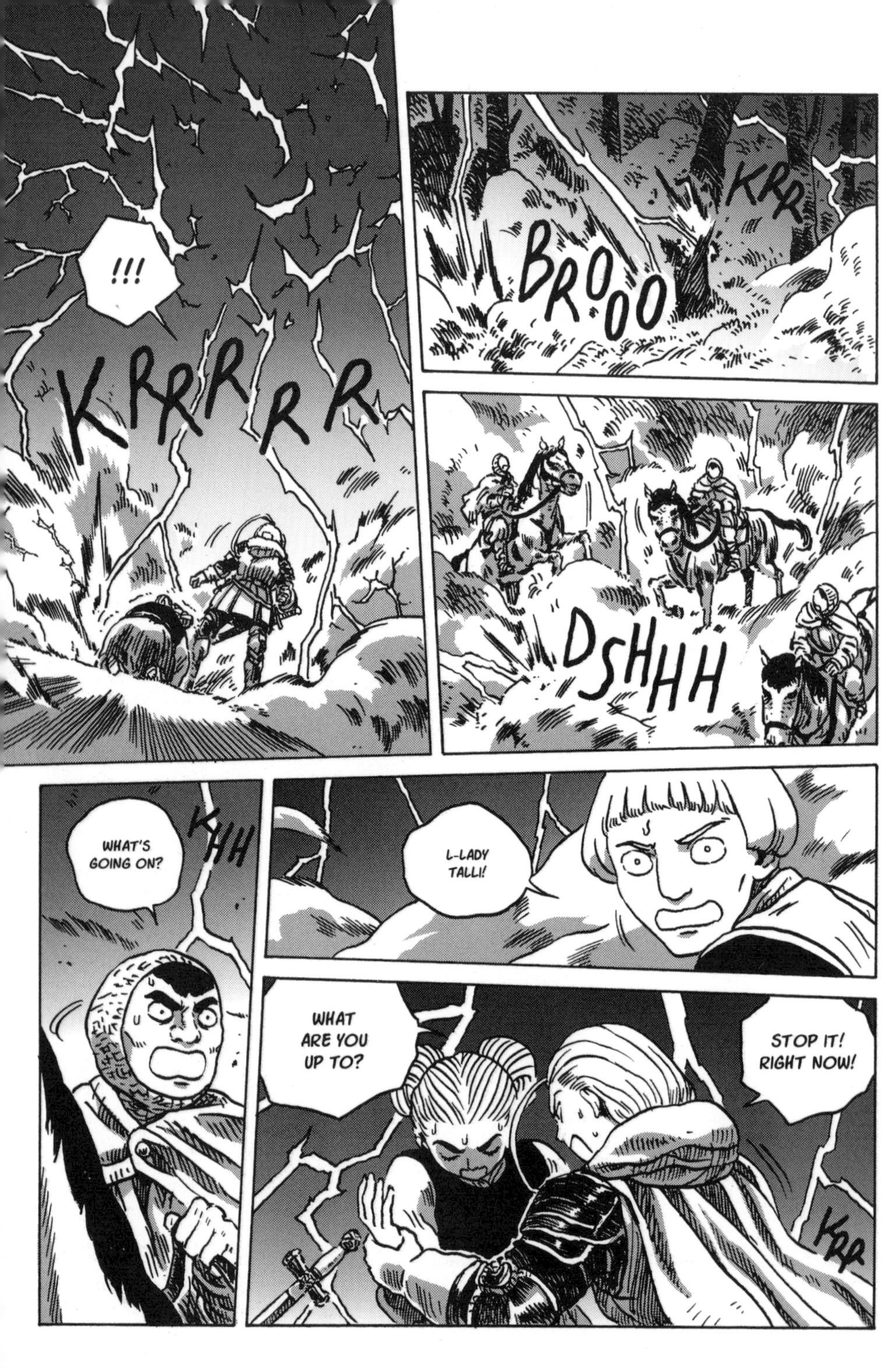
!!!
KRRRRRR
BROOOO
KRRR
DSHHH
WHAT'S GOING ON?
KHH
L-LADY TALLI!
WHAT ARE YOU UP TO?
STOP IT! RIGHT NOW!
KRR

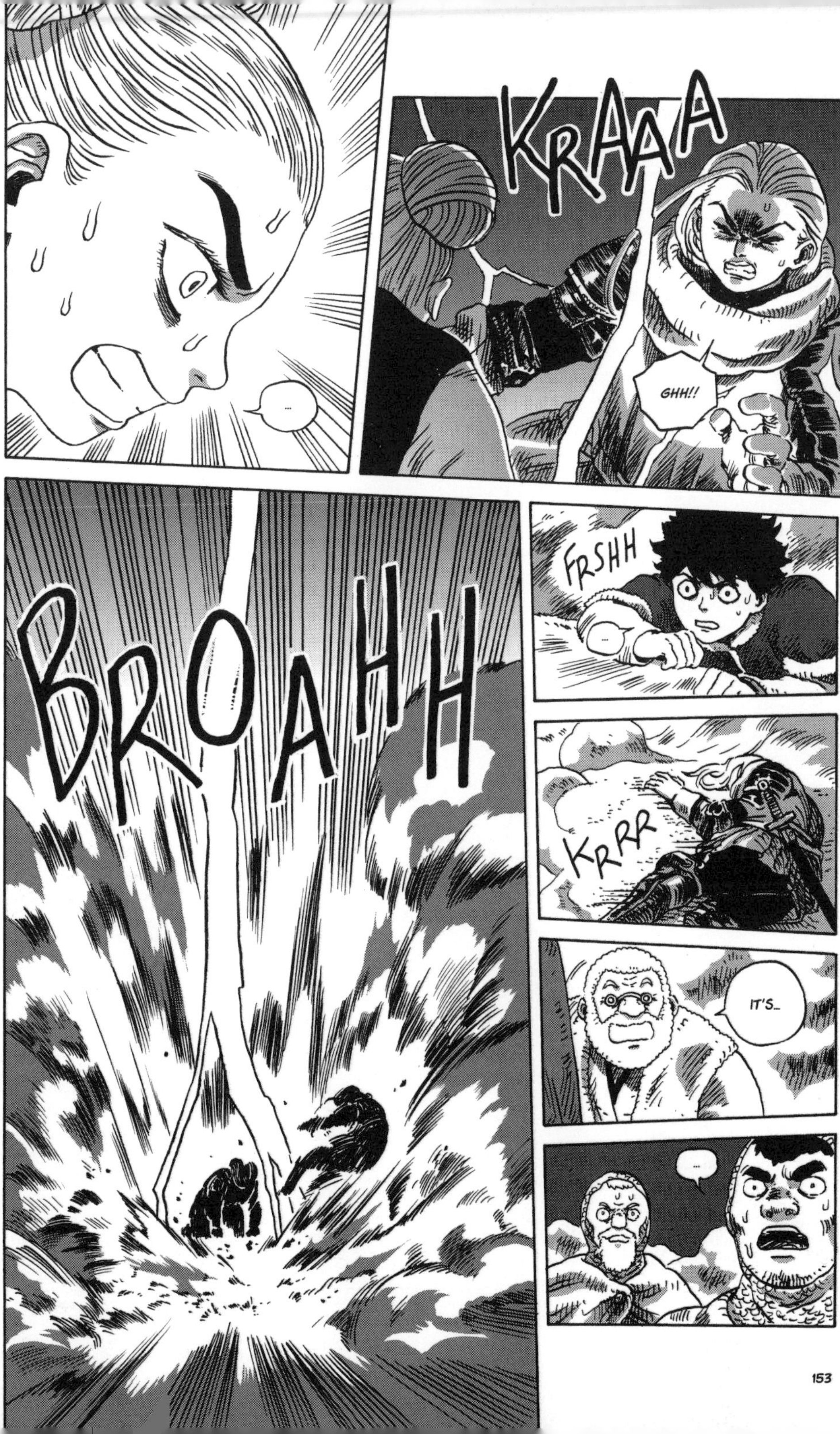
...
KRAAA
GHH!!
BROAHH
FRSHH
...
KRRR
IT'S...
...

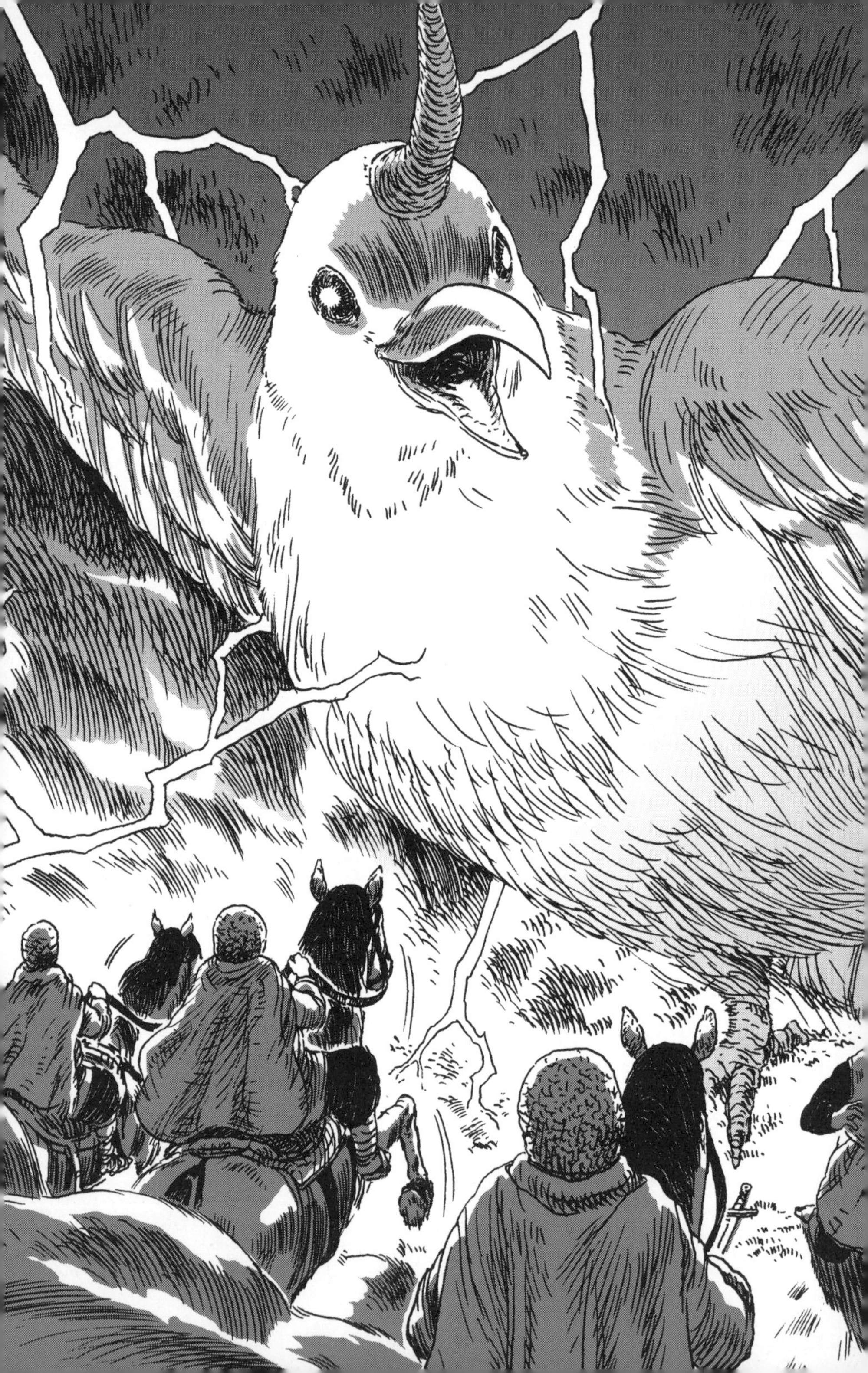

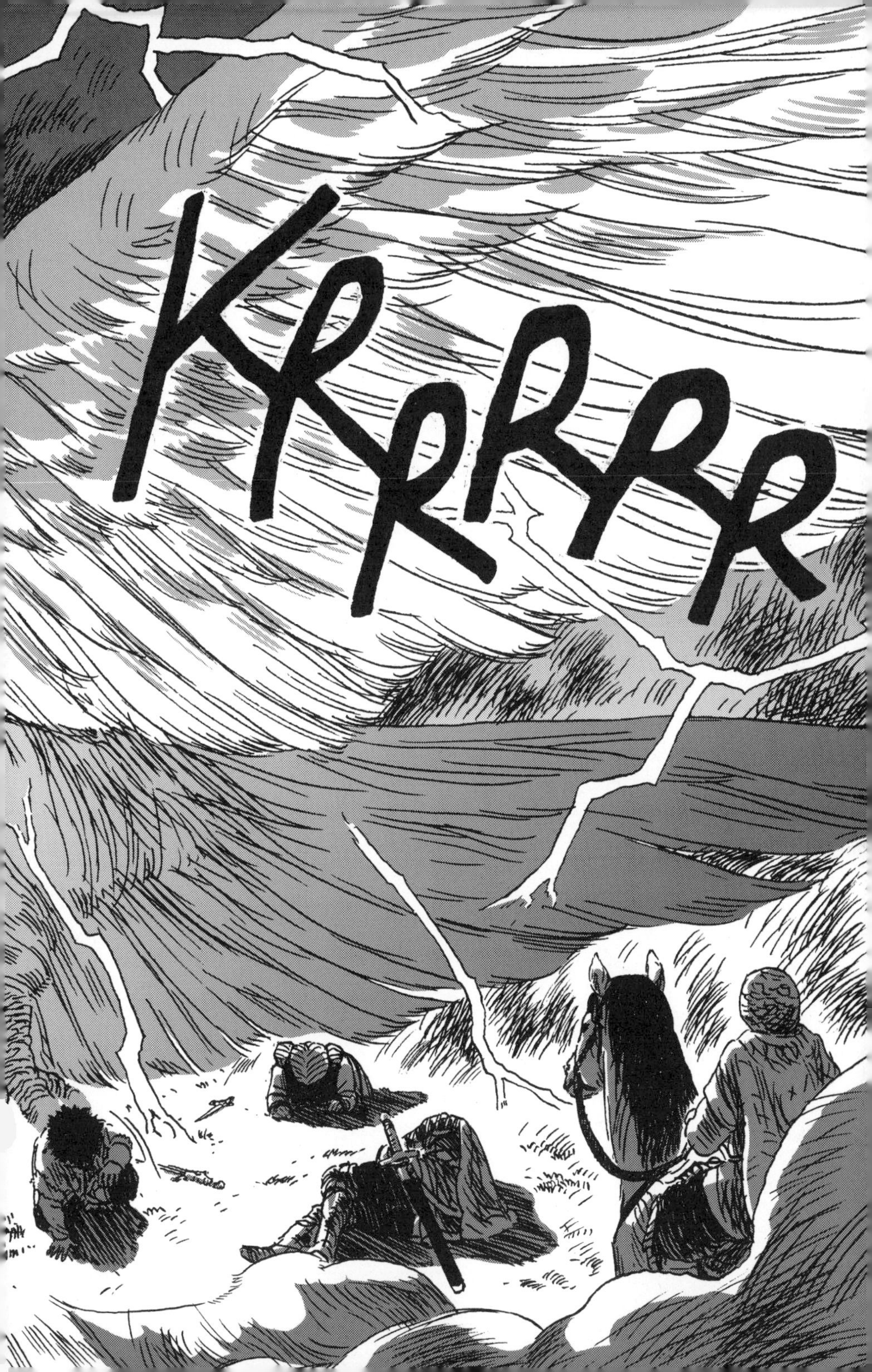
KRRRRR

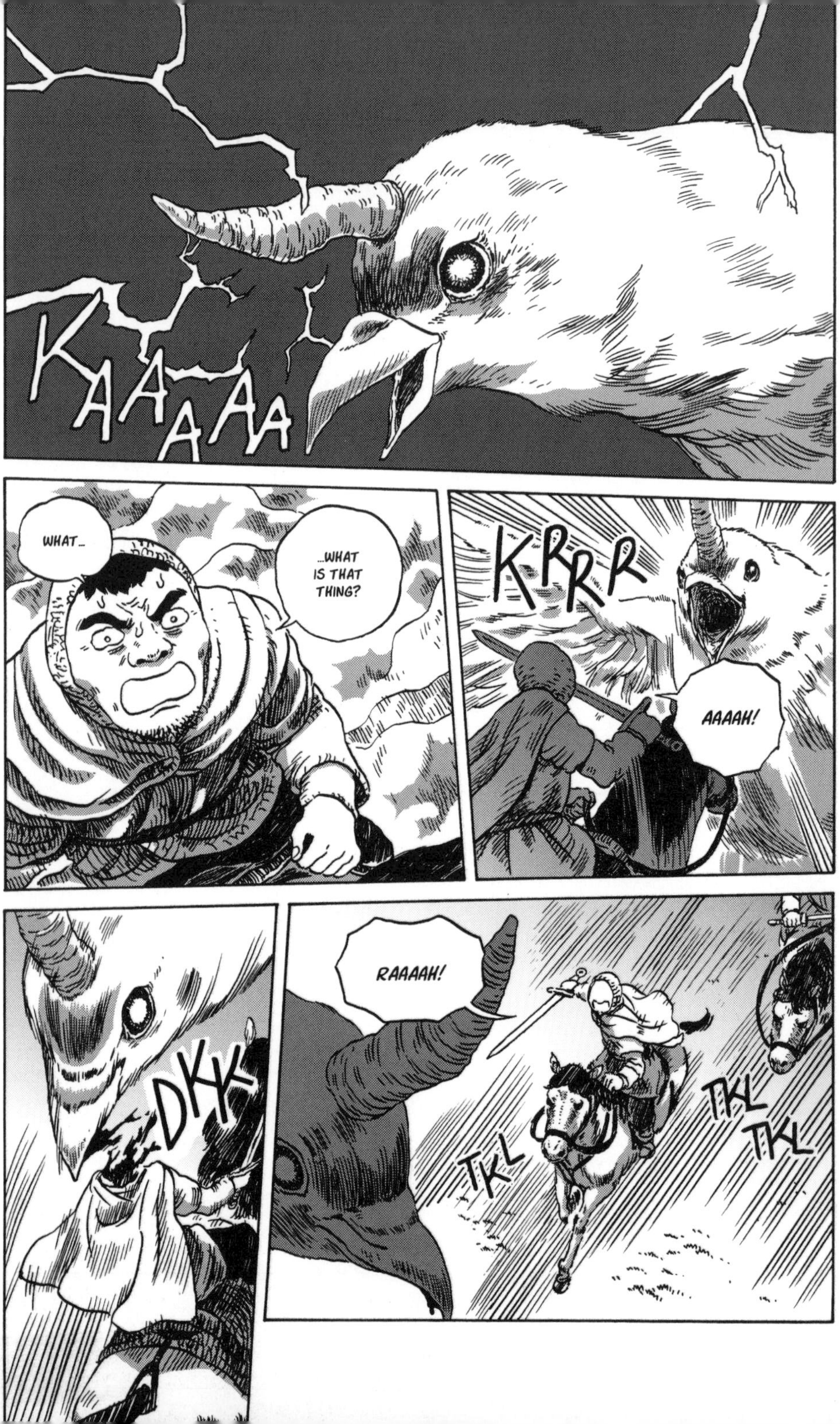
KAAAAAA
WHAT...
...WHAT IS THAT THING?
KRRRR
AAAAH!
DKKL
RAAAAH!
TKL
TKL
TKL

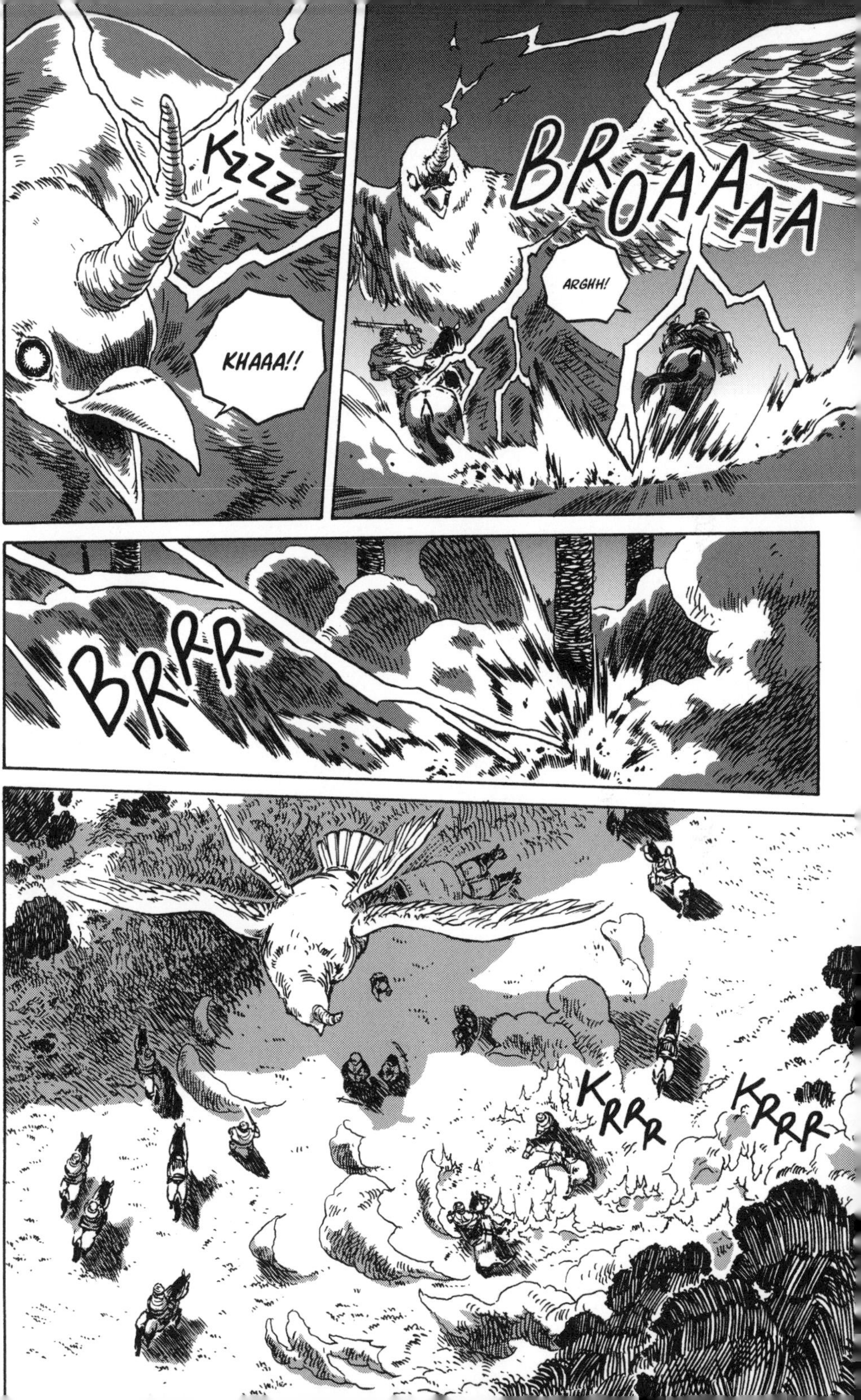
KZZZZ
KHAAA!!
BROAAAAA
ARGHH!
BRRR
KRRR
KRRRR

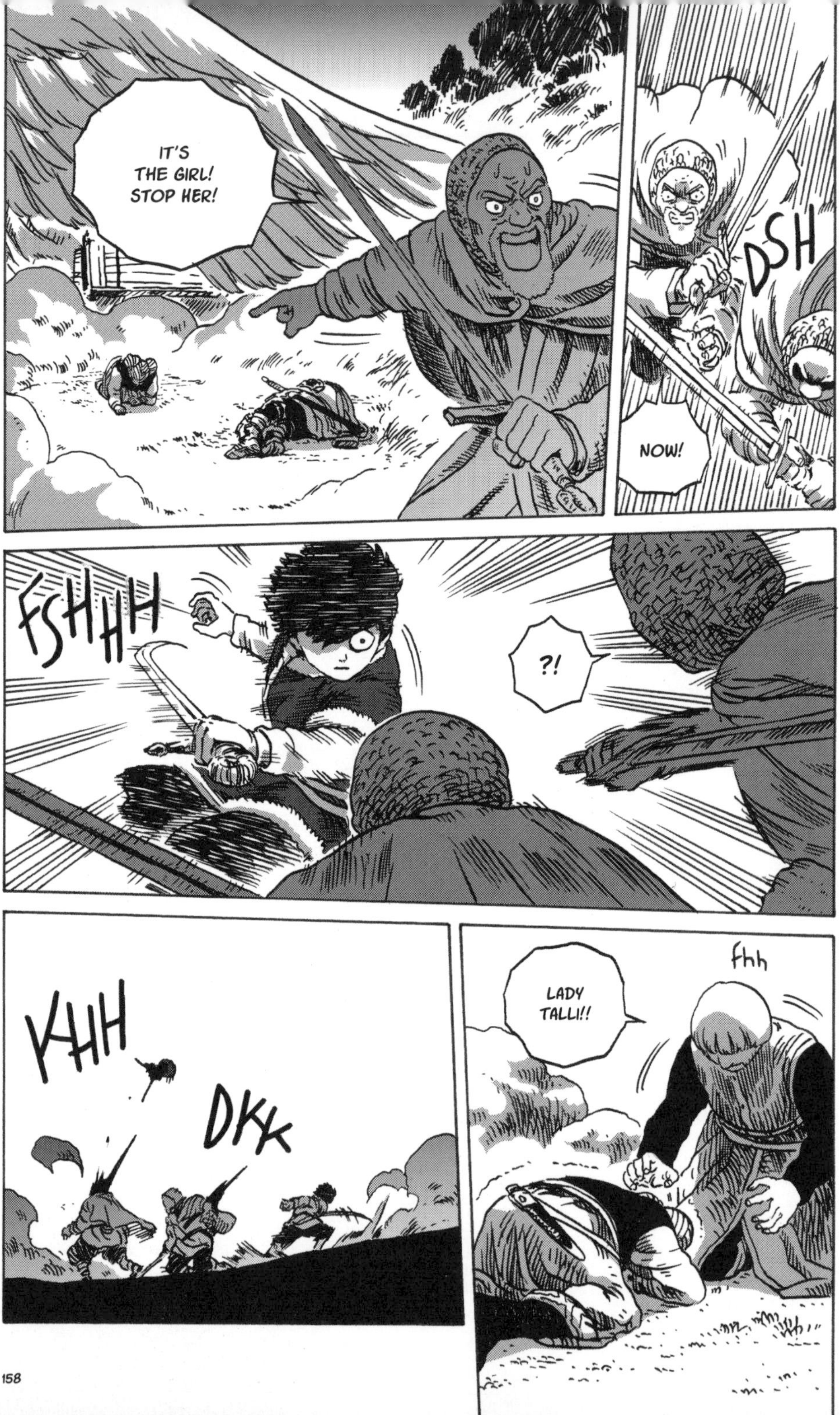
IT'S THE GIRL! STOP HER!
DSH
NOW!
FSHHH
?!
KHH
DKK
fhh
LADY TALLI!!

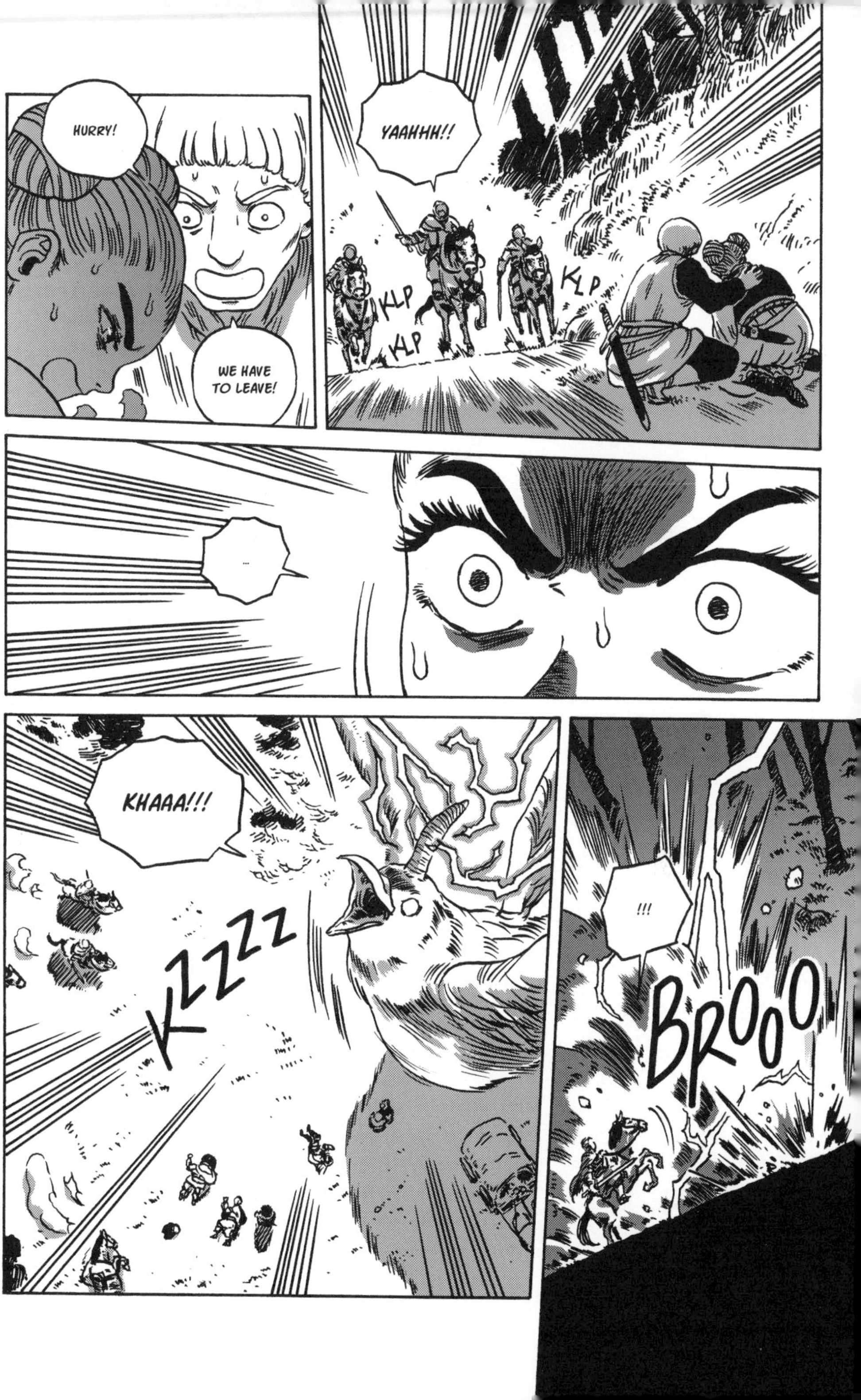
HURRY!
WE HAVE TO LEAVE!
YAAHHH!!
KLP
KLP
KLP
...
KHAAA!!!
KZZZZ
!!!
BROOOO

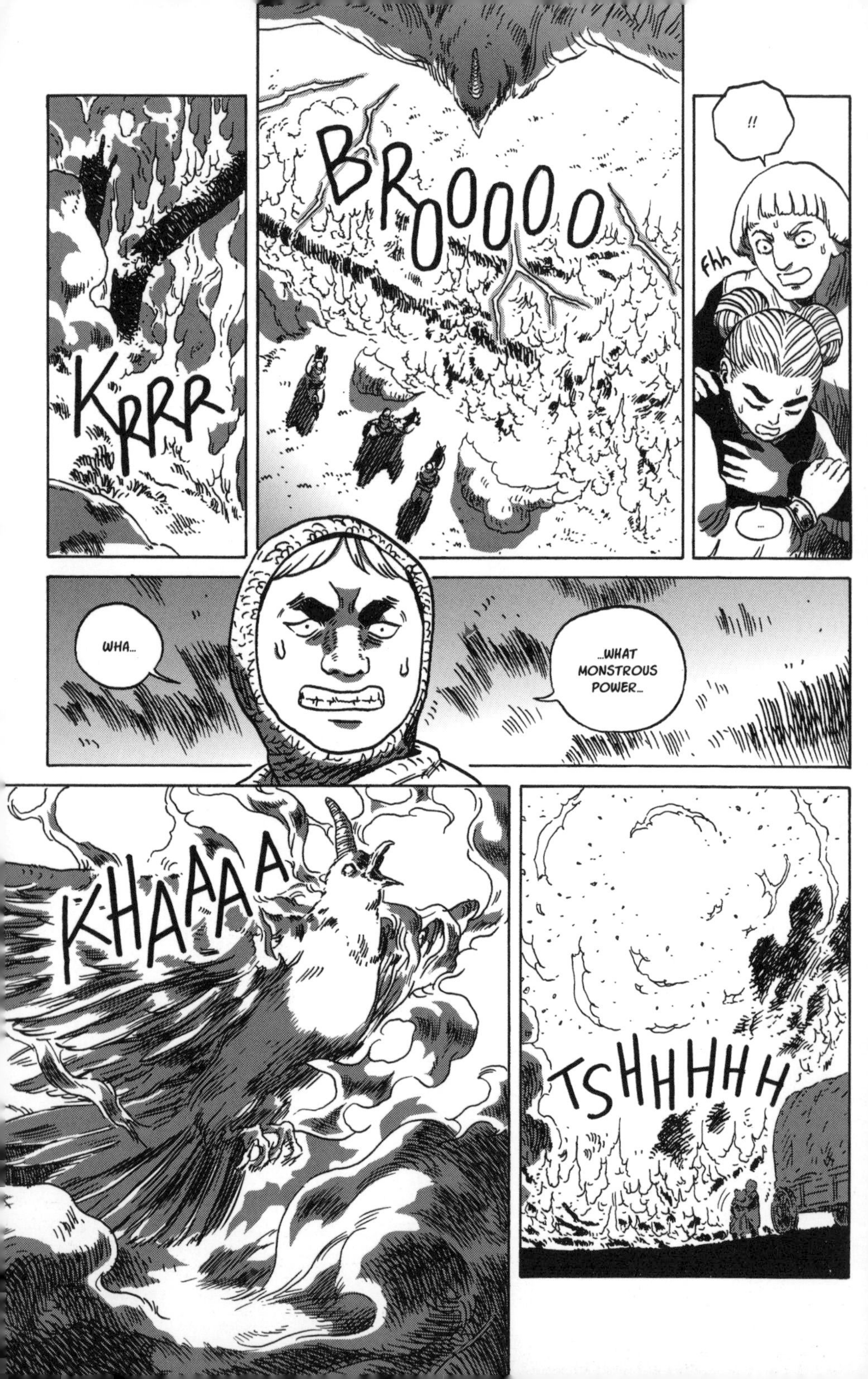
KRRR
BROOOOO
!!
fhh
...
WHA...
...WHAT MONSTROUS POWER...
KHAAAA
TSHHHHH

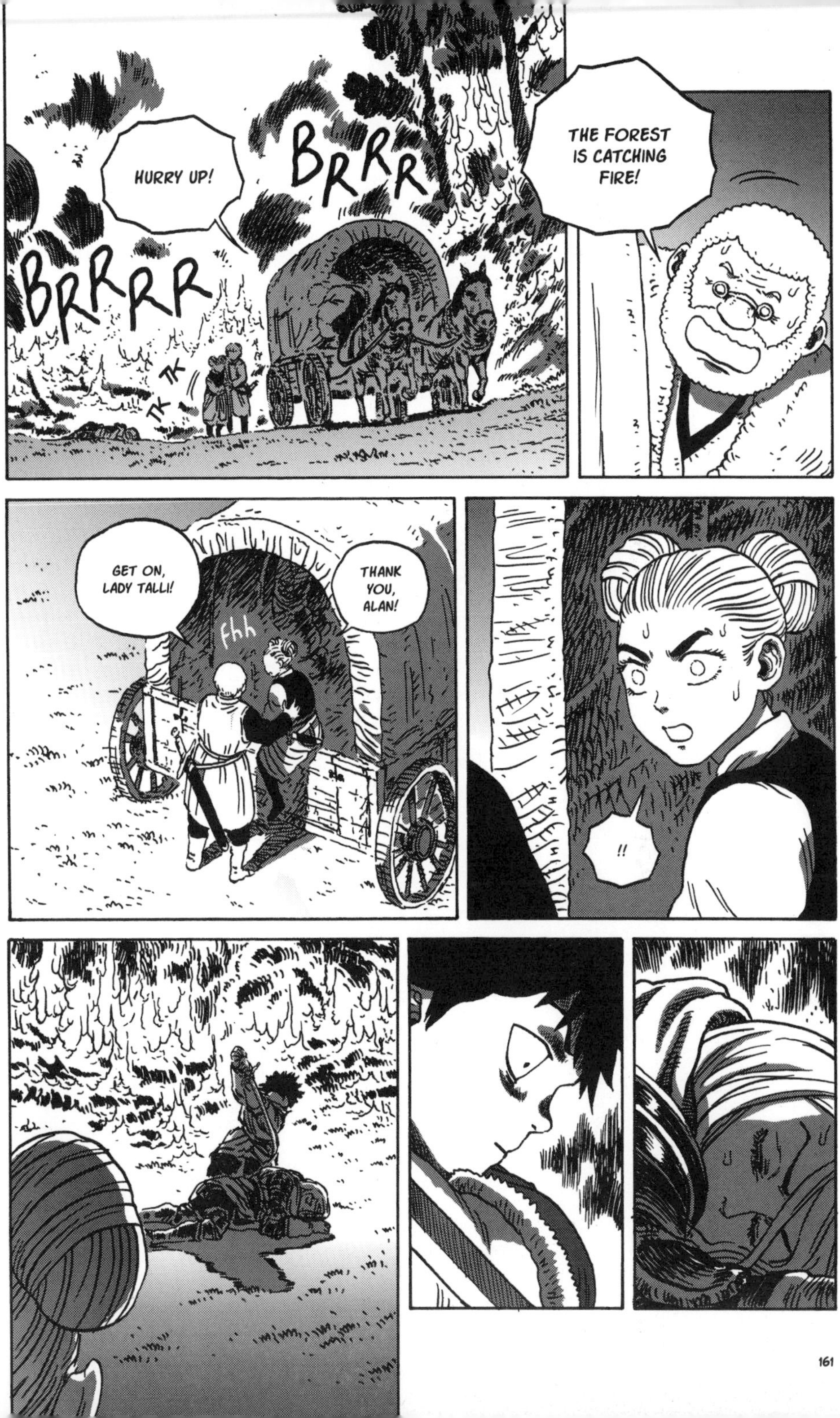
BRRRR
HURRY UP!
BRRR
TK TK
THE FOREST IS CATCHING FIRE!
GET ON, LADY TALLI!
THANK YOU, ALAN!
fhh
!!

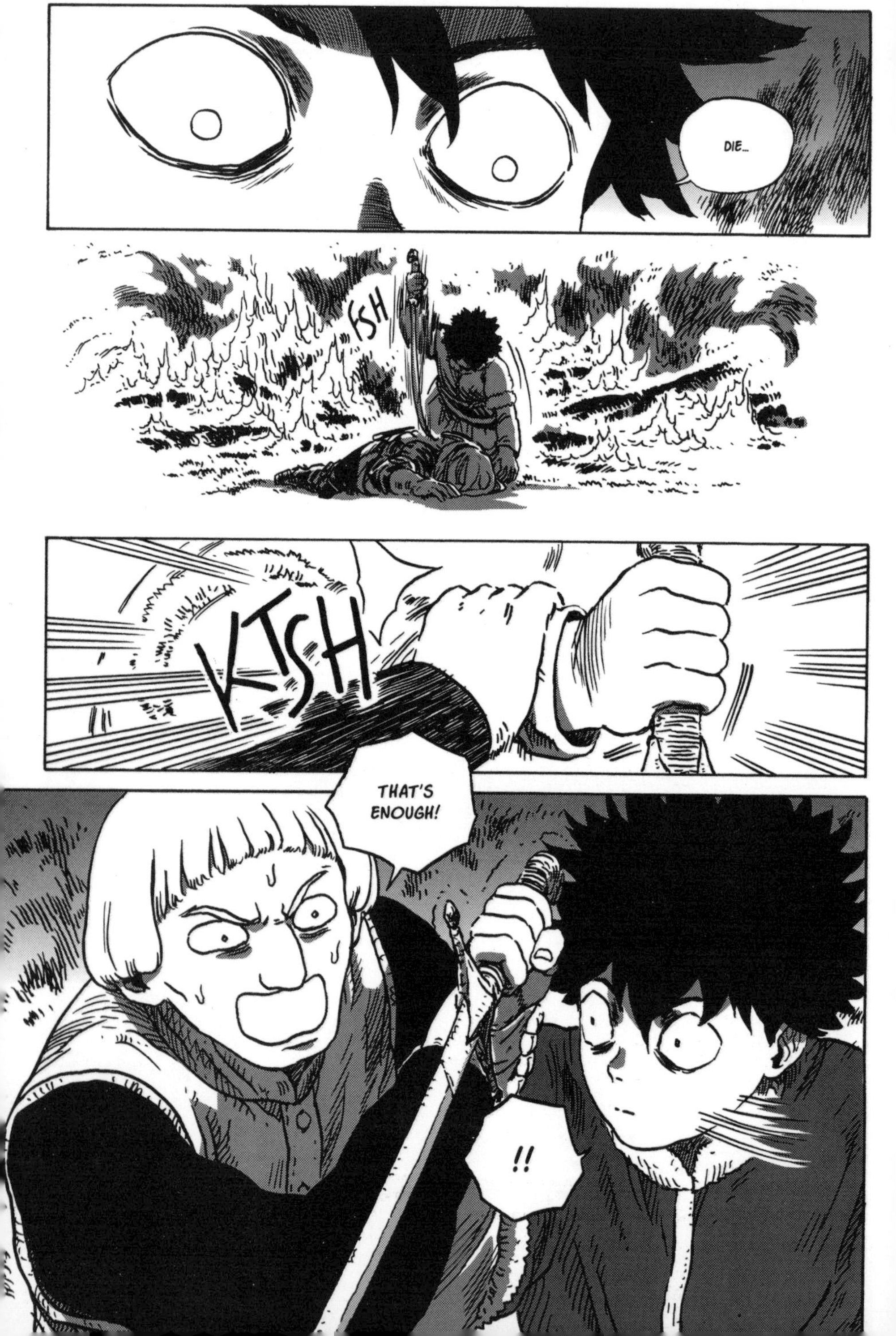
DIE...
FSH
KTSH
THAT'S ENOUGH!
!!

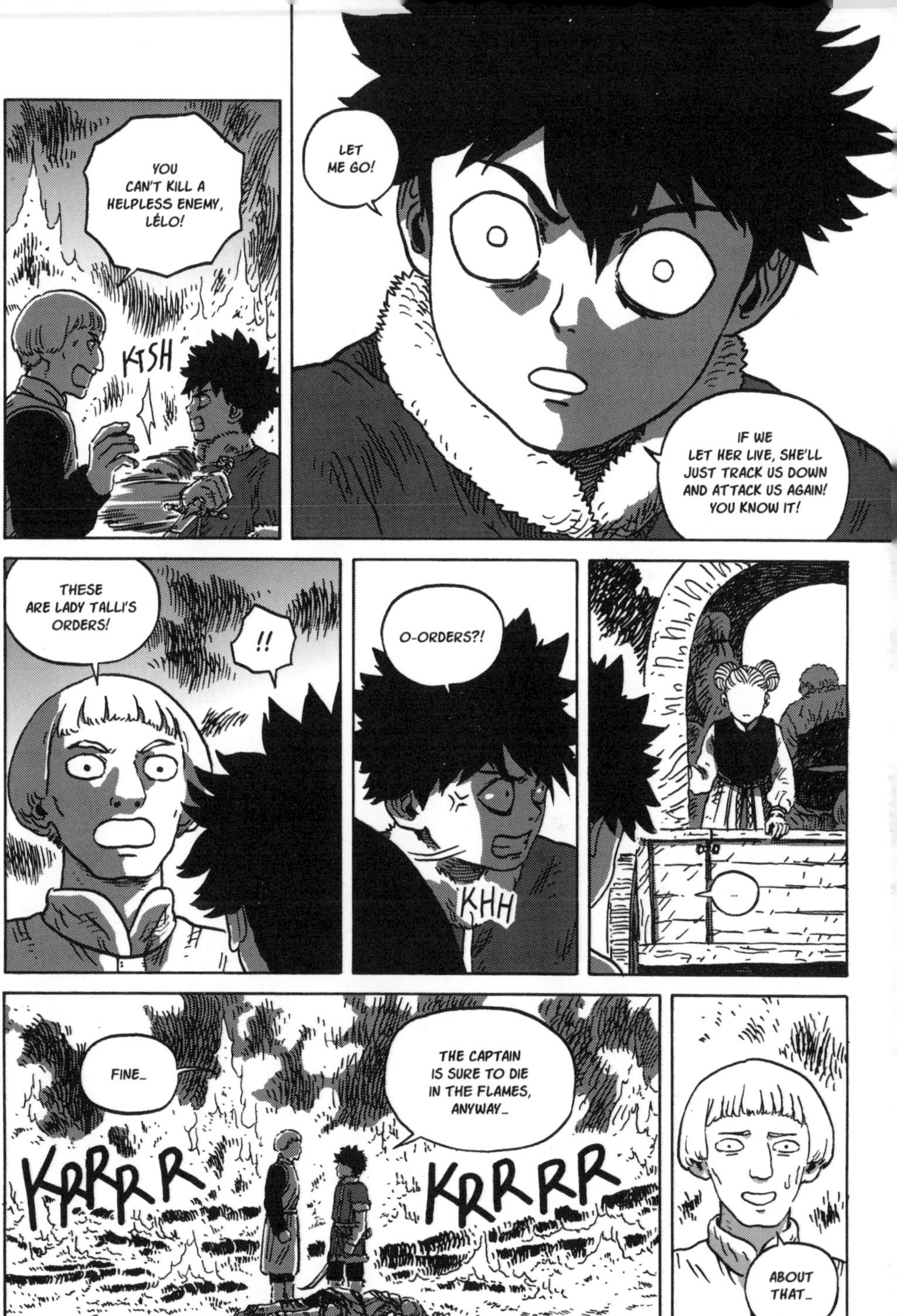

YOU CAN'T KILL A HELPLESS ENEMY, LÉLO!
KTSH
LET ME GO!
IF WE LET HER LIVE, SHE'LL JUST TRACK US DOWN AND ATTACK US AGAIN! YOU KNOW IT!
THESE ARE LADY TALLI'S ORDERS!
!!
O-ORDERS?!
KHH
...
FINE...
KRRRR
THE CAPTAIN IS SURE TO DIE IN THE FLAMES, ANYWAY...
KRRRR
ABOUT THAT...

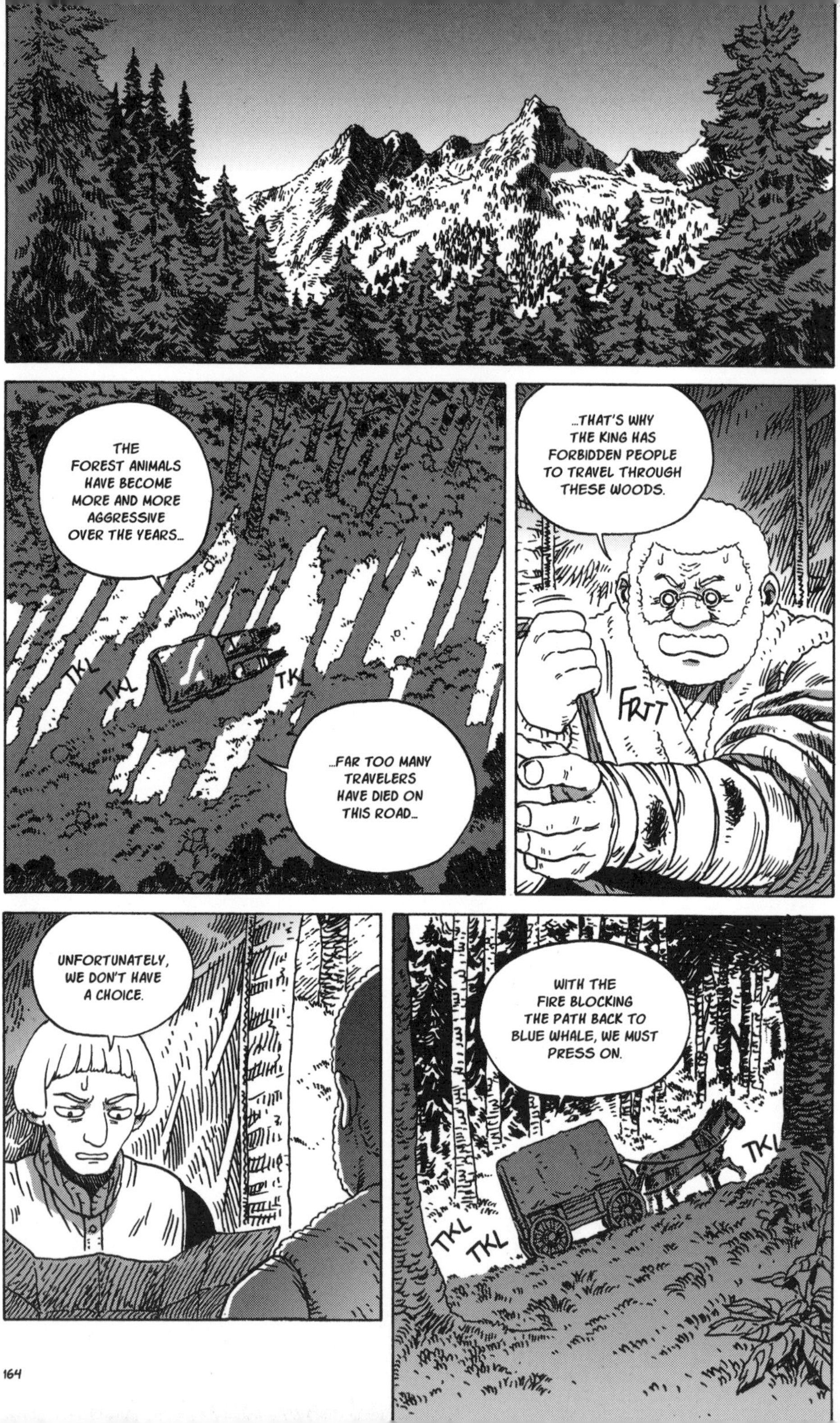
THE FOREST ANIMALS HAVE BECOME MORE AND MORE AGGRESSIVE OVER THE YEARS...
TKL
TKL
TK
...FAR TOO MANY TRAVELERS HAVE DIED ON THIS ROAD...
...THAT'S WHY THE KING HAS FORBIDDEN PEOPLE TO TRAVEL THROUGH THESE WOODS.
FRTT
UNFORTUNATELY, WE DON'T HAVE A CHOICE.
WITH THE FIRE BLOCKING THE PATH BACK TO BLUE WHALE, WE MUST PRESS ON.
TKL
TKL
TKL

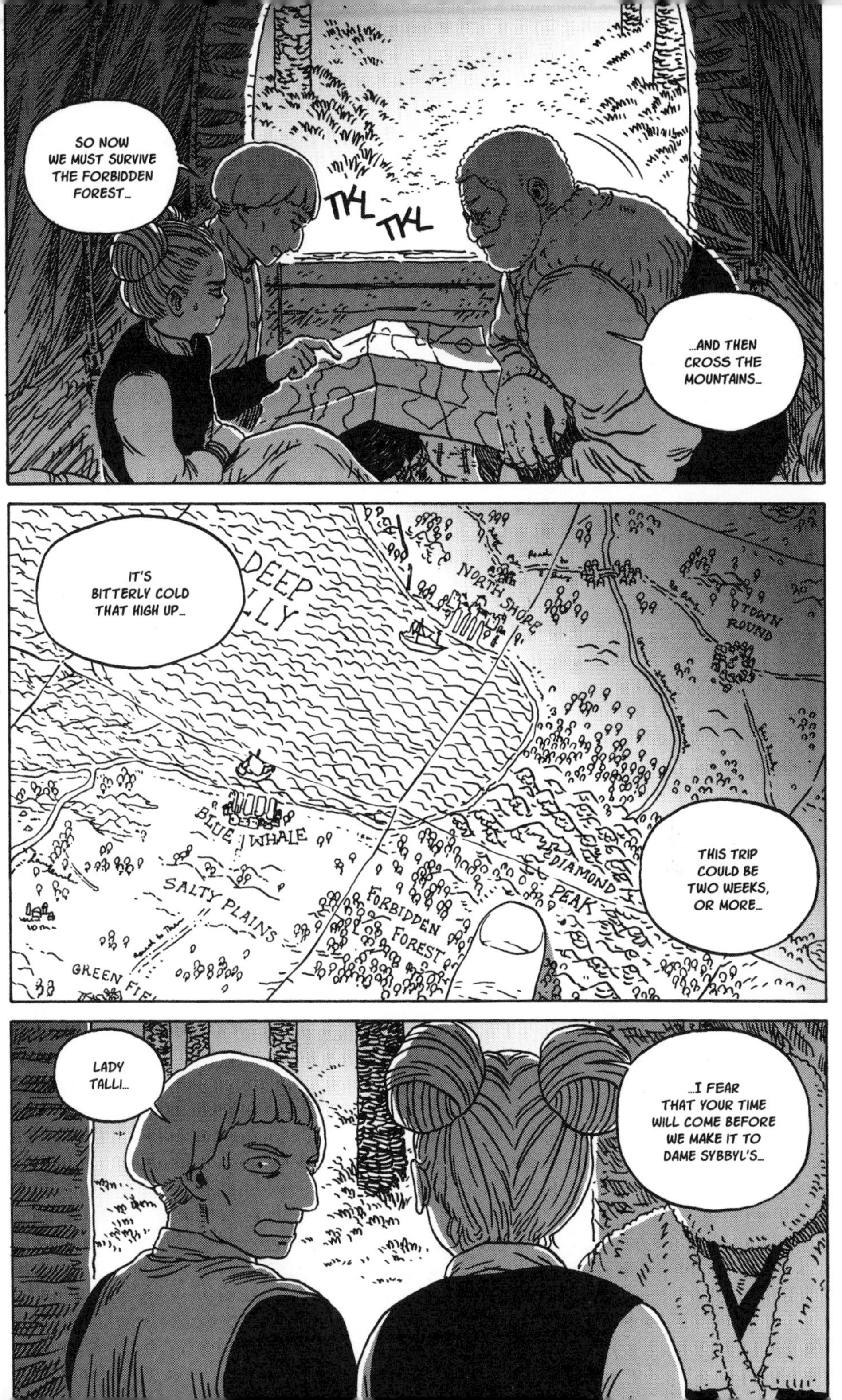
SO NOW WE MUST SURVIVE THE FORBIDDEN FOREST...
TKL TKL
...AND THEN CROSS THE MOUNTAINS...
IT'S BITTERLY COLD THAT HIGH UP...
DEEP
NORTH SHORE
TOWN ROUND
BLUE WHALE
SALTY PLAINS
FORBIDDEN FOREST
DIAMOND PEAK
THIS TRIP COULD BE TWO WEEKS, OR MORE...
LADY TALLI...
...I FEAR THAT YOUR TIME WILL COME BEFORE WE MAKE IT TO DAME SYBBYL'S...

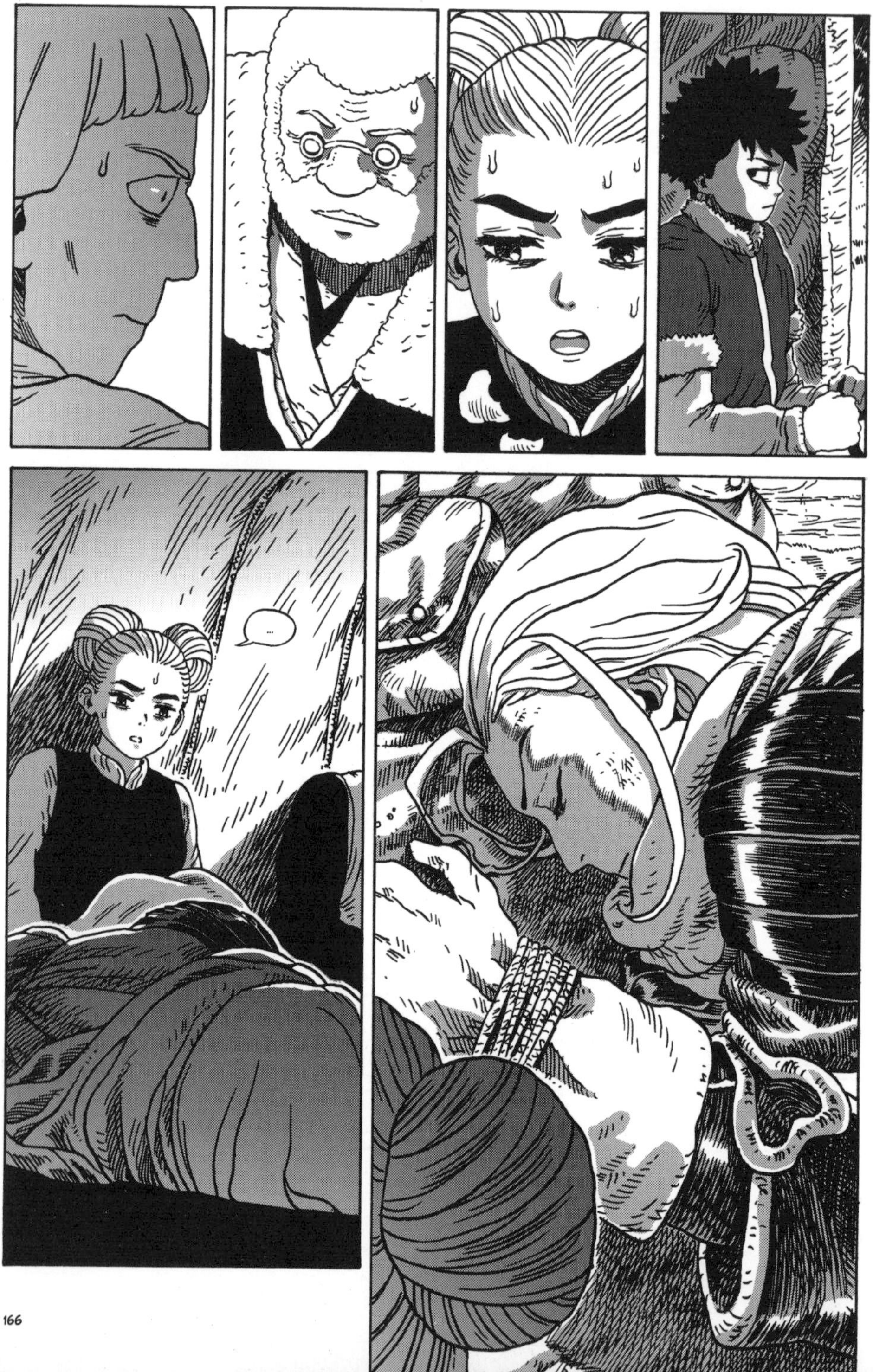
...

TO BE CONTINUED...

The Making of Talli

PART ONE

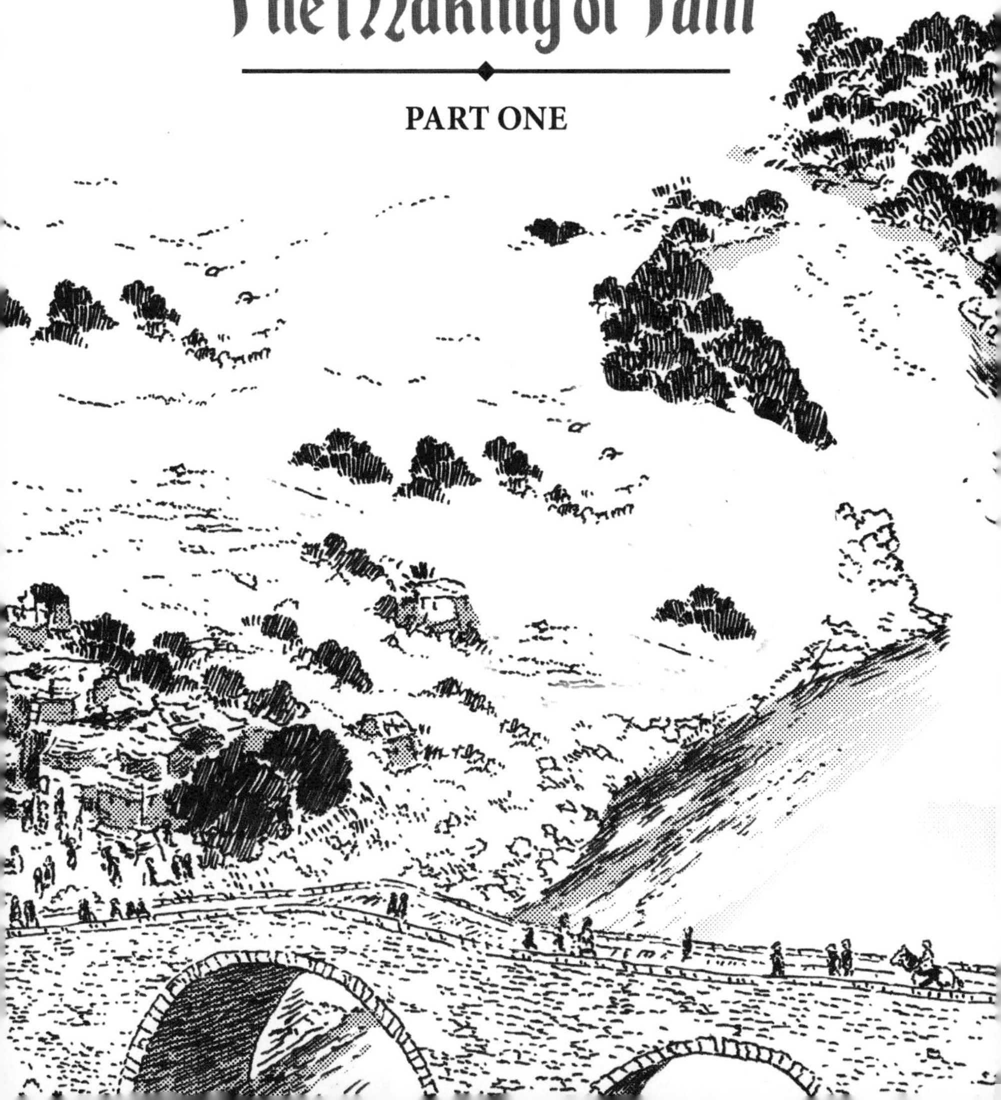

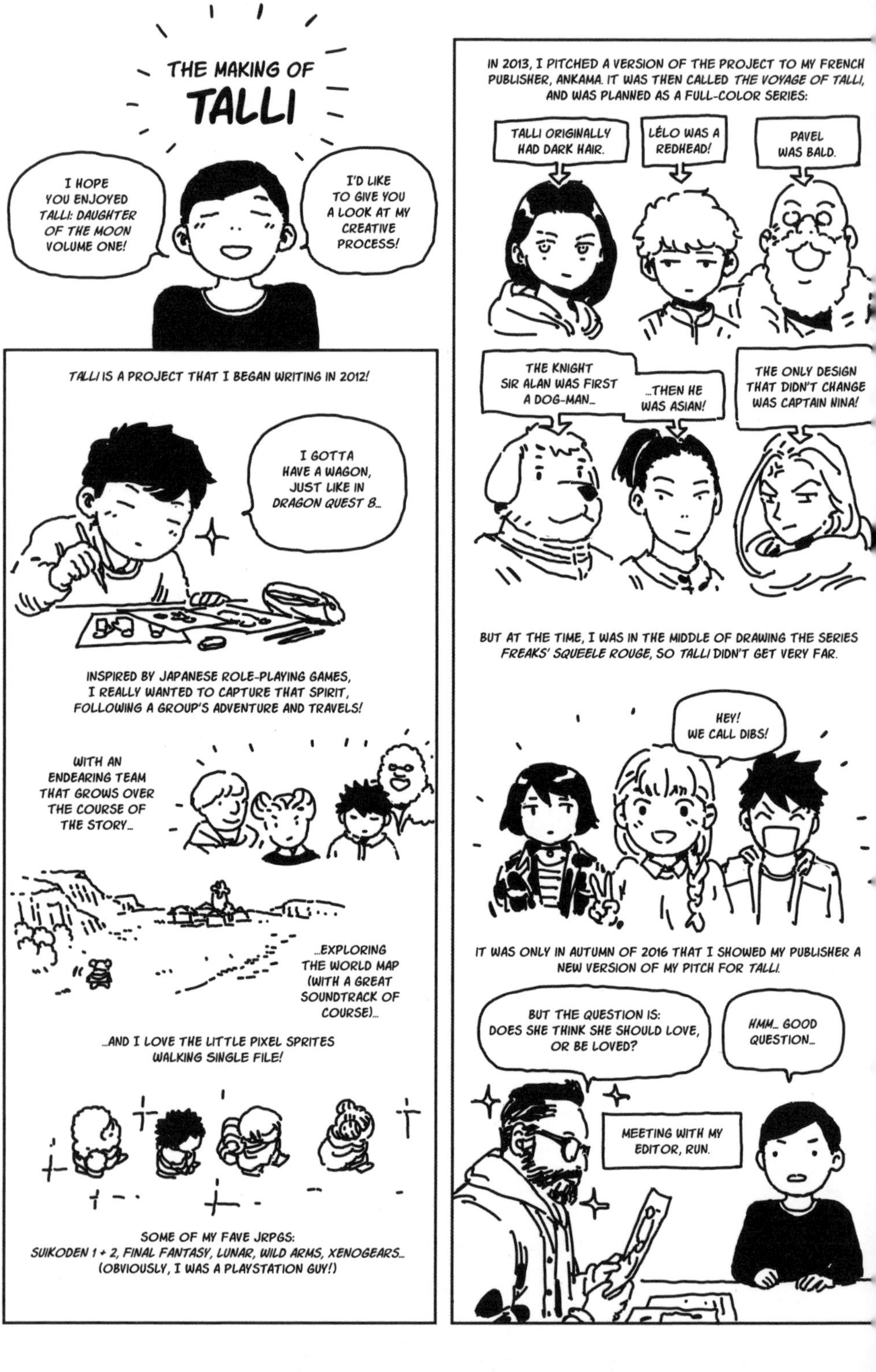
THE MAKING OF TALLI
I HOPE YOU ENJOYED TALLI: DAUGHTER OF THE MOON VOLUME ONE!
I'D LIKE TO GIVE YOU A LOOK AT MY CREATIVE PROCESS!
TALLI IS A PROJECT THAT I BEGAN WRITING IN 2012!
I GOTTA HAVE A WAGON, JUST LIKE IN DRAGON QUEST 8...
INSPIRED BY JAPANESE ROLE-PLAYING GAMES, I REALLY WANTED TO CAPTURE THAT SPIRIT, FOLLOWING A GROUP'S ADVENTURE AND TRAVELS!
WITH AN ENDEARING TEAM THAT GROWS OVER THE COURSE OF THE STORY...
...EXPLORING THE WORLD MAP (WITH A GREAT SOUNDTRACK OF COURSE)...
...AND I LOVE THE LITTLE PIXEL SPRITES WALKING SINGLE FILE!
SOME OF MY FAVE JRPGS:
SUIKODEN 1 + 2, FINAL FANTASY, LUNAR, WILD ARMS, XENOGEARS...
(OBVIOUSLY, I WAS A PLAYSTATION GUY!)
IN 2013, I PITCHED A VERSION OF THE PROJECT TO MY FRENCH PUBLISHER, ANKAMA. IT WAS THEN CALLED THE VOYAGE OF TALLI, AND WAS PLANNED AS A FULL-COLOR SERIES:
TALLI ORIGINALLY HAD DARK HAIR.
LÉLO WAS A REDHEAD!
PAVEL WAS BALD.
THE KNIGHT SIR ALAN WAS FIRST A DOG-MAN...
...THEN HE WAS ASIAN!
THE ONLY DESIGN THAT DIDN'T CHANGE WAS CAPTAIN NINA!
BUT AT THE TIME, I WAS IN THE MIDDLE OF DRAWING THE SERIES FREAKS' SQUEELE ROUGE, SO TALLI DIDN'T GET VERY FAR.
HEY! WE CALL DIBS!
IT WAS ONLY IN AUTUMN OF 2016 THAT I SHOWED MY PUBLISHER A NEW VERSION OF MY PITCH FOR TALLI.
BUT THE QUESTION IS: DOES SHE THINK SHE SHOULD LOVE, OR BE LOVED?
HMM... GOOD QUESTION...
MEETING WITH MY EDITOR, RUN.

SIGNING THE CONTRACT ON *TALLI* ALSO MARKED THE MOMENT THAT I LEFT MY HOMETOWN OF LYON AND MOVED TO PARIS, WHERE I LIVED WITH SOMEONE FOR THE FIRST TIME.

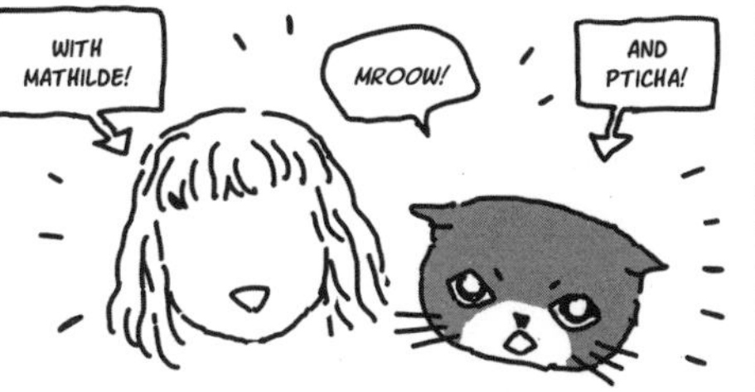
WITH MATHILDE!
MROOW!
AND PTICHA!

IT WAS GREAT TO TALK THINGS THROUGH WITH MATHILDE, SHE ALWAYS HAD GREAT IDEAS!

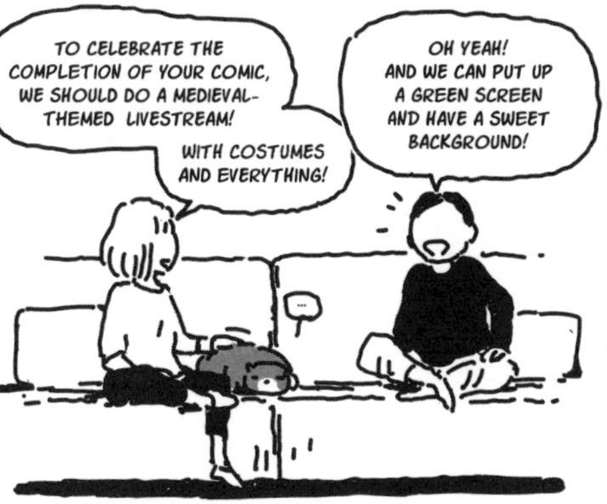
TO CELEBRATE THE COMPLETION OF YOUR COMIC, WE SHOULD DO A MEDIEVAL-THEMED LIVESTREAM!
WITH COSTUMES AND EVERYTHING!
OH YEAH! AND WE CAN PUT UP A GREEN SCREEN AND HAVE A SWEET BACKGROUND!
...

FUN FACT: I SLEEP IN A LOFT, BUT THE CEILING IS REALLY LOW, SO AT FIRST I HAD THE IMPRESSION OF BEING IN A COFFIN... IT TOOK ME A FEW DAYS TO GET USED TO IT.

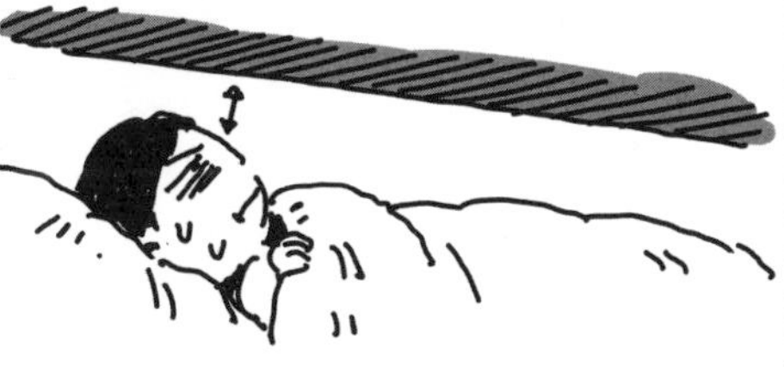

WE LIVE IN THE ASIAN QUARTER OF BELLEVILLE! VERY CONVENIENT FOR EATING OUT!

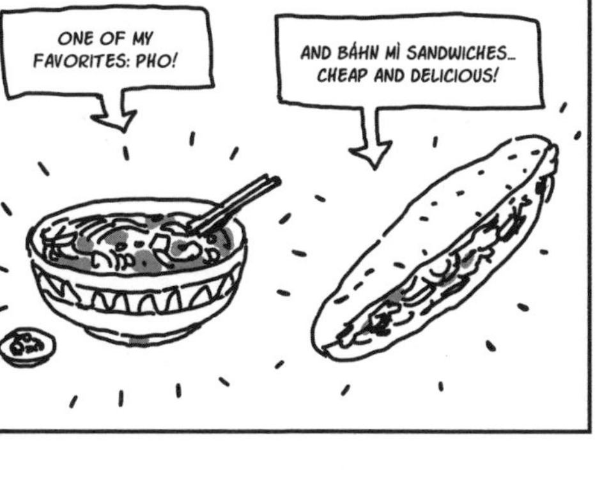
ONE OF MY FAVORITES: PHO!
AND BÁHN MÌ SANDWICHES... CHEAP AND DELICIOUS!

LIVING IN PARIS ALSO MEANS PLENTY OF NIGHTS OUT WITH FRIENDS, TALKING ABOUT OUR PASSIONS OVER DRINKS!

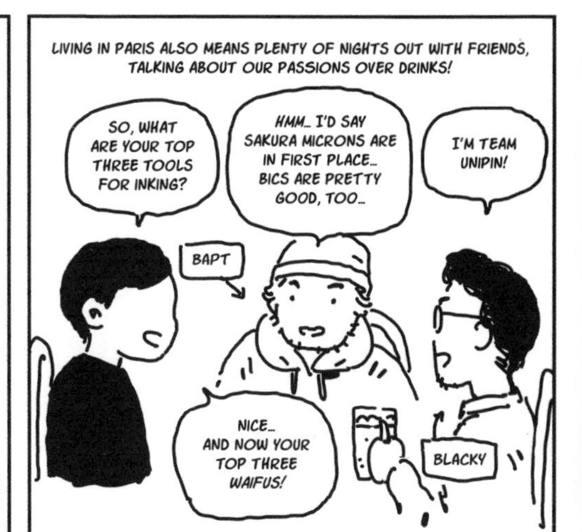
SO, WHAT ARE YOUR TOP THREE TOOLS FOR INKING?
HMM... I'D SAY SAKURA MICRONS ARE IN FIRST PLACE... BICS ARE PRETTY GOOD, TOO...
I'M TEAM UNIPIN!
BAPT
NICE... AND NOW YOUR TOP THREE WAIFUS!
BLACKY

AND *STREET FIGHTER 5* PARTIES...

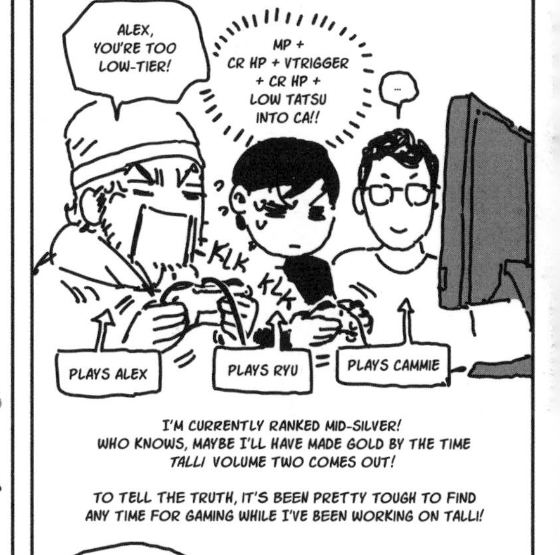
ALEX, YOU'RE TOO LOW-TIER!
MP + CR HP + VTRIGGER + CR HP + LOW TATSU INTO CA!!
...
KLK
KLK
PLAYS ALEX
PLAYS RYU
PLAYS CAMMIE

I'M CURRENTLY RANKED MID-SILVER! WHO KNOWS, MAYBE I'LL HAVE MADE GOLD BY THE TIME *TALLI* VOLUME TWO COMES OUT!

TO TELL THE TRUTH, IT'S BEEN PRETTY TOUGH TO FIND ANY TIME FOR GAMING WHILE I'VE BEEN WORKING ON TALLI!

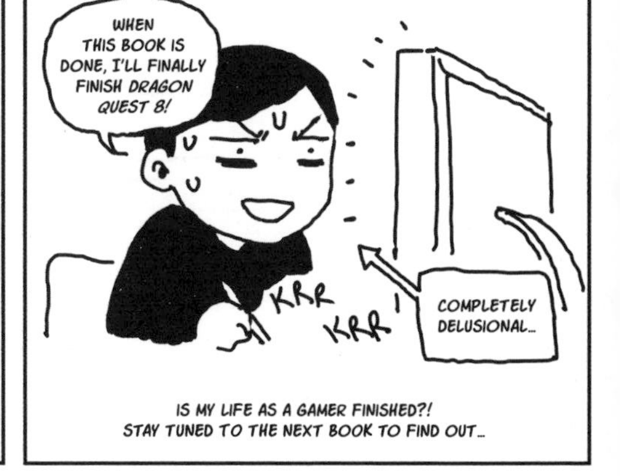
WHEN THIS BOOK IS DONE, I'LL FINALLY FINISH *DRAGON QUEST 8*!
KRR
KRR
COMPLETELY DELUSIONAL...

IS MY LIFE AS A GAMER FINISHED?! STAY TUNED TO THE NEXT BOOK TO FIND OUT...

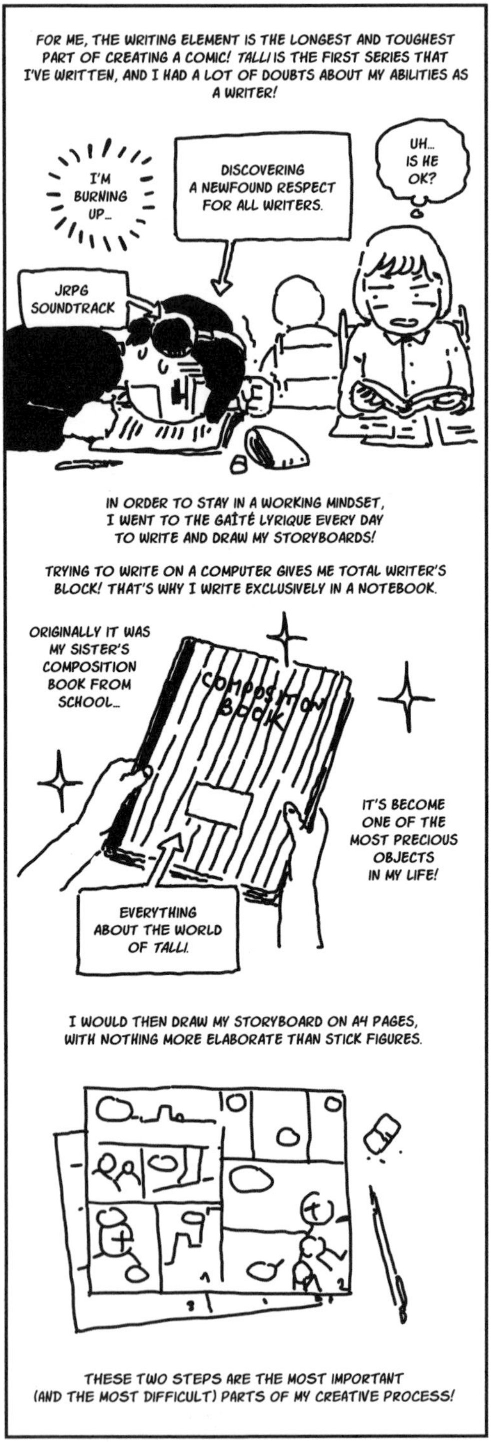
FOR ME, THE WRITING ELEMENT IS THE LONGEST AND TOUGHEST PART OF CREATING A COMIC! TALLI IS THE FIRST SERIES THAT I'VE WRITTEN, AND I HAD A LOT OF DOUBTS ABOUT MY ABILITIES AS A WRITER!
I'M BURNING UP...
DISCOVERING A NEWFOUND RESPECT FOR ALL WRITERS.
UH... IS HE OK?
JRPG SOUNDTRACK
IN ORDER TO STAY IN A WORKING MINDSET, I WENT TO THE GAÎTÉ LYRIQUE EVERY DAY TO WRITE AND DRAW MY STORYBOARDS!
TRYING TO WRITE ON A COMPUTER GIVES ME TOTAL WRITER'S BLOCK! THAT'S WHY I WRITE EXCLUSIVELY IN A NOTEBOOK.
ORIGINALLY IT WAS MY SISTER'S COMPOSITION BOOK FROM SCHOOL...
COMPOSITION BOOK
IT'S BECOME ONE OF THE MOST PRECIOUS OBJECTS IN MY LIFE!
EVERYTHING ABOUT THE WORLD OF TALLI.
I WOULD THEN DRAW MY STORYBOARD ON A4 PAGES, WITH NOTHING MORE ELABORATE THAN STICK FIGURES.
THESE TWO STEPS ARE THE MOST IMPORTANT (AND THE MOST DIFFICULT) PARTS OF MY CREATIVE PROCESS!

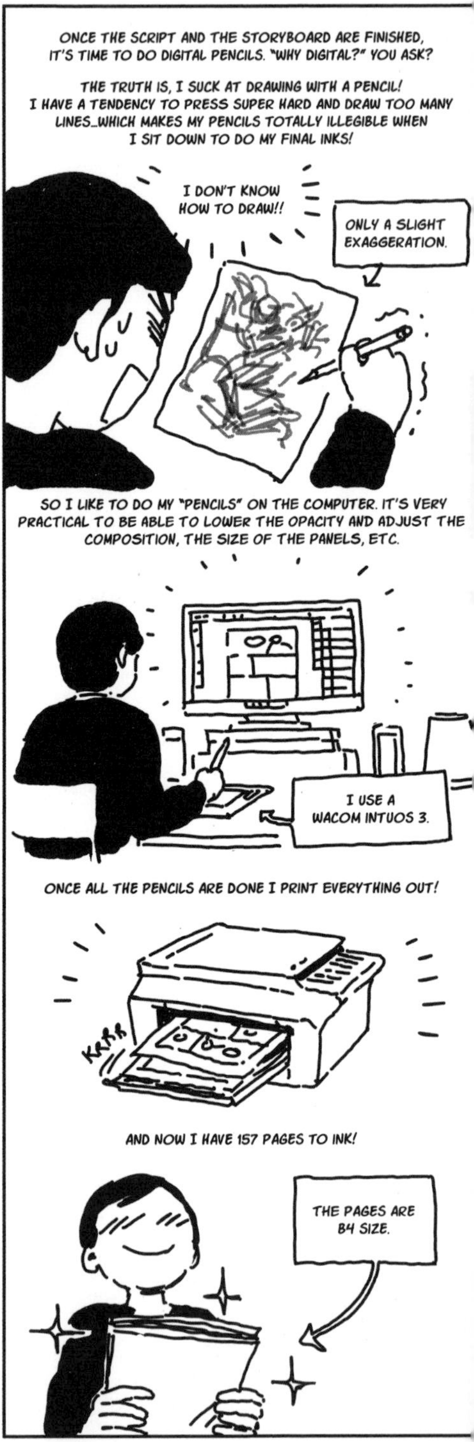
ONCE THE SCRIPT AND THE STORYBOARD ARE FINISHED, IT'S TIME TO DO DIGITAL PENCILS. "WHY DIGITAL?" YOU ASK?
THE TRUTH IS, I SUCK AT DRAWING WITH A PENCIL! I HAVE A TENDENCY TO PRESS SUPER HARD AND DRAW TOO MANY LINES...WHICH MAKES MY PENCILS TOTALLY ILLEGIBLE WHEN I SIT DOWN TO DO MY FINAL INKS!
I DON'T KNOW HOW TO DRAW!!
ONLY A SLIGHT EXAGGERATION.
SO I LIKE TO DO MY "PENCILS" ON THE COMPUTER. IT'S VERY PRACTICAL TO BE ABLE TO LOWER THE OPACITY AND ADJUST THE COMPOSITION, THE SIZE OF THE PANELS, ETC.
I USE A WACOM INTUOS 3.
ONCE ALL THE PENCILS ARE DONE I PRINT EVERYTHING OUT!
KRRR
AND NOW I HAVE 157 PAGES TO INK!
THE PAGES ARE B4 SIZE.

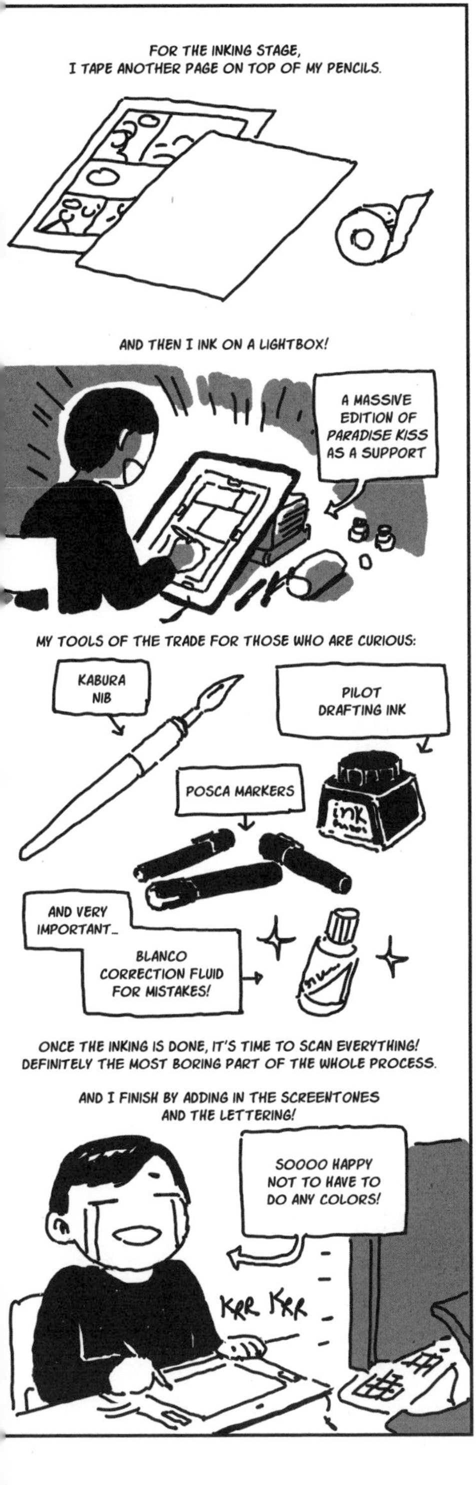
FOR THE INKING STAGE,
I TAPE ANOTHER PAGE ON TOP OF MY PENCILS.
AND THEN I INK ON A LIGHTBOX!
A MASSIVE EDITION OF PARADISE KISS AS A SUPPORT
MY TOOLS OF THE TRADE FOR THOSE WHO ARE CURIOUS:
KABURA NIB
PILOT DRAFTING INK
POSCA MARKERS
ink
AND VERY IMPORTANT...
BLANCO CORRECTION FLUID FOR MISTAKES!
ONCE THE INKING IS DONE, IT'S TIME TO SCAN EVERYTHING!
DEFINITELY THE MOST BORING PART OF THE WHOLE PROCESS.
AND I FINISH BY ADDING IN THE SCREENTONES
AND THE LETTERING!
SOOOO HAPPY NOT TO HAVE TO DO ANY COLORS!
KRR KRR

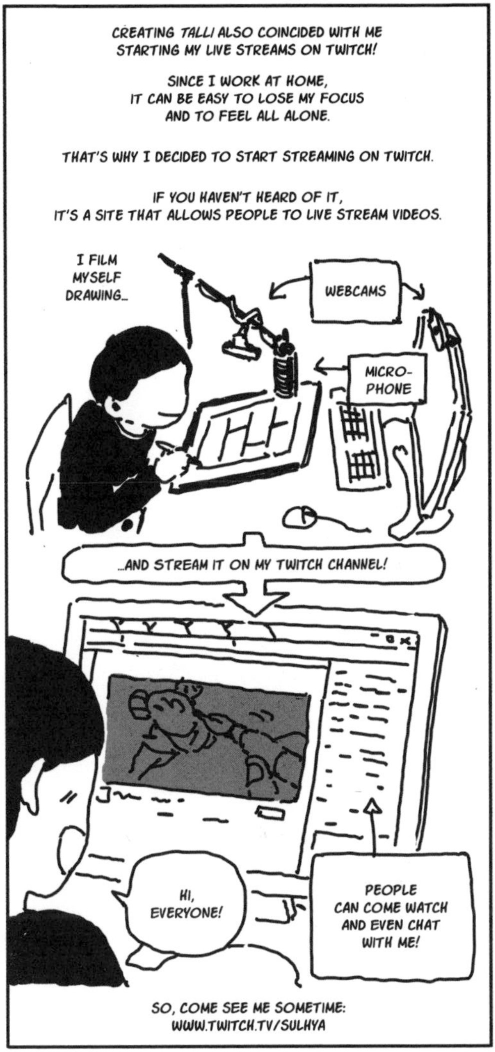
CREATING TALLI ALSO COINCIDED WITH ME
STARTING MY LIVE STREAMS ON TWITCH!
SINCE I WORK AT HOME,
IT CAN BE EASY TO LOSE MY FOCUS
AND TO FEEL ALL ALONE.
THAT'S WHY I DECIDED TO START STREAMING ON TWITCH.
IF YOU HAVEN'T HEARD OF IT,
IT'S A SITE THAT ALLOWS PEOPLE TO LIVE STREAM VIDEOS.
I FILM MYSELF DRAWING...
WEBCAMS
MICRO-PHONE
...AND STREAM IT ON MY TWITCH CHANNEL!
HI, EVERYONE!
PEOPLE CAN COME WATCH AND EVEN CHAT WITH ME!
SO, COME SEE ME SOMETIME:
WWW.TWITCH.TV/SULHYA

THANKS SO MUCH FOR READING THE FIRST VOLUME OF *TALLI!* I HOPE YOU LIKED IT! I'D LIKE TO THANK MY FAMILY FOR THEIR SUPPORT, MY FRIENDS AT POCKET DOJO FOR THEIR PASSION, MATHILDE AND PITCHA FOR THEIR PRESENCE, AND MY LOYAL VIEWERS ON TWITCH! A VERY SPECIAL THANK YOU TO DAMIEN AND ELSA FOR THEIR HELP! THANKS TO THE TEAM AT ANKAMA EDITIONS, AND THANK YOU TO MY EDITOR RUN FOR BELIEVING IN *TALLI* AND IN ME! SEE YOU SOON IN VOLUME TWO!

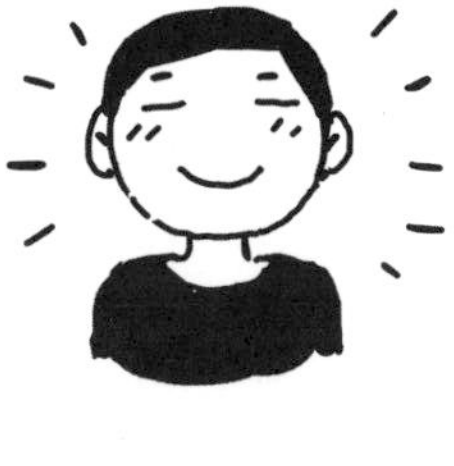